NEW YORK REVIEW BOOKS
CLASSICS

PRISONER OF LOVE

JEAN GENET (1910–1986) was born in Paris. Abandoned by
his mother at seven months, he was raised in state institutions
and charged with his first crime when he was ten. After spending
many of his teenage years in a reformatory, Genet enrolled in
the Foreign Legion, though he later deserted, turning to a life of
thieving and pimping that resulted in repeated jail terms and,
eventually, a sentence of life imprisonment. In prison Genet
began to write—poems and prose that combined pornography and
an open celebration of criminality with an extraordinary baroque,
high literary style—and on the strength of this work found himself acclaimed by such literary luminaries as Jean Cocteau, Jean-
Paul Sartre, and Simone de Beauvoir, whose advocacy secured
for him a presidential pardon in 1948. Between 1944 and 1948
Genet wrote four novels, *Our Lady of the Flowers*, *Miracle of the
Rose*, *Funeral Rites*, and *Querelle*, and the scandalizing memoir
A Thief's Journal. Throughout the Fifties he devoted himself to
theater, writing the boldly experimental and increasingly political
plays *The Balcony*, *The Blacks*, and *The Screens*. After a silence
of some twenty years, Genet began his last book, *Prisoner of
Love*, in 1983. It was completed just before he died.

AHDAF SOUEIF is a novelist and a writer on political and cultural
affairs. Her latest novel, *The Map of Love*, was shortlisted for the
Booker Prize in 1999. She was born in Egypt and lives in Cairo
and London.

PRISONER OF LOVE

JEAN GENET

Translated from the French by
BARBARA BRAY

Introduction by
AHDAF SOUEIF

NEW YORK REVIEW BOOKS

New York

This is a New York Review Book
Published by The New York Review of Books
435 Hudson Street, New York, NY 10014
www.nyrb.com

Library of Congress Cataloging-in-Publication Data
Genet, Jean, 1910–
  [Captif amoureux. English]
  Prisoner of love / Jean Genet ; translated from the French by Barbara
Bray ; and with an introduction by Ahdaf Soueif.
    p. cm.
  ISBN 1-59017-028-8
  1. Genet, Jean, 1910-—Political and social views. 2. Genet, Jean,
1910-—Journeys—Arab countries. 3. Genet, Jean,1910-—
Journeys—United States. 4. Palestinian Arabs—Politics and
government. 5. Authors, French—20th century—Biography. 6. Afro-
Americans—Politics and government. 7. Arab-Israeli conflict. 8. Black
Panther Party. I. Bray, Barbara. II. Title.
  PQ2613.E53 Z46313 2003
  848'.91209—dc21

                              2002014859
ISBN 978-1-59017-028-1

Book design by Lizzie Scott
Printed in the United States of America on acid-free paper.
1 0

CONTENTS

"Put all the images in language in a place of safety and make use of them, for they are in the desert, and it's in the desert we must go and look for them."

—JEAN GENET

Manuscript note at the top of the final proofs of this book.

INTRODUCTION

W HEN *Prisoner of Love* was first published in France in 1986, *Le Matin* declared that "Genet was assuredly one of the greatest French prose poets of this century, reaching the same heights as Proust and Céline. *Un Captif amoureux* has all the sacred fire and poetry of his earlier works." Yet today several bibliographies do not list the book, and even readers familiar with Genet are sometimes unaware of its existence. I was amused to see that when the French theatrical Compagnie Lara adapted *Captif* into a play and performed it in April 2002 as part of the Prague Writers' Festival (dedicated to Genet), the performance was mentioned in the British press as "a new production of Genet's last play."

In fact Genet's last play, *The Screens*, about the Algerian revolution, was written on the eve of Algerian independence from France in 1961. Three years later, following the death of his companion of some nine years, the high-wire artist Abdallah Bentaga, Genet (having, it is said, destroyed his manuscripts) left France. His relationship with his homeland had never been simple. Born in 1910 and abandoned as an infant to the *assistance publique*, he had by the age of fifteen been jailed for petty theft. At nineteen he was sent to Syria as a volunteer for the Foreign Legion, which he deserted seven years later, setting off on a *vagabondage* across Europe towards France and jail once more. Genet's extraordinary 1940s saw him in and out of prison while producing the great narratives that won him the admiration and solidarity of Cocteau, Sartre, and André Breton: *A Thief's Journal, Miracle of the Rose, Our Lady of the Flowers, Funeral Rites,* and *Querelle.* In the 1950s he created the plays which are his great bequest to

European postwar theater: *The Balcony*, *The Maids*, and *The Blacks*, followed in 1961 by *The Screens*.

"Obviously," Genet said in an interview in the early 1980s, "I am drawn to peoples in revolt . . . because I myself have the need to call the whole of society into question." But if all Genet's preceding work subverted the values and arrangements of society, *The Screens* was the first to engage with a specific revolt. Perhaps it was this that then drew other "transgressors" to appeal to him. And Genet responded. He wrote an *hommage* for the young revolutionary Daniel Cohn-Bendit in 1968, smuggled himself across the Canadian border into the US to speak on behalf of the Black Panthers at Stony Brook in March 1970, and, in the autumn of that year, turned up in the Palestinian bases in Jordan. He was to stay until the end of May 1971 and then—intermittently—through the end of 1972. His involvement with the Palestinians is the story of *Prisoner of Love*.

But Genet did not, as it were, go home and start writing. Another ten years were to pass before he started work on the new book. During this time he was to say in an interview for Australian radio: "I no longer have the need to write. . . . I have nothing further to say." Then, in September 1982, Genet (at the request of his Palestinian friend Leila Shahid) visited Beirut and found himself in the middle of the Israeli invasion of the city. He was, it seems, one of the first foreigners to enter the Palestinian refugee camp of Chatila after the Christian Lebanese Phalange, with the compliance of the Israeli command, tortured and murdered hundreds of its inhabitants. There, pushing open doors wedged shut by dead bodies, Genet memorized the features, the position, the clothing, the wounds of each corpse till three soldiers from the Lebanese army drove him at gunpoint to their officer: " 'Have you just been there?' [the officer] pointed to Chatila. 'Yes.'—'And did you see?'—'Yes.'—'Are you going to write about it?'—'Yes.' "

The essay "Four Hours in Chatila" was published in 1983, and in October of that year Genet began writing *Prisoner of Love*. It is as if, through the long years of virtual silence, everything was being saved up for this last book which he finished just before his death of throat cancer in 1986. Serious and playful, romantic and unflinching, literary and factual, *Prisoner of Love* is a coming together of everything that was Genet: his art, his politics, and his humanity.

But Genet is at pains to point out that "I'm not an archivist or a historian or anything like it." *Prisoner of Love* accumulates its power through a staggering display of leaps between times, places, styles, and modes of consciousness. Taking in events from the beginning of the twentieth century to the time of writing, shifting from polemic to lyrical, from exposition to prophecy, fusing disparate bits of the world into living images, it resists definitions and summaries. "This," said Genet, "is *my* Palestinian revolution, told in my own chosen order."

His revolution is—at the beginning, amidst the hills of Ajloun—"a party that lasted nine months. To get an idea of what it was like, anyone who tasted the freedom that reigned in Paris in May 1968 has only to add physical elegance and universal courtesy." And at the heart of the party were the young guerrillas, the fedayeen.

The party, however, was being held in grim circumstances. Expelled from their lands in 1948 and again in 1967, these Palestinians were refugees in King Hussein's Jordan. Radicalized by the Arab states' defeats in both wars, they had started to take matters into their own hands by forming guerrilla organizations. In 1970 there were at least five such organizations operating in Jordan and the King had started to fear them. Their raids across the border brought Israeli attacks on Jordanian villages, and there were several skirmishes between the fedayeen and Hussein's Bedouin troops.

Although Arab governments tried to contain the conflict, it escalated until, on September 6, the Popular Front for the Liberation of Palestine, led by George Habash, hijacked three airplanes. They demanded the release of some one hundred Palestinians from Jordanian jails and blew up one of the planes—after releasing the passengers and crew. On September 16 the King launched a full-scale attack on the Palestinians. In the civil war that raged for ten days, some three thousand Jordanian and two thousand Palestinian fighters were killed. It was at the end of this "Black September" that Genet arrived at Ajloun: "War was all around us. Israel was on the watch, also in arms. The Jordanian army threatened. But every fedayee was just doing what he was fated to do." What they did was train, discuss revolution—and make music. One of Genet's recurring images is his memory of two young fighters "drumming on wood, inventing more and more cheerful rhythms" on a pair of deal coffins—coffins that were clearly destined to be either their comrades' or their own, for "nearly all of them were killed, or taken prisoner and tortured."

The root *fda* in Arabic signifies something relinquished in the certainty of gaining something more precious: a ransom, perhaps, or a sacrifice. "What made the fedayeen supermen," Genet wrote, "was that they put the predicament of all before their own individual wishes. They would set out for victory or death, even though each still remained a man alone with his own sensibilities and desires." In them he rediscovered one of the central themes that had occupied his earlier work. In *Miracle of the Rose* Genet had written, "Only children who want to be bandits in order to resemble the bandit they love . . . dare have the audacity to play that character to the very end." In the Palestinian fedayeen in 1970 he found young men—boys almost—with the audacity to play the revolutionary to the very end. And with them, this "pink and white" sixty-year-old French eminence, although he never thought of himself as Palestinian, felt "at home."

One of the unique qualities of this book is that Genet never exhibits any of the characteristics we have learned to expect from white men or women writing about Arabs. He has no inclination to "go native," and he never goes in for generalizations on "Arab customs" or the "Arab mind" in either his descriptions of the Palestinians or his reflections on them and his feelings for them. More than that, his opening scene, where he finds himself sipping tea among the women in the camp at Baqa—women who laugh and joke when he asks if their husbands would mind his presence among them—is set up as a swipe at "orientalist" references and as a joke at his own expense: "Something told me my situation was not what I'd have expected from my previous knowledge of the East: here was I, a man, alone with a group of Arab women. And everything seemed to reinforce this topsy-turvy vision of the Orient."

From then on, in image after image, Genet fuses together his own French, Catholic world and this new one he is experiencing: the Bedouins dance, "twelve or fourteen soldiers holding arms like Breton bridegrooms"; an annex of the Fatah office makes him think of "the 1913 Russian Ballet: with five Parisian stage-hands standing by, several Nijinskys in striped costumes flecked with moss and dead leaves waiting to leap on-stage in *Le Prélude à l'après-midi d'une faune*"; a Circassian village on the Golan Heights, after six years of Israeli occupation, is like a village "in Normandy after the landing at Avranches. Looted by the Yanks." And then, in what becomes a motif of the revolution throughout the book, the image of a young fedayee, Hamza, and his mother is "linked to that of the Pietà and Christ."

But if Genet was *bouleversé* by the fedayeen—as his friend Leila Shahid put it—he retained a clear eye for the circumstances surrounding them: "[The fedayee's] brightness protected him, but worried the Arab régimes.... What was it the Arab world so urgently needed, that the Palestinian resistance should come into being?" In training not just his eye, but his heart and his genius on the Palestinian revolution, Genet also sees the world surrounding it: the Palestinian leaders who are the "servants of two masters," the Arab rulers "faithful allies of America," America—"Does she support Israel, or just make use of her?"—and Israel—"If you're against Israel you're not an enemy or an opponent —you're a terrorist. Terrorism is supposed to deal death indiscriminately, and must be destroyed wherever it appears. Very smart of Israel to carry the war right into the heart of vocabulary...." And the revolution itself?

> There's a shop in Châtellerault where I once saw a knife as small as a penknife with blades that opened slowly one after the other and then gently shut again, after having threatened the town in all directions.... Open, this small provincial masterpiece swelled up until its forty-seven blades resembled a porcupine at bay or the Palestinian revolution. That too was a miniature threatening in all directions: Israel, America, the Arab kingdoms. Like the penknife in the window it turned on its own axis and no one wanted to buy it.

Time and time again as I read *Prisoner of Love* I found myself wishing that Genet were alive today. As Edward Said wrote in 1990, he "fully intuited the scope and drama" of what the Palestinians were living through, recording "a seismographic reading, drawing and exposing the fault lines that a largely normal surface had hidden." And in doing this he was also reading the future. It could be said that for Genet the enemy was always the rigid form: a movement that became a government, a revolution that turned into an authority. The Palestinians were the antithesis of rigidity; he was captivated by the flexibility of their identity. It could embrace, it seemed, anyone who wanted to be part of it: German and Cuban doctors, a French priest, a nun, two young Frenchmen called Guy, a young Israeli who had renounced Zionism; everyone was welcome at the party. And—as is testified to by Genet's failure to realize that the fedayee leader he knew as Abu Omar was in fact a Christian—"Palestinian" always came before "Christian" or "Muslim."

Yet this openness itself, Genet saw, could in the prolonged absence of victory prove a weakness. In a passage just after the middle of the book he examines the French expression *entre chien et loup*—meaning "dusk": a time when one creature might metamorphose into another. For a moment Genet pulls back from his image: "In order to record the next phase of the story," he suggests, "perhaps I ought to draw back at first and take a run at it." What he's taking a run at is his fear of the fedayeen metamorphosing into Islamic militants; the "logical conclusion" of his feeling that "the expression *entre chien et loup*, instead of connoting twilight, describes any, perhaps all, of the moments of a fedayee's life." The proposition brings "howls of protest . . . from the PLO officials." But Genet's premonition is so strong that—uncharacteristically—he records the exact date of its occurrence: "As one of their leaders told me today, 8 September 1984, that such a thing was impossible, let's pretend this digression was never either written or read."

This remarkable passage is very much Genet at work. Like a miraculous street artist he beckons us over to watch as he paints prophetic lines and shadows on the pavement. The image complete, he walks away with a shrug.

But what he has to say is of tremendous importance, and he knows it. There is no doubting that once again he has nailed his colors to the mast of the oppressed, to the "metaphysical revolution of the native"—in this instance the Palestinian, as before it had been the Black Panthers and before that the Algerian revolution. Said reports that in Beirut in the fall of 1972, speaking of Sartre's strong pro-Israeli stance, Genet had said, "He's a bit of a coward for fear that his friends in Paris might accuse him of anti-Semitism if he ever said anything in support of Palestinian rights." Genet would probably not have been surprised to see otherwise admiring critics, like Edmund White, fearful that such an accusation might be leveled against them, seeking to separate the genius of the book, somehow, from its politics. Similarly Clifford Geertz has written that "Genet is, for all his empathy for the Palestinians' predicament, not so much a partisan . . . as a connoisseur of pure rebellion." Genet himself would have rejected such expedient distinctions. "It's not the justice of their [the Palestinians'] cause that moves me," he writes, "it's the rightness."

And yet, if the Palestinians found in Genet a passionate friend and a thoughtful interpreter, Genet, writing in the early 1980s, found in them the subject that would draw from him a powerful and layered articulation of the themes that had informed his work of the 1940s and 1950s: the heroism of the outlaw, the beauty of the constant, willful overturning of the established order, the transfiguration of eroticism into chastity, the power of a nonreligious spiritual life, the weightlessness of death, the continuation of a feeling beyond the life of the individual who felt it, and the tensile and creative relationship between the image and its reality.

This is a book about the Palestinian revolution (with some pages about the Black Panther movement), but it is also about art and about representation. In *The Balcony*, *The Maids*, and *The Blacks* the central theme is the relationship of appearance to reality. For Genet the image is central both to art and to life. It can make reality more bearable and keep memory alive:

Every district in the camp tried to reproduce a village left behind in Palestine. . . . Nazareth was in one district, and a few narrow streets away Nablus and Haifa. Then the brass tap, and to the right Hebron, to the left a quarter of old Jerusalem. Especially around the tap, waiting for their buckets to fill, the women exchanged greetings in their own dialects and accents, like so many banners proclaiming where each patois came from.

But its mask can also be used to manipulate reality to sinister ends. Genet cites the murder of three Palestinian leaders in Beirut by three pairs of Israeli commandos camping it up as ringletted queens who

> kissed one another on the lips to shock the bodyguards into thinking they were just shameless, giggling Arab pansies.... Newspapers all over the world described the assassination, but none of them called it terrorism on another country's sovereign territory. No, it was considered as one of the Fine Arts, deserving the relevant Order and receiving it.

Then, and most importantly, there is the image which needs to be created in order to convey reality, to make it, so to speak, real. "It's not enough just to write down a few anecdotes. What one has to do is create and develop an image or a profusion of images." And this is the task that Genet has set himself in *Prisoner of Love*. For an image, he suggests, is "the only message from the past that's managed to get itself projected into the present." It is a measure of Genet's pinpoint accuracy, the hardheaded realism that accompanies his poetics of the image, that today—two decades on—the Palestinians are more than ever embroiled in an "image" battle, while Genet's friend, the onetime Black Panther leader David Hilliard, is embarking on a fight to rescue the image of his group from a new and different group calling itself by the same name. "This is about more than the ownership of a trademark," Hilliard is quoted as saying, "it's about who controls and defines history."

In his 1982 interview for Australian radio, Genet insisted that the work he had done of his own accord—the novels written in prison—had been done in the certainty, because of the certainty, that it would never be read. His plays he dismissed as having been written on commission, except for *The Screens* which—because of its cast of 107 characters—he had thought would never be performed. In *Prisoner of Love* the possible absence of a reader is at once reassuring and troubling: "This book will never be translated into Arabic, nor will it ever be read by the French or any other Europeans. But since I'm writing it anyway ... who is it for?"

Sartre had written—in praise of Genet's work—that "he reduces the episode to being merely the manifest illustration of a higher truth. ... He reconstructs the real on every page ... in such a way as to produce for himself proof of the existence of God. That is, of his own existence." It is not surprising that, in 1982, Genet brushed this aside with "[Sartre's] book called *Saint Genet* was really about himself." For in the work that he was about to embark upon, unconstrained and uncommissioned, Genet was engaged upon a project at once more artful and more truthful. The Palestinians, he saw, were no good at making images:

> The ... journalists, describing the Palestinians as they were not, made use of slogans instead. I lived with the Palestinians, and my amused astonishment arose from the clash between the two visions. They were so opposite to what they were said to be that their radiance, their very existence, derived from that negation. Every negative detail in the newspaper, from the slightest to the boldest, had a positive counterpart in reality.

It is this reality that Genet devoted his final years to recording. He feared the revolution's defeat and "the evidence, rarely accurate but always stirring, vouchsafed to the future by the victors." Age and illness were against him. Pain was there too. In the last months he refused painkilling drugs to retain the lucidity that he needed to create, for the future, his image of the reality of the Palestinian revolution: "Would Homer have written or recited the *Iliad* without Achilles' wrath? But what would we know about Achilles' wrath without Homer?" Genet the great subversive image-maker knew that he had found his subject and his subject had found him.

—AHDAF SOUEIF

TRANSLATOR'S NOTE

It is easier to understand the oddities and above all to appreciate the beauties of Genet's last work if one knows something about the history of its text.

Genet worked on *Un captif amoureux* for several years, sometimes from notes written at the time of the events described, more often from memory. During the last two years, when he knew his days were numbered, he devoted all his remaining time and strength to the book, doing without pain-killing drugs so as to stay as lucid as possible.

His accidental death while the book was being prepared for the press presented his French publisher with a problem.

At best Genet had cared as little for accepted rules of grammar and composition as for conventions of conduct, but a deliberately subversive style had been raised by physical and psychological factors to a level of anarchy unusual even for Genet.

Rough inter-cutting of different elements and chronologies; articulation of argument through bizarre images rather than logic; abrupt linking together of usually unrelated themes—often such features still seemed to need a finishing, integrating touch.

Even possible errors of transcription, both from the original manuscript and from such proofs as Genet lived long enough to correct, could not be decisively checked: the whereabouts of the original manuscript were by then, typically, unknown.

Establishing a definitive text would be a matter of long search and research, and would be eventually attempted for a scholarly edition of Genet's collected works. Meanwhile, Genet had been very eager for the book to appear. His publishers therefore chose to fulfil his wish and to publish the existing text as it stood.

Prisoner of Love will be truly translated only if and when a more perfect original is achieved. Till then, it seemed worth trying to reflect as well as possible the astonishing trajectory of Genet's imagination. At its most inspired moments it produces new and exhilarating insights into the way mind may function—a twentieth-century "dissociation of sensibility." And perhaps, after all, disdain for "finish" was only one aspect of the state of being that enabled Genet to set down his last, strange, "Metaphysical" poetry.

—BARBARA BRAY

A NOTE ON THE TEXT

AFTER ASSEMBLING the various elements for his last book, Genet hesitated for a long time before choosing its definitive form.

He had at one point proceeded to compose the work by juxtaposing, on each page, several texts arranged in columns or in the form of squares on a chessboard, to make use of the interplay between red and black typography. He decided instead on a more readable presentation of a continuous text that he wrote, integrating earlier fragments, during the last two years of his life. Consequently, the story unfolds on many levels and in various time periods, a practice that could already be noted in his "Four Hours at Shatila." Above all, he played very freely with the subtleties of writing to express the nuances of his thought and his sometimes contradictory positions and reflections.

The translator's task of transposing a book's complexity into another language is especially difficult when the book's disorganized appearance nonetheless represents the intention of an author who conceived it as an essentially literary work.

The French edition was printed according to the author's instructions on the two sets of proofs that he read and corrected.

Genet perhaps wanted this work, which was revised until it reached its definitive state, to be marked by the independence of his personal reflection and his poetic vision.

—LAURENT BOYER,
for Éditions Gallimard

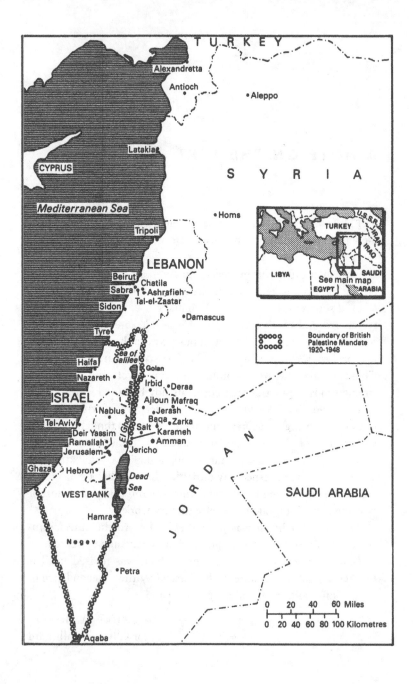

PRISONER OF LOVE

ONE

THE PAGE that was blank to begin with is now crossed from top to bottom with tiny black characters—letters, words, commas, exclamation marks—and it's because of them the page is said to be legible. But a kind of uneasiness, a feeling close to nausea, an irresolution that stays my hand—these make me wonder: do these black marks add up to reality? The white of the paper is an artifice that's replaced the translucency of parchment and the ochre surface of clay tablets; but the ochre and the translucency and the whiteness may all possess more reality than the signs that mar them.

Was the Palestinian revolution really written on the void, an artifice superimposed on nothingness, and is the white page, and every little blank space between the words, more real than the black characters themselves? Reading between the lines is a level art; reading between the words a precipitous one. If the reality of time spent among—not with—the Palestinians resided anywhere, it would survive between all the words that claim to give an account of it. They claim to give an account of it, but in fact it buries itself, slots itself exactly into the spaces, recorded there rather than in the words that serve only to blot it out. Another way of putting it: the space between the words contains more reality than does the time it takes to read them. Perhaps it's the same as the time, dense and real, enclosed between the characters in Hebrew.

When I said the Blacks were the characters on the white page of America, that was too easy an image: the truth really lies where I can never quite know it, in a love between two Americans of different colour.

So did I fail to understand the Palestinian revolution? Yes, completely. I think I realized that when Leila advised me to go to the West Bank. I refused, because the occupied territories were only a play acted out second by second by occupied and occupier. The reality lay in involvement, fertile in hate and love; in people's daily lives; in silence, like translucency, punctuated by words and phrases.

In Palestine, even more than anywhere else, the women struck me as having a quality the men lacked. Every man, though just as decent, brave and considerate, was limited by his own virtues. The women—they weren't allowed on the bases but they did all the work in the camps—added to all their virtues a dimension that seemed to subtend a great peal of laughter. If the act they put on one day to protect a priest had been performed by men it would never have carried conviction. Perhaps it was women, not men, who invented the segregation of women.

By the time we'd had our very light lunch it was about half-past twelve. The sun shone down vertically on Jerash and the men were taking a siesta. Nabila and I were the only two people awake and, not wanting to be in the shade, we decided to go to the camp at Baqa nearby. At that time Nabila was still an American. She got divorced later so as to stay with the Palestinians. She was thirty years old, with the beauty of a heroine in a Western. In blue denim jeans and jacket, her black hair falling loose to the waist but cut in a fringe in front, she was a shocking figure to be walking around the camp at that hour. Some Palestinian women in national dress spoke to her, and must have been astonished to hear the boyish figure answer like an Arab of their own sex and with a Palestinian accent.

Whenever three women get talking, after a few polite exchanges they are joined by five more, and then seven or eight. Although I was with Nabila I was forgotten, or rather treated as non-existent. Five minutes later we went into a Palestinian woman's house for a glass of tea—an excuse for continuing the conversation in a room that was cool and out of the sun. The women spread out a blanket for the two of us to sit on, added a few cushions, but remained standing themselves as they made the tea or coffee. No one took any notice of me except Nabila, who, remembering I was beside her, passed me a little glass. All the talk was in Arabic. My only interlocutors were the four walls and the whitewashed ceiling.

Something told me my situation was not what I'd have expected from my previous knowledge of the East: here was I, a man, alone with a group of Arab women. And everything seemed to reinforce this topsy-turvy vision of the Orient. All but three of the women were married, probably each to a different man. Perched there like a pasha on my cushions, I was in a rather dubious position. I interrupted the torrent of words they were exchanging with Nabila and asked her to translate.

"You're all married. Where are your husbands?"

"In the mountains!"

"Mine works in the camp!"

"So does mine."

"What would they say if they knew a man was here alone with you, sprawled on their blankets and cushions?"

They all burst out laughing.

"They *will* know!" said one. "We'll tell them, to embarrass them and have a good laugh at their expense. We'll tease our wonderful warriors! And perhaps they'll get cross and pretend to find boys more amusing."

The women all seemed to have nothing to do, and to talk a lot as they did it. But in fact each of them looked after one or two male offspring, changing their nappies and suckling or bottle-feeding them so that they would grow up into heroes and die at twenty, not in the Holy Land but for it. That's what they told me.

This was at Baqa Camp in 1970.

The fame of heroes owes little to the extent of their conquests and all to the success of the tributes paid to them. The *Iliad* counts for more than Agamemnon's war; the steles of the Chaldes for more than the armies of Nineveh. Trajan's Column, *La Chanson de Roland*, the murals depicting the Armada, the Vendôme column—all the images of wars have been created after the battles themselves thanks to looting or the energy of artists, and left standing thanks to oversight on the part of rain or rebellion. But what survives is the evidence, rarely accurate but always stirring, vouchsafed to the future by the victors.

Without warning we were on the alert. Europe received a jolt, and I'm still amazed. Three years before—I quote—"some film directors in Tel Aviv had scattered boots, helmets, guns, bayonets and human footprints on the sands to simulate a débâcle later edited in a studio in Los Angeles."

There was nothing new about the representation of battles, whether victories or defeats. Each side had its tricks and its experts, and artists attached to its army to cover the Egyptian campaigns. Draughtsmen and painters depicted after the event whatever the victor permitted. In 1967, I was told, Israel prepared, shot and cut in advance a film showing Egypt's defeat, and on the seventh day showed it to all the world's television, proclaiming their victory over the Arabs. When Nasser died the brilliance of his funeral eclipsed his death. The cradle, the football, you could call it the coffin, pitched and tossed in the air and practically flew over the heads of the crowd, which though visibly angry was perhaps at the same time amused.

Hussein, Boumédienne, Kosygin, Chaban-Delmas, Haile Selassie the Lion of Judah and other heads of state or government were lifted up by fists packing—flesh and bone together—fifteen kilos; by shoulders inured to the crates of Cairo shipping agents or the assembly lines of truck factories. The celebrities were picked up and then set down on the rostrum as delicately as a silk stocking held between finger and thumb. But the toughs of Egypt kept the coffin for themselves.

It was a good game. The ball disappeared into the scrum, then reappeared in another corner of the screen. Several players grappled for possession. Whose furious kick would send it flying into eternity? The pall-bearers walked faster and faster, as if dead drunk, their mad rush forcing the Koran to follow. Legs, feet, throats and the bier all got carried away. The bearers hurried the coffin along more nimbly than the All Blacks, and then it was swallowed up in the crowd. The whole world was following the match on the screen, and could imagine the bier passing from foot to foot, fist to shoulder, crotch to hair, until from the soil of Egypt the crowds, the pall-bearers, the reciters of the Koran, the coffin and the rugby players all vanished, leaving nothing but haste ever accelerating until it reached the grave. The sound of the gun salute was drowned by falling spadefuls of earth. Despite the guard, two or three thousand feet, relieved of their load, danced on the grave till morning, moving at the absolute speed that must belong to the One God. I couldn't help thinking of a World Cup in Oriental Funerals: this one would certainly have scored.

Not long after, in September 1970, when Hussein of Jordan was in danger of being beaten by the fedayeen, America came to his aid. Neither Nasser's morale nor his heart having held out, the rugby match at once muscular and sentimental that we saw on television was a ceremony designed to wipe out the débâcle of 1967 and conceal those ushered in by 1970. Was the deceased only in hiding? The earnestness of the spectacle on the screen was as naïve as the kisses showered on the lips, hair, gold chain, ear-ring and eyes of a player who's just scored a goal. Is the spectator's applause for the goal or for the kisses? Has one out of ten sweating lads disappeared beneath the rest? Is he hiding? The Raïs's body had vanished. He who was the sun of a people would merge into the cedar of his coffin, and all would be ratified by time. The Arab people was skewered on an age of nations. The countries of the world were getting restive. New wars would be needed. Nasser would come in handy again, transfigured by comic strips.

Even before I got there I knew my visit to the banks of the Jordan, to the Palestinian bases, could never be clearly expressed. I had greeted the revolt as a musical ear recognizes a right note. I often left my tent and slept under the trees, looking up at a Milky Way that seemed quite close through the branches. At night the armed sentries moving around over grass and leaves made no sound. They tried to merge into the tree-trunks. They listened.

The Milky Way rose out of the lights of Galilee and arched over me and the Jordan Valley before breaking up over the desert of Saudi Arabia. Lying there in my blanket I may have entered into the sight more than the Palestinians themselves, for whom the sky was a commonplace. Imagining their dreams, for they had dreams, as best I could, I realized I was separated from them by the life I'd lived, a life that was blasé compared with theirs. Cradle and innocence were words so chastely linked, for them, that to avoid corrupting either they avoided looking up. They mustn't see that the beauty of the sky was born and had its cradle in the moving lights of Israel.

In one of Shakepeare's tragedies the archers loose their arrows against the sky, and I wouldn't have been surprised if some of the fedayeen, feet firmly on the ground, but angered at so much beauty arching out of the land of Israel, had taken aim and fired their bullets at the Milky Way—China and the socialist countries supplied them with enough ammunition to bring down half the firmament. But could they fire at stars rising out of their own cradle, Palestine?

"There was only one procession. Mine. I led it on Good Friday in a white surplice and black cope. I really haven't got time to talk to you," said the priest, already red with anger.

"I saw two. One with a banner of the Virgin Mary..."

"No. What you refer to as the second procession and the Virgin Mary—they were no such thing. Those louts marching along blowing bugles? Fishermen of some sort who'd have done better to stick to their own concerns. They enjoy causing a scandal."

But two processions had passed one another before my very eyes, the first led by the Lebanese priest, the second preceded by the blue and white banner of the saint and, according to the irate cleric, made up of hooligans and sailors quick-marching to the harbour.

I heard later, from a Benedictine, that there really were two processions. The first, despite the accompanying band, moved slowly, with an assumed melancholy. A group of musicians and male and female singers were performing what should have been a joyful requiem when this lachrymose parade was intercepted by another, composed of jaunty young men charging along blowing bugles. At their head was a stout young fellow holding up a picture of the Virgin Mary.

I recognized her from the folded hands, the white-edged clouds against the blue sky, the golden stars as in a Murillo, and the toes resting on a sharp-looking crescent. But I ought to have realized the truth from the stars, the blue of the sky, the quick marching, the bugles, the gaiety, the sweaters and rubber boots of the sailors, the absence of women—in fact the whole procession, and in particular, as my informant pointed out, the stars and the moon, ought to have enlightened me.

Although they described a perfect orbit around the lady, the stars were exactly the same in number as those in Ursa Minor. The blue was that of the sea. The fringed clouds were gentle waves. The crescent was Islam. The buglers played a merry tune because they were on the right road, and they didn't think twice about cutting the other mournful procession in two. The strapping lads in their gumboots were fishermen, and the picture of the woman, who didn't have a halo like the Virgin Mary, symbolized the Pole Star.

This was what the Benedictine told me to start with. He went on to say that the lady in the picture was neither virginal nor Christian but belonged to the pre-Islamic "Peoples of the Sea." Her origins were pagan, and she'd been worshipped by sailors for thousands of years. In the dimmest of nights she infallibly showed them the North, and because of her the worst-rigged ship was sure to reach harbour safe and sound.

But the Benedictine couldn't tell me why the second procession was so cheerful that particular day, the day the Son died, leaving behind one who'd been a mother at sixteen and was very like the lady on the banner. Since he didn't want to go into it, I told myself, silently, that perhaps the buglers' high spirits that Good Friday represented the triumph of paganism over the religion of the Son.

That night at Ajloun I saw the Pole Star to my right in its place in Ursa Minor and the Milky Way dissolving into the Arabian desert, and I couldn't but wonder that, in a Muslim country where, as I still believed, woman was something remote, I was able to conjure up in my mind's eye before falling asleep a procession of men, apparently unmarried, who'd captured the image of a beautiful lady. But she represented the Pole Star, eternally fixed immeasurable distances away in the ether, and belonged, like every woman,* to a different constellation. The fishermen were masturbators rather than mates, and the word polar applied as much to the woman as to the star.

Though I was lying still in my blankets as I looked up into the sky, following the light, I felt myself swept into a maelstrom, swirled around and yet soothed by strong but gentle arms. A little way off, through the darkness, I could hear the Jordan flowing. I was freezing cold.

It was for fun as much as anything that I'd accepted the invitation to spend a few days with the Palestinians. But I was to stay nearly two years. Every night as I waited half dead for the capsule of Nembutal to send me to sleep, I lay with my eyes open and my mind clear, neither afraid nor surprised, but amused to be there. On either side of the river men and women had been on the alert for ages. Why should I be any different?

Meagre though it seemed at the time, I'd had the privilege of being born in the capital of an empire that circled the globe, while at the same time the Palestinians were being stripped of their lands, their houses and even their beds. But they'd come a long way since then!

"Stars, that's what we were. Japan, Norway, Düsseldorf, the United States, Holland—don't be surprised if I count them up on my fingers—England, Belgium, Korea, Sweden, places we'd never even heard of and couldn't find on the map—they all sent people to film us and photograph us and interview us. 'Camera,' 'in shot,' 'tracking shot,' 'voice off'—but gradually the fedayeen

---

*The Palestinians, who were often invited to China, will quote the Thoughts of Mao at me; one of those most frequently quoted refers to women as "half of the stars."

found themselves 'out of shot' and learned that the visitors spoke 'voice off.'

"A journalist who'd been driven around for a few yards by Khaled Abu Khaled would claim to be a friend of Palestine. We learned the names of towns we'd never dreamed of, and how to use apparatus we'd never seen before. But no one on the bases or in the camps ever actually saw a foreign film or photograph, television programme or newspaper article about us. We knew *we* existed, we must be doing surprising things since people came from such far-off places to see us—but did the far-off places exist?

"And the journalists used to stay about two hours: they had to catch a plane in Amman to cover the Lord Mayor's Show in London in six hours' time. Most of them thought Abu Amar and Yasser Arafat were two different people, possibly enemies. Those who got that right would multiply the numbers of Fatah and the ALP* by three or four because they counted all the members' pseudonyms as well as their ordinary names.

"We were admired so long as our struggle stayed within the limits set by the West. But nowadays there's no question of going to Munich, Amsterdam, Bangkok and Oslo. We did get as far as Oslo once, and it snowed so hard we could make snowballs as it fell and chuck them at one another. In our own sands, on our own hills, we were a fable. When we went down the steeps of the Jordan at night to lay mines, and came up again next morning, were we ascending from Hell or descending from Heaven? Whenever a European, man or woman, looked at us . . ."

This story had to be transmitted through another fedayee acting as interpreter, but the fedayee who told it gave me the impression he'd recited it often. It all came out so pat I was able to grasp what he said without waiting for the translation. Did he see that from my expression? At any rate he started to address me directly.

"Whenever Europeans looked at us their eyes shone. Now I understand why. It was with desire, because their looking at us produced a reaction in our bodies before we realized it. Even with our backs turned we could feel your eyes drilling through the backs of our necks. We automatically adopted a heroic and therefore

---

*Palestine Liberation Army.

attractive pose. Legs, thighs, chest, neck—everything helped to work the charm. We weren't aiming to attract anyone in particular, but since your eyes provoked us and you'd turned us into stars, we responded to your hopes and expectations.

"But you'd turned us into monsters, too. You called us terrorists! We were terrorist stars. What journalist wouldn't have signed a fat cheque to get Carlos to sit and drink one or two or ten whiskies with him! To get drunk together and have Carlos call him by his name! Or if not Carlos, Abu el-Az."

"Who's he?"

In 1971 Hussein's prime minister, Wasfi Tall, was killed in Cairo—had his throat cut, I believe—by a Palestinian who scooped up his blood and drank it. His name was Abu el-Az. He's in prison now in Lebanon, held by the Phalangists. The fedayee who was talking me was one of his colleagues—I shan't give his name. I'd thought before then that "drinking someone's blood" was just a figure of speech for "killing," but according to his friend Wasfi Tall's murderer had lapped up his gore.

"Israel calls everyone in the PLO terrorists, leaders and fedayeen alike. They show no sign of the admiration they must feel for you.

"As far as terrorism is concerned, we're nothing compared to them. Or compared to the Americans and the Europeans. If the whole world's a kingdom of terror we know whom to thank. But you terrorize by proxy. At least the terrorists I'm talking about risk their own skins. That's the difference."

After the 1970 agreement the streets of Amman were policed by patrols of fedayeen and Bedouin, often mixed. The airy, quizzical fedayeen could read and understand all the international signs and symbols, while the Bedouin turned them over gingerly in their slender, desert aristo fingers and handed back residence permits, passes, safe-conducts, driving licences and car papers upside down. Their dismay was obvious. And after being humiliated by the Palestinians in 1970, they were only too delighted to kill them in June 1971. There was no reason for the slaughter, but there was joy in it.

Today almost the whole of Amman is like the district which is still called Jebel Amman and remains the most fashionable part of the city. The walls of the houses were built of stone embossed on the outer surface, sometimes in the style called diamond point. In 1970 the solidity of this luxury district was in sharp contrast to the canvas and corrugated iron of the camps. The fact that the tents were of many colours, because of the patches, made them pleasing to look at, especially to a Western observer. If they looked at them from far enough away and on a misty day, people thought the camps must be happy places because of the way the colours of the patches seemed to match: those who lived beneath such harmony must be happy, or they wouldn't have taken the trouble to make their camps such a joy to the eye.

Who, reading this in the middle of 1984, when it was written, can help saying the Palestinian camps have increased and multiplied? Just as they did before, perhaps four thousand years ago or more, they seem to have sprung up all over the world, in Afghanistan, Morocco, Algeria, Ethiopia, Eritrea. Whole nations don't become nomads by choice or because they can't keep still. We see them through the windows of aeroplanes or as we leaf through glossy magazines. The shiny pictures lend the camps an air of peace that diffuses itself through the whole cabin, whereas really they are just the discarded refuse of "settled" nations. These, not knowing how to get rid of their "liquid waste," discharge it into a valley or onto a hillside, preferably somewhere between the tropics and the equator.

From the sky, from the pressurized air of the cabin, we see quite plainly that while the fortified countries and cities, tied to the ground like Gulliver, made use of their nomads—the privateers, the navigators, the Magellans, Vasco da Gamas and Ibn Battutas; the explorers, the centurions, the surveyors—they despised them too. And it got better and more comfortable still for the banks when, thanks to the gold in their cellars, money could "circulate" by means of bits of paper.

We oughtn't to have let their ornamental appearance persuade us the tents were happy places. We shouldn't be taken in by sunny photographs. A gust of wind blew the canvas, the zinc and the corrugated iron all away, and I saw the misery plain.

The words sailors use were probably arrived at quite naturally; but what a strange language they spoke when they were lost. They weren't yet poets—landsmen moving over and resting on peaceful earth, with plenty of time to imagine the wide expanses of ocean and its abysses and whirlpools. They were just simple mariners travelling around the world without a hope, unless heaven or their mothers' prayers intervened, of an unexpected return to known shores and familiar hearths. Yet what curious words they found for a beach or a piece of wood or canvas—words like fo'c'sle and poop and topgallant.

The surprising thing is not the wildness of their invention, but that the words still live on in our language instead of having sunk like a wreck. Invented in wandering and solitude, and therefore in fear, they still make us reel and our vocabulary pitch and toss.

When you go from Klagenfurt to Munich you take a little train that snakes loop after loop through the hills, and the Austrian ticket-collector walks down the corridor with the gait of a sailor in a rough sea. It's the only relic of the sea in the mountains of the Tyrol, all that remains of a terrestrial and maritime empire on which the sun never set. But Maximilian and Charlotte had the same rolling gait when they sailed to Mexico.

"The deep" is as expressive a term as most of the old but unforgotten phrases used in navigation. When sailors lost their way in loneliness and fog, water and endless pitching, perhaps hoping never to emerge, they also ventured verbally, making such discoveries as shoals, Finisterres, breakers, tribes, baobabs, Niagaras, dogfish. It was in a vocabulary that would have sounded strange in the ears of their widows, remarried by now to some shoemaker, that they told travellers' tales no one can explore without both dread and delight.

Perhaps the waters of the deep are as impenetrable as the darkest night: no eye can pierce its thousand walls, and colour there is first impossible and then superfluous.

Amman can be described in these terms. It's made up of seven hills and nine valleys, the latter consisting of deep crevasses that banks and mosques can never fill. When you come down from the best districts of the city—the highest and most wealthy—you descend into the deep, surprised at being able to do so without a diving suit. You notice your legs are more sprightly, your knees more supple, your heartbeat quieter, but the shouts of the passers-by and the noise of the traffic—and sometimes of bullets—seem to struggle against one another like rival teams in some new game. Now the shouting predominates for a moment, now the traffic din, producing a confusion in which nothing is clear except what's called a muffled roar, though it's really your own hearing that's impaired.

So much for your ears. As for the eye, in the shops of the "deep" it encounters windows all grey with dust. Of course the dust was still Arab even though the goods I saw on display were Japanese, but the even layer of particles, soft to the eye as the down in an ass's ear, was a kind of darkness. Not total darkness, though. A sort of submarine gloom. You might say the grey dust made Amman a city of the deep.

What did it mean, the soft film falling on the latest models of Japanese electronics from that most chic of archipelagos? Did it signify the rejection of an absurd but creeping sophistication? An attempt to bury it for ever? Was it the symbol of the inevitable future awaiting everything? A way of taming the fiercest technology?

But would astronomy ever have become almost as pointless a branch of knowledge as theology if sailors, despite their dread of the deep and its reefs, hadn't told of the heavens and its galaxies?

From Amman, city of the kingdom of David, a Nabatean, Roman, Arab city going back into the mists of time, there arose an age-old accumulation of stench.

When we gave up believing in a Providence that steered us by the shoulder, we had to fall back on chance.

It was by chance I found out about the two networks by which some young men from North Africa who wanted to die for Fatah—the only organization every Arab had heard of in 1968—made their way to Egypt. Bourguiba, preferring diplomacy to war, had banned the volunteers from Tunisia, though they did pass through. Did he shut his eyes to it? Did approaching senility make him take too long an afternoon nap?

Some strange words ask to be understood more than others equally unfamiliar. Even if you hear them only once their music stays with you. The word fedayeen was one of these. In the train from Sousse to Sfax I met a group of six young men, laughing and eating cheese and sardines. They were in high spirits because the recruiting board had found them unfit for military service. From what they said I gathered they had pretended to be mentally defective or mad, or deaf from self-abuse. They must have been about twenty. I left them behind when I got off the train at Sfax, but a few hours later met them once more by a fountain, again eating food out of tins. Instead of returning my smile or my greeting they seemed embarrassed. Some started to study the holes in their Gruyère. Others, who had recognized me, began a whispered but urgent conversation from which I learned—unless someone told me directly—that they'd got off the train at Sfax too, but on to the rails rather than the platform, so as not to be seen by the station master.

The next day a lorry took them to Médenine, where they stayed in a small hotel. They crossed the Libyan frontier during the night.

This was in the early summer of 1968. I often used to go to Sfax. A waiter in my hotel asked me if liked Tunisia. That's how, after a preliminary exchange of glances, amorous encounters always begin. I said I didn't.

"Come with me this evening," he said.

We met outside a bookshop.

"I'll read, and translate to you as I go along."

The shopkeeper handed us some slim volumes of Arabic poetry hitherto safely concealed, as he thought, under piles of other books. Then he opened a door and showed us into a small room, where the young man read me the first poems dedicated to Fatah and the fedayeen. What impressed me most was the elaborate decoration at the beginning, to the right, of each line of verse.

"Why are they hidden?" I asked.

"The police don't allow them to circulate openly. The southern part of the country is being developed by engineers from America and Vietnam. Bourguiba doesn't want any trouble with the US or Israel. And our government has recognized Saigon.

Come with us tomorrow. Three of us are driving forty kilometres out of town."

"What for?"

"You'll see. And hear."

The poems, at least in translation, left me unmoved, except for the beauty of the calligraphy. They were about struggle and disaster, but I couldn't make anything of the imagery, which was all about doves and damsels and honey.

The next day at about five in the evening the youths drove me out into the desert. They stopped the car where two tracks crossed. At six o'clock we listened to Bourguiba delivering a speech in Arabic on the radio. Every so often the boys would interrupt with sarcastic comments. Afterwards we started to drive back to Sfax.

"What did you come all the way out here for?" I asked.

"For two years we've amused ourselves listening to Bourguiba speechify in the desert," they said.

Then, more seriously, they showed me a place where two tracks met in the sand. One went south with the caravans of female camels, the other went north through Tunisia. Both came from Mauretania, Morocco and Algeria and led to Tripoli, Cairo and the Palestinian camps. Those who took the northern route hitch-hiked or jumped rides on the train. The ticket collectors looked the other way, as I was told by a ticket collector himself. The young men who went south mingled with the Bedouin caravans. King Idriss's border was open to them, and after a few weeks' military training in Tripoli they went on to Cairo by train, and then on again, I forget how, to Damascus or Amman.

I don't mean to say a whole flood of fighters from four or five North African countries used this illegal detour to come to the aid of the Palestinian camps. But that was how I learned of the appeal the Palestine resistance exercised on the Arab nation as a whole, and of the reverberations and almost immediate response it awakened. Of course the fedayeen had to be helped to reject the Zionist occupation, America or no America; but I sensed additional motives. Each of the Arab peoples wanted to throw off old yokes: when Algeria, Tunisia and Morocco shook their leaves they'd brought down the French who'd been hiding in the foliage. Cuba had got rid of its Americans in the same way. In South

Vietnam they were only hanging by a cobweb. And Mecca, not so much sought after as it has become since, still didn't have many pilgrims.

It was about then that the minister Ben Salah introduced the figures 49 and 51 into Tunisian conversation. Fifty-one per cent of the country's profit went to the government, forty-nine per cent to private individuals. Fifty-one per cent of the population was male, forty-nine per cent female. Perhaps as a joke Ben Salah cut the merchants down to size: souks and French trees were pruned back and carpet sellers grew thin and seemed to be searching the ground for their lost branches. Bourguiba's sky-blue eye was fixed exclusively on Washington. Meanwhile, in every village along the coast and from north to south, potters indefatigably turned out millions of jars—replicas of the age-old amphorae that sponge fishers are always finding at the bottom of the sea, full of oil preserved by the mud since the days of ancient Carthage. Every morning there were more jars, still warm from the just-quenched oven. I could see Tunisia dwindling away: all its clay being sold to girls from Norway in the form of terracotta amphorae. In the end, I thought, it'll disappear altogether.

A few weeks later, about the middle of May 1968, I came across the same slim volumes of Arabic poems to the glory of Fatah, but without the decorations, in the courtyard of the Sorbonne in Paris. I think the stand they were on was close to Mao's. That August the Soviet Union nipped the Prague Spring in the bud.

The young Tunisians I saw in the south of the country then were about eighteen or twenty: the rutting season, the age of conquest for its own sake and for the sake of sex; the age for making fun of the moral values your parents talk about and never practise. The younger generation were all the more wild and even brazen because Nasser encouraged their rebelliousness, and because they were preparing to die. As you'll have realized, while some of the young men in Tunisia were as I've described, the rest were preparing to be a nation of waiters—a hierarchy of waiters and head waiters in cafés and restaurants. Floor waiters in hotels were the highest on the ladder to Heaven. They went about almost naked, and those who were good-looking, even though some of them were married, would often leave the country, travelling first class with some Swiss banker, or more rarely some Swiss banker's wife.

So 1968 ended, and in Amman the Palestinians' struggle against King Hussein, muted at first, grew more intense.

I'm still itching to say a few more words about amphorae. I saw them being made. The clay was on the wheel and the potter was turning it with his foot. He reminded me of a countrywoman working a sewing machine. But when the amphora was almost finished the potter took it off the wheel, threw it into a box and broke it. An assistant kneaded the still malleable pieces together and added them to the mass of clay still waiting to be worked.

What had happened was that at the last moment the potter had made an irreparable mistake. Because he was tired, or for some other reason, one of his fingers, or more likely his thumb, had pressed down too hard and produced a hole or some similar flaw in the side of the jar. So he had to start all over again, or the amphora wouldn't live up to its supposed three thousand years.

Even now—they'll never grow up—Japanese potters still play with accidents. Whether it arises from the clay, the wheel, the kiln or the glaze, they watch out for any irregularity and sometimes even emphasize it. In any case they use it as a starting point for a new adventure. The shape and colour may be perfectly classical, but spoiled by a scratch or being under- or over-fired. So they pursue and develop the flaw, struggling fiercely, lovingly with and against it until it becomes deliberate, an expression of themselves. If they succeed they're overjoyed: the result is modern. Never Tunisian. But not many Swiss bankers take up with Japanese potters.

To the other reasons I've given for the more lively part of Tunisian youth going to fight with the Palestinians, we might add that it was fed up with age-old amphorae.

In their own country the young Tunisians I mentioned before could easily look around and find others to lord it over: the fellahs from some god-forsaken part of the south as yet unrecorded on the rainfall map couldn't express themselves very well; French tourists were equally impressed by dusky eyes and by their gift of the gab. Their rapid prattle sounded as if it might owe something to amphetamines, but in fact this forked generation had merely learned to string phrases together from French television news-readers: "Problems concerning the social fabric and rising delin-quency aside, it will depend entirely upon ourselves to succeed at all levels in obtaining the highest possible output, creating a market in quality products even though the imminence of new scientific developments might call for ultra-sophisticated state-of-the-art equipment." But outside Tunisia none of these squirts ever breathed a word, either in Arabic or in French. It was deeds that were needed, and gutsy ones—but siesta starts at two in the afternoon.

Bourguiba was asleep on his back.

It had been so pleasant dreaming about the Palestinians, and nobody knew yet, except in Israel, that all the Arab countries of Asia would expel them. No one knew, but everyone wanted them to be driven out and was secretly working for it.

One Palestinian alone was enough to cause a commotion. Their arrival in Tunis in 1982 was a facer for the languid Tunisians, part Turk, part wop, part Breton: more than a thousand Palestinians and, in their midst, Arafat himself.

It's at this point, neither sooner nor later, that I must say what Fatah was. But already those who dreamed up the various names of the Palestine movements were using Arabic as if they were both philologists and children. So while I'm going to try to ex-plain the word, I know I can never bring out all its meaning.

The consonants F, T and H, in that order, form a triliteral root meaning fissure, chink, opening; also a breakthrough before a vic-tory, a victory willed by God. Fatah is connected with the word for key, which in Arabic is *meftah*—the three basic letters pre-ceded by *me*. The same triliteral root gives *Fatiha*, that which opens, the name of the first surat of the Koran. The first surat itself begins with Bismillah.

Fatah, then, or rather F.T.H., corresponds to the initials of the Flasteen (Palestine) Tahrir (liberation) Haraka (movement). In their French or logical order the three letters would give Haftha, which if it exists at all is meaningless. To get F.T.H. the order had to be reversed. Some overgrown children must have had a good laugh over that.

I see three hidden meanings in the three words Fatah, meftah and fatiha. Fatah—chink, fissure, opening—suggests the expectation, the almost passive expectation, of a God-willed victory. Mefta —key—suggests almost visibly a key in an opening or lock. Fatiha also means an opening, but a religious one, the first chapter of the Koran. So behind the three words derived from the same root as Fatah lurk the ideas of struggle (for victory), sexual violence (the key in the lock), and battle won through the grace of God.

The reader probably sees this digression as a mere diversion, but I was so intrigued by the choice and composition of the word Fatah that I extracted the three above meanings from it, having put them there myself. The word itself occurs three times in the Koran.

The image of the fedayee grows more and more indelible: he turns into the path, and I'll no longer be able to see his face, only his back and his shadow. It's when I can neither talk to him any more, nor he to me, that I'll need to talk about him.

The disappearance seems to be not only a vanishing but also a need to fill the gap with something different, perhaps the opposite of what is gone. As if there were a hole where the fedayee disappeared, a drawing, a photograph, any sort of portrait, seems to call him back in every sense of the term. It calls him back from afar— again, in every sense of the word. Did he vanish deliberately in order that the portrait might appear?

Giacometti used to paint best around midnight. He spent the day gazing intently, steadily. I don't mean he was absorbing the features of the model—that's something different. Every day Alberto looked for the last time, recording the last image of the world.

I first met the Palestinians in 1970. Some of the leaders got excited and almost insisted I finish this book. But I was afraid the end of the book might coincide with the end of the resistance. Not that my book would show it as it actually was. But what if my decision to make my years with the resistance public were a sign that it was soon to disappear? Some inexpressible feeling warned me that the rebellion was fading, flagging, was about to turn into the path and disappear. It would be made into epics. I looked at the resistance as if it were going to vanish at any moment.

To anyone looking at their pictures on television or in the papers, the Palestinians seemed to girdle the earth so fast they were everywhere at once. But they saw themselves as swallowed up by all the worlds they travelled through. Perhaps both we and they are wrong, or rather caught between an old illusion and a new variety, as when Ptolemy's ancient theory collided with Copernicus's novel and probably equally temporary truth.

The Palestinians imagined they were being hounded on all sides—by Zionism, imperialism and Americanism. One day towards evening when things were at their quietest, we were safe inside the stone walls of our apartment in the middle of the Palestine Red Crescent building in Amman and I was writing down some addresses from Alfredo's dictation. Suddenly the air was rent by a cry, or rather a shriek. It was the lady of fifty.

She was a Palestinian who'd gone to live in Nebraska when she was very young and got rich there. What I remember about her is her face, her American accent and her black clothes. She always dressed entirely in black, whether it was a blouse and a full skirt or a blouse and a narrow skirt; whether she chose a long seroual or a coat lined or edged with fur; whether the material was thick or thin. Her shoes and stockings, her jet necklaces, her hair and the scarf she tied over it—all were black. Her face was stern, her speech brief, curt and guttural. The director of the Red Crescent had arranged for her to have a bedroom and the use of the lounge in our flat. All he told us about her was that one day in Nebraska, at home watching television, she saw some pictures of fedayeen who'd been killed by King Hussein's Bedouin. She switched off the television and the electricity, collected her handbag, passport and cheque-book, bolted and barred the front door, called in at the bank, went to the travel agent's and booked a ticket to Amman, and finally took a taxi straight from Amman airport and came and offered her services to the Red Crescent.*

The Red Crescent were in a quandary, because apart from signing cheques—and she ruined herself doing that—this immensely wealthy Palestinian could do only one thing: even in the most uncomfortable conditions, sit in front of the television and watch American films.

We didn't talk to her much. She spoke only American and just a bit of Arabic. But we found out from her shriek, the meaning of which we learned soon afterwards, how stupefied the Palestinians were when they suddenly found out that the whole world was against them.

Twiddling the knobs of the television to find something to pass the time, she could only find dialogue in Arabic. Then she thought she'd been rescued from the boredom of the evening, from Alfredo's and my silence and from the distant murmur of Amman, when someone on the screen spoke a whole sentence in Brooklyn slang. But—and this was why she'd shrieked—the other person answered in Hebrew: the television had picked up Tel Aviv. Her Palestinian hand, trembling with rage, cut off the sound in mid sentence.

Silence fell again. The Palestinians might whizz non-stop from Oslo to Lisbon, but they knew they were being kept track of in the hated language.

The villas in Jebel Amman had very large rooms. Each house had four salons: a Louis Quinze, a Directory, an Oriental and a Modern—and sometimes even a "modern style" or *art nouveau* one as well. The nursery was done out in chintz, the nanny's room in cretonne. The domestics—cooks, gardeners, valets and so on—slept out in the suburbs, in the camp at Wahadat, or twenty kilometres away in the camp at Baqa. Special servants' buses took them out every evening, standing up and already asleep, and brought them back again the next morning, standing up and not

---

*The Muslim counterpart to the Red Cross.

yet awake. A night porter stayed on duty to have tea and rolls ready for the masters when they woke up.

In this world of refugees, masters and servants were equal. The word refugee, later to become a title of distinction, was now a title-deed to one of the strong, stone-built, wind-proof villas. But it was a title that threatened, though not yet too ominously, the camps of shreds and patches.

"I'm your equal because I'm a refugee. I'm your superior because my house is built of stone. Don't do anything to hurt or disturb me—I'm a refugee and a Muslim just like you."

Caught up in the to-ing and fro-ing between camp and villa, the servants seemed to bear their indignity proudly. But the year 1970 upset everybody. Wealthy Palestinians let their servants sleep in for a while. Others, by way of precaution, started to eat the same food as their staff. In September, democracy became fashionable almost overnight. Surreptitiously at first, then openly, the daughters of the house made their own beds or even emptied the ashtrays in the lounge. The reason was that all the menservants had taken up their guns ready for the fighting in Amman. They became heroes or, better still, died and became martyrs. For various reasons that time was always to be known as Black September.

Many German families offered to take in wounded fedayeen from mobile hospitals like the one run by Dr. Dieter. All I'll say of him here is that in 1971 he set up a training school for nurses in the camp at Gaza. He took me to the camp one day after finishing his rounds among the sick and wounded. We went into one of the houses, all of which consisted of a single room. We were greeted by the political officer of the camp and the mothers and fathers of all the girls who wanted to learn the rudiments of nursing.

Naturally we drank tea, and then Dr. Dieter, standing at a blackboard fixed to the wall, began his lecture by drawing a rough sketch of a male body, complete with sexual organs. Not only did nobody laugh or smile; there was a sort of holy hush. The interpreter was a Lebanese. Dieter demonstrated the circulation of the blood with coloured chalks, showing the veins in blue and the arteries in red. He put in the heart and lungs and other vital parts, and indicated where tourniquets should be applied. After the brain, skull, lungs, aorta, arteries and thighs he came to the male sexual organs.

"A bullet or shell splinter can lodge here," he said.

So he drew a bullet near the penis. He didn't attempt to conceal anything, with his hand or his voice or his words. Both the official and the families approved of his frankness. His main concern was the shortage of doctors and nurses, male and female, in the camps.

"After twenty lessons the girls will know the basic necessities, but I shan't award certificates—the political and military chiefs are against it. The girls are being trained to go with the fedayeen and look after the wounded, not to Jebel Amman to administer aspirin and footbaths to the wives of millionaires."

There are lots of Palestinians in the Rhineland. They work in factories and speak good German, with the verbs at the ends of the sentences. The young ones born of German mothers learn Arabic and the history of Palestine, and call all the butchers in Düsseldorf, with their bloody aprons, Hussein.

As soon as I arrived on the bases at Ajloun I noticed a sergeant who was both a Palestinian and black, and whom the fedayeen spoke to or answered, if not scornfully, at least with a tinge of irony. Was it the colour of his skin? A fedayee who spoke French told me it wasn't, but he smiled as he said it.

It was the month of Ramadan, and the soldiers could be divided up into very devout, not very devout and indifferent. The latter ate during the fast.

One evening the sergeant, knowing I was a Christian, laid a cloth on the grass and set out a bowl of soup and a pot of vegetables. He himself remained standing, obeying the Koran. I had to choose quickly. To refuse would be to snub a Black; to accept would make the favour too obvious. Eating just a little struck me as an elegant compromise. A few bits of bread dipped in the soup were all I wanted anyway. There were a couple of soldiers standing behind me, and when I'd eaten what I thought was a polite amount I got up, and the sergeant told the soldiers to finish what I'd left.

I could feel my cheeks flushing. I ought to have told the sergeant the fedayeen must eat with me, not after, and above all not finish my leavings—but how could I say that to a Black? The main thing was not to make too much fuss. I said nothing. Should I sit down with the fedayeen and ask them for a bit of bread? The fedayeen had noticed what was happening. But not the black sergeant, as far as I could see.

When they look back, do the Palestinians see themselves with the same features and gestures, the same attitudes of body and limbs, in the same get-up, as fifteen years ago? Do they see themselves from behind, for instance, or in profile? That image of themselves they conjure up amid the events of the past—is it younger?

Which of them remembers the scene I witnessed under the trees at Ajloun a few days after the fighting in Amman? The fedayeen had built a little arbour with a roof of leaves, and inside was a table—three planks laid shakily on four roughly stripped branches—with four benches fixed in the ground around it. The month of Ramadan had brought the expected surprise of a crescent moon open towards the west. We'd eaten our evening meal out on the moss near the arbour and were sitting replete around a bowl still warm but empty, listening to someone reciting verses from the Koran. So it must have been about eight o'clock.

"The man's a monster," Mahjoub told me. That evening he'd seemed the hungriest of us all. "He's the first head of state since Nero to set fire to his own capital."

What national pride I still possessed allowed me to reply:

"Excuse me, Dr. Mahjoub—we did just as well as Nero long before Hussein. A hundred years ago Adolphe Thiers asked the Prussian army to shell Versailles, Paris and the Commune. He did the job even more thoroughly than Hussein. And he was just as small."

The evening star was out. Mahjoub, slightly taken aback, went to bed in his tent. A dozen or so soldiers aged between about fifteen and twenty-three almost filled the arbour, but they made room for me. One fedayee stayed on sentry duty by the door. Then two men came in. They were fighters, still quite young but with downy moustaches on their upper lips to show how tough they

were. They weighed one another up, as the phrase goes, each trying to intimidate the other. Then they sat down facing one another, lowering themselves casually but stiffly on to the benches
and hitching up their trousers to preserve a non-existent crease.

I was sitting silent and alert, as I'd been told, on the third bench.
The newcomer sitting next to me took his hand out of the left-
hand pocket of his leopard trousers and, with a movement at once
very human and yet seeming to belong to some rare ceremonial,
produced a small pack of fifty cards which he got his partner to cut.
Then he fanned the cards out in front of them. One of the two swept
them up and arranged them in a pack again, examined it, then
shuffled the cards in the usual way and dealt them out between
the two of them. Both looked serious and almost pale with suspicion. Their lips were tight, their jaws set. I can still hear the silence.
Card-playing was officially forbidden on the bases: Mahjoub had
referred to it as "a middle-class pastime for middle-class people."

The game began. Gambling, and for a stake, filled both their
faces with greed. They were equally matched, and first one and
then the other grabbed the kitty. Around the two heroes, everyone tried to catch a brief glimpse of their swiftly concealed hands.
Against all the rules the onlookers behind each contestant made
signals to the player opposite, who pretended to take no notice. I
think they must have been playing a game something like poker.
I was impressed by the way they both stared blankly at their
hands, concealing their agitation and anxiety; by their brief hesitation over whether to take one, two or three cards; and by the
speed of those thin fingers, the bones so fine it seemed they might
break when the winner turned the cards over and gathered them
in. One of the players dropped a card on the floor and picked it
up so nonchalantly it reminded me of a film in slow motion. The
indifference, even disdain, on his face when he saw what it was
made me think it must be an ace.

I thought people would think he'd been cheating, imitating
an "accident" familiar to card-sharpers. What little Arabic I knew
consisted mainly of threats and insults. But the words *charmouta*
and *hattai*, muttered between the players' clenched teeth and lips
gleaming with saliva, were quickly bitten back.

The two players stood up and shook hands across the table,

without a word, without a smile. Such dreary ceremony can be seen only in the casinos of Europe or Lebanon. Tennis matches can end like this too, but only in Australia. Sometimes a laugh is provided by a well-dressed lout who bends the cards lengthwise, either backwards or forwards. According to its position on the table a card may be either the boat in which the cheat himself sails, or the first half of the beast with two backs, or a woman pressed down on the beach and opening herself up. If the croupier notices the resulting smiles where no smiles should be, he brings out a fresh pack of cards, his face and eyes as expressionless as someone doing up his flies in public.

Obon is the name the Japanese give to another kind of game. Obon is the feast of the dead, who come back amongst the living for three times twenty-four hours. But the person who's returned from the grave is present only through the deliberately clumsy actions of the living. I interpret these as meaning: "We are alive and we laugh at the dead. They can't take offence because they're only skeletons condemned to remain in a hole in the ground."

It's merely their absence that the children, those underminers of ceremony, will bring up and install in their apartments. "We'll stay in the graveyard—we shan't be in anyone's way. We'll only be present if your awkwardness gives us away." The invisible dead are seated on the finest cushions and offered good things to eat and gold-tipped cigarettes to smoke such as Liane de Pougy was offered when she was twenty-three.

The kids pretend to limp. It seems that in the month leading up to Obon they practise limping, the better to leave the absent corpse behind in the races. These come to a sudden end—shin-bones, skulls, thigh-bones and finger-bones fall to the ground, and all the living laugh. An act of irony and affection had been enough to give the dead person a taste of life.

The game of cards, which only existed because of the shockingly realistic gestures of the fedayeen—they'd played at playing, without any cards, without aces or knaves, clubs or spades, kings or queens—reminded me that all the Palestinians' activities were like the Obon feast, where the only thing that was absent, that could not appear, was what the ceremony, however lacking in solemnity, was in aid of.

The science of shrieking seems almost as well known in the Arab world as the art of giving birth standing up, with the woman, her legs apart, holding on to a rope attached to the ceiling.

"Jean, did you hear that woman? She must be an Arab. That shriek's exactly like the one my grandmother let out when she did my father out of his inheritance."

"What was the inheritance?"

"The eighth part of an olive grove."

"What does that amount to?"

"Three and a half kilos of olives."

It doesn't take Muhammad many words to tell of his poverty, his father's dependency, the shriek of the old Arab woman. The shriek itself may have been natural, but its shrillness was learned when she was a girl. No one teaches R'Guiba, the watchman, how to shout a warning—he learns it in his youth when his voice is still high, and it comes back to him when he's on watch and some danger threatens, even after his voice has broken.

The Syrians often let out the same cry as the shamming Palestinians when a one of swords or any of the same suit comes up. All except the seven are of ill omen: the one means excess, the two softness, the three distance, the four absence or loneliness, the five defeat, the six effort, and the seven—the famous Seven of Swords*—means hope, and it's the one card in the pack that's greeted with kisses. The eight means complaint, the nine masturbation, and the ten desolation and tears—and the cry that met this card, dejected rather than aggressive, was not at all like the cry of delight that greeted the appearance of clubs, the symbols of happiness.

At the camp at Baqa the humiliated got their own back. The Japanese, Italians, French, Germans and Norwegians were the first film cameramen, photographers and sound engineers on the scene. The air, which had been light, became heavy.

---

*Mary of the Seven Swords, stepdaughter of Lady Music. (*The Satin Shoe*, Paul Claudel).

Those who'd never been asked to pose themselves but who would be stars if they got a picture of a star—which here meant every Palestinian wearing combat dress and carrying a Kalashnikov—thought they had their victims just where they wanted them. With the irritability more or less natural to the inhabitants of a vexed archipelago, the Japanese threatened in English to go back to Tokyo without any pictures and leave Japan ignorant of the Palestinian Revolution. Little did they know that the famous terrorists of Lodz were in training ten kilometres away, with maps of Israel and plans of the airport in their overall pockets.

The French made one fedayee pose twelve times for a single picture. Dr. Alfredo put a stop to this farce with three sharp words.

To show they knew how to take low-angle shots the Italians told the fighters to unload their guns and take aim, then threw themselves down and took pictures lying on the ground. But the spirit of revenge produced a delightful chaos.

A photographer is seldom photographed, a fedayee often, but if he has to pose he'll die of boredom before he dies of fatigue.

Some artists think they see a halo of solitary grandeur around a man in a photograph, but it's only the weariness and depression caused by the antics of the photographer. One Swiss made the handsomest of the fedayeen stand on an upturned tub so that he could take him silhouetted against the sunset!

What is still called order, but is really physical and spiritual exhaustion, comes into existence of its own accord when what is rightly called mediocrity is in the ascendant.

Betrayal is made up of both curiosity and fascination.

But what if it were true that writing is a lie? What if it merely enabled us to conceal what was, and any account is, only eye-wash? Without actually saying the opposite of what was, writing presents only its visible, acceptable and, so to speak, silent face, because it is incapable of really showing the other one.

The various scenes in which Hamza's mother appears are in a way flat. They ooze love and friendship and pity, but how can one simultaneously express all the contradictory emanations issuing from the witnesses? The same is true for every page in this book where there is only one voice. And like all the other voices my own is faked, and while the reader may guess as much, he can never know what tricks it employs.

The only fairly true causes of my writing this book were the nuts I picked from the hedges at Ajloun. But this sentence tries to hide the book, as each sentence tries to hide the one before, leaving on the page nothing but error: something of what often happened but what I could never subtly enough describe—though it's subtly enough I cease to understand it.

Hicham had never been shown any consideration by anyone, old or young. No one took any notice of him, not because he was nothing, but because he did nothing. But one day his knee hurt him and he put himself down for medical inspection the following day. He went, and was given the number fourteen. Fifteen was a fedayee officer, a captain. After seeing thirteen patients Dr. Dieter read out Hicham's name and number, but he was so flustered by hearing his own name pronounced by a doctor he didn't realize it referred to him. He nudged number fifteen, the officer who was supposed to come after him.

"No—you first," said Dieter. "You with the bad knee."

An official told Hicham to go first, and so he did. And I was told that after that day, when a German doctor made him go before a captain, Hicham started to throw his weight about. He knew he hadn't gone up in rank, but the fact that the official had briefly given him precedence made him throw out his chest. Not long afterwards he relapsed into obscurity again: the officers forgot to return his salute. There was no such thing as pride to be seen in Baqa Camp.

Outside the arbour, under the trees, indifferent to the phantom game of cards, ten or so fedayeen waited their turn for a shave. They looked tired, but fairly relaxed. The lengthy ceremonial had begun. First every man had to bring a little bundle of dead branches. A fire was lit with a handful of leaves and the water put to boil in an old tin can. They were on such friendly terms with each other they might easily have taken it in turns with the one mirror and shaved themselves. But the mirror was only as big as the palm of a man's hand, and it was a sort of rest, added to that of the evening itself, to leave your beard and your face in the hands of the fedayee known as the barber. The touch of a hand, whether friendly or indifferent, but anyway different from one's own, was the start of a wave that soothed every organ in the seated body and reached right down to the weary toes. They took turns to be shaved. The whole thing usually lasted from eight o'clock to ten, and took place three times a week.

But why the game of cards?

"I leave the fighters completely free."

Mahjoub and I were walking under the trees at night.

"I should hope so."

"The only thing I've forbidden is cards."

"But why cards?"

"The Palestinian people wanted a revolution. When they find out the bases on the Jordan are gambling dens they'll know brothels will be next."

I defended as best I could amusements I personally wasn't interested in, but was sorry Mahjoub took it on himself to ban something that helped the men pass the time.

"Gambling often leads to fighting."

It was easy to quote chess as an example of the pitiless struggle between the USSR and the Western powers. Mahjoub said a curt goodnight and went to bed. The fedayeen knew. The show they'd put on for me demonstrated their disillusion, for to play only with gestures when your hands ought to be holding kings and queens and knaves, all the symbols of power, makes you feel a fraud, and brings you dangerously close to schizophrenia. Playing cards without cards every night is a kind of dry masturbation.

At this point I must warn the reader that my memory is accurate as far as facts and dates and events are concerned, but that the conversations here are reconstructed. Less than a century ago it was still quite normal to "describe" conversations, and I admit I've followed that method. The dialogue you'll read in this book is in fact reconstituted, I hope faithfully. But it can never be as complex as real exchanges, since it's only the work of a more or less talented restorer, like Viollet-le-Duc. But you mustn't think I don't respect the fedayeen. I'll have done my best to reproduce the timbre and expression of their voices, and their words. Mahjoub and I really did have that conversation; it's just as authentic as the game of cards without cards, where the game existed only through the accurate mimicry of hand and finger and joint.

Is it because of my age or through lack of skill that when I describe something that happened in the past I see myself not as I am but as I was? And that I see myself—examine myself, rather—from outside, like a stranger; in the same way as one sees those who die at a certain age as always being that age, or the age they were when the event you remember them for happened? And is it a privilege of my present age or the misfortune of my whole life that I always see myself from behind, when in fact I've always had my back to the wall?

I seem to understand now certain acts and events that surprised me when they happened there on the banks of the Jordan, opposite Israel—acts and events unrelated to anything, inaccessible islets I couldn't fit together then but which now form a clear and coherent archipelago.

I first went to Damascus when I was eighteen years old.

Arab card games are very different from those played by the French and the English. They're closer to the Spanish—an inheritance from Islam preserved by the fingers of urchins playing La Ronda.

Mahjoub in Jordan and one-armed General Gouraud in Damascus both banned card-playing for different reasons, as they thought. Gouraud must have been afraid of clandestine gatherings that must *ipso facto* be anti-French. So the Syrians played cards at night in the little mosques of Damascus, by the light of a candle end or a wick dipped in a drop of oil. My presence must have reassured them. If some sappers on patrol in the narrow streets were surprised by the light and came to see what it was, I could explain we were there for religious reasons, to pray for France.

After the game, to make sure I wouldn't forget them, the Syrians would show me the ruins. I'm sure they'd been deliberately left as they were by Gouraud, the big boss, who refused to have them cleared away so that the citizens of Damascus should shake in their shoes for ever. In the morning, at the dawn prayer, the players used to go home linking little or forefingers. I can still see the Swords and the Seven of Swords.

In the very small fraction of Fatah that I knew I counted up eight Khaled Abu Khaleds. The number of *noms de guerre* was astonishing. False names were originally intended to conceal a fighter; now they adorned him. His choice was a pointer to his fantasies, which were paralleled by such designations as Chevara (a contraction of Che Guevara), Lumumba and Hadj Muhammad. Every name was a thin, sometimes transparent, mask beneath which there was another name, another mask, of the same or different stuff but of another colour, through which could be glimpsed a further name. Khaled just concealed a Maloudi, itself imperfectly covering an Abu Bakr, which again was superimposed on a Kader. The layers of names corresponded to layers of personas, and what they hid might be someone quite simple but was usually someone complex and weary. In such cases the name might belong to a deed admissible in one place and forbidden in another.

I, in my ignorance, accepted appearance and reality with equal politeness, and felt slightly irritated whenever I discovered someone's original name. A lot could be said about those two words, appearance and reality! Some of the names were invented, some came from garbled memories of American films; all tried to cover up whatever might remain of the misdeed.

I thought I could hear echoes of it in the phraseologies and absurdly sweeping slogans attributed to the sort of figures that haunt the imagination of nations in revolt.

Who said what?

"I'd make a treaty with the devil to fight against you."

"Who sups with the devil must use a long spoon."

"You don't ask for freedom. You take it."

"We'll fight two or three or four or five or ten Vietnams if necessary."

"We have lost a battle but not the war."

"I do not confuse the American people, whom I love and admire, with their reactionary government."

The paternity of such sayings is not very clear. The fourth is supposed to belong to Guevara. The fathers of the third were Abd el-Kadr and Abd el-Krim, and of the second Churchill, Stalin and Roosevelt. It's said the first had Lumumba for a sire but was legitimized by Arafat, and this made it possible for Khaled to say to me:

"Israel is the devil we have to work with to conquer Israel."

It seemed to me he said it in one go, without any punctuation or pause for breath until the burst of laughter at the end. Take it as it is, and as you like.

One very conventional image reigned, trivial as the posters in the Paris Métro.

"From camp-fire to camp-fire there echoed calls to arms, *noms de guerre* and songs. Anyone who was twenty then saw the world as being consumed or at least licked by flakes of fire, like the R of Revolution ever being devoured but never burned away by eternal flames."

What I saw at once was that every "nation," the better to justify its rebellion in the present, sought proof of its own singularity in the distant past. Every uprising revealed some deep genealogy whose strength was not in its almost non-existent branches but in its roots, so that the rebels springing forth everywhere seemed to be celebrating some sort of cult of the dead. Words, phrases, whole languages were disinterred.

One day in Beirut, when I'd managed to make some sort of a joke, a Lebanese smiled at me and said almost fondly:

"You're getting to be a real Phoenician!"

"Why a Phoenician? Can't I be an Arab?"

"No, not any more. We haven't been Arabs since Syria invaded Lebanon." That was in 1976. "The Syrians are Arabs. The Lebanese Christians are Phoenicians."

The youngest generation were a lot of moles. What an example, after two thousand years of travelling the earth's surface on horseback, on foot or by sea, to go back and burrow among molehills for the remains of some temple! Not only the search itself but also the wholesale identifying of one people with another, root and branch, struck me as undignified, a pretentious vulgarity worthy of Paris. It's a form of laziness to think nobility is proved by ancestry, and when I knew them the Palestinians didn't go in for it. The danger then was that they might see Israel as a sort of super-ego.

1972 was before the Syrians' battle for the Palestinian camp at Tal-el-Zaatar. That didn't take place till 1976. But the Palestinians did show me the Phalangist barracks overlooking the camp.

This book could be called *Souvenirs*, and I'll lead the reader back and forth in time as well as, inevitably, in space. The space will be the whole world, the time chiefly the period between 1970 and 1984.

Pierre Gemayel's militia, modelled on Hitler's SA and founded at about the same time, was called the Phalange—Kataeb in Arabic. Black shirts, brown shirts, blue shirts—the famous "Azul legion" that froze to death among the fairy-tale snows of white Russia—green shirts, grey shirts, shirts of steel . . . In the place of the Nazis' anthem I heard the Phalangists'.

In 1970 the tall lads marched along singing the praises of the Immaculate Conception. I was enchanted. I could calculate their cruelty from their stupidity. Something half-way between monks and hoodlums, they swung along, chins jutting out, to a military march, some obliging musician having converted the tempo of the hymn into the solemn beat of an irresistible advance into immortality. From their full, slightly negroid lips the songs issued forth with a fine foolishness. The Virgin Mary must have trembled at the thought of all those adolescent dead about to land in Heaven at any moment. But it was tragic too, the obvious virility of the young men lauding the gentleness of an invisible goddess, a smart young woman smothered in wreaths of white roses. Marching along in quick time, the strapping youths struck me as unreal, of another world—which as a matter of fact was where they soon went.

They marched in martial fashion. But wars aren't fought by marching in martial fashion. Real warriors probably never march in time. I was trying to impart some dignity to the ponderous, rather theatrical gait of the Kataeb—like something from the

Beirut Opera. It was dictated by a leader for whom this sort of outmoded spectacle was appropriate; he never marched himself, but he did think in double time.

The newspaper-seller's two sons answered me shyly. They were both Phalangists, and as they spoke they each touched, or rather clutched, a gold medal of the Virgin of Lourdes in the same way as a native of Mali on the banks of the Niger might clutch his gri-gri—a few magic words in Arabic on very thin paper, perhaps Rizla, rolled up in a red woollen holder.

"Why are you touching that?"

"To remind me to say my morning prayer from the Koran."

The Cross and the image of the Virgin Mary, especially if they are engraved, or better still embossed, in gold—the Phalangists touch such talismans to preserve their strength. But what is it they are really touching—the Cross, the Virgin Mary, gold, or the sex of the world? If a Phalangist kills anyone he doesn't do so of his own accord but on orders from God and in defence of His Mother, His Son, and the gold presented by one of the Magi. The Phalangists' God is the Lord of Hosts who makes haste to help them against the threat of the Other—Allah.

In 1972 I saw a member of the Kataeb kiss a young Lebanese woman. Between her tanned breasts, evidence of topless sunbathing, shone the little gold gibbet, studded with diamonds and rubies. But instead of Christ it had a black, egg-shaped pearl. The young man's lips seemed to swallow the pearl, his tongue to caress the skin of the girl's breast. She laughed. Three Phalangists in turn bowed their heads in that communion, and without a trace of self-consciousness the girl said:

"May Jesus protect you and His Mother give you victory."

Having pronounced this blessing she went chastely on her way.

Francisco Franco was in power. On my way to the abbey of Montserrat I went through rocks, boulders and ripe wheat. Churches are always decorated in red for Pentecost, and the columns in the chapel were hung with cerise silk banners embroidered with gold, or what glitters like gold these days. The Abbot assisted in the celebration of the mass.

After having looked on with some emotion—the significance of which, before my meeting with Hamza and his mother, will appear later—as the black Virgin proffered her child (as it might have been some hoodlum showing a black phallus), I sat down on a bench. The church was full of men and women in mourning. Most of the congregation were very young. The Abbot and his two acolytes, heirs of Cisneros the grand inquisitor, wore copes of cerise silk. Children's voices, crystal frail and slightly raw, sang a mass by Palestrina. I kept thinking how the name started with the same six letters as Palestine. Then came the famous kiss of peace: after the elevation the Abbot kissed each of the acolytes on both cheeks, and they conveyed the salutation to each of the monks sitting in the choir. Then two choristers opened the screen doors and his reverence came down among the congregation, kissing some of us. I was one of those who received a kiss, but I broke the chain of fraternity by not passing it on. The clergy emerged from the choir and went down the nave towards the main doors, followed by the congregation, men and women mingled together and I among them.

Then, for me alone, a wonderful thing happened. The doors seemed to open by themselves, as if pushed from without—the opposite of what happened on Palm Sunday, when the clergy, having gone out through the sacristy, knocked at the church door three times in memory of the Messiah's entry into Jerusalem, asking to be let into the nave. Now, at Whitsuntide, the doors opened inwards, while inside the lighted chapel the Abbot with his crozier and all the clergy wanted to be let out.

The countryside started at the church porch, and to a triumphal tune the procession moved through the wheat and through the rye, as far as the rocks that the first Saracens in Spain shrank from scaling in about the year 730. For some time everyone had been singing the *Veni Creator Spiritus*. And I remembered—I thought it had significance only for me—that it was sung at weddings as well as at Whitsun.

The monks and the acolytes sprinkled the fields with holy water, and the Abbot, thinking to bring the country peace, blessed it with one hand, the index and middle finger raised and singing at the top of his voice. He sounded crazy to me—the whole crowd was crazy, almost delirious. A little rain, just a few drops, would have been a relief to all of us. But the Catalan countryside cowered there in the sun like every other living thing in Spain. God who created heaven and earth must have had some fun carving out those red phalloid rocks which perhaps, despite the legend, were crowned with Arabs the moment they appeared, but which the Abbot now blessed as freely as he blessed the wheat.

The sun blazed down. It was noon. Suddenly we turned our backs on nature, over which and for which the nuptial chant, Latin and Gregorian, had risen up, and were led by our shepherd back to the church. But our going back into the shade was not so much a return into the Temple as the closing in around us of a night forest, where groves and thickets and clearings lay waiting for us in the moonlight.

A ring of young men and girls in the woods on a moonlit night—are they there to pray, or, when all Islam is governed by lunar cycles, to fuse their strength together into a single malediction? Is it Christian to place the feet of married couples on the inside of the Crescent? I could think of nothing to compare with what I was feeling. Something other than the Eternal was present. What terror was ever like this? Mont Blanc advancing upon me? Grock entering the circus ring and producing a child's violin from his trousers? Or a policeman's hand falling on my shoulder? And the hand saying quietly: "Got you!"

The word paganism sounds a challenge to any society. The word atheist is less dangerous—it's too close to Christian moralism, or at least the kind that reduces Christ to the thorn in His kingly and godly crown, to be a threat. But paganism puts the unbeliever back amid the so-called "mists of time," when God didn't yet exist. A sort of intoxication and magnanimity allows a pagan to approach everything, himself included, with equal respect and without undue humility. To approach, and perhaps to contemplate. No doubt I overrate paganism, which I seem to have been confusing with animism. But in describing that ceremony at Montserrat I tell of the cave I emerge from, the cave I sometimes find myself in again through some fleeting emotion.

I tried in the *Review of Palestinian Studies* to show what was left of Chatila and Sabra after the Phalangists had been there for three nights. They crucified one woman alive. I saw the body, with the arms outstretched and covered with flies, especially round the tips of her hands: there were ten blackening clots of blood where they had cut off the top joints of her fingers.

Was that how the Phalangists got their name, I wondered. In that place, at that time, in Chatila on 19 September 1982, it seemed to me it must have been a game. To cut off someone's fingers with secateurs like a gardener trimming a yew—these Phalangist jokers were just gardeners larking about, converting a landscape garden into a formal one. But this impression disappeared as soon as I had time to think it over, and then I saw quite a different scene in my mind's eye. You don't lop off either branches or fingers for nothing.

Their windows were shut but the panes were broken, and when they heard the gun-fire and saw the camps lit up by flares, the women knew they were trapped. Jewel cases were emptied out on to the tables. Like people pulling on gloves so as not to be late for a party, the women stuck rings on all the fingers and even the thumbs of both hands, perhaps five or six rings to a finger. And then, covered with gold, did they try to escape? One, hoping to buy the pity of a drunken soldier, took a cheap ring set with an imitation sapphire off her forefinger. The Phalangist, drunk already, grew drunker still at the sight of all her jewellery, and to save time took out his knife (or a pair of secateurs found near the house), cut off the top two joints of her fingers, and pocketed them and their adornments.

Pierre Gemayel went to see Adolf Hitler in Berlin, and what he saw there—brawny blond young men in brown shirts—made up his mind: he would have his own militia, based on a football team. As a Lebanese Christian he wasn't taken seriously by the other Christians, for whom force could come only from finance. The Maronites' mockery drove Pierre and his son Bechir straight into the arms of the Israelis and led the Phalangists to make use of cruelty, a shadow of force more effective in those parts than force itself. Neither Pierre nor his son could have exercised power if some other power—Israel—hadn't sponsored and backed them up. And Israel and its cruelty were sponsored in turn by the United States.

So I was getting to know them better, these Phalangists who kissed gold crosses between girls' breasts, whose thick lips clung to medals of the Virgin on gold chains, and lingered over the hand of a Patriarch devoutly masturbating the shaft of his golden crozier.

I opened my eyes wide to gaze at the "Real Presence" in the monstrance, where sumptuously, humbly but boldly the "bread" was displayed. How many individual shipwrecks the Church is made up of . . .

The Muhammadan steeds rode hell for leather. Were they running away? We stood behind the Abbot in the chapel. The black Virgin and her negro Jesus had resumed their former pose. But would I be experiencing the thrill I felt that Whitsun if I hadn't given a twenty-year-old Muslim a lift in my taxi from Barcelona, and he hadn't stayed on with me throughout the ceremonies?

The original kiss bestowed by the Abbot in the chapel and multiplied like the Nazarene's loaves by the lakeside or like the petals of a flower, each subsequent kiss having the same virtue as the first, reminds me of the chief of the pseudo-tribe giving each of the sixteen worthies fewer kisses than the one before.

"To each according to his deserts." But perhaps the noblest of the sixteen worthies was he who was given a single kiss. I knew nothing about it. Perhaps just a single kiss was the sign of the highest veneration, in a progression descending by intervals of sixteen to the One?

One night just before dawn in January 1971, four months after Black September, three separate groups of fedayeen who'd been on the march for some time, transferring from one base to another, were singing to each other from their various hills. Between each song I could hear the silence of the morning, dense with all the daytime sounds that hadn't yet burst forth. I was with the group nearest the Jordan. As I squatted down, resting, I was drinking tea—noisily, for it was hot and in those parts it's the custom to proclaim the pleasures of tongue and palate. I was also eating olives and unleavened bread. The fedayeen were chatting in Arabic and laughing, unware of the fact that not far away was the spot where John the Baptist baptized Christ.

The three hilltops, each invisible to the other two, hailed one another in turn—it was about then, or a little later, that Boulez was working on *Repons*—and in the east the yet unrisen sun was tingeing the black sky with blue. Even the uncertain voices of the young lions of fourteen were pitched low to improve the polyphonic effect (usually they all sang in unison), and also to prove their general maturity, their fighting spirit, their courage, their heroism—and perhaps also, by this discreet emulation, to prove their love for the heroes.

One group would be silent, waiting for the other two to answer, which they always did together, though each of the three groups sang in a different mode. In certain passages, though, a boy fighter would decide to add some trills a couple or two and a half tones higher than the rest; then the others would fall silent, as if making way for an elder. The contrast between the voices underlined the contrast between the terrestrial kingdom Israel and the landless land with no other prop than the warbling of its soldiers.

"Were these kids fighters, then—fedayeen, terrorists, who steal out in the dead of the night or in broad daylight and plant bombs all over the world?"

In between the verses winging from hill to hill I thought all was utterly silent. But then between the second and third verses I heard the voice of a stream. I never made out whether it was near or far away, but from its murmur I took it to be clear and secret, and it rose up modestly between two hills and two groups of singers. It was only between the fifth and sixth verses that the stream's voice rose and filled the whole valley. Then, as if meaning spread from the stream of water to the stream of voices, the singing grew hoarser and louder, driving out the childish tones and becoming rough, imperious and, finally, quite wrathful.

It seemed absurd that a dictator should silence lovers. But probably they hadn't heard either the stream or the torrent.

The night wasn't dark enough: I could make out the shapes of trees, kitbags, guns. When my eyes got used to a very dim patch and I peered hard, I could see, instead of the patch, a long shadowy path ending in a sort of intersection from which other even darker paths branched out. The call to love came not from voices or things, perhaps not even from myself, but from the configuration of nature in the darkness. A daylight landscape, too, sometimes issues the order to love.

The improvised trills—all the singing was improvised—were devoid of consonants and mostly very high pitched. It was as if three scattered Queens of the Night, wearing faint moustaches and battle dress, came together in the morning to carol with the confidence, recklessness and detachment of prima donnas, oblivious of their weapons and their clothes. Oblivious too of the fact that they were really soldiers, who at any moment might be silenced for ever by a hail of bullets from Jordan as accurate and melodious as their own singing. Perhaps the Queens believed their camouflage uniform made their singing infrasonic?

The legendary pre-Islamic hero Antar, buried deep in memory, might have come to life again at any moment. I remembered how at eighty years old he rose in his stirrups to sing the praises of his dead beloved and of their happy home. And a blind man, guided only by the voice, drew his bow and slew Antar with an arrow in the groin. The voice had replaced the sightless eyes to guide the dart.

The voices, that morning at least, were as sure as the sound of oboes, flutes and flageolets—sounds so true you could smell the wood the instruments were made of, feel its grain. Just as in Stravinsky's own voice, cracked yet delightful, I recognized the sound of the instruments in *The Soldier's Tale*. I remember the rough, so-called guttural Arabic consonants being contracted, elided or prolonged till they were soft as velvet.

A great light in the east: day came to the hills before the sun rose. I was under some old olive trees that I knew well.

We made our way round another hill, the same one as before, though I'd thought we were several hills further on. This was a pathetic trick to make the enemy think the Palestinians were everywhere at once. For ten years, against the hyper-sensitive equipment of Israel, the Palestinians used ruses that were both dangerous and useless, but often amusing and even poetic.

To my question, "What song were you singing?," Khaled replied:

"Everyone invents his own. One group introduces a subject, the group that answers first gives the next subject, the third group gives the first an answer that's also a question, and so on."

"What's it usually about?"

"Love, of course! And occasionally the revolution."

I made another discovery: some voices, inflexions and quarter-tones sounded familiar. For the first time in my life I was hearing Arab singing coming freely out of people's mouths and chests, borne on a living breath that machines—discs, cassettes, radios—killed at the very first note.

That morning I'd heard a great improvisation performed among the mountains, in the midst of danger; yet heedless of the death that lurked everywhere for warrior musicians whose bodies might soon lie decomposing in the midday sun.

Let us not dwell on the well-known fact that memory is unreliable. It unintentionally modifies events, forgets dates, imposes its own chronology and omits or alters the present of the writer or speaker. It magnifies what was insignificant: everyone likes to witness things that are unusual and have never been described before. Anyone who knows a strange fact shares in its singularity.

And every writer of memoirs would prefer to stick to his original plan. Fancy having gone so far only to find that what lies beyond the horizon is just as ordinary as here! Then the writer of memoirs wants to show what no one else has ever seen in that ordinariness. For we're conceited, and like to make people think the journey we made yesterday was worth writing up today. Few races are naturally musical: every people and every family needs its own bard. But the writer of memoirs, though he doesn't advertise the fact, wants to be *his* own bard: it's within himself that his tiny, never-finished drama takes place. Would Homer have written or recited the *Iliad* without Achilles' wrath? But what would we know about Achilles' wrath without Homer? If some undistinguished poet had sung of Achilles, what would have become of the glorious, peaceful but shortish life Zeus allowed him?

English aristocrats and English mechanics alike can all whistle Vivaldi and the songs of sparrows and other English birds. The Palestinians were inventing songs that had been as it were forgotten, that they found lying hidden in themselves before they sang them. And perhaps all music, even the newest, is not so much something discovered as something that re-emerges from where it lay buried in the memory, inaudible as a melody cut in a disc of flesh. A composer lets me hear a song that has always been shut up silent within me.

A few days later I saw Khaled again. I thought I'd recognized his voice in one of the choirs on the three hills. What subjects had he chosen?

"I'm getting married in a month's time," he answered, smiling, "so the two hills opposite mine were making fun of my fiancée. They said she was ugly and stupid and had a hump and couldn't read or write. And I had to defend her. I told them when the revolution's over I'll throw them all in jail."

He unslung his carbine from his shoulder and added it to the pile of guns stacked on their butts on the grass. His teeth flashed under his moustache.

I wrote that in February 1984, fourteen years after the singing on the hills. I never made any notes at the time, along the roads or tracks or on the bases. Nor anywhere else. I record an event because I was present when it happened and I was lastingly affected by it. I think my life is made up of impressions as strong as that, or even stronger.

"Why not now?"

"You know very well we haven't got any prisons."

"What about a mobile one?"

"Design one for us!"

"So then what happened?"

"They answered, and the sun came up, and we sang the dawn prayer. Then they pulled my leg about what they said I used to get up to on the sly with King Hussein and Golda."

"And then?"

"I doubled their sentences."

"What happened next?"

"They said they'd really been singing about their hill, which was called The Fiancée (*Laroussi*)."

He was silent, smiling slightly. Then he asked shyly:

"It was a good song, wasn't it?"

Looking at his hand, with its thick palm and powerful thumb, I realized the strength of his song and of his spirit.

"Maybe you didn't catch all the words? At one point I described all the cities in Europe where we've carried out attacks. Did you hear how I sang 'München', in German, in all sorts of different keys?"

"And you described it?"

"Yes, street by street."

"Do you know it?"

"After singing about it for so long, yes—like the back of my hand."

Still smiling, he told me more about his views on the art of singing, and added seriously:

"The stream was an awful nuisance."

"In what way?"

"It got in our way. Once it took over it wouldn't let anyone else get a word in."

So he had noticed the voice I'd thought so secret and unobtrusive that mine was the only ear to hear it.

But if such elusive sensations are perceptible to organs other than mine, perhaps what I took to be my own exclusive knowledge is available to everyone, and I have no secret life . . .

In the evening the fedayeen usually rested from the day's work: fetching and carrying supplies and guarding the base, the gun emplacements, the radio and telephone network, and everything else to do with security; not to mention the permanent alert against the ever-dangerous Jordanian villages. One evening Khaled Abu Khaled asked me about the fighting methods of the Black Panthers.

My answer was slowed down by the meagreness of my Arabic vocabulary. He was surprised to hear about the activities of the urban guerrillas.

"Why do they do that? Haven't they got any mountains in America?"

Perhaps because it seemed to lack depth, the Panther movement spread fast among the Blacks, and among young Whites impressed by the guts of its leaders and grass-roots activists and by its novel and strongly anti-establishment symbolism. Afro hair-dos, steel combs and special handshakes were also the insignia of other black movements more orientated towards Africa—an imaginary Africa that combined Islam and spirit-worship. The Panthers didn't reject those emblems, but added to them the slogan "All Power to the People"; the image of a Black Panther on a blue background; leather jackets and blue berets; and above all the open carrying of weapons.

To say the Party had no ideology because its "Ten Points" were either vague or inconsistent and its Marxism-Leninism was unorthodox is neither here nor there. The main object of a revolution is the liberation of man—in this case the American Black— not the interpretation and application of some transcendental ideology. While Marxism-Leninism is officially atheist, revolutionary movements like those of the Panthers and the Palestinians seem not to be, though their more or less secret goal may be to wear God down, slowly flatten Him out until He's so drained of blood and transparent as not to be at all. A long but possibly efficient strategy.

Everything the Panthers did was aimed at liberating the Blacks. They used rousing images to promote the slogan "Black is Beautiful" which impressed even black cops and Uncle Toms. But swept along, it may be, by the momentum of its own power, the movement overshot the goal it had set itself.

It grew weak, with the harsh weakness then in fashion, shooting cops and being shot by them.

It grew weak through its rainbow fringe, its fund-raising methods, the quantity and inevitable evanescence of its TV images, its use of a rough yet moving rhetoric not backed up by rigorous thought, its empty theatricality—or theatricality *tout court!*— and its rapidly exhausted symbolism.

To take the elements one at a time: the rainbow fringe probably acted as a kind of barrier between the Panthers and the Whites, but in addition to being frivolous it also infiltrated the Panthers themselves.

As for the movement's fund-raising methods, enthusiasm was quickly aroused among rich bohemians, black and white: cheques flowed in, jazz and theatre groups contributed the takings from several performances. The Panthers were tempted to spend money on lawyers and lawsuits, and there were various unavoidable expenses. But they were also tempted to squander money, and they yielded to the temptation.

Television images had the advantage of being mobile, but they were still only two-dimensional, and had more to do with dreams than with hard fact.

The Panthers' rhetoric enchanted the young—both black and white took it up. But the words "Folken," "Man" and "Power to the People" soon came to be a thoughtless habit.

Theatricality, like TV, belongs to the realm of imagination, though it uses ritual means.

The Panthers' symbolism was too easily deciphered to last. It was accepted quickly, but rejected because too easily understood. Despite this, and precisely because its hold was precarious, it was adopted by the young in the first instance—by young Blacks who replaced marijuana with outrageous hair-styles and by young Whites still used to a language of Victorian prudishness. They laughed when first Johnson and then Nixon were publicly called mother-fuckers, and supported the Panthers because they were the "in" thing. The Blacks were no longer seen as submissive people whose rights had to be defended for them, but determined fighters, impulsive and unpredictable but ready to fight to the death for a movement that was part of the struggle of their race all over the world.

Maybe the explosion was made possible by the Vietnam war and the resistance the Viets put up against the Yanks. The fact that Panther leaders were allowed to speak—or were not prevented from speaking—at anti-war meetings seemed to give them a right to take part in the country's affairs. Later—and this shouldn't be underrated—some Black veterans joined the Party when they came home, bringing with them their anger, their violence and their knowledge of firearms.

Probably the Panthers' most definite achievement was to spotlight the fact that the Blacks really existed. I had the opportunity of seeing this for myself. At the Democratic Convention in Chicago in 1968 the Blacks were still if not timid at least cautious. They avoided broad daylight and definite statement. Politically they made themselves invisible. But in 1970 they all held their heads high and their hair stood on end, though the real, fundamental activity of the Panthers was almost over.

If the white administration hoped to destroy them by inflation followed by deflation, it was soon proved wrong. The Panthers made use of the inflation period to carry out many acts, perform many gestures that became symbols all the stronger for being weak. They were quickly adopted by all the Blacks and by White youth. A great wind swept over the ghetto, carrying away shame, invisibility and four centuries of humiliation. But when the wind dropped people saw it had been only a little breeze, friendly, almost gentle.

The image I want to record here came to me in a crowd of others which gradually yielded to it in vividness, force and persuasiveness as my decision to write became clear and concentrated on that image alone—the image of night at the Pole.

The Lufthansa plane took off from Hamburg on the evening of 21 December 1967 and took us first to Copenhagen, where because of a fault in the navigation equipment we had to go back to Hamburg. We left again on the morning of the twenty-second. Apart from three Americans, five Germans and myself, all the passengers were taciturn Japanese. Nothing of note happened till we got to Anchorage, but there, just before we landed, the air hostess spoke a few greetings in English and German, and then said "Sayonara."

The clear voice, the long-expected strangeness of the language, the limpid vowels gliding over the consonants, the word itself floating through the darkness while the plane was just about to leave Western longitudes, gave me the feeling of utter newness that we call presentiment.

The plane took off again. Or did it? The engines were running, but I hadn't felt the jolt, great or small, that usually accompanies take-off. And it was so dark I couldn't see if we were moving or not. Everyone was silent, sleeping perhaps or taking their own pulse. Through the window I could see a red sidelight on the wing-tip. One of the hostesses told me we'd passed the Pole and were "coming down" on the eastern part of the globe.

The fatigue of the journey, the change of route, the movement of the plane, the darkness that seemed to stretch as far as Japan, the thought of being on the east of the world, the idea that at any moment there might be an accident whereas every other moment proved there hadn't been one yet, the echo in my mind of the word "Sayonara"—all these things kept me awake.

The word made me feel my body being stripped bit by bit of a thick black layer of Judaeo-Christian morality, until it was left naked and white. I was amazed at my own passiveness. I was a mere witness of the operation, conscious of the well-being it produced without taking part in the process. I knew I had to be careful: the thing would only be a complete success if I didn't interfere. The relief I felt was rather a cheat. Perhaps someone else was watching me.

I'd fought so long against that morality my struggle had become grotesque. But it was vain. Yet a word of Japanese spoken in the fluent voice of a girl had been enough to trigger off the operation. What also struck me as surprising was that in my past struggles I'd never invented, or by learning Japanese discovered, that simple, rather amusing word, the meaning of which I still didn't know. I was intrigued by the medicinal power of a mere word irrespective of its content. A little while later it seemed to me that "Sayonara" (as the "r" sound doesn't exist in Japanese it sounded like "Sayonala") was the first touch of cottonwool that was going to cleanse my wretched body—wretched because of the long degrading siege it had had to withstand from Judaeo-Christian ethics.

This deliverance, which I'd expected to be lengthy, irksome

and deep, as if carried out with a scalpel, began with a sort of game—an unfamiliar word placed cunningly after some English and German ones. And that welcome, addressed to all the passengers, was the start for me of a clean-up that, while only superficial, would free me from a moral system that clung to the skin rather than burned into the flesh. I ought to have realized before that it would be got rid of not by a solemn surgical operation but by the application of good strong soap. My inside wasn't affected.

Nevertheless I got up to go and have a crap in the rear of the plane, hoping to get rid of a tapeworm three thousand years long. I obtained almost immediate relief: all would be well—my liberation had begun by tweaking the nose of propriety. An agile aesthetic had loosened the grasp of an onerous ethic. But I didn't know anything about Zen, and I don't know why I wrote that. The plane flew on through the night, but I had no doubt that when I got to Tokyo I'd be naked and smiling, ready and willing to slice off the heads of first one and then another customs officer or else laugh in their faces.

The customs people didn't even look at the little Japanese girl whose death I'd both hoped for and feared. I'd thought her fragile bones and already flattened features cried out to be crushed. The German crew's heavy boots matched the muscles in their hips and thighs, the sturdiness of their torsos, the tendons in their necks, their grim expressions.

"Such frailty is a kind of aggression and just asks to be suppressed."

But I probably had that thought in some other form, presumably haunted by images of emaciated Jews naked or almost naked in the concentration camps, where their weakness was regarded as a provocation.

"To look so frail and crushed is a sort of plea to be crushed. If we were to crush her, who would know? There are already more than a hundred million Japanese alive today."

But she was still alive and speaking Japanese.

All decisions are made blindly. If even one judgement left the judges exhausted after sentence was pronounced, their officers aghast, the public flabbergasted and the criminal free, unreason would have been at the root of both judgement and freedom. Fancy taking as much trouble over a judgement as some idiot does over a poem! Where will you find a man determined to earn his living by not judging? How many forsake the narrow byways of the law to wear themselves out arriving at an elaborate judgement which may only prove that to plan carefully is a recipe for failure? A judge hidden in anonymity is a judge only in name. When the judge calls the criminal's name out he stands up, and they are immediately linked by a strange biology that makes them both opposite and complementary. The one cannot exist without the other. Which is the sun and which the shadow? It's well known some criminals have been great men.

Everything happens in the dark. At the point of death, however insubstantial those words and however unimportant the event itself, the condemned man still wants to determine for himself the meaning of his life, lived in a darkness he tried not to lighten but to make more black.

Stony-Brook is a university about sixty kilometres from New York. The university buildings and the houses where the professors and students live stand in the middle of a forest. The Panthers and I were to give a couple of lectures there, one for the students and the other for the professors. The idea was to talk about Bobby Seale and his imprisonment, and the real risk that he might be sentenced to death. We were also going to discuss Nixon's determination to wipe out the Black Panthers' Party, and the black problem in general; to try to sell some copies of the party weekly; and to collect one lecture fee of five hundred dollars from the professors and another of one thousand dollars from the students. And we meant to see if we could recruit some sympathizers from among the small number of black students.

Just as I was getting into the car to leave party headquarters in the Bronx, I asked David Hilliard if he was coming with us.

He smiled faintly and said he wasn't, adding what seemed to me an enigmatic comment:

"There are still too many trees."

I left, together with Zaïd and Nappier, but all through the journey I kept thinking of what he had said. "There are still too many trees." So, for a Black only thirty years old, a tree still didn't mean what it did to a White—a riot of green, with birds and nests and carvings of hearts and names interwined. Instead it meant a gibbet. The sight of a tree revived a terror that was not quite a thing of the past, which left the mouth dry and the vocal cords impotent. A White sitting astride the beam holding the noose at the ready—that was the first thing that struck a negro about to be lynched? And what separates us from the Blacks today is not so much the colour of our skin or the type of our hair as the phantom-ridden psyche we never see except when a Black lets fall some joking and to us cryptic phrase. It not only seems cryptic; it is so. The Blacks are obsessionally complicated about themselves. They've turned their suffering into a resource.

The professors at Stony-Brook were very relaxed and gave us a warm welcome. They couldn't understand why I didn't try to distance myself from the Panthers by using a less violent rhetoric. I ought to have calmed down the Panther leaders, made them understand . . . Both cheques were made out to me, though they were given to the Panthers. I was touched by this fine distinction. A blonde lady professor said:

"We have to protest against the shooting down of the Panthers—at the rate things are going it'll be our own sons next."

On reflection I have to say this: from its foundation in October 1966 right up to the end of 1970 the Black Panthers' Party kept on surpassing itself with an almost uninterrupted stream of images. In April 1970 the Panthers' strength was still as great as ever. University professors could find no arguments against them, and so inevitable was their revolt that the Whites, whether academics or laymen, were reduced to mere attempts at exorcism. Some called in the police. But the Panther movement, though both cheerful and touching, was never popular. It called for total commitment, for the use of arms, and for verbal invention and insult that slashed the face of the Whites. Its violence could only be nurtured by the misery of the ghetto. Its great internal liberty arose from the war waged on it by the police, the government, the white population and some of the black middle classes. The movement was so sharp it was bound to wear out quickly—but in a shower and clatter of sparks that made the Black problem not only visible but crystal clear.

Very few American intellectuals understood that the Panthers' arguments, not being drawn from the common fund of American democracy, were bound to seem very sketchy, and the Panthers themselves ignorant and simple-minded. They didn't realize that, at the stage the Panthers were at, the force of what was called Panther rhetoric or word-mongering resided not in elegant discourse but in strength of affirmation (or denial), in anger of tone and timbre. When the anger led to action there was no turgidity or over-emphasis. Anyone who has witnessed political rows among the Whites—the Democratic Convention in Chicago in August 1968, for example—and who cares to make a comparison, will have to admit that the Whites aren't overburdened with poetic imagination.

It's clear now that the Panthers' party alone couldn't have been responsible for the riot of colour in the fabrics and furs affected by the young Blacks. The Whites knew that beneath this bold provocation there lay a will to live, even at the cost of life itself. The outrageous young Blacks of San Francisco, Harlem and Berkeley were simultaneously concealing and hinting that a weapon was being aimed at the Whites. Because of the Panthers those Blacks who were still called "Toms"—the ones with jobs in government or the law, the mayors of mainly black cities, who'd been elected or appointed just for show—were now "seen" and "looked at" and "listened to" by the Whites. Not because they took orders from the Panthers or because the Panthers took orders from them, but because the Panthers were feared.

Sometimes the results were unfortunate for the ghetto. Some black leaders who were listened to by the Whites were tempted to try to extend their influence and crush offending Blacks, for love not of justice but of power. They were able to prop up American law and order. But between 1966 and 1971 the Panthers emerged as young savages threatening the laws and the arts in the name of a Marxist-Leninist religion about as close to Marx or Lenin as Dubuffet is to Cranach.

You had to get some sleep, though, in the end. In the small hours, after discussions and disputes, whisky and marijuana, you had to go to bed. There were plenty of stomach ulcers among the Panthers.

The young Black in jail for having taken drugs, then stolen and raped and beaten up a White—you might think he's the son of some polite black man who obeys the laws of Church and State. But in fact, as he himself well knows, he's one who three hundred years ago killed a White; took part in a mass runaway, robbing and pillaging and pursued by hounds; charmed and then raped a white woman, and was hanged without trial. He's one of the leaders of a revolt that took place in 1804, his feet are chained to the walls of his prison, he's one who bows his head and one who refuses to bow his head. White officialdom has provided him with a father he doesn't know, black like himself, but perhaps fated to finalize the break between the original Negro, who has gone on existing, and himself.

This method is at once convenient and inconvenient for the Whites. It's convenient because it allows the government to strike down or kill people without being held responsible. But it's inconvenient because responsibility for the "crimes" of the Blacks rests with individuals and not with the whole black community, and when an individual is sentenced he is drawn into the American democratic system. So that makes the Whites miserable: are they to condemn the Negroes as a whole or just a Black? Because of the Panthers some very good Blacks were taken over, but by their action these same Panthers showed that "once a Negro always a Negro."

But a touch of garlic helps . . .

In the Palestinian camps the boys between seven and fifteen who were trained to be soldiers were known as young lions. The arrangement seems very open to criticism. It was useful psychologically, but only up to a point. The boys' minds and bodies might have been hardened through difficult sports of ever-increasing complexity, calling for immediate reactions to overcome cold, heat, hunger, fear and surprise. But training conditions, however harsh, will always be different from the situation soldiers find themselves in when confronted with other soldiers determined to kill—even if the enemy consists of children. The leaders of the young lions, knowing they are training kids, give even their sternest orders a tinge of almost maternal gentleness.

"Every Palestinian knows how to shoot from the age of ten," Leila told me proudly. She still thought shooting consisted of raising your gun to your shoulder and pulling the trigger. Real shooting means aiming at the enemy and killing him, and the boys—like the fedayeen—were using obsolescent weapons. But where were they supposed to be shooting? At whom? And above all under what conditions?

In the microscopic patch of land allotted to the young lions, more a playground than a battleground, there was a reassuring, nursery atmosphere, never the terror or intolerable cruelty caused by a certain something you'll never know about the enemy. The lessons in guerrilla warfare were rudimentary. I saw the young lions going through the same barbed-wire entanglements so often without being presented by any new problems—i.e. without having to circumvent any surprise that might have been worked out in the recesses of Israeli brains—that the boys seemed to me to serve the same Potemkin-like purpose as the bases themselves. The young lions' camps tried to prove to the journalists from all over the world who came on organized visits that generations of Palestinians were being born with guns in their hands, their eyes on the target, and recapture of the occupied territories in their hearts. Only journalists from the Communist countries were prepared to be taken in.

In its declarations on the subject, Israel always referred to this undying hatred. (On the maps, a blank surrounded on one side by the blue of the Mediterranean, in the east by Lebanon and in the south by the kingdom of Jordan represented what was known as Palestine until 1948, and was supposed to obliterate what the world now called Israel.) Mere photographs of the young lions in their camps were enough to show, if not the vulnerability of

Israel, at least the constant danger that threatened it. And yet there was no comparison between Israel's own preparations and actions and these camps of boy soldiers solemnly hoisting their triangular flag every morning. I was present several times at this ceremony. The size of the flag matched that of the kids: it was very small. But no one's surprised when schoolchildren wave tiny paper flags as a queen goes by, her little smile answered by an even smaller one from the children. In the young lions' camps the symbol of the homeland was feeble, but I dare say that as they grew older the symbols grew larger.

If the training camp was suddenly shrouded in smoke the children were neither frightened nor surprised; it was part of an organized plan. But what would happen when Israel destroyed the sun and turned broad day into night?

What does it mean—"a touch of garlic helps"? Insipid food can be brightened up by a dash of spice, and some of the young lions, when put in temporary charge of the other boys, would, being older and more depraved, introduce an element of sadistic pleasure. A nasty addition, perhaps, but stimulating.

Cleanliness is congenital to the Palestinians, and anyone facing death can only do so after a thorough washing and scouring.

Again it was Khaled who put me in the picture. Two twenty-year-old fighters—from among those who'd been singing with him in the mountains—were washing one another carefully out in the open not far away from us. The other fedayeen seemed not to notice and certainly not to look at them. By washing and scouring I mean the almost maniacal attention they paid to personal hygiene and to the work it involved, which seemed to be sacred in the sense of paramount. First with a towel and then with their hands they rubbed their skin till it shone, passing the cloth between their toes several times to make sure all the dirt was removed. Then came the private parts, the trunk and the armpits. The two soldiers helped each other, one pouring on clean water after the other had soaped himself.

They were only a few yards away from the other soldiers, but what they were doing separated them for ever from the rest, making them at once huge as mountains and distant as ants. Each scoured his own body like a housewife cleaning a saucepan, washing it in detergent and rinsing it till it sparkles. And theirs struck me as different from the usual Muslim ablutions.

Obediently copying the attitude of the fedayeen, I left the two to their solitude and their work, neither of which could be shared. One of them started to sing, and the other joined in. The first picked a small pouch up from the ground nearby, zipped it open, took out a pair of dressmaking shears, and proceeded very carefully, still singing—improvising as usual—to cut his toe-nails, paying particular attention to the corners, which were liable to make holes in his socks. Then he did his finger-nails, and after that, still singing, washed his hands, his face and his shaven pubis, trying to find, and soon finding, words that applied to Palestine itself.

I don't know why they didn't go down that night into Israel. The pre-funerary toilette wasn't called for, and so they became a couple of unconsecrated fedayeen just like the others again. They'd have to start all over again the next time they were chosen.

It was with a roar of laughter designed to show she had the same "collar of Venus" as Lannia Solha that Nabila told me about the death of a Palestinian woman eighty years old. She was very thin round the stomach, and put on a sort of bodice with four rows of splinter grenades inside. She was probably helped by other women of her own age or younger, used to her sex, her thinness and her white hair. Then, weeping real tears, she approached a group of Amal fighters who were laughing as they rested from shooting Palestinians. The old woman wept and moaned for some time, until the group of Amals kindly went up to her to see if they could help her. She kept mumbling phrases in Arabic that the Shiites couldn't hear, so they had to gather round close.

When I read in the papers about a virgin of sixteen blowing herself up in the middle of a group of Israeli soldiers, it doesn't surprise me very much. It's the lugubrious yet joyful preparations that intrigue me. What string did the old woman or the girl have to pull to detonate the grenades? How was the bodice arranged to make the girl's body look womanly and enticing enough to rouse suspicion in soldiers with a reputation for intelligence?

I was listening on a Walkman in a hotel room, but imagining a real funeral in a church with a coffin surrounded by wreaths and eight candles and a real dead body inside, even if the box is closed—and then the *Requiem* descended on me with full choir and orchestra. The music conjured up not death but a life, the life of the corpse, present or absent, the one for whom the mass is sung. But I was listening through headphones.

Mozart, using the Roman liturgy and Latin phrases that I followed with difficulty, asked for eternal rest, or rather another life. But as there had been no ceremony, and I could see no church door, graveyard, priest, genuflexions or censer, at the sound of the "Kyrie" I started to hear a pagan madness.

The troglodytes came dancing out of their caves to welcome the dead woman, not in the light of sun or moon but in a pearly mist that generated its own light. The caves looked like the holes in a huge Swiss cheese, and the cavemen, phantoms without your human dimensions, cheerful and even laughing, swarmed around greeting the newcomer, the "maiden" whatever her age, so that she might adapt easily to the after-life, accept like a welcome gift either death or the new eternal life, happy and proud to have been plucked up out of the world below.

The days of wrath, the tubas, the trembling of the kings—it wasn't a mass but an opera lasting less than an hour, the time it might take someone to die, performed and heard in dread of losing this world and finding oneself in what other? And in what form? The journey through the underworld, the terror of the grave, all that was there, but above all the gaiety, the laughter overlaying the fear, the haste of the dying woman to quit this world and leave us to the bleak courtesies of everyday while she went laughing up—not down but up—to the light. Laughing, and perhaps, who knows, sneezing as well.

That was what I heard, from the "Dies Irae" to the famous eighth bar of the "Lacrimosa" which I could never distinguish from those that followed—music that permitted hilarity and even liberty, that dared all.

When after long days of doubt and anxiety a youth—transsexual is rather a horrible word—decides on a sex change, once the decision is made he is filled with joy at the thought of his new sex, of the breasts he'll really stroke with hands too small and damp, of the disappearance of body hair. But above all, as the old sex fades and, he hopes, finally drops off useless, he'll be possessed with a joy close to madness when he refers to himself as "she" instead of "he," and realizes that grammar also has divided into two, and the feminine half has turned a somersault so that it applies to him, whereas the other half used to be forced on him. The transition to the non-hairy half must be both delightful and terrible. "I am filled with thy joy..." "Farewell to half of me—I die to myself..."

To leave behind the hated but familiar masculine ways is like forsaking the world and going into a monastery or a leper-house. To quit the world of trousers for the world of the brassière is a kind of death, expected but feared. And isn't it also comparable to suicide, with choirs singing the "Tuba mirum"?

A transsexual is thus a sort of monster and hero combined. An angel too, for I don't know if anyone would ever actually use his new sex even once, unless the male member withered quite away, or, worse, fell off, and the whole body and its purpose became one great female organ. He'll start to be frightened when his feet refuse to get smaller: you won't find many high-heeled shoes in size 9 or 10. But happiness will prevail over all else—happiness and joy.

The *Requiem* says as much: joy and fear. And so the Palestinians, the Shiites and the Fools of God, who all fell laughing upon ancient cavemen and gold court shoes size 9 or 10, came together in a thousand roars of onward-rushing laughter, mingled with the fierce retreat of trombones. Thanks to joy in death or in the new, despite bereavement, and in contrast to ordinary life, all moralities had broken down. What prevailed was the joy of the transsexual, of the *Requiem*, of the kamikaze. Of the hero.

In contrast to the disagreeable practice of drying your Western hands in a blast of hot air to avoid wetting a clean towel, you must have experienced, especially as children, the pleasure of staying out in the rain, preferably in the summer when the water that drenches you is warm. I've never been able to find out which way the wind's blowing by wetting my finger and holding it up, nor the direction of the rain, unless it's as slanting as the last rays of the sun. And when I realized, at the first hail of bullets, that I was going towards them, I laughed like a boy taken by surprise. As I crouched in the shelter of a wall I felt a sudden idiotic delight at being safe, while certain death awaited two yards beyond the wall. I was enjoying myself. Fear didn't exist. Death was just as much a part of life as the shower of steel and lead nearby. All I could see on the faces of the fedayeen were happy smiles or a calm that might have been blasé. Abu Ghassam, the fedayee who'd grabbed my sleeve and pulled me to safety, looked both irritated and relieved.

"A nice thing," he must have been thinking, "getting shot at without warning, and on top of that having to look after a European." He'd been made responsible for me because he knew some French.

I noticed that none of the soldiers attempted to go into the buildings to find shelter from which to shoot back and perhaps protect the inhabitants, though they were armed and laden with ammunition, with cartridge belts crossed over their chests. All—except me—were very young and unseasoned.

I felt weighed down by a kind of despondency, which in other places and by other people has been called defeatism. The famous last words, "It is finished," probably express my mood better. They weren't even fighting any more near Jerash. All that was still standing out were the columns of the temples left by the Romans. The front of the house was being riddled with bullets, but as our wall was at right angles to it no one was in any danger. Death was close, but being held at bay. If I moved forward two yards I'd be killed.

And it was there more strongly than anywhere else that I heard the call across a horizontal abyss, more urgent and more apt to enfold me for ever than any vertical gulf shrieking my name. As on other days, the shooting went for some time. The young fedayeen laughed. Apart from Abu Ghassam none of them knew any French, but their eyes told me everything.

Would Hamlet have felt the delicious fascination of suicide if he hadn't had an audience, and lines to speak?

———

But why had the voice of the stream grown so loud that night, so loud that it got on my nerves? Had the choirs and the hills come close to the water without anyone realizing? More likely the singers' voices were tired, or they just started to listen to the voice of the stream, either because they liked the sound of it or because they disliked it.

Two images help me tell you what I remember. First the image of white clouds. Everything I saw in Jordan and Lebanon remains shrouded in dense clouds that still swirl down on me. I seem able to pierce them only when I grope blindly after some vision, though I don't know which. I want it to appear to me as fresh as when I first experienced it as participant or witness: the vision, for example, of four hands drumming on wood, inventing more and more cheerful rhythms on the planks of a coffin. And then the mist parts. Swiftly, or as deliberately as the rise of a theatre curtain, the context of the four rhythm-creating hands emerges as clear as when first I saw it. I make out, whisker by whisker, the two black moustaches; the white teeth; the smile that ceases only to come back broader still.

The second image is that of a huge packing case. I open it and find nothing but shavings and sawdust inside. My hands sift through them, I'm almost desperate at the thought of finding nothing else when I know they're used to protect valuables. Then my hand touches something hard and my fingers recognize the faun's head, the handle of the silver teapot that the shavings and sawdust at once guard and conceal. I had to search through the almost impenetrable packing in order that the teapot might reach me undented. The teapot stands for the Palestinian events which I thought were lost in sawdust and clouds, but which were preserved for me in their morning freshness as if someone—my publisher, perhaps?—had wrapped them up safe so that I might describe them to you as they were.

Clouds are very nutritious.

———

Anyhow, I remember my astonishment and saying to myself: "If the fedayeen really perceive what I think I'm the only one to see, I must hide what I feel, because they often shock me. Then pretence is prudence as much as politeness."

Despite the frankness of their faces, gestures and actions, despite their openness, I soon realized I caused as much astonishment as I felt, if not more. When so many things are there to be seen, just seen, there are no words to describe them. A fragment of hand on a fragment of branch; an eye that didn't see them but saw me and understood. Everyone knew I knew I was being watched.

"Are they just feigning friendship, pretending we're comrades? Am I visible or transparent? Am I visible because I'm transparent?

"The fact is I'm transparent because I'm too visible—a stone, a clump of moss, but not one of them. I thought I had a lot to hide. They looked like hunters: at once suspicious and sympathetic."

"No man who's not a Palestinian himself ever does much for Palestine. He can leave her behind and go to some nice quiet spot like the Côte d'Or, or Dijon. But a fedayee has to win, die or betray."

This is a basic truth never to be forgotten. There's only one Jew, a former Israeli, among the leaders of the PLO: Illan Halery. The PLO and the Palestinians trust him because he's completely rejected Zionism.

Either a Palestinian falls and dies or, if he survives, he's sent to prison for a few sessions of torture. After that the desert takes him and keeps him in the camps near Zarka. We'll find out more later what a fedayee's "slack periods" were like.

A team of German doctors is always to be found where there's torturing going on. They may be serving commercial interests back home: supplying the camps with instruments of torture, selling medicines and the latest wonders of physiotherapy, and getting those who don't succumb to torture out of the country to safety. Then they're sent to hospital in Düsseldorf, Cologne or Hamburg, and if they come out they learn German and snow and the winter wind; they look for a job, and sometimes marry a single wife.

I was told that was what had happened to Hamza. It was a

theory held by several Palestinian leaders. But after December 1971 I didn't meet anyone who could tell me for sure that Hamza was still alive.

But what were the "slack periods" like? The expression conceals what is perhaps a Palestinian soldier's guiltiest secret. What are the daydreams of a revolutionary who rebels in the desert with no experience of the West and practically none of his own shadow, the East? Where do they get their assumed names from? What effect does novelty have on them? And so on . . .

The emblem was easy to decipher—a gilt aluminium crown in the kingdom of Jordan. How is one to describe the king? Something Glubb Pasha left behind on the throne. In 1984 people talked about him like this:

"How's the 'Monarch'?"

"What's the 'Monarch' doing?"

"What does the 'Monarch' think?"

"Where's the 'Monarch' gone?"

"The 'Monarch' was in a good temper."

"The 'Monarch' pees standing up—he's the same as everyone else. Does he think he's Bismarck?"

But in the Palestinian camps, in private conversation where people feel safe from the Moukabarats,* in European countries where former fedayeen have taken refuge, it wouldn't occur to anyone except the children not to call him just the Butcher of Amman.

"It's not an insult. The poor fellow likes blondes and has an erection when he sees his own massacres through the open window. 'I screw blondes—and screw you too! I murder and slay—and that goes for you as well!' He's got his Circassians and Moukabarats and Bedouin to do it with."

"His Majesty is so natural—it's really touching! I'm often with His Majesty. He sometimes perches his ass right on the edge of

---

*The secret police of the kingdom of Jordan.

his chair, he's so shy! The reason His Majesty's so amiable is that His Majesty was educated in England. His Majesty listens to a few words, then gets up and goes. He says a few words in English, as naturally as the royal princess. And yet His Majesty's a Bedouin."

"His Majesty takes great pride in being no more and no less than a Bedouin from the Hejaz. He enters. All the lights in the room go out. Then he approaches, a little oil lamp with a mauve silk shade holding out his hand for people to kiss."

"King Hussein relies on this defence: that if he hadn't subdued the Palestinians, Tsahal would now be in Riyadh."

"He's been unlucky. Move your chair closer—walls have ears—and listen.

"His grandfather, King Abdullah, was assassinated as he left the mosque in Jerusalem. Blood."

"His father went mad. Blood."

"Glubb Pasha, his mentor, was kicked out. Blood."

"King Talal, his father, died out of his mind in Switzerland. Blood."

"The Palestinians. Blood."

"Muhammad Daoud, his prime minister, was given a slap in the face by his sixteen-year-old daughter. Blood."

"Wasfi Tall, his other prime minister, was assassinated in Cairo. Blood."

"Poor King Hussein, what a lot of corpses in his little arms."

That was the tune being sung in Amman in July 1984.

Prismatic vision might teach us a lot. A few years ago, in various parts of the Arab world, you might come across a lady, a sort of benevolent schoolmistress devoted to those of low degree. She was the same to everyone, man, woman or child, no matter what their rank: the fact was, she was born a princess of Orleans. Her condescension was invisible to Arab emirs and Arab beggars alike. But she knew she was a princess, related to the royal houses of Europe, and a village famine and a sheikh's family relationship to the Prophet were of equal importance to her.

Who or what made me come back to this house? The wish to see Hamza again after fourteen years? The wish to see his mother, whom I could easily have imagined older and thinner without coming all this way? Or was it the need to prove to myself that I belonged, in spite of myself, to the class, proscribed but secretly desired, of those who when it comes to other people make no distinction between the highest and the humblest? Or was it that without our realizing it an invisible scarf had been woven between us, binding us all to one another?

The princess wouldn't have bothered to join in the mockery of Hussein: he wasn't an Orleans.

A shanty town within a kingdom. In a piece of broken mirror they see their faces and bodies piecemeal, and the majesty they see there takes shape before them in a half-sleep; and always this sleep leads up to death.

Everyone prepares for the Palace, and by the age of thirteen they all wear silk scarves made in France and specially designed for the shanty towns of the kingdom: the colours and patterns have to be as obvious as kiss curls. So some trade does take place between the shanty town and the outside world, though it's limited to the sale of scarves, brilliantine, scent, plastic cuff-links and counterfeit watches from a counterfeit Switzerland in exchange for the currency brothels have to offer. The scarves and machine-embroidered shirts must be becoming and set off the little ponces' pretty faces.

Scarves, shirts and watches all have one function—they are signs informing Palace and police representatives of the character of whoever contacts them. One applicant is determined to risk his life, another offers his mother or sister or both, another the kind of sex marketable in Europe, another some inside knowledge, some ass or eye or amorous whisper—and each ties round his neck the scarf that corresponds to his particular stock-in-trade.

Though born of a chance coupling and raised under the rusty sky of the shanty town, every one of them is good looking. Their fathers are from the South. The boys soon acquire the arrogance of males destined for tasks and fates outside both the shanty town and the kingdom. Some are fair, with a flashy beauty, a provocation that will last another couple of years.

"It's not only our eyes, Jean. It's our curls (those on their heads), our necks, our thighs as well. You're probably not familiar with the fairness of our thighs?"

Whether the king's Palace was an abyss into which the shanty town might be drawn, or the shanty town an abyss drawing down the Palace and its paraphernalia, in any case one wonders which was real and which only a reflection. Anyhow, if the Palace was the reflection and the shanty town the reality, the reflection of the reality was only to be found in the Palace, and vice versa. You could see that if you visited first the Palace and then the shanty town. The two powers were so evenly balanced you wondered if it wasn't a case of mutual mesmerism, that familiar, flirtatious but bitter confrontation linking the two palaces. The king's palace seemed to look with envy at the poverty of men and women wearing themselves out in the attempt to survive, longing to betray—but whom?—and knowing that possessions and luxury would go up in smoke if ever they decided they had nothing to lose.

What inspired leap launched the naked child, warmed by the breath of an ox, nailed with nails of brass, hoisted up finally, because he had been betrayed, into universal glory? Isn't a traitor one who goes over to the enemy? That among other things. The Venerable Peter, abbot of Cluny, in order to study the Koran better, decided to have it "translated." Not only did he forget that in passing from one language to another the holy text could only convey what can be expressed just as easily in any tongue—that is everything except that which is holy; but he was probably actually motivated by a secret desire to betray. (This may manifest itself in a sort of stationary dance, rather like the desire to pee.)

The temptation to "go over" goes with unease at having just one simple certainty—a certainty that's bound *ipso facto* to be uncertain. Getting to know the other, who's supposed to be wicked because he's the enemy, makes possible not only battle itself but also close bodily contact between the combatants and between their beliefs. So each doctrine is sometimes the shadow and sometimes the equivalent of the other, sometimes the subject and sometimes the object of new day-dreams and thoughts so complex they can't be disentangled. Once we see in the need to "translate" the obvious need to "betray," we shall see the temptation to betray as something desirable, comparable perhaps to erotic exaltation. Anyone who hasn't experienced the ecstasy of betrayal knows nothing about ecstasy at all.

The traitor is not external but inside everyone. The Palace got its soldiers, informers and whores from that part which was still desirable of a population that had been knocked over backwards, and the shanty town responded with all kinds of mockery.

The shanty town, a medley of monsters and woes seen from the Palace, and in turn seeing the palace and *its* woes, knew pleasures unheard of elsewhere. One went about on two legs and a torso, around dusk—a torso from which a wrist stuck out with a hand on the end like a stoup, a begging bowl made of flesh that demanded its mite with three fingers you could see through. The wrist emerged from a ragged mass of crumpled, worn-out, dirty American surplus, merging ever more completely with the mud and shit until it was sold as rags, mud and muck combined.

Further on, also on two legs, is a female sex organ, bare, shaven, but twitching and damp and always trying to cling on to me. Somewhere else there's a single eye without a socket, fixed and sightless, but sometimes sharp, and hanging from a bit of sky-blue wool. Somewhere else again, an arse with its balls hanging bare and weary between a pair of flaccid thighs.

Treason was everywhere. Every kid that looked at me wanted to sell his father or mother; fathers wanted to sell their five-year-old daughters. The weather was fine. The world was disintegrating. The sky existed elsewhere, but here there was only an inexplicable lull in which nothing survived but bodily functions. Beneath the tin roofs the light was grey by day and by night.

A pimp went by dressed like someone in an American film of the thirties. He looked tense, and to keep up his courage he was whistling as though he were walking through a forest at night. This was the middle of the brothel for Arabs who were stony broke. Whether hell or the depths of hell, place of absolute despair or of rest in the midst of perdition, this red-light quarter for some incomprehensible reason prevented the shanty town from sinking further into and merging with the mud on which it had been almost delicately poised. It calmly linked the shanty town to the rest of the world, and hence to the Palace. It was a place for making love, and pimps and madams, whores and customers restricted themselves to what is called normal love and is therefore incomplete. No sodomy or cocksucking here, only quick reciprocal fucking lying down or standing up, without any devouring of arses or dicks or cunts—only married, patriotic, Swiss mountain love.

Erotic fantasies were more intricate and more sought after in the bedrooms and corridors of the Royal Palace, with its mirrors, whole walls of mirrors, in which the smallest caress was repeated to infinity—that infinity where you can make out every detail of a tiny ultimate image. The mirrors were set at strange angles designed to include a view of the shanty town. Need it be said that the residents of the Palace were more sophisticated than those of the shanty town? And did the people in the shanty town know they were there in the mind of the Palace, ministering to its pleasure?

Everyone felt relieved at his own rottenness, soothed at escaping from moral and aesthetic effort. What crawled towards the brothels was a mass of desires craving quick fulfilment, dragging itself along on a thousand legs, seeking and finding some damp and quivering hole where the frustration of a week would vanish in five jolts and in as many seconds.

If a stranger, Arab or otherwise, came here, he'd see the survival of a closely guarded civilization, one with a familiar, almost pious contact with rejection, with what Europe calls dirt. The alarm clock was always set. In five minutes the customer disposed of his dreams. A youth of eighteen who wanted to go into the king's army or join the society of police informers might come across his own father having a crap: then the budding spy would kick his squatting parent's teeth in—or walk by, pretending to believe he was a Norwegian.

The absence of morality scares everyone, but it doesn't put them off. Excrement is consoling, it corresponds to something in our comfortable souls, it stops us from finishing ourselves off. A prick moves, seeks a way to fulfil itself. What's needed for that: to do away with the pride of self, of having a surname, a first name, a family tree, a country, an ideology, a party, a grave, a coffin with two dates—birth and death. Birth and death, those accidental dates; but it's difficult to put down to chance the Transcendent Absolute that governs Heaven and Earth in Islam.

The system of exchange between the Palace, the King, the Court, the Stables, the Horses, the Officials, the Footmen and the Tanks on the one hand, and the Shanty town on the other, is a complex one, but though it's not obvious it's sure. It allows the surface of both places to remain unruffled. There's never any friction, and this is why: the splendour of the Palace is a kind of poverty. The rank of the Sun King and his courtiers is purely mythical. The brutality of the police derives simply from their readiness to obey too promptly and too well. The shanty town slows down, tempers and filters this naïve zeal. The handsome youths, the issue of strange couplings, go through the brothels where faces and bodies are lit up by what used to be. With their good looks goes the utmost scorn, and as they are sturdy too, their masculinity is proud, even regal. To preserve its power the Palace covets the force that comes forth at night from the shanty town.

"I am the force. The tank."

At this point in my fantasy I begin to wonder who was its author. A god perhaps, but not just any old god—the one not to be reborn but born for the first time on a heap of ox and ass dung, to go through this shambles of a world somehow, to rub along somehow, to die on the cross and become the force.

"Could *you* sell your mother?"

"I have! It's easy to sell a cunt when you've emerged from one on all fours."

"What about the Sun?"

"For the moment we're brothers."

The poverty of the villages leads to the capital, to the sky of rusty tin and the rubbish that serves to produce a few handsome boys. The Palace consumes a great deal of youth.

"It's to maintain some sort of order, whether muddy or lacerated by the Sun."

What sort of beauty is it these lads from the shanty town possess? When they're still children a mother or a whore gives them a piece of broken mirror in which they trap a ray of the sun and reflect it into one of the Palace windows. And by that open window, in the mirror, they discover bit by bit their faces and bodies.

The king was in Paris when the Bedouin troops dug up the bodies of the fedayeen killed between Ajloun and the Syrian frontier, to kill them again, or as the ritual expression put it, "to get rid of a hundred spare bullets." Had he abandoned his massacres for three days in order to try out a new Lamborghini? His brother, the regent, stayed behind in Amman. The camp at Baqa, twenty kilometres from the capital, was suddenly completely surrounded by three rows of tanks. The parleying between the women from the camp and the Jordanian officers lasted two days and two nights. The old women awakened pity, the younger ones desire. They all displayed whatever might still touch the soldiers: children, breasts, eyes, wrinkles.

Of this gesture of sacred prostitution the men of the camp appeared to know nothing. They turned their backs on it; little groups of them went about the muddy alleys in silence, fingering their amber beads and smoking. Imagine the thousands of gold-tipped Virginia cigarettes thrown away as soon as lit. The emirates supplied the Palestinians with cigarettes to teach them the geography of the Gulf.

The men refused to talk to Hussein's officers. I think to this day that the fedayeen (all the men in the camp were fedayeen) had made an agreement with the women, young and old, by which the women were to talk and the men to be silent so as to impress the Jordanian army with their determination, real or assumed. I think now it was assumed. But the Bedouin officers didn't know they were witnessing a performance designed to conceal an escape.

To prevent the Jordanians from entering the camp, the Palestinians had to hold out another day and night. The women yelled, the children they carried on their backs or led by the hand were frightened and yelled even louder. Pushing prams full of children, bags of rice and sacks of potatoes, the women went through the barbed wire fences while the men, still silent, went on fingering their beads.

"We want to go back home."

They were on the road that leads to the Jordan. The officers were very perplexed.

"We can't fire on women and prams!"

"We're going home."

"What do you mean—'home'?"

"Palestine. We'll walk. We'll cross the Jordan. The Jews are more humane than the Jordanians."

Some of the Circassian officers were tempted to shoot at them and their kids, proposing to walk forty kilometres to cross the Jordan!

"Sire—a word of advice. Don't shoot."

That's what Pompidou is supposed to have said to Hussein.

Though the French ambassador in Amman was rather simple, Pompidou knew through his spies about the women's revolt. A French priest whose name I've forgotten because he's still alive acted as "post-box" between some Palestinian leaders and what may then have been called the French left, which had links with the left in the Vatican. When the Jordanian authorities heard he was in the camp they ordered the army and political chiefs to hand him over to the Jordanian police.

The Law Courts in Brussels, the Albert Memorial in London, the altar to the Motherland in Rome, and the Opéra in Paris are supposed to be the ugliest buildings in Europe. A sort of grace once mitigated one of them. When a car emerges from the arches of the Louvre facing the avenue de l'Opéra, the Opéra itself, or Palais Garnier, is visible at the end of the street. It has a kind of grey-green dome on top, and I think that's what you see first.

When the women of Baqa left the camp claiming they were going home to Palestine, King Hussein was going up part of the avenue de l'Opéra on his way to lunch at the Elysée Palace. I've been told the grey-green dome was the first and perhaps the only thing he saw: it had "PALESTINE WILL OVERCOME" painted on it in huge white letters. Male dancers, ballerinas and stagehands from the Opéra had gone up on the roof and written the message the night before the procession, and the king saw it. Nowhere in the world seemed safe from the terrorists: the Paris Opéra, haunted both by Fantômas and, in its cellars, by the Phantom, was now haunted in its attics by the fedayeen. The brief warning lasted a long while despite rain and sun, and despite orders from Pompidou. He must have laughed.

But twenty times or more on the grey walls of Paris, near the Opéra and elsewhere, I saw Israel's answer to that message. Sprayed on hastily, unobtrusively, almost shyly, it read: "Israel will live." It happened two or three days after what in my memory I still refer to as "Palestine: the last dance at Baqa." How immensely more forceful was this response!—response rather than answer. Or rather, what a contrast between the limited declaration of "will overcome" and the almost eternal claim of "will live." In the field of mere rhetoric, in the twilight of Paris, Israel and its furtive sprayings went immensely far.

If people can understand a nation dying for its country, as the Algerians did, or for its language, as the Flemings of Belgium and the Irish of Ulster are still doing, they ought to be able to accept that the Palestinians are fighting against the Emirs for their lands and their accent. The twenty-one countries in the League, including the Palestinians, all speak Arabic, but the accent, though subtle and not easily perceived by an untrained ear, does exist. The division of the Palestinian camps into districts transferring, reflecting and preserving the geography of the villages back in Palestine was no more important to them than the preservation of their accent.

This is roughly what Mubarak told me in 1971. When I offered to give an Arab a lift and drive him a hundred and sixty kilometres on his way, he asked me to wait there, and then ran off. He ran more than two kilometres in less than a quarter of an hour, and came back with his only treasure: a not quite new shirt wrapped up in a newspaper. *Filiumque*, and another religion bursts into flame. A stress on the first or the penultimate syllable of a word, and two nations refuse to get along. Something that seemed to us of no value had become that man's one treasure, for which he was ready to risk his life.

Accents apart, an extra letter added to a forgotten or garbled word could be enough to cause a tragedy. During the 1982 war the lorry drivers were either Lebanese or Palestinians. An armed

Phalangist would hold out his hand with something in it and ask, "What's this?"

According to your answer you would either be waved on or get a bullet in the head. The word for a tomato in Lebanese Arabic is *banadora*; in Palestinian Arabic it's *bandora*. One letter more or less was a matter of life or death.

Every district in a camp tried to reproduce a village left behind in Palestine and probably destroyed to make way for a power station. But the old people of the village, who still talked together, had brought their own accent with them when they fled, and sometimes local disputes or even lawsuits too. Nazareth was in one district, and a few narrow streets away Nablus and Haifa. Then the brass tap, and to the right Hebron, to the left a quarter of old El Kods (Jerusalem). Especially around the tap, waiting for their buckets to fill, the women exchanged greetings in their own dialects and accents, like so many banners proclaiming where each patois came from.

There were a few mosques with their cylindrical minarets and two or three domes.

When I was in Amman the dead were buried on their sides, facing Mecca. I attended several funerals, and I know that at Thiais, as at Père-Lachaise, there was a compass showing the direction of Mecca. But the grave, or rather compartment, was more like a narrow pipe, so that people sometimes had to trample on the deceased to make him lie down and sleep.

All over the world and in every age, plays upon words, accents or even letters have often caused quite bitter conflict. Every thief has had dealings in his time with the sort of judge who's out to get us. They had a special way of reading out our record in court.

"Theft!"—triumphantly.

"Theft!" again.

A pause, and then suddenly in a quiet voice, enunciating every letter and leaving the bench in no doubt of our eternal guilt.

"Theft*s-s-s* . . ."

A pause. Theftss. And that was that.

Once again in the history of the revolt, the women acted as a diversion. First paramount object: not to hand over the Christian priest. Second paramount object: to save the camp. It appealed to their love of adventure, of drama, of dressing up and using different voices and gestures. The women jumped for joy; the men's rôle was to lie low and act the coward. On the theme, "Let's pretend to be outraged because the Bedouin want to get at our wives," the women wrote a script and proceeded to perform it.

The regent phoned Hussein. Pompidou made his famous remark. Night fell, as it always does, and five banners depicting from right to left God the Father, the Lamb, the Cross, the Virgin and the Child appeared according to plan, facing the Jordanian tanks. Then came children in red robes and long white lace tops, carrying a kind of golden sun. The whole procession advanced singing, probably in Greek, towards the three lines of tanks.

Every Jordanian soldier was supposed to keep his eyes and ears open in the dark and capture the French priest dead or alive. They'd all goggled before at such ceremonies taking place around the little Greek church in Amman. So they didn't notice an elderly peasant in corduroy trousers and a red scarf round his neck making his way alone through the barbed wire.

The women, with their sleeping children, stayed out by the tanks all night. In the morning, smiling and cheerful, they took the Jordanian officers by the hand and led them into every house in the camp, opening boxes of matches and packets of salt to show there wasn't any priest hidden inside.

A week after Hussein returned home a reconciliation was celebrated between the fedayeen and the Bedouin army, just roundly tricked by the women as well as by the men, who could now talk and smile freely again. It was like the Field of the Cloth of Gold or some other scene during the Western Middle Ages in which ostensibly friendly kings embraced so warmly you couldn't tell which one was going to stifle the other. Or like the reconciliation between China and Japan, or between the two Germanies, or between France and Algeria, Morocco and Libya, de Gaulle and Adenauer, Arafat and Hussein. I don't see any end to these hypocritical kisses.

We expected a party, and we got one.

Hussein sent boxes and baskets of fruit. Arafat brought hampers of bottles from the Gulf: coconut milk, mango and apricot juice and so forth. All in the open space outside the camp where the women and howling infants had spent that night.

Did it really all happen as I say it did?

A few months before, a few soldiers and even fewer officers had deserted from the Bedouin Army. I met some of them, including a very fair young second lieutenant with blue eyes. If I ask him where he got his fairness and sky-blue eyes, I thought, he'll say from the cornfields of Beauce and the Franks who fought in the first Crusade. How could an Arab be fair?

"Where did you get your fair hair?" I asked aloud.

"From my mother. A Yugoslav," he answered in French without an accent.

Some of the officers who'd remained "loyal" to Hussein had probably looked the other way so as not to see the priest leave the camp. He made his way out unmolested in his greenish jacket, his red knitted muffler and a cap from the Manufacture d'Armes et de Cycles at Saint-Etienne in the Loire. The Palestinians escorted him to Syria, where he caught a plane to Vietnam.

I went early, with an Egyptian friend, to get a closer view. The wooden tables were covered with white cloths and laden with mountains of oranges and bottles of fruit juice. But the crowd had got up even earlier than I had. There was a battalion of desert Bedouin, each with two bandoliers crossed over his chest; two lots of fedayeen, unarmed; and photographers from all over the world, journalists, and film directors from ·various Arab and Muslim countries.

The Bedouin dancing is chaste because it takes place between men, mostly holding one another by the elbow or forefinger. But it's also erotic because it takes place between men, and because it's performed before the ladies. So which sex is it that burns with desire for an encounter that can never be?

Can there be a party where no one gets drunk? If a party isn't designed to make people drunk, it's best to turn up intoxicated. Can there be a party where no prohibition is flouted? What about the *Fête de l'Humanité* at La Courneuve?

As alcoholic drinks are sinful according to the Koran, the intoxication that morning came from the singing, the insults and the dancing. Or, if you prefer, from the insults in the form of singing and dancing.

I was below the open space, looking up at it obliquely.

As the fedayeen stood there almost stiffly in their civilian clothes, the Bedouin soldiers began to dance, accompanied only by their own shouts and cries and the thud of their naked feet on the concrete. So as not to be restricted they'd taken off their shoes, but they still wore their puttees. I knew then that the Bedouin were making use of the dance in the same way as the Palestinians had made use of their wives a week before: the dancing was a display, almost a confession, of the femininity that contrasted so strongly with their burly chests. But these were crisscrossed with bandoliers so full that if one bullet had exploded the whole battalion would have gone up in smoke. And in their acceptance of, even desire for, that annihilation lay the source of their virility and their valour.

This is how they danced. First in a single row, which then split into two. Then a line of ten, twelve or fourteen soldiers holding arms like Breton bridegrooms would be joined by a similar line, also holding arms, all dressed in long tunics buttoned up down to their calves, or rather their puttees. Each man wore a turban and a moustache, but beneath these there wasn't a row of teeth to be seen. Knowing they were the victors, the Bedouin soldiers didn't smile, though their colonels did. The troops themselves were too shy, and had probably already learned that smiles unleash anger.

To a heavy double beat, reminiscent of Auvergne, the Bedouin threw up their knees and shouted:

"Yahya-l-malik!" (Long live the king!)

Facing them, but some distance away, Palestinians in civilian clothes performed a clumsy imitation of the Bedouin dance and answered with a laugh:

"Abu Amar!" (Yasser Arafat!)

The rhythm was the same, because "Yahya-l-malik" is pronounced "Yayal malik." Four syllables uttered by the Jordanians and four uttered by the Palestinians. The same rhythm and almost the same dance, for it was just a vestige, a stump of a dance, the weary echo of a few steps from a forgotten dance, to satisfy bureaucratic requirements and officials with badly knotted ties. There was nothing left of the original gloomy ritual, with the Bedouin advancing menacingly, backed up and protected by their accomplice the desert. Their "yahya" was not so much a tribute to their king as an insult spat out at the Palestinians. The latter were more and more entrammelled in the clumsiness, the inferiority, of their own contribution to the show.

As they danced the Bedouin were surrounded by the desert and the mists of time. And I wonder even now whether one day, as they dance, weighed down with bullets and gunpowder, ever more vigorous, ever more rigorous, they won't rip apart the Hashemite kingdom they seem to be defending. And after that, destroy America, conquer heaven, meet the fedayeen there and speak the same language.

Languages may be an easily learned method of communicating ideas, but by "language" shouldn't we really mean something else? Childhood memories: of words, and above all of syntax, conveyed to the young almost before vocabulary, together with stones and straw and the names of grasses, streams, tadpoles, minnows, the seasons and their changes. And the names of illnesses: a woman was said to be "dying with her chest," a phrase beside which such words as tuberculosis or galloping consumption were banal. The cries and groans we invent while making love, going back to our childhood with its moments of wonder and its flashes of comprehension.

"You're as red as a crayfish!"

But a crayfish isn't red—it's grey, almost black! We've seen it shrinking back in the stream, and it's grey. Yes, but wait—by the time you ate it it had been in boiling water, which had turned it red and dead. Bedouin and fedayeen didn't speak the same language. But a "red crayfish" would have been just as incomprehensible to either.

The Palestinians, dancing worse and worse, were on the point of collapse. Then came a sharp blast on a whistle: the camp commander had seen what was happening, and he waved them towards the tables and the fruit. Saved! In this context the word means that face was saved: the dancers pretended they were dying of thirst, and fell upon the bottles and the oranges. At no time did Bedouin and Palestinians address a word to each other.

Hatred between factions can be something terrible, even if it's kept up artificially. Some figures: the Bedouin army consisted of 75,000 men in all, from about 75,000 families, which makes a total population of about 750,000. That was the official figure for the "pure Jordanian" population. The Bedouin, who in a way had answered the questions I'd been asking myself a few days earlier, had conquered through dancing.

The Palestinians, isolated by this archaeo-virility, had distanced themselves from the Bedouin and their obscure privileges, but this didn't impress Israel. Meanwhile every life, the only treasure of anyone on either side, was lived in its unique and solitary splendour.

The figures I've quoted date from 1970.

The sun had just risen over Ajloun and was still among the trees.

"You must see her," they said. "Come with us and we'll translate."

At six in the morning I was pretty angry with the thirteen or fourteen lads who'd woken me up.

"Here, we've made you some tea," they said.

They threw off my bedclothes and hauled me out of the tent. If I went a couple of kilometres with them up the path among the hazel trees I'd see the farm and the farmer's wife.

The hills near Ajloun, south of the Jordan, are like the hills in the Morvan, with the odd foxglove or honeysuckle though fewer tractors in the fields and not a single cow.

The land around the buildings was well looked after: that's what I noticed first. In the little kitchen garden in front of the house there was parsley growing, and courgettes, shallots, rhubarb and black beans, and a creeping vine with bunches of white grapes already basking in the sun.

The farmer's wife was standing in the romanesque arch of the doorway, watching us approach, the band of youngsters and the old man. Judging by her wrinkles and the wisps of grey hair escaping from her black headscarf, I'd have said she was in her sixties.

Later on I'll say that Hamza's mother was actually about fifty in 1970. When I met her again in 1984 she had the face of a woman of eighty—I don't say she "looked" eighty, because creams and salves and massage and various other artificial treatments against wrinkles and excess fat make one forget the ever-swifter flight towards decrepitude and death. I *had* forgotten. In Europe people do forget how a peasant woman's face disintegrates in the sun and the cold, with weariness and poverty and despair. And also how, at the last gasp, there may be a sudden flash of childlike mischief, as at a last little treat.

She held out her hand and greeted me without a smile, but put a finger that had touched my hand to her lips. I did the same, and she greeted each of the fedayeen in the same way, courteous but reserved, almost wary. She was a Jordanian: neither proud nor ashamed of it, but simply making it plain. As she was alone in the house we couldn't go into the main room, and besides: "There isn't room for five, let alone fifteen."

She spoke easily. Later I was told her Arabic was as fine as that spoken by professors. She went barefoot on the straw. She seldom read a newspaper. The only available space on the farm big enough to hold us all was a perfectly round sheepfold adjoining the house.

"Where are the sheep?"

"One of my sons is out with them. My husband's taken the mule up the mountain."

So the Jordanian farmer I said good morning to without thinking every day was her husband. He used to lend the mule to the fedayeen, who took several barrels every day up to some soldiers posted on a rock, keeping watch over the silent village.

But everything was silent. The Jordanian peasants stayed out of sight. Now and then, through binoculars, I could see a woman in a black headscarf throwing grain to her hens or milking a goat, but she soon went back into her house and shut the door. The men must have been waiting inside with their guns kept trained on successive targets—on the Palestinian bases and patrols.

On the morning before our visit to the farm, two fedayeen had gone smiling into the courtyard of a house where they were celebrating a wedding. Custom prescribed that all visitors, even casual passers-by, should be offered food and drink, and the people there were all smiles. Except to the Palestinians, at the sight of whom the smiles faded. They left, feeling hurt.

The farmer's wife offered us all coffee, and went inside to make it—into her main and perhaps her only room. The sheepfold consisted of a circle marked out on the ground and covered with straw. A stone ledge built into the inside of the wall served as a bench. We sat down, the boys joked with each other, and the farmer's wife brought in a tray with a coffee pot and fifteen empty glasses piled up on it.

"But there are sixteen of us."

I thought I hadn't heard aright: a woman on her own would never sit down with us here. But we all wanted her to be the sixteenth. Neither offended nor coy, she declined. But she didn't mind sitting on the raised sill of the entrance for a moment. Not a hair strayed out of her headscarf: she must have set herself to rights in the mirror while the coffee was brewing. I was opposite her as she sat outlined in the doorway. I noticed her large feet, bare but as if of bronze, protruding from under a full black closely pleated skirt. The oracle of Delphi had just sat down in the sheepfold. When spoken to she answered in a clear, resonant voice. A fighter who knew French translated for me; he told me in a whisper he thought her Arabic was probably the most beautiful he'd ever heard.

"My husband and I both agree that the two halves of our people have only one country—this one. We were only one people when the Turks founded the Empire. We were only one before the French and the English drew lines we don't understand over us with their rulers. Palestine was put under the English mandate, and now it's called Israel; they gave us an Emir from the Hejaz—Hussein is his great-grandson. You've brought a Christian to see me: tell him I greet him in friendship. Tell him you are our brothers, and it hurts us to be living in houses while you are living in tents. As for the man who calls himself the king, we can do without him and his family. Instead of looking after his father in his palace, he let him die in a prison for madmen."

Patriotism is generally an inflated assertion of imaginary superiority or supremacy. But rereading what I've written here I feel I was convinced by what the farmer's wife said. Or rather I was touched, as by a prayer in a vast church. What I heard was like a chant expressing the aspirations of a whole people. We should always remember that the Palestinians have nothing, neither passport nor territory nor nation, and if they laud and long for all those things it's because they see only the ghosts of them. The Jordanian woman sang without either bombast or platitude. Her strong and musical utterance was neither dull nor declaratory but almost drily factual; her voice remained even, as if stating the obvious.

"But Hussein's a Muslim just like you," joked one of the boys, trying to provoke her.

"Perhaps, like me, he's fond of the smell of mignonette," she answered. "The resemblance goes no further than that."

She sat in the doorway and spoke in that calm fearless voice for nearly an hour. Then she rose and straightened up, signifying she had work to do on the farm.

I went over and congratulated her on her garden.

"We're from the South," she said. "My father was a Bedouin soldier. He was given the farm a few weeks before he died."

Her voice never showed either pride, humility or anger. She answered all our questions and remarks with patience and politeness.

"Do you know who taught us to farm?" she said. "The Palestinians, in 1949. They showed us how to turn the soil, how to choose the seeds, and when to water them."

"I noticed your vine," I said. "It's very handsome, but why does it crawl along the ground?"

For the first time, she smiled. Broadly.

"I know that in Algeria and France the vines are propped up and grow like runner beans. You make wine out of them. For us that would be a sin. We eat the grapes. And they taste best when they ripen on the ground."

She touched fingertips with each of us, and watched us go.

It wasn't impossible that, deep down, every Palestinian blamed Palestine for lying down and submitting too easily to a strong and cunning enemy.

"Why didn't she rise up in revolt? Volcanoes might have erupted, thunderbolts might have fallen and set fire to everything . . ."

"Thunderbolts? Haven't you realized yet that Heaven's on the side of the Jews?"

"But just taking it lying down! Where are the famous earthquakes?"

Even their anger, not merely verbal but born out of suffering, increased their determination to fight.

"The West goes out of its way to defend Israel . . ."

"The arrogance of the strong will be met with the violence of the weak."

"Even blind violence?"

"Yes. For a purpose that's both blind and lucid."

"What do you mean?"

"Nothing. I'm just getting worked up."

None of the fedayeen ever let go of his gun. If it wasn't slung over his shoulder he held it horizontal on his knees or vertical between them, not suspecting this attitude was in itself either an erotic or a mortal threat, or both. Never on any of the bases did I see a fedayee without his gun, except when he was asleep. Whether he was cooking, shaking out his blankets or reading his letters, the weapon was almost more alive than the soldier himself. So much so that I wonder whether, if the farmer's wife had seen boys without guns coming towards her house, she wouldn't have gone indoors, shocked at the sight of young men walking about naked. But she wasn't surprised: she lived surrounded by soldiers.

When, after leaving her place, we reached the turning by the little hazel copse, the fedayeen ran off and left me by myself on the road. Each tried not to be seen by the others, but I could just make them out from flashes of white shirt when, calm as babies on the pot, they squatted down to defecate. I suppose they wiped themselves clean with leaves plucked from the lower branches. Then back they came on to the road in good order, buttoned up neatly, still carrying their guns and still singing an impromptu marching song. When we got back we made ourselves some tea.

When I thought about her afterwards the farmer's wife sometimes struck me as a woman of great courage and intelligence; but at other times I couldn't help seeing her as a perfect example of dissimulation. Were she and her husband, with the hidden consent of the whole population of Ajloun, acting a part—he pretending, to the point of obsequiousness, to be a friend of the Palestinians, while she more subtly used argument and political acumen? Were they really a couple of collaborators, as the word was used by Frenchmen of other Frenchmen who consorted with the Germans? Had they been instructed to feign sympathy with the fedayeen in order to pass on information to the Jordanian army? If so, perhaps it was they who supplied the details that made the massacres of the fedayeen possible in June '71.

I still wonder why that farmer's wife was so much against Hussein. Was part of her family Palestinian? Did she have a score to settle? Did she remember being rescued from danger by some Palestinians? I still wonder about it.

All the pretence, misunderstanding and eyewash were quite evident to the journalists, who either went along with it deliberately or were dazzled by the glare given off by all rebellions. But although the very naïvety of the deceits ought to have warned them, I can't remember one newspaper article expressing surprise at the collusion and childishness involved. Perhaps the papers, who'd spent real money sending all those reporters and photographers and cameramen such a long way, insisted on sensational events to justify the expense. No question of applying the Paris cops' motto, "Move on, please, there's nothing to see."

Journalists weren't allowed anywhere near the bases—Halt! Secret! No Entry! The bases were forbidden territory, perhaps because, as everyone guessed though they didn't dare say so, there wasn't anything to see.

And perhaps this book I'm writing, an upsurge in my memory of some delightful times, is also—but would I say so?—just a collection of past moments designed to conceal the fact that there was nothing to see or hear. Are these pages only a barricade to hide the void, a mass of minor details designed, because they themselves are true, to lend plausibility to the rest?

I felt rather uncomfortable about the way the PLO were using the same devious and cynical methods of keeping military secrets as ordinary states successfully established, though I had to admit I couldn't see any alternative.

As a matter of fact I never saw or heard anything that couldn't perfectly well have been repeated. But mightn't that have been due to my extreme naïvety and fits of absent-mindedness? While visiting a base I was quite capable of poring at length over the manoeuvres of a colony of processionary caterpillars, themselves so clueless that they'd chosen to live among fedayeen growing colder and hungrier by the hour. Did Abu Omar see me as a real colleague who happened to be rather featherbrained, or as a dim old man who if anything important happened wouldn't understand, let alone disclose it, but just put it on a par with the comings and goings of the caterpillars?

The fedayee who'd translated the farmer's wife's Arabic so efficiently brought the almost involuntary distance between us to a rather abrupt end. I was invited to a birthday dinner by a former Turkish officer who turned out to be his father.

Until about 1970 Amman, which like other Arab capitals retained the dusty dullness of a small Bedouin township, was still a wreck. Now, after all the storms that have raged around Beirut, Amman is dangerously overblown.

The stream, in a voice that was low at first, has told how all the Arab countries mistrusted the Palestinians. Not one of them bothered to give any real help to that tortured people, tormented by its enemy, Israel, by its own political and revolutionary factions, and by the inner conflicts of each of its citizens. Every country felt threatened by a people without a country.

Lebanon, the so-called Switzerland of the Middle East, would disappear when Beirut disappeared under the bombs. The phrase "carpet of bombs," repeated over and over again by the papers and the radio, was perfectly apt.

And the more Beirut collapsed, its houses bent double as if they had stomach-ache, the stronger, the more portly, the fatter, grew Amman. As you went down into the old city you saw little bureaux de change cheek by jowl, straight out of the City of London. As soon as the sun got too hot their smiling moustachioed owners put up their steel shutters, went out in their damp short-sleeved shirts to their air-conditioned Mercedes, and drove home to take an afternoon nap in their villas in Jebel Amman. Nearly all of them, and their wives (in the plural), were fat. The wives looked through *Vogue* and *House and Garden*, ate chocolates and listened to *The Four Seasons* on cassettes. Vivaldi was all the rage when I got there in 1984; Mahler was just arriving as I left.

Ruins achieve glory and everlastingness through those who laid them low. And mending a broken column or a chipped capital is a kind of reparation. Because of its Roman remains Amman, for all its dust and dirt, had something.

I went through quite a large orchard near Ashrafieh and the fedayee-cum-interpreter was waiting for me at the house. It was not unlike the Nashashibis' place, all on one floor. The main reception room was on the same level as an orchard of apricot trees. Omar's father was sitting in an armchair smoking a hubble-bubble. The carpet was so vast and thick and had such a beautiful pattern I was tempted to take off my shoes.

"But they'll smell my dirty feet, my postman's feet that have trudged for miles . . ."

A small table laden with honey cakes was already set out on the carpet.

"I hope you like oriental pastries."

Omar's father was tall and lean and stern looking. His hair and moustaches were white and trimmed quite short.

"Don't listen to my son. He's made up his mind not to like them because there's nothing Marxist-Leninist or scientific about their ingredients or the way they're cooked. Make yourself comfortable."

When I reached the cushions on the far side of the carpet I stretched out and propped myself up on my elbow. Omar, Omar's father and Mahmud, another fedayee, were all three squatting down in their socks, their three pairs of shoes left on the marble surround. I laughed at the bubbles inside the hookah.

"You find it amusing? Strange?" asked the ex–Turkish officer.

"I feel as if I were looking at my stomach after I've drunk a bottle of Perrier."

Faint smiles from Omar and Mahmud. Very faint. Almost invisible.

"Maybe what you're really thinking is: there's your stomach, but it's my mouth producing the storm in it."

It wasn't what I was thinking, but it did echo my feelings, impossible to put into words, as I reclined there on the carpet under the Murano chandelier, talking to a former Turkish officer whom I later discovered to be eighty years old.

The limits of convention in conversation are very fluid, perhaps as fluid as geographical frontiers, but as with the latter it takes a war, with deaths, casualties and heroic survivors, to move them. When they do move, it's to make way for new frontiers which are also traps. So I still know next to nothing about the Moslem Brotherhood.

"Last year, in Cairo, a writer asked me to correct an article he'd written in French," a Moroccan lawyer told me. "It was about forty pages long, but by page two I was completely stunned. The whole thing was full of hate. Things like: 'We must fight everything that isn't Islam. For the time being we'll act through strikes . . . Nothing is more offensive to man but pleasing to God than the fetid breath of a starving atheist or of a brother who's been on hunger strike for ten days.' "

The Moroccan's grimace of disgust struck me as more far-fetched than the Egyptian's tirade. He'd refused to correct the article.

But when they spoke to me, a Frenchman, every member of the Moslem Brotherhood kept within the usual bounds. So I never gained access to their infernal secrets, as a reader in the old days might be admitted to the forbidden books in the *enfer* of the Bibliothèque Nationale.

The Turkish officer didn't seem to mind what he said. (And here, in reconstructing Monsieur Mustapha's conversation, I have to go in for a bit of forgery, filling in the gaps with the help I got later from Abu Omar and Mubarak. Otherwise all I'd have would be an unintelligible sketch of ruins drawn in the dark. I reproduce the content correctly, but in references to people who are still alive I've changed first names, surnames and initials.)

"It was in Constantinople that I began to speak your language. I hope I've improved in it since then. But I was born in Nablus and our family name is Naboulsi. It's a famous family, and since eight minutes past eight this morning I've been eighty years old. In 1912 I was a student in Berlin and an officer in the Ottoman army. In 1915, at the beginning of the war, when I suppose you were a French child and already my enemy, we—"

Here he smiled as sweetly as a saint or a baby: "We—forgive me: that word doesn't link you to me, it excludes you, because in this context 'we' means the Germans and the Turks—we were serving under Kaiser Wilhelm II. We weren't yet fighting your Maréchal Franchet d'Esperey. He came later. So Turkish is my first language, but as well as Arabic I also speak German. And English. You must be the judge of my French. Don't think too badly of me for talking about myself this evening—it's my birthday until midnight. In 1916 I was posted to intelligence."

Each sentence gulped down the one that went before without leaving time for digestion. My job was to listen.

"The war you Europeans say is over will last a long time yet. A Muslim I was and a Muslim I remained in the Empire, though we knew a transcendental God was unfashionable. But now—does being a Muslim mean any more than just saying so? Anyway, I'm still an Arab and a Muslim in the eyes of both Arabs and Muslims. But as regards Palestine... As a Turk I was a Palestinian. Now I'm practically nothing. Except perhaps through my youngest son—through Omar. I'm still a Palestinian through someone who's betrayed Islam for Marx.

"I believe, like you, in the virtues of treason, but I believe even more—though, alas, obscurely—in fidelity. As you see, I'm left in peace in my house in Amman, but here I'm a Jordanian, fallen stage by stage from the Khedive to Hussein, from the empire to the provinces."

"Are you still a Turkish officer?"

"You could say so. I have the courtesy title of colonel. That means about as much to me as if Monsieur Pompidou made me a duke in the French Section of the Workers' International or the Prince of Air Inter. In theory I obey the last scion—why don't I say sprig or twig?—of a Hashemite dynasty from the Hejaz, because since 1917 I've had to . . . No, it was 1922, the time when Ataturk did a deal with Europe . . ."

"You don't like Kemal Ataturk?"

"It's not true, the famous scene where he's supposed to have thrown down a copy of the Koran in the Assembly. He'd never have dared—the chamber was full of Muslim deputies. But he proved later on that he hated us."

"At the end of his life he got Antioch and Alexandretta back for Turkey."

"The French gave them to Turkey. They shouldn't have done it. They're Arab territories. The people there still speak Arabic. But as I was saying, after 1922 I had to stop taking orders from the Ottomans and take them from the English, from Abdullah, and from Glubb, who stripped me of my officer's rank because I'd served under Ataturk. He really did it because I'd done my military training in Germany."

"France has had its 'lost soldiers,' too."

"What a fine name! But all soldiers are lost.

"It's only just turned ten. I've still got till midnight. When I came back to Amman, the very town where I'd fought the English under Allenby, my eldest son, Ibrahim, whose mother, my first wife, is German, arranged for me to buy our house back. For that's what I had to do. Then one day I was playing backgammon in a café near your hotel—the Salah-ed-Din, I believe?—when I was recognized. I spent five months in prison. You've been luckier . . . you only spent a few hours with Nabila Nashashibi—one of her brothers told me. After that I was free. Free! Free not to cross the Jordan or see Nablus again. Not that I care, of course."

He put the mouthpiece of the hubble-bubble back in his mouth. I took sneaky advantage of the brief silence.

"But you're still a Turkish officer?"

"Discharged, as they say, a long time ago. My enemy was Ismet Inonu, less brutal but more bitter than Kemal. It was at his funeral in Ankara thirty years ago that I last wore Turkish uniform in public. My first wife keeps it in Bremen. She lives there with my son Ibrahim."

He sang it softly:

"It was at his funeral in Ankara thirty years ago that I last wore Turkish uniform in public."

Then, to another rhythm:

> "It was at his funeral
> in Ankara
> Thirty years ago
> That I last wore, that I last wore, Kara,
> Turkish uniform
> In public."

He went on:

"That tune haunts me. It's a sort of cavatina. The first musical table mat we had in Constantinople—Istanbul to you—used to play it."

"When you fought for the Turks against the English, didn't you feel you were fighting the Arabs in Lawrence and Allenby's army?"

"Did I hear you mention feelings? My dear Monsieur Genet, you don't suppose that in the army, where they like to give orders and be obeyed, and to obey, ah yes, to obey, and win medals—you don't suppose people in the army have feelings, do you?"

He and I both laughed politely. Omar and Mahmud didn't join in.

"And nothing was as clear-cut as that small but immodest archaeologist makes out. Lawrence embroidered everything—even when he's sodomized he presents it as heroism. And look at what's happening in Amman and Zarka now: all the officers and men of Palestinian origin have somehow received orders, or at least been advised in pressing terms, to desert from the Jordanian army—which is still made up of groups from Glubb's Arab

Legion, young Bedouin and Palestinians—and join the PLA* And how many have done so?'†

"Not many."

"Very few. But why? Out of disloyalty to the Palestinian homeland? Out of cowardice? To avoid having to fight against former brothers-in-arms? Out of loyalty to King Hussein? I'm a very old soldier, and I know all those things can come into it. I was an Arab officer in the Ottoman army. When your historians talk of Lawrence bringing about a general Arab revolt, let's cheerfully admit it was thanks to gold, to the coffers of gold sent by His Majesty George V. Of course there were solemn discussions in which ambition skulked in the disguise of rhetoric about freedom and independence, patriotism and magnanimity. But despite the fine words, ambition itself was disfigured by demands for posts, governorships, commissions, missions—and other things I can't remember. But I can remember the gold. My blue eyes saw it, my fingers touched it. The discussions! What a joke! About gold! About gold coins in pockets.

"My son told me you went to see a farmer's wife last week. I understand she's the daughter of a Bedouin NCO who was dazzled by British gold. He was dazzled by gold, but so were our emirs, who were also impressed by sashes and garters and ribbons—medals for the puffed-out chests of Bedouin who can be bowled over by a Lebel rifle. Just look at what's going on around you. Or keep your eyes closed, you who see nothing but poetry: Omar belongs to Fatah—do you think the fedayeen rush to join it out of altruism?"

He raised his voice, but it was mournful as he called out to the two young men: "Omar! Omar and Mahmud! Tonight you may smoke."

For my benefit he added, leaning back on his cushions of embroidered silk, "They wouldn't have smoked in the presence of my white hairs when I was a diwan."

---

*Palestine Liberation Army. Not to be confused with the Palestine Liberation Organization, led by Yasser Arafat.

†Leila told me that in fact many soldiers and officers deserted. But how many is many?

We took no notice of this slip of the tongue, and fell silent. Perhaps he thought an apology would only make it worse; perhaps I liked the idea of talking to an old Turk who thanks to his dreams and my passivity saw himself as a former vizir.

Hands were already fishing in pockets for lighters and American cigarettes.

"One day you'll understand what the English were like.

"But look at the Circassians. Let's talk about them for a bit. Abdulhamid needed a reliable army (Muslim but not Arab) to fight against the rebel Bedouin. So he thought of the Circassians in the Russian Empire. The Khedive offered them the best land in this region—here in Jordan and in what later became Syria—land where springs were few but bountiful. They may have abandoned their land in Golan"—he pronounced it "Jolan"—"to the Jews, but they still have their villages near Amman. And who were the Circassians? A kind of Muslim Cossack good at slaughtering Bedouin. And now they're their generals, ministers, ambassadors and postmasters who work for Monsieur Hussein and protect him against the Palestinians."

The two young men went behind a pillar to smoke. I saw this same deference to the Arab aristrocracy, or what set itself up as that, not only in the faces, words and behaviour of the fedayeen but also when Samia Solh entered the lounge of the Strand Hotel in Beirut. But the description of that evening can wait. The Turk was forging ahead.

"If justice had been done we ought to have lost the war in our officers' messes, with their countless trays of mezze and glasses of arak. We didn't think of anything but food. Amid all the plates and liqueurs and jokes our discussions would have flagged if we hadn't had a star to guide us. What we were debating was this: Should we, as Arab officers in the Turkish army, be hoping for and doing our best to promote the downfall of the Empire and the victory of England and France? I admit what was admissible in our debates, and say nothing about our revolting ambitions should Ludendorff defeat you on the Somme.

"The English had despised us under Muhammad Ali. The French had done so in Algeria and Tunisia. Right through the 1914–18 war the mosques in Tunisia prayed for our victory. Perhaps because the Bey was of Turkish origin. Anyhow, Tunis prayed for Germany and Turkey to conquer your countries. The Italians had despised us since 1896 in Eritrea. Ought we have wished all those Christians success?"

"The Germans were Christians, too."

Monsieur Mustapha paused for a few seconds to whistle the cavatina the musical plate-warmer used to play.

"No Arab country was a German colony. And Boche engineers built our roads and railways. Have you see the Hejaz railway?"

"Not this time. I did when I was eighteen. I did my military service in Damascus."

"In Damascus! You must tell me about it. What year?"

"1928 or '29."

"Did it leave you with happy memories? . . . No, don't talk about that country, or about yourself and your love affairs. I know all about it. Let's get back to the debate that fired our Arab consciences every hour of every day. I remember Ataturk with a certain amount of respect. He didn't like the Arabs and scarcely knew their language,* but he saved what he could of the Ottoman world.

"The way you humiliated the Empire, with the last Caliph escaping on an English ship, a prisoner and a deserter like Abd el-Kader! England with its Glubb here, and its Samuel in Palestine. And Frangié in Lebanon, and Aflak and his ridiculous Baas in Syria. And Ibn Saud in Arabia . . ."

"What ought we to have done in '14—and '18?"

Under the Murano chandelier, on the Smyrna carpet, Omar's father stood up and looked at me.

"We knew before 1917, long before the Balfour decision, that during the war some rich landowners . . ."

For the first time I heard the Sursok family mentioned.

". . . some rich landowners had already made contacts with the object of selling whole villages to the Jews, good and bad land all mixed up together. We know the names of the Arab families who gained by it . . ."

"They had friends in the Porte . . ."

---

*Is this a legend? Ataturk was almost taken prisoner because he spoke Arabic so badly. And I've heard he couldn't understand it very well, either.

"Undoubtedly. And the English, who were anti-Semitic but re-alistic, wanted a European colony near Suez to help them stand guard over what lay east of Aden."

The ebony and mother-of-pearl clock struck midnight. The Turkish officer had reached the sixteenth hour of his eightieth birthday. Omar asked him respectfully whether he hadn't been afraid of offending me, a stranger. The old man looked at me kindly, I thought.

"Not for a moment," he said. "You're from a country that will still be in my heart even after I'm dead: the country of Claude Farrère and Pierre Loti."

They brushed against death every day, every night, hence the airy elegance beside which dancing is heaviness itself. And with them animals and somehow things also were tamed.

Among groups ranging in size from ten to ten thousand, death didn't mean anything any more: you couldn't feel a quadruple grief when four friends died instead of one, a sorrow a hundred times deeper when a hundred died. Paradoxically, the death of a favourite fedayee made him all the more alive, made us see details about him we'd never noticed before, made him speak to us, answer us with new conviction in his voice. For a short time the life, the one life of the now dead fedayee took on a density it had never had before. If while he was still alive the twenty-year-old fedayee had made a few undemanding plans for the next day—washing his clothes, posting a letter—it seemed to me those unfulfilled intentions were accompanied now by the smell of decomposition. A dead man's plans stink as they rot.

But what did they mean to do with this grey head, with its grey skin, grey hair, grey unshaven beard—this grey, pink, round head for ever in their midst? Use it as a witness? My body didn't count. It served only to carry my round grey head.

It was much simpler with the Black Panthers. They'd found a waif, but instead of being a child the waif was an old man, and a White. Childish as I was about everything, I was so ignorant of American politics it took me a long time to realize Senator Wallace was a racist. It was like the fulfilment of an old childhood dream, in which strangers, foreigners—but probably more like me than my own compatriots—opened up a new life to me.

This childishness, almost innocence, was forced on me by the Panthers' kindness, which it seemed to me they bestowed on me not as a special favour but because it was natural to them. To be adopted like a child when one was an old man was very pleasant: it brought me both real protection and education in affection. The Panthers were well known for their talent as teachers.

The Panthers protected me so well I was never afraid in America—except for them. And as if by magic neither the white administration nor the white police ever made trouble for me. Right at the start, before I was adopted by David Hilliard, someone almost always went with me if I wanted to see Harlem. Until one day I went on my own into a bar that served Blacks only. It was probably attached to a brothel, for pretty girls kept coming in with black pimps. I ordered a Coca-Cola. My accent and the order in which I spoke the words made everyone burst out laughing.

I was deep in discussion with the barman and a pimp when two Panthers who were looking for me found me in "the jungle of the cities."

The Whites' recoil from the Panthers' weapons, their leather jackets, their revolutionary hair-dos, their words and even their gentle but menacing tone—that was just what the Panthers wanted. They deliberately set out to create a dramatic image. The image was a theatre both for enacting a tragedy and for stamping it out— a bitter tragedy about themselves, a bitter tragedy for the Whites. They aimed to project their image in the press and on the screen until the Whites were haunted by it.

And they succeeded. The theatrical image was backed up by real deaths. The Panthers did some shooting themselves, and the mere sight of the Panthers' guns made the cops fire.

"Was the Panthers' failure due to the fact that they adopted a 'brand image' before they'd earned it in action?"—that's a rough summary of a question I was asked by a paper called *Remparts* (Ramparts). But the world can be changed by other means than the sort of wars in which people die. "Power may be at the end of a gun," but sometimes it's also at the end of the shadow or the image of a gun. The Panthers' demands, as expressed in their "ten points," are both simple and contradictory. They are like a screen behind which what's done is different from what's seen to be done.

Instead of seeking real independence—territorial, political, administrative and legal—which would have meant a confrontation with white power, the Black underwent a metamorphosis in himself. He had been invisible; he became visible. And this visibility was accomplished in various ways. Black is not a colour itself, but with a pigmentation showing every shade of density the Black can wear clothes that are veritable feasts of colour. Against a black skin, light or dark, matching tones or contrasts of gold and azure, pink and mauve are all equally striking. But the set cannot disguise the tragic scene being played before it. The eyes are alive, and give forth a terrifying eloquence.

Did this metamorphosis bring about any change?

"Yes, when the Whites were affected by it. The Whites changed because their fears were no longer the same."

Deaths and other acts of aggression showed the Blacks as more and more threatening, less and less in awe of the Whites. The Whites sensed that a real society was coming into being not far away. It had existed before, but then it had been timid attempt at counterfeiting white society. Now it was breaking away, refusing to be a copy. And not only outwardly, in everyday life, but also inwardly, in the creation of a myth for which Malcolm X, Luther King himself, and N'Krumah all acted as models.

It was almost certain that the Panthers had just won a victory, and by means that seem derisory: silks, velvets, wild horses and images that brought about a metamorphosis in the Black. The method—for the moment—was traditional: international conflict, national liberation and perhaps class struggle.

Was it only a kind of theatre?

Theatre as it's usually understood involves an acting area, an audience, rehearsals. If the Panthers acted they didn't do so on a stage. Their audience was never passive: if it was black it either became what it really was or booed them; if it was white it was wounded and suffered. No imaginary curtain could be brought down on their performances. Excess in display, in words and in attitude swept the Panthers to ever new and greater excess.

Perhaps it's time to mention their lack of a country, though what follows is only a suggestion.

For every well-defined people—and even for nomads, for they don't visit their grazing areas merely at random—land is the necessary basis of nationhood. It is more. It's territory, it's matter itself, it's the space in which a strategy may be worked out. Whether still in its natural state, cultivated or industrialized, it is land that makes the notions both of war and of strategic withdrawal possible. Land may or may not be called sacred—the barbaric ceremonies that are supposed to make it so are of little importance. What matters is that it provides a place from which you can make war and to which you can retreat. But both the Blacks and the Palestinians are without land. Their two situations are not completely identical, but they are alike in that neither group has any territory of its own.

So where can these virtual martyrs prepare their revolt *from*? The ghetto? But they can't take refuge there—they'd need ramparts, barricades, bunkers, arms, ammunition, the support of the whole black population. Nor can they sally forth from the ghetto to wage war on white territory—all American territory is in the hands of the American Whites.

The Panthers' subversion would take place elsewhere and by other means: in people's consciences. Wherever they went the Americans were the masters, so the Panthers would do their best to terrorize the masters by the only means available to them. Spectacle. And the spectacle would work because it was the product of despair. The tragedy of their situation—the danger of death and death itself; physical terror and nervous dread—taught them how to exaggerate that despair.

But spectacle is only spectacle, and it may lead to mere figment, to no more than a colourful carnival; and that is a risk the Panthers ran. Did they have any choice? But even if they themselves had been the masters, or had had sovereignty over some territory, they probably wouldn't have formed a government complete with president, minister for war, minister of education, field marshals and Newton as "supreme commander" as soon as he got out of jail.

The few Whites who sympathized with the Panthers soon ran out of steam. They could follow them only on the plane of ideas, not into the depths, where a strategy had to be worked out whose only source was the Blacks' imagination.

So the Panthers were heading for either madness, metamorphosis of the black community, death or prison. All those options happened, but the metamorphosis was by far the most important, and that is why the Panthers can be said to have overcome through poetry.

I went back to the tents of Ajloun by the Salt road, and the first thing I saw was Abu Kassem with his arms in the air. He was hanging out his washing on a string tied to a couple of trees. The spring was nearby. Before the Amman massacre the Jordanian ministers' servants used to water their horses there. The fedayeen now lived in the ministers' houses. Where had Abu Kassem got the clothes pegs? And why had he been doing his washing? He answered me, unsmiling, with a quote from the catechism.

"A fedayee can look after himself and can always find whatever he needs. There are the pegs—if you've got any washing to do you can use them. You won't find any others—you're not a fedayee."

"Thank you—I never wash. You're joking, Kassem, but you look very grim."

"M'hammad's going to the Ghor tonight."

The Ghor is the Jordan valley.

"Is he your friend?"

"Yes."

"How long have you known he was going?"

"Twenty minutes."

"Is that his washing?"

"His and mine. The men must be clean tonight."

"Are you worried, Kassem?"

"Anxious. I'll be anxious until he comes back or until I have to give up hope."

"You love M'hammad that much, and you a revolutionary?"

"When you're a revolutionary yourself you'll understand. I'm nineteen, I love the revolution, I'm devoted to it and hope to work for it for a long time to come. But here we're in a way off duty. We may be revolutionaries but we're only human. I love all the fedayeen, and you too. But here under the trees all night and day, I can be more friendly with one of the commandos than with the rest if I want to. I can break a bar of chocolate into two, but not into sixteen. So I make my choice."

"You're all revolutionaries, but you like just one of them the best?"

"We're all Palestinians. But I choose to belong to Fatah. Hasn't it ever struck you that revolution and friendship go together?"

"Yes. But what about your leaders?"

"Even if they're revolutionaries they're like me and have their preferences."

"And would you go so far as to call the friendship you speak of, love?"

"Yes. It is love. Do you think at a time like this I'm afraid of words? Friendship, love? One thing is true—if he dies tonight there'll always be a gulf at my side, a gulf into which I must never fall. My leaders? When I was seventeen they thought I was grown-up enough to be allowed to join Fatah. And I've stayed in Fatah even though my mother needed me. I'm nineteen now, and no less grown-up than I was before. I may be a revolutionary, but in moments of relaxation I turn to friendship—friendship's restful, too. I'll be worried tonight, but I'll get on with my work. I learned two years ago what I have to do when it's my turn to go down to the Jordan, so I know all about it. Now I'd better hang this last vest up to dry."

There were ten or twelve camps in Jordan. Jebel Hussein, Wahadat, Baqa, Gaza Camp and Irbid were the ones I knew best. Life in the camps was less elegant, that's to say less stripped down to essentials, than on the bases. Less volatile, too. The women were all very serene, but even the thinnest carried a characteristic feminine weight. I don't mean the physical weight of breasts, hips and thighs, but that of the womanly gestures conveying certainty and repose.

A lot of foreigners, that is non-Palestinians, not only visited the camps but also went "up," paradoxically, to the "bases" overlooking the Jordan—fortified positions commanding the river from the mountains. The fedayeen came back to the camps to rest—or to get laid, as Westerners say, or to get medicine to cure the effects of that activity.

Nearly every camp had a tiny infirmary-cum-pharmacy full— it was so small—of old cartons of unidentified and useless drugs from Germany, France, Italy, Spain and Scandinavia. Nobody could read the lists of ingredients or the instructions for use.

When a few tents were burned down at Baqa Camp, Saudi Arabia flew some houses made of corrugated iron straight out from Riyadh as a gift, and the old women greeted their arrival as if they were young princesses, with a sort of impromptu dance. It was like the dance Azeddine invented in honour of his first bicycle. The corrugated iron or aluminium houses reflected the glare of the sun. Imagine a cube with one side missing for the floor and another with a doorway cut in it. In such a room an eighty-year-old couple would have cooked in the midday sun in summer and frozen at night in the winter.

Some Palestinians had the bright idea of filling the corrugations on the roof and sides of one house with loose black earth, held in place with wire netting. Then they sowed seeds in the soil and watered it every evening, producing a carpet of green dotted with poppy flowers. The place became a little grotto pleasant to be in, winter or summer. But there weren't many imitations of those horse-covered hills.

What was to become of you after the storms of fire and steel? What were you to do?

Burn, shriek, turn into a brand, blacken, turn to ashes, let yourself be slowly covered first with dust and then with earth, seeds, moss, leaving behind nothing but your jawbone and teeth, and finally becoming a little funeral mound with flowers growing on it and nothing inside.

When I looked at the Palestinian revolution from a viewpoint higher than my own, it was never desire for territory, for land more or less derelict and unfenced kitchen gardens and orchards, but a great movement of revolt, a challenge over rights which reached to the limits of Islam, not only involving territorial boundaries but also calling for a revision, probably even a rejection, of a theology as soporific as a Breton cradle.

The dream, but not yet the declared aim, of the fedayeen was clear: to do away with the twenty-two Arab nations and leave everyone wreathed in smiles, childlike at first but soon foolish. But they were running out of ammunition and their main target, America, was endlessly resourceful. Thinking to walk tall, the Palestine revolution was sinking fast. Training people to sacrifice themselves results not in altruism but in a kind of fascination that makes them jump off a cliff not to help but merely to follow those who have already leapt to their deaths. Especially when they foresee, not through thought but through fear, the annihilation to come.

A little further back, when I was talking about the deference, almost sycophancy, in the fedayeen's behaviour towards members of the Palestinian traditional or banking aristocracies, I said I'd return to the subject of Samia Solh.

I'd already seen wounded commandos lying between white sheets in hospital in Southern Lebanon, overawed by elderly women with made-up eyes, lips and cheeks, who tinkled like tambourines whenever they moved, so many were their gold bracelets, chains, necklaces and ear-rings.

"Your janglings will either wake them up or kill them," I said to one.

"Not a bit of it! We wave our arms about because we're Latins. Or at least Mediterranean—Maronites, Phoenicians. We do our best to restrain ourselves, but we can't help showing pity at the sight of all this suffering. And then naturally our jewellery makes a noise! But our martyrs love it. Some of them tell me they've never been as close to anything so rich and beautiful in their lives. Let their poor eyes at least be filled with happiness."

"Don't argue with strangers, Mathilde. Let's go on to the surgical ward."

Later on I had the chance all too often to observe at close quarters such elderly ladies, from what remains of the leading Palestinian families.

Perhaps a goose cassoulet provides the best metaphor for what a handsome old Palestinian lady looked like. The faces and the manners of these rich dames made you think of something cooked very fast at times but mostly simmered very slowly to produce those round cheekbones and retain that pink skin. The misfortunes of their people at once sharpened and softened their features; they were preserved in suffering as the goose's flavour is preserved in its own fat. So they were—one of them especially—adorably and selfishly sweet. The object of their sweetness was to keep sufferings that were too raw at a distance. They kept themselves up to date about the sufferings in Chatila as they did about the price of gold and the exchange rate of the dollar—through the stitches of a piece of embroidery or tapestry. They knew about suffering, but through a cushion, or a gown a hundred or a hundred and twenty years old, worked by dead fingers, watched by now sightless eyes. They cultivated politeness as a kind of ornament.

If Venice happened to crop up in conversation they never mentioned Diaghilev. Instead they made elegant reference to the Lagoon, the Grand Canal, the glass factories at Murano, and funerals at which the coffin was borne along in a gondola.

"Like Diaghilev's," you might say.

"I watched it go by from a balcony at the Danieli."

These princesses with wrists strong enough to wear solid gold chains contemplate their people from their chaises-longues, through pearl-handled lorgnettes. They watch the fighting through their windows, and the sadness in their eyes grows ever more affected.

I myself watched the sea and Cyprus in the distance through the window of a prefab, and waited for the fighting, but I didn't turn into a juicy old princess. The resemblance never troubled me: I didn't fancy either the smooth looks or the easy life of the line of Ali.

Yet like them I'll have looked on at the Palestinians' revolt as if from a window or a box in a theatre, and as if through a pearl-handled lorgnette.

How far away I was from the Palestinians. For example, when I was writing this book, out there among the fedayeen, I was always on the other side of a boundary. I knew I was safe, not because of a Celtic physique or a layer of goose fat, but because of even shinier and stronger armour: I didn't belong to, never really identified with, their nation or their movement. My heart was in it; my body was in it; my spirit was in it. Everything was in it at one time or another; but never my total belief, never the whole of myself.

There are so many ways of being married. But what struck me as really strange, every day, day and night, every hour, every second, there under the trees, were the doings of that curious couple, Islam and Marxism. In theory everything about it was incompatible. The Koran and *Das Kapital* were foes. Yet harmony seemed to result from their contradictions. Anyone giving out of generosity seemed to have done so out of a love of justice resulting from an intelligent reading of the German tome. We sailed along madly, sometimes slowly, sometimes fast, with God always bumping into the domed forehead of Marx, who denied him. Allah was everywhere and nowhere, despite all the prayers towards Mecca.

Louis Jouvet was a famous actor in France in the late forties, and when he coolly asked me to write him a play with only two or three characters in it I answered with equal detachment. I realized his provocative question was asked only out of politeness. And I detected the same politeness in Arafat's voice when he said:

"Why don't you write a book?"

"Why not?"

We were only exchanging courtesies; neither of us was bound by promises forgotten before they were uttered. My certainty that there was nothing at all serious either in Arafat's question or in my answer was probably the real reason why I forgot to bring pen and paper with me. I didn't believe in the idea of that or any other book; I meant to concentrate on what I saw and heard; and I was as interested in my own curiosity as in its objects. But without my quite realizing it, everything that happened and every word that was spoken set itself down in my memory.

There was nothing for me to do but look and listen. Not a very laudable occupation. Curious and undecided, I stayed where I was, at Ajloun. And gradually, as with some elderly couples who started off indifferent to one another, my love and the Palestinians' affection made me stay on.

The policy of the superpowers, and the PLO's relations with them, spread over the Palestinian revolt, and us with it, a kind of transcendental influence. A tremor starting in Moscow, Geneva or Tel Aviv would rumble on via Amman to reach out under the trees and over the mountains to Jerash and Ajloun.

The complex old Arab and Palestinian aristocracies worked alongside the modern authorities, parallel to and, as I once thought, superimposed on them.

From Ajloun, Palestinian patriotism looked like Delacroix's *Liberty on the Barricades*. Distance, as often happens, lent a touch of divinity. But the birth of that patriotism had been obscure, even dubious.

The Arab Peninsula had long been entirely under Turkish rule, mild for some people, harsh according to most. Then between 1916 and 1918 the English, with their coffers full of gold, promised the Arabs independence and the setting up of an Arab kingdom if the Arab-speaking people rose against the Turks and the Germans. But even before this, rivalries among the leading Palestinian, Lebanese, Syrian and Hejazi families had led to their seeking now Turkish and now English support, not to obtain greater freedom for the new Arab nation, as yet unborn though perhaps about to be conceived, but so that they could cling on to power. Among these illustrious clans were the Husseini, Jouzi, N'seybi and Nashashibi families. Others either awaited the victory of the Emir Faisal or worked against it.

Nothing was said clearly. No leading Palestinian family actually declared itself, but all of them probably had a representative in either the Turkish or the Anglo-French camp.

That had been roughly the set-up in 1914.

But the families who'd rashly chosen the English camp, which was also that of the Emir Faisal, were obliged to turn against the English when they found out that the Jewish National Home was to be recognized as an independent state.

With the exception of some wealthy Syrian and Lebanese families such as the Sursoks and the incredible descendants of Abd el-Kadr, all the hereditary "leading" Palestinian families claimed to be at the fore-front of the struggle, leading the country simultaneously against Israel and the British.

The Husseini family*—sons, grandsons, nephews and great-nephews of the Grand Mufti of Jerusalem—has produced many martyrs to the Palestinian cause. (When I use words like "martyr" I don't adopt the aura of nobility that the Palestinians attribute to them. From a slightly mocking distance, I merely make use of the vocabulary. I shall give my reasons later.)

Madame Shahid (the name means "martyr'), née Husseini, a niece of the Grand Mufti, told me with what I took to be pride how the Khedives had sorted things out in Jerusalem.

"There was such chaos and muddle around the Holy Sepulchre, such mean and petty rows about who was to celebrate the most masses, who was to occupy the church the longest—Roman Catholics, Russian Orthodox, Greeks, Maronites, those with hair or those with tonsures—and what liturgies they were to follow—the French, Italian, German, Spanish and Coptic bishops and the Greek and Russian priests all wanted to use their own languages—that the Khedives decided two or three Muslim families should be put in charge of the keys of the Holy Sepulchre and of the Church of the Ascension. I can remember the sound of the carriage on the cobblestones as my father drove home with the key of Christ's tomb, and how glad my mother was to have him back safe and sound."

---

*The still numerous Hussein family are connected only distantly, if at all, with the present King of Jordan, though both the Palestinian and the Hejazi families claim to be "Ashraf"—that is, descended from the Prophet.

The "leading families" still took part in the struggle, but not all their members were equally devoted to the cause. Some merely made use of it, rallying round or distancing themselves as it suited their interests. The Husseini and Nashashibi families both include many heroes, though they were rivals under the Turks.

Members of the Leading Families didn't spare one another. One of their privileges was to tell of anything that might harm their rivals, whether it was true or false. But I never heard any such allegations among the fedayeen. Perhaps I missed them through not understanding the language better. I heard plenty of insults against the army chiefs, though: the fighters made no secret of their contempt. They often talked to me about it, but they never said a word against one another. Judgement was shrewdly conveyed without a word being spoken.

Nor did the fedayeen know anything of the ornaments that generation after generation of the leading families had added to the Muslim epic. None of them could have told me the story Madame Shahid related.

"When Sultan So-and-So [some name I've forgotten] entered Jerusalem he decided, before any other ceremony, to say a prayer. As there was no mosque there yet the people suggested he should pray in a Christian church, but he refused, saying, 'If I did, some future governor might use it as an excuse to seize the church on the grounds that it had been used to worship Allah.' So he prayed in the open, and it was there that the Muslims later built the Mosque of the Rock."

That story's about as true as the French legend of St Louis dispensing justice under an oak tree and blessing the acorns.

With such embroideries Madame Shahid, a Palestinian, tried to bolster up the legend of a tolerant Islam. At the same time (the way the English tend the graves in their churchyards) she polished up the reputation of a sultan who might have had some connection with her own family fifteen hundred years ago. Such fairy tales were unknown to the fedayeen.

Lawrence promised Faisal sovereignty for the Arab people, but England didn't keep the promise. The League of Nations gave

France mandatory powers over Lebanon and Syria, while England got Palestine, and Jordan went to Iraq. The rivalry between the leading families was transformed into patriotism; their senior members became war-lords, regarded as bandit chiefs by England and France, and, after 1933, as Hitler's lackeys in the Middle East. The Palestine resistance was beginning.

One day a hotel porter told me he was waiting to hear from Canada about a job he was hoping to get in a big hotel there, "instead of staying here with no future." As we were talking a bent old waiter went by and disappeared into the staff quarters.

"That's my future if I stay," said the porter scornfully. "Sixty years a servant."

"And never a day's rebellion!"

He slapped his hand angrily on the desk.

"Yes, sixty years and never a day's rebellion! I'd go anywhere rather than that."

Guests at the Strand Hotel in Beirut included political and military officials of the PLA and PLO, politicians of all nationalities who wanted to meet Arafat, journalists more or less friendly with or accepted by the Resistance, and a few German writers sympathetic to its cause. You might have a whisky or two with Kadoumi's bodyguards in one of the lounges there.

Samia Solh, sister-in-law to Prince Abdullah of Morocco, had just been ushered in by the manager. Just before she sat down she let her ankle-length mink coat, lined with white silk, slip to the floor, forming a sort of plinth. She stepped over it, and a bellboy picked it up and bore it off on outstretched arms to the cloakroom.

I was eighteen when I was taken to see four men who'd been hanged in Cannon Square, here in Beirut. (I was told they were thieves, but I think now they were rebel Druses.) My eyes had been as quick to seek out the dead men's flies as the eyes of the guests were now to fasten first on the famous hips, then on the reputedly very quick tongue and lips of the lovely but dim Samia.

"A week ago I was with Muhammar in Tripoli," she said. "We hit it off straight away."

Not dreaming that ten years later the PLO would be banned from Libya, its offices in Tripoli closed, the Palestinian officers listened to the lady entranced, with a reverence so hushed that her would-be intimate murmur rang out like a lecture at the Collège de France. Her peals of laughter were designed to draw attention to her triple collar of Venus, but they sounded coarse rather than crystalline when punctuated by Kaddafi's given name.

No one was allowed to talk to her. Only the radio dared to comment, as it calmly did on the latest massacres on the banks of the Jordan and the ease with which fedayeen were picked off by Israeli soldiers.

No one touched those hips, that throat, those lips. I can understand now—I wondered at the time—how a fedayee might have been excited by all that beauty, the result of massages, applications of dandelion juice, anointings with royal jelly and other products of shameless chemists. But the attentions the fedayeen paid her that evening were an eye-opener to me. Their tribute wasn't to the vixen wiggling her hips, though. It was to the fact that she brought History into the reinforced concrete hotel. It was in the Strand that the leaders of the PLO used to meet, among them Kamal Udwan, Kamal Nasir and Muhammad Yusif al-Najjar—I'll tell later on how they were killed by Israelis pretending to be queers, perhaps in retaliation for the murders at Munich during the 1972 Olympics.

"Verdun is very well laid out—a mixture of crosses and crescents forming one huge graveyard. There was slaughter there, carried out by God Himself. Senegalese, Madagascans, Tunisians, Moroccans, Mauritians, New Caledonians, Corsicans, men from Picardy, Tonkin and Réunion all clashed fatally with Uhlans, Pomeranians, Prussians, Westphalians, Bulgarians, Turks, Serbs, Croats and men from Togoland. Thousands of peasants from all corners of the globe came here to die, to kill and be killed, to be swallowed up in the mud. So many that certain poets—only poets think such thoughts—have seen the place as a kind of magnet attracting soldiers from everywhere, a magnet pointing to some other Pole Star, symbolized by another virgin.

"Our Palestinian graves have fallen from planes all over the world, with no cemeteries to mark them. Our dead have fallen from one point in the Arab nation to form an imaginary continent. And if Palestine never came down from the Empire of Heaven to dwell upon earth, would we be any less real?"

So sang one of the fedayeen, in Arabic.

"The lash of outrage was urgent. Yet here are we, a divine people, on the brink of exhaustion, sometimes close to catastrophe, and with about as much political power as Monaco," answered another.

"We are the sons of peasants. Placing our cemeteries in heaven; boasting of our mobility; building an abstract empire with one pole in Bangkok and the other in Lisbon and its capital here, with somewhere a garden of artificial flowers lent by Bahrain or Kuwait; terrorizing the whole world; making airports put up triumphal arches for us, tinkling like shop doorbells—all this is to do in reality what smokers of joints only dream of. But has there ever been a dynasty that didn't build its thousand-year reign on a sham?"

So said a third fedayee.

Everywhere Obon, the non-existent dead Japanese, and the card-game without cards.

One afternoon under the trees.

"We'll wrap ourselves up a bit more tightly in our blankets and go to sleep. The next day we'll wake up an exact replica of the Jews. We'll have created a Palestinian, not an Arab, God, and a Palestinian Adam and Eve, a Palestinian Cain and Abel."

"How far have you got?"

"To the word replica."

"With God, the book, the destruction of the Temple and all that?"

"A New Israel, but in Romania. We'll occupy Romania or Nebraska, and speak Palestinian."

"When you've been a slave it's lovely to be just a down and out. When you've been a Palo* it's lovely to turn into a tiger."

"Having been slaves, shall we be terrible masters when the time comes?"

"Soon. In a couple of thousand years. If I forget thee, El Kods ..."†

The two fedayeen were exchanging quips across the camp. All the time they went on smiling, smoothing their moustaches with thumb, forefinger or tongue, flashing their teeth, lighting cigarettes.

Holding out a lighter, cupping the flame with your hand, moving it near the tip of the other's cigarette, accidentally letting the light go out and then striking it again—all this means more than the mere offer of a smoke when the emirs shower down packets of cigarettes by the million.

Small gestures, whether difficult or easy, can show esteem or real friendship: a smile, the loan of a comb, helping someone brush his hair, a look in a tiny mirror.

But the greenstuff was so ubiquitous and intrusive I longed for a whiff of Bovril.

I see I often mention the trees. That's because it was a long time ago—fifteen years—and they've probably been cut down by now.

They didn't shed their leaves even in the winter, though they did go yellow. Does this strange phenomenon occur anywhere else? Was it really strange?

I talk about the trees because they were the setting of happiness—happiness in arms. In arms because there were bullets in the guns; but I don't remember ever experiencing so deep a peace.

War was all around us. Israel was on the watch, also in arms. The Jordanian army threatened. But every fedayee was just doing what he was fated to do.

All desire was abolished by such liberty. Rifles, machine-guns, Katyushkas—every weapon had its target. Yet under the golden trees—peace.

---

*Palestinian.

†El Kods = Jerusalem in Arabic.

There are the trees again—I haven't really conveyed how frag-ile they were. The yellow leaves were attached to the branches by a fine yet real stalk, but the forest itself looked as frail to me as a scaffolding that vanishes when a building's finished. It was insub-stantial, more like a sketch of a forest, a makeshift forest with any old leaves, but sheltering soldiers so beautiful to look at they filled it with peace.

Nearly all of them were killed, or taken prisoner and tortured.

Ferraj's group of about twenty fedayeen were camped in the forest some distance from the asphalt road from Jerash to Ajloun.

Abu Omar and I found them sitting on the grass.

Abu Hani was the colonel in command of the whole sector, an area about sixty kilometres long and forty wide, with the Jordan on two sides and the Syrian frontier on the other. The first thing the colonel did if ever there were any visitors was impress them with his rank. I remember him as short and covered with braid, a cane under his arm and stars on his shoulders. His face was too red; he was bad tempered rather than bossy, but inclined to be stu-pid. Rather like the portraits of Charles X, only not so tall.

Ferraj was twenty-three. He soon steered the conversation in the direction he wanted.

"Are you a Marxist?"

I was rather surprised, but didn't attach much importance either to the question or to the answer.

"Yes," I said.

"Why?"

I was still not really interested. Ferraj's young face looked open and guileless. He was smiling, but anxious to hear what I'd say. After a while I told him nonchalantly:

"Perhaps because I don't believe in God."

Abu Omar translated immediately and correctly.

The colonel jumped. I mean he'd been sitting on the reddish grass or moss like the rest of us, but now he actually leapt to his feet and yelled:

"That's enough!"

He was talking both to the fedayeen and to me.

"Here you can talk about everything. Absolutely everything. But don't call in doubt the existence of God. I won't have any blasphemy. We don't take lessons from the West any more."

Abu Omar, a practising Christian, went on translating as calmly as before, though he was rather vexed. Ferraj, looking across at me and not up at the colonel, didn't raise his voice either. He answered gently but with a touch of irony, rather as one might address a harmless madman:

"You don't have to listen. It's quite easy. Your HQ's only a couple of kilometres away—you can be there in a quarter of an hour without even hurrying. And then you won't hear anything. But we're going to keep the Frenchman here till five in the morning, to hear what he's got to say and tell him what we think. We'll be free to say what we like."

So that night I was either going to be given my pass, or rejected.

Abu Hani went off, having said he must have a report on what I said during the night.

"I'm responsible for the discipline in this camp."

The next morning he came back to Ferraj's base and shook hands with me. He claimed to know what had been said.

Our vigil in the tent under the trees had lasted till quite late. Each of the fedayeen asked me questions as he prepared tea or coffee or his own argument.

"But it's you who ought to be talking to me—telling me what you mean by revolution, and how you intend to bring it about."

Perhaps they were carried away by the lateness of the hour, or by a time that was getting more and more confused—the grey, intoxicating time outside space, which upsets the clocks of the memory and seems to set words free.

It was like closing time in a bar, when you can suddenly hear the sound of the pinball machines. Something makes everyone very lucid and interested, and because the waiters are sleepy you go and continue the discussion outside.

Through the walls of the tent we could hear the cries of the jackals. Perhaps because we were so tired, time and space ceased to exist, but the fedayeen, relishing and borne along by their youthful eloquence, went on talking.

Abu Omar translated.

"Because Fatah's not only a war of liberation but also the beginning of a revolution, we'll use the violence to get rid of privilege, starting with Hussein and the Bedouin and the Circassians."

"But how?"

"The oil belongs to the people, not to the princes."

I remember that phrase very clearly. The odd thought struck me, though I partly believed it too, that a very poor people may need to indulge in the luxury of having fat princes over them, waddling through their cool invisible gardens, just as other poor folk save up and even ruin themselves for Christmas. The inhabitants of some countries let themselves be eaten up by fleas at night and flies in the daytime in order to fatten the flocks of their pious rulers.

But my thought was too disagreeable for that night, and I kept it to myself.

Arabian tobacco smoke was pouring out of our mouths and nostrils.

"We must get rid of Hussein, America, Israel and Islam."

"Why Islam?"

As soon as we arrived I'd noticed his big black beard and burning eyes, his gleaming black hair and swarthy skin. And his silence, that seemed all the more intense for having now been broken. It was he who'd asked the question, in a voice that was strong but almost crystal clear.

"Why do you have to get rid of Islam? How can you get rid of God?"

He was talking chiefly to me. He went on:

"You're here, not just in an Arab country, or in Jordan, or on the banks of the Jordan, but with the fedayeen. So you must be a friend. When you came"—he smiled—"you from France and I from Syria—you told us you didn't believe in God. But if you ask me, if you didn't believe in Him you wouldn't have come."

He went on smiling.

"I claim to be a good Muslim. If you agree, we'll have a debate, you and I, in front of everyone. Are you game?"

"Yes."

"Stand up then, and we'll meet each other halfway and embrace. Let's start out as friends and stay friends during and after the discussion. A year ago I was sent to China for three months, and this is what I remember from the thoughts of Mao Tse-tung: Before you argue, show that you're friends with a kiss on both cheeks."

He spoke easily. While he was slightly taken aback by the strangeness of my position, you could tell he spoke from absolute certainty himself, demanding answers from God as of right. The fedayeen were utterly silent as he and I went and embraced in the middle of the tent and then returned to our places. We addressed ourselves to the theme that oil was something that must be made use of.

Of course. A few experts would take care of the oil industry. But it seemed the fedayeen thought all Arabia's oil was in one bottomless pit, a sort of Danaïds' well, like the Englishman's chest of gold coins that was never empty despite the Turko-Arab officers' full pockets, holsters and saddlebags.

"If God didn't exist, you wouldn't be here," said Abu Gamal, the Syrian. "And the world would have had to create itself, and the world would be God, and the world would be good. But it isn't. The world's imperfect, so it can't be God."

Abu Omar translated into French. I answered flippantly: I was tired and rather light-headed.

"If God made the world he made a pretty poor job of it, so it comes to the same thing," I said.

"But we're here to remedy that," said the Syrian. "We're free both to suffer and to cure."

I could see by now that the earth was flat and Lorraine was still called Lotharingia. I felt like invoking Thomas Aquinas. Abu Gamal and I jousted on without either of us suspecting we were heading inevitably for heresy. What mattered to me was not any particular argument, nor even the discussion itself—it struck me as scholastic and colourless—but a sort of kindness and strength, a combination of conviction and openness in which everyone present shared. We *were* free—free to say anything we liked. We mightn't have been actually drunk, but we'd taken off, knowing Abu Hani was sleeping his head off, probably alone, a couple of kilometres away.

Almost roughly I interrupted Ferraj to say something to Abu Gamal.

"When you started by putting the discussion under the aegis of God you cut the ground from under my feet—I don't claim the patronage of anyone so grand. And your God is all the grander because you can increase His dimensions as much as you like. But the reason you also insisted on beginning with the seal of friendship is that even though you're a Muslim you've got more faith in friendship than you have in God. For here we all are, armed, an unbeliever among believers, and yet I'm your friend."

"And where does friendship came from but God? . . . To you, to me, to all of us here this morning. Would you be our friend if God hadn't inspired you with friendship for us, and us with friendship for you?"

"So why doesn't He do the same to Israel?"

"He can whenever He wants to. And I believe he will."

Then we took it in turns to talk about irrigating the desert.

"We'll have to get rid of the princes," said Ferraj. "They own the desert. And we'll have to learn hydraulics. The trouble is the princes are descendants of the Prophet."

"We'll show them they're sons of Adam like the rest of us."

That was Abu Gamal.

Then to me:

"If a Jordanian soldier—a Muslim, that is—threatened you, I'd kill him."

"I'd try to do the same if he threatened you."

"And if he killed you I'd avenge you by killing him," he laughed.

"It must be difficult to stay a Muslim. I respect you for your faith."

"Thank you."

"Respect me for being able to do without it."

A dangerous leap. He hesitated, but in the end no, he wouldn't.

"I'll pray to God to *give* you faith."

Everyone in the tent burst out laughing, even Abu Omar and Abu Gamal. It was nearly four in the morning.

The whole gathering was highly diverted at the notion of all these young drinkers of tea and orange juice spending the night lecturing and being lectured to by an elderly Frenchman, an outsider suddenly set down under the trees in a winter that had begun with Black September. There I was in the midst of a bunch of terrorists whose mere names made newspapers tremble like leaves in their readers' hands. And there were they, laughing without cynicism, verbally inventive, a bit wild, but as proper as a bunch of seventeen-year-old seminarists. Their exploits on land and in the air were reported with fear and disgust, or at least a good imitation of it. But vague moral condemnation didn't bother them. That night, from dark to dawn . . .

Time had undergone a curious transformation since I arrived in Ajloun. Every moment had become "precious," so bright you felt you ought to be able to pick it up in pieces. The time of harvest had been followed by the harvest of time.

But I managed to surprise them by swallowing eight capsules of Nembutal.

I slept peacefully in a deep underground shelter inside the tent. Farcical as it had been to enter the United States after the American consul in Paris had refused me a visa, it was even stranger to be here, sleeping quietly in the midst of this free and easy egalitarianism. But there was nothing dramatic about it. These gentle terrorists might have been camping on the Champs Elysées, with the rest of us watching them through binoculars for fear of getting wet—for they peed both far and high.

Just before I lay down on the blankets spread for me in the shelter, the fifteen or twenty terrorists peered in amazement at my medicine bottle, at the eight Nembutal capsules I took, and at the tranquil expression on my face. As I gulped the poison down they gazed at my Adam's apple with amazement and perhaps admiration. They must have been thinking:

"To put away a dose like that without showing any fear—that must be French courage. We have a hero among us tonight."

The hours we spent in friendly argument, the long nights of stupefied weariness in which we got to know one another, come back to me as a vague babble which I re-create as I write.

Every mosque, however small, had a fountain—a little trickle of water, a bowl or stagnant pool for the ritual ablutions. In the forest, whether to shave his pubic hair or to prepare himself for prayer, a pious fedayee in his late teens would make himself a miniature Ganges out of leafy branches and a green plastic pail, a minute Benares of his own under a cork-oak, beech or fig-tree. It was such a good imitation of India that as I went by I could almost hear the Muslim murmur, as he offered up his cupped palms, "Om mani Pad me Om." The Muhammadan forest was full of standing Buddhas.

Unless:

Wherever there was a drop of flowing or standing water there was a spring: here (though less than in Morocco) Islam stumbled over paganism at every step. Here, where Christian beliefs are held to blaspheme a God as solitary as the vice to which the same adjective is applied, paganism provides a touch of darkness at noon, of sunlight in shadow, of dampness drawn up from the Jordan. It's a dampness from which the kind fairy with the magic wand catches hayfever; a dampness that leaves behind it the print of a human foot.

Because they never owned anything, the fedayeen imagined the luxury they wanted to rid the world of. That's what I meant—what I wanted both to say and to conceal—by the "quiet periods" I mentioned above: the day-dreams people have to work off somehow when they've neither the strength nor the opportunity to make them come true. It's then they invent the game of revolution, which is what revolt is called when it lasts and begins to be structured, when it stops being poetic negation and becomes political assertion.

If such imaginary activity is to be of any use it has to exist. But gradually people learn to do without it, like a detachable lining in the West. Then our preoccupation with merely imaginary wealth and power is supposed to help us create weapons with which to destroy real wealth and power when we meet them.

But except for a worn-out cushion on a sofa in some old Turkish house, there wasn't any red velvet in Jordan. So the fedayeen were forced to invent the powers it possesses.

Why that material, that colour? Is there really any connection between them and power? It seems there might be. The all but absolute reign of the Sun King called for red velvet, and both the first and the second Emperor of France were crowned amid velvet and red. Other materials are less stifling and their colours more amiable. But red velvet!

The soft stone of which the villas of Amman are built crushed the commandos, but it didn't weigh as heavily on them as it did on the women and old men left behind in the camps.

Whenever I go back to Amman I feel as if I'm buried alive.

"It's depressing and pathetic. But if it weren't depressing there wouldn't be any poetry—the poetry comes from the poor." (This from Monsieur El Katrani, talking about the Tuileries Gardens in Paris at night.)

Some of the fedayeen asked me to bring them the works of Karl Marx back from Damascus. In particular *Das Kapital*. They didn't know he wrote it sitting on his backside on pink silk cushions— wrote it in fact to fight against soft pink silk, and soft mauve silk, and against little tables and vases and chandeliers and chintz, and silent footmen and portly Regency commodes.

In Jordan we had Roman columns, most of them lying flat, having fallen and been set up again and fallen again. But they're not luxury. They're History.

These were the Palestinians' enemies, in order of importance: the Bedouin, the Circassians, King Hussein, the feudal Arabs, the Muslim religion, Israel, Europe, America, the Big Banks. Jordan won, and so victory went to all the rest, too, from the Bedouin to the Big Banks.

One night in December 1970 Mahjoub called a meeting in a cave and spoke to the fedayeen.

"You're now observing a cease-fire. I'm supposed to inform you officially. And so I have. But you're fighters, so use your heads. You've got sisters and cousins married to Jordanians—do what's necessary to get hold of their guns. That's just a suggestion—think of better ones for yourselves. Hussein's government has banned any further operations against Israel on the Occupied Territories carried out from bases in Jordan."*

The men weren't happy with this. They all made the same objection.

"What's a soldier without his gun?" "A disarmed fighter is like a man naked and impotent."

For three hours Mahjoub tried, in vain, to convince them there in the cave, illuminated by torches and by lighters lighting American cigarettes. As we emerged I must have been the only one affected by the loveliness of the sky, unless the beauty of the night and of the promised land aggravated the fedayeen's pain.

The day after the next they all had to hand in their arms. The dumps had been prepared. If it was a long time till the fighting started again, the greased and dismantled guns would be out of date.

All the fedayeen in Jordan were to be allowed to stay on the alert in the quadrilateral formed by the Jordan river, the Salt–Irbid road, the Syrian frontier and the Salt–Jordan road. Ajloun was roughly in the middle.

Something was going on inside us. Some organ was troubled, and troubled us. Or else we suddenly saw the world more clearly, or thought we did. Then a place, often an empty space without people or animals or so much as a caterpillar, but with moss and pebbles and grasses broken by something in flight, would suddenly all sweetly come together and shift without moving. It has just, or for a long time, been eroticized.

So it was with the fields around Ajloun. They were waiting for a sign. But from whom?

---

*The PLO had agreed with Hussein that a Palestinian militia should remain, but with their weapons discreetly hidden. We were meeting in the cave, so that Mahjoub could make this clear to the stubborn fedayeen, for whom a weapon not brandished aloft lost its power: what Mahjoub was suggesting was almost as painful to them as being asked to shave off their moustaches.

The fedayeen moved silently from one commando camp under the trees to another, some dreaming but armed, others unarmed but on the alert, stealthy. They delivered boxes of grenades, cleaned their revolvers.

They were humiliated by defeat. For they'd won glory by making life difficult for Hussein and his Bedouin. They'd hijacked El Al and Swissair planes over the desert. They'd learned of the death of many of their comrades at the hands of the Israeli enemy lurking beyond the Jordan. They'd sensed the menacing silence of the Jordanian villages; perhaps, too, the thoughts of the women and children left behind in the camps. And they weren't yet dry from the shame of not having dared shoot out the tyres when a chrome and white Cadillac, with red leather upholstery, roof open and headlights blazing in broad daylight, was driven by a Bedouin chauffeur in a red and white keffieh full tilt past the soldiers, who had to jump out of the way.

"I'm the Emir Jaber's driver and I've come to find out how His Royal Highness's secretary's nephew is—"

The rest was swallowed up in the sound of grinding gears and screaming tyres.

Although it was done very discreetly, we could tell from the security precautions set up in the middle of the night that the Soviet ambassador to Cairo was about to arrive for a meeting with Arafat at some still secret destination in the Ajloun hills.

He came by helicopter.

We weren't really surprised by the unannounced visit: the Palestinian problem had ceased to be merely regional, and the great powers were beginning to take an interest in the recently created and still insignificant PLO.

But we wanted to use the occasion to try to see things from a higher vantage point, though it wouldn't be easy to attain vertical take-off right away. Every fedayee felt free ranging over this area on foot or by car, never letting go of the surface. It was the surface that concerned us, and we learned its contours as we moved over them. Each fedayee's horizon was taught him by his eyes and feet. He had only to look in front of him to see where he was going, and behind him to see where he'd come from. Neither a radio nor a newspaper linked him to the rest of the revolution; just occasionally an order for a mission.

They were all taken aback, even the leaders, when I said I was going to attend the meeting in Kuwait.

"What are you going to do in Kuwait? Stay with us. Who else will be there anyway? Mostly Europeans. They'll all be talking in English, and you don't speak English."

"I've got a visa for Kuwait in my passport and my room is booked. And here's the letter inviting me."

"All right, if you're obstinate—a couple of fedayeen will drive you to Deraa."

"Why two?"

"We always go in pairs, as a precaution. Cross the frontier at Deraa as best you can, and from there two others will drive you to Damascus. You can catch a plane from there to Kuwait. On your way back after the conference there'll be a car at Damascus Airport to drive you to Deraa, and you'll find a couple of fedayeen waiting there to bring you back here."

It was decided I should stay in Ajloun.

But, above our heads, PLO diplomacy was active, even though it came up against Hussein and his advisers in the American embassy. The comings and goings of diplomats between Amman, Tel Aviv and Washington were common knowledge, not in factual detail but through gossip. We came and went in the area I've described, regarding ourselves as free, though for security reasons we always moved at ground level. We were obeying the orders of colonels who never rose any higher than their maps, which had ascended from the horizontal to so high on the wall that you needed a pointer to show the north—the Jordan river and the towns just within the occupied territories.

Did the Palestinians realize that by omitting the name and geography of Israel from their maps they were at the same time abolishing Palestine? They either coloured Israel blue and threw it into the sea, or made it black and turned it into the Greeks' kingdom of the Shades.

Arafat and the rest of the PLO, with their agreements and their disagreements, functioned at quite a different altitude altogether:

they flew from one capital to another. Perhaps Palestine was no longer a country to them, but something to be expressed in fractions, a tiny element in a grand operation being waged between East and West.

But we all knew deep down that the peace we felt, the peace we enjoyed, was due to the PLO.

We hadn't heard about Kissinger's trip to Peking, or his return to Pakistan the next day. How could we have known, on this cliff edge, that China's aid to the PLO was being reduced? What was China, viewed from here? First and foremost a name: Mao.

Many Palestinians—ordinary fedayeen as well as important leaders—were invited to Peking. And to Moscow. I still believe they confused China itself with the organized crowds and ardent demonstrations that sent them home with accounts and images of some sort of paradise. I was told dozens of times how marvellous the old men looked as, grave or smiling, they silently performed their Swedish drill every morning in T'ien an Men Square. The fedayeen also told me about the athletic ancients' long thin beards. Here a beard is more like an article of clothing.

I may never know whether I ought to call it the Palestinian Resistance or the Palestinian Revolution. And should I really use capitals? There aren't any capital letters in written Arabic.

At the beginning of this book I tried to describe a game of cards in an arbour. As I said, all the gestures were genuine but the cards were not. Not only were they not on the table, but they weren't anywhere; it wasn't a game of cards at all. The cards were neither present nor absent. For me they were like God: they didn't exist.

All that pretence for its own sake—the invitation to me, the preparations, the performance itself, the excitement designed to show me what was missing—can you imagine what it would do to anyone who went through those motions every evening? Withdrawal symptoms for cards, as if they were cocaine. The end of the game was its beginning: nothing at the start and nothing at the finish. What I was seeing was an absence of images: no bastos, no knights, no swords. I wonder if Claudel knew the game the Moors used to play in Spain?

Didn't the new occupiers know what would happen to the Palestinian people when they drove them out of Palestine? That unless they destroyed themselves they'd occupy another territory belonging to another people?

"Why haven't they just melted away?"

To which one could only reply:

"Has a people on the march ever melted away? Tell me where. And how."

I still don't know what the fedayeen's own inmost feelings were, but as far as I could see their land—Palestine—was not merely out of reach. Although they sought it as gamblers do cards and atheists God, it had never existed. Vestiges of it remained, very distorted, in old people's memories. But in our memory things are usually seen as smaller than they really were, and increasingly so with age. Unless, on the other hand, recollection lights them up and makes them larger than life. In either case the dimensions of memory are seldom accurate.

And here everything had changed—the names of things, all their dents and protuberances. Every blade of grass had been grazed; more of the forest was eaten up every day in the form of paper, books and newspapers. The fedayeen's goal had been transformed into something impossible for them to imagine. Everything they did was in danger of becoming useless because they'd substituted the rehearsal for the performance. The card players, their hands full of ghosts, knew that however handsome and sure of themselves they were their actions perpetuated a game with neither beginning nor end. Absence was in their hands just as it was under their feet.

"Some officers clearly hankered after the solid equipment, the steel carapaces and complex instruments of the military academies in Europe, America and the USSR. They mistrusted the word guerrilla—that 'little war' in which you had to find allies in fog, damp and the height of rivers, in the rainy season, the long grass, the owl's cry, and the phases of the sun and moon. They knew you could command only if you stood to attention and gave orders to someone doing the same. But military academies are not places for getting discipline, obedience and victory out of half-educated men, mischievous Arabs at home among mosses and lichens. How to glide from tree to tree and rock to rock, freezing at the slightest sound—no ordinary officer could have taught that."

That's still the opinion of some Palestinians, who miss the combined guile and integrity of battle, and perhaps sometimes its comradeship.

"The Bedouin on the one hand and the Israelis on the other all slaughter civilians with tanks and planes. A hundred guerrilla fighters have only to slip into Israel and shells rain down on the civilians in the Palestinian camps.

"In the Moroccan Navy, sailors with syphilis are called 'Admirals.' Their medical cards are marked with crosses and stars. The first cross indicating the pox is greeted with ecstasy, like a goal at a football match, as proof of virility. The first sore is a sacred stigma.

"Everyone—doctors, nurses and cooks—took excellent care of us. I was a four-star admiral. Five stars meant the Empire. And death. The famous leper king, who's known even in Islam, had two stigmata: one from his anointing and the other from leprosy. I wonder whether the fiercest officers, the ones who wanted heavy artillery, tanks, cannon and even the atomic bomb, hadn't really got their eye on a state funeral rather than on dying for their country."

It wasn't only the graduates of Saint-Cyr who thought guerrilla warfare lacked nobility. The Soviet Union also refused to take it seriously and referred to it as terrorism. If the Palestinian army is ever to win it'll have to become a ponderous machine, with every colonel's chest covered with gongs from all the right countries.

One evening when the Ramadan fast ended, two of the leaders gave a party near a spring close to the river Jordan. There was only a bit more honey cake than usual and some freer laughter. They welcomed one guest, a long-haired young man called Ishmael, by throwing their arms round him.

I was too used to nicknames and aliases to be surprised at this one.

(It was here, not far away from the place between the Damia

and Allenby bridges where John had once baptized Jesus, that the fedayeen decided to change my first name to Ali.)

Ishmael had straight brown locks like Napoleon's down to his shoulders.

"He's a Palestinian who's doing his military service in the Israeli army. He speaks perfect Hebrew," one of the leaders told me.

I said I thought the young man's profile was more Jewish than Arab.

"He's a Druse, but for goodness' sake don't mention it. As soon as he saw you were a Frenchman his expression changed." (I still don't know what he meant by this.) "He takes great risks to pass us information."

As I ate I smiled, and asked Ishmael, in French, to sing us the Israeli national anthem.

He looked surprised, as if he understood, but he had the presence of mind to ask for my question to be translated into Arabic. In answer to something Mahjoub said, he had spoken in English:

"Classical war, I don't know. Classical or romantic."

This struck me as rather affected.

When he left at nightfall to get back into Israel without being spotted by the Jewish sentries, he kissed everyone goodbye except me.

His profile was Hebraic but his speech rhythms were Western.

Not long before, at Jerash, a Sudanese lieutenant of thirty had been astonished to hear me speak, and Abu Omar reply, in French.

"Everything that happens here is because of you," said the Sudanese. "You're responsible for the Pompidou government."

He said other things too, which I've forgotten. But I'll never forget that black face, with its gleaming hair and cheeks slashed with tribal scars, speaking to me not only in French but in slang, with a suburban accent and a Maurice Chevalier vocabulary. And to talk to me he airily stuck his hands in his trouser pockets.

When Abu Omar explained to him in Arabic that I wasn't at all close to the French government, he calmed down and we became great friends. Whenever I met him it was a smile that approached, and I knew he was cooking up some new story specially for me.

"It's very lucky we can understand one another. If it weren't for us Sudanese you wouldn't speak French, only some provincial patois."

"Explain."

"Every province in France used to speak its own jargon—you were barbarians. When you were strong enough to land in our country you were still only the linguistic equivalent of a game of patience. The Basque soldiers spoke Basque, the Corsicans Corsican. And soldiers from Alsace, Brittany, Nice, Picardy, the Morvan and the Artois all poured into Madagascar, Indochina and the Sudan. But to conquer us you needed a common language. So they all had to learn Parisian French—the language of their officers, trained at Saint-Cyr. Wandering about two by two in the native quarter they had to have at least a few key expressions:

" 'The Legion! Help!'

" 'Here, boys!'

" 'Two of us are in trouble!'

" 'Get a move on!'

" 'The Zouaves! Help!' "

It was an amusing theory, correct or no. Jules Ferry was Minister of Education before he became Minister for the Colonies.

The light, sensitive French that gradually spread all over France may have been born of the terrified trembling bequeathed to mainland France by little soldiers from Brittany, Corsica and the Basque country, conquering and dying in the colonies. Dialect had to go away so that an almost perfect language might be fashioned beyond the seas and come home.

The counterpart to this epic is perhaps the following passage, from Morocco in 1917:

"My fine fellows! Raring to go! When I told them I was going to give them arms and ammunitions they'd have worshipped me if I'd let them. But I'm always as cool as a cucumber. The man who'll get round me hasn't been conceived yet, let alone born. They like a scrap, my lads, and I lead them to it. They expected sabres and I give them guns. They'll wipe out all the Boches. They've got as far as the Somme, guns blazing."

This summarizes the main points of a speech printed in *L'Illustration*. "They" got as far as the Somme. "They" got off the train, marched a couple of hundred yards in silence, breathing loudly. There were about a thousand of them. The first wave lay down without a word, then the second wave, then the third. "They" died in slow motion. A gust of wind laden with gas shut them up for good. Just north of Abbeville lay a huge grey Moroccan carpet.

It was Mubarak who told me all this. As a Sudanese officer he tended to sympathize with Kaddafi. I had no news of him for some time. As with Hamza, I knew only his first name. After some hesitation he chose Habash instead of Arafat. I wish I could tell you how handsome he was, how gentle, with those cheeks slashed with sacrificial scars.

It was Georges Habash's FPLP* that kept three plane-loads of passengers sweltering in the sun for three days at Zarka airport.

Coming back to the fedayeen bases after a fortnight in Damascus, I found them very thinly spread out, and was struck by the weakness of the new arrangement. Was it the work of someone foolish, inexperienced, obstinate—some Palestinian no good at either strategy or tactics?

It made me think of a papier-mâché wall. What could you expect when there were only six or seven of you all alone, with six or seven small guns? Physically, even the enemy were a kilometre away from the area allotted to the fedayeen. But they were well trained, equipped with heavy artillery and helped by ballistics experts. It was rumoured that Hussein's army had American and Israeli aides. (In 1984 some Palestinians confirmed this. Jordanian officers scornfully denied it.)

I thought of that fedayeen position fourteen years later amid the ruins of Beirut, when Jacqueline was telling me about a trip she'd made to southern Lebanon.

"After the massacres at Sabra and Chatila, Palestinian soldiers and civilians were shut up for hours in cells or hotel rooms in Tyre and Sidon. Then, in Tyre and Sidon and the coast villages in between, came the ceremony of the hoods. Israeli officers and men made the inhabitants of villages and districts file past a man wearing a hood over his head. The spy didn't say anything for

---

*Popular Front for the Liberation of Palestine.

fear of being recognized—he just pointed a gloved finger at the guilty parties. What were they guilty of? Of being Palestinians, or Lebanese friends of Palestinians, or likely to become so, or knowing how to handle explosives."

"Weren't any of the hooded men recognized?"

"No. At first it was rumoured that they were renegade Palestinians, but a few days later the truth, or what might have been the truth, came out. It was an Israeli soldier under the hood, and he just pointed people out at random. The other members of a victim's family were also suspect, so they kept quiet. By the time it leaked out that the renegade Palestinian was really an Israeli the damage was done. No one dared denounce the trick in case after all the man had been a Palestinian, some friend or relation."

"And did the play-acting last long?"

"Two or three weeks. Long enough. Everyone suspected everyone else. Then came the business of the rooms."

It was a Lebanese woman who told me about that. The Palestinians—soldiers, civilians and women—would be crammed into one cell or room. Then cries of terror and moans in Arabic, weeping, shrieks and finally death rattles would be heard from outside. Amid all this came the sound of Arab voices alleging atrocious crimes and vendettas against their Arab relatives; and of fedayeen accusing their officers of betraying their comrades and giving away military secrets.

All this was rehearsed and tape-recorded by Arabic-speaking Israeli soldiers, then played into the rooms. At every so-called act of treachery a kind of incidental music of amused, sarcastic or affectedly contemptuous laughter could be heard, with Israeli officers making comments in Hebrew on the confessions. During the next two days the same recording would be broadcast through loudspeakers in village squares.

The object was to intimidate the Lebanese people, Shiite or otherwise, and in particular the Palestinians. This was in September 1982. Perhaps that enormous bluff, the Arabic cry of "Remember Deir Yassin!," was recorded in a studio in Tel Aviv.

It was the memory of this that caused a Frenchman to say:

"The big Israeli demonstration in 1982 against the Lebanese war was planned before the invasion began. Everything was worked out in advance: the invasion, the raids on Beirut, the murder of Bechir Gemayel, the massacres at Chatila, the ostentatious horror of world press and television—even the world's revulsion, the demonstration itself and the final whitewash. All to make Israel's face look less dirty—"

This made his wife say, "Ssh . . ."

"They made us run away from Deir Yassin with a lorry and a loudspeaker."

I've often thought about that radio producer, perhaps an NCO in Tsahal, re-rehearsing a shriek or death-rattle that didn't ring true. Perhaps he got the cast to wear Arab dress, to make their moans more convincing. Maybe he was a well-known director from the Habima Theatre in Tel Aviv.

But let's get back to 1971. The location of all those thin-spread fedayeen bases in and around Ajloun was known to within a yard by the Jordanian army. And the Circassian officers, with the help of their Bedouin troops, had set up loudspeakers transmitting voices that, under cover of distance, indistinctness and dark, might be taken for the voices of Palestinian resistance leaders.

"We're all encircled. Surrender is inevitable. We must hand our weapons over to the king's army. The king has promised that every fedayee who presents himself unarmed will have his gun returned to him the next day. The fight is over. No one will be ill treated. I speak in the name of the king and of Abu Amar [Yasser Arafat]."

Imagine the effect, on often very young soldiers, of those voices at once distant and close; giant voices thundering through the dark forest and mountains between ten o'clock and midnight; the voice of the mountains themselves. The voices came from the other side of the Jordan. The quality of the sound was so poor they were unidentifiable.

It was in July 1971 that Hussein's troops encircled the fedayeen. Officially three or four hundred of them were killed, while thousands were sent as prisoners to various jails in the kingdom or the camp at Zarka. The rest managed to escape through Irbid to Syria. Some crossed the Jordan and were disarmed; these got a very friendly welcome from Israeli officers and men. But having fled after listening to their leaders' alleged betrayal, they must have felt very lonely living with their own real treason.

Two Frenchmen who'd been fighting as and with the fedayeen got as far as Irbid. They lie buried in the cemetery there, among the Palestinian martyrs.

To me there is something other than fear and cowardice in the fedayeen's flight; something great. What they were running away from was the sudden appearance of the unexpected. Death, the expected, hadn't come. They were prepared for bullets, wounds and suffering. They weren't prepared for midnight clamour that later turned out to be the sound of a helicopter still on the ground, but magnified ten-fold and with some artillery and machine-gun fire thrown in. No real bullets or shells, though, and after a while a sudden silence in which to hear their treacherous leaders telling them too to betray.

Panic is really the word, and I should write it quickly, for it was that which made legs run of their own accord, fleeing not death but the unexpected. Perhaps that was what embarrassed me so much when I saw the *achebals*, the young lions, in training: they couldn't be trained for the inadmissible—for fleeing into Israel, as one might commit suicide.

"Against Israel I'd make a pact with the devil."

There it was twice: the voice of the leaders telling the fedayee to be a traitor, and sending him into a real alliance with the devil, Israel.

Trying to escape and find some refuge from the voice, perhaps they didn't realize they'd crossed into Israel. Perhaps they thought they were still in Palestine—which in fact they were.

I mentioned panic, but I don't know if people still fear Pan—if the god still summons them on the unequal reeds of his flute, with notes so persuasive that whoever hears and tries to follow them may end up none knows where.

Mist rose up and veiled the moon. If the huge voice reverberating from hill to hill was the voice of God, the fedayeen, ignorant of the miracles of electricity and acoustics, ran to shelter in His bosom. Perhaps the French slang expression, *jouer des flûtes* (literally "make with the pins," that is, run away) has some such divine origin.

Even if the body, the arms and legs, didn't realize it, the fear had come from across the Atlantic. I often went to Amman, where the Boeings used to fly over my hotel, bringing gifts of arms from America to Hussein.

The two young Frenchmen buried in Irbid—the first name of both was Guy—were about twenty years old. Their woman friend, also French, was with them. They used to help the Palestinians rebuild their collapsed walls, thus learning bricklaying and Arabic simultaneously. I met the two Guys at Wahadat: they were like two children of May 1968—liberated but full of antiquated platitudes.

"Hussein must be brought down because he's a fascist. And he must be replaced with a régime that's revolutionary but not Soviet."

"What sort of régime?"

"One based on the Situationists, for instance."

But describing dramatic moments of the resistance, as I've been doing, doesn't give any idea of its everyday atmosphere. That was youthful and lighthearted. If I had to use one image for it I'd suggest this:

Not a series of shocks, but one long-drawn-out, almost imperceptible earthquake traversing the whole country. Or: A great yet almost silent roar of laughter from a whole nation holding its sides, yet full of reverence when Leila Khaled, grenade at the ready, ordered the Jewish crew of the El Al plane to land in Damascus. Then there were the three planes—they belonged to Swissair, I think—full of Americans of both sexes, that landed at Zarka on Habash's orders and stood there side by side in the sun for three days.

A few days later came what might be called the children's revolt. Some Palestinian boys and girls of about sixteen, together with a few young Jordanians of both sexes, all laughing and smiling and shouting, "Yahya-l-malik!" (Long live the king!) went up to a line of Jordanian tanks in the streets of Amman and offered the occupants of one of them a bunch of flowers. The men in the tank, surprised but pleased, opened the turret and stretched out their arms to take the bouquet. But one of the girls dropped it inside at the feet of the crew, together with a grenade, and the tank exploded. The girl's friends whisked her away into a sidestreet, where she waited to get her breath back and to be supplied with a further series of flowers and grenades.

It was in Amman, of course, that I heard about it. Was the resistance starting to go in for such ingenious cruelties? Was an official uprising in preparation? Had the things I was told about really happened? At any rate, the slap in the face the king's prime minister had received from his daughter was echoing still.

Those children make me think of a fox devouring a chicken. The fox's muzzle is covered with blood. It looks up and bares its perfect teeth—white, shiny and sharp. You expect it to beam like a baby at any moment.

An ancient people restored to youth by rebellion and to rebellion by youth can seem very sinister.

I remember like an owl. Memories come back in "bursts of images." Writing this book, I see my own image far, far away, dwarf size, and more and more difficult to recognize with age. This isn't a complaint. I'm just trying to convey the idea of age and of the form poetry takes when one is old: I grow smaller and smaller in my own eyes and see the horizon speeding towards me, the line into which I shall merge, behind which I shall vanish, from which I shall never return.

Going through Jerash on my way back from Damascus, I thought I'd look up Dieter, the German doctor who'd started a little hospital in the camp at Gaza. I was met by another doctor, a Lebanese with a kind face.

"Dr. Dieter isn't here any more," he said. "He's in Germany. You were a friend of his, weren't you? Well, he was sent to prison and tortured, and the West German ambassador finally managed to get him repatriated.

"This is what happened. One day the Jordanian army entered the camp at Gaza, looking for fedayeen probably, and beat up the women and children—anyone they found alive. When they heard there were casualties, Dieter, together with the male nurse and the nun who worked in the hospital here, all set out for Gaza with their instrument cases and urgent medical supplies—surgical spirit, bandages and so on. But as soon as they started to tend the wounded they were surrounded by troops. The Jordanians laid about them in their usual way, and Dieter and the two nurses were put in the prison you went to with Nabila Nashashibi and Dr. Alfredo. I advise you not to make yourself too conspicuous in Amman."

If only he'd put up some resistance . . . But for all his devotion to the sick and his enormous energy and endurance, Dieter was a very ethereal kind of German. He'd sit up late at night with patients who came to see him just because they were lonely, helping them with a few words or an aspirin. He was fair-haired, uncompromising and delicate.

I'd already heard in Damascus that the Bedouin had won. The Lebanese doctor's story told me something else: the Palestinians were lost.

The head man at Baqa camp, an Arab said to be a hundred years old, used to set out very early for his constitutional. Barefoot, wearing a white *abaya* and with a white scarf wound round his wrinkled head, he'd leave his house at or even before dawn. Obedient to the call from a nearby minaret, he'd stop to say the first prayer of the day, then continue slowly and peacefully on his way towards the Jordanian lines. All the Jordanian officers and men would say good morning to the still hale centenarian, but he didn't return their greeting until he was on his way back, when he went through the Bedouin lines for the second time.

"I let them give me a little cup of coffee. One of the officers has been in Tunisia and he puts some orange-flower water in it. Very nice."

"The officer?"

"The coffee. It bucks me up for the journey home."

At sunset the old boy made his way calmly back to the camp. The Jordanians could see his white figure, almost upright without the aid of a stick, growing ever smaller in the distance, until at last it vanished into the dusk, together with its long black shadow.

He counted the steps on the outward journey, and checked them on the way back. They were the first steps of a smiling, sly and still cautious resistance. From his paces the distance between the camp and the first lines of the Jordanian army, and thus the right bearings for the guns, could be calculated. The fedayeen used to bring the old man a tin bowl of soup, and he'd sometimes listen for the first shots before going off to bed in his tiny room.

One day I tried to find out if he'd counted up right or if his age was only a legend. Karim often talked to him, so I asked Karim. He said the old chief was sixty, not a hundred, but because of his deep wrinkles and white moustache and eyebrows he was able to conceal his real age. He used his furrowed brow for cover as the fedayeen used the ravines.

Nothing escaped him. When he came back he'd seen and remembered everything: the state of the Jordanians' weaponry, the colour of their shoes, changes in the vegetation, the names and numbers of the enemy's tanks. And times, down to hours and minutes—he could repeat them all. He had two wives in a large tent on the other side of the camp. Seven of the fedayeen on the bases were his sons.

The Legion of Honour is worn on the left, isn't it? No one noticed that he wore it, among other medals, on his right breast. Was it dangerous for him to wear it in the desert? How did he die? Of old age? Weariness? A bullet? Perhaps he isn't dead at all! His boldness was breathtaking.

His eyes used to smile whenever they lighted on me: I was an impostor, too. I had neither pencil nor paper and didn't write anything down, but perhaps he observed me and guessed.

28 September 1970 was just a point on the straight line measured by the Gregorian calendar, but for millions it became a password charged with emotion.

In her youth Golda Meir was elected "Miss Palestine." Palestine was "Flastine" to the "Flestini" themselves.

These lines, this whole book, are only a diversion, producing quick emotions quickly over. Others were produced in me by the words "Islam" and "Muslim."

You get to Ajloun by the road that goes from Baqa past the American satellite-tracking radar to the Jordan.

A month after the battle every reminder of the Palestinians had been burned or buried or taken away, apart from empty or half-empty cigarette packets and charred shrubs. The fedayeen had been either killed, taken prisoner, or left at the Saudi Arabian frontier after a spell in Jordanian jails that were worse torture to them than the desert. The experts from the FBI were more comfortable there in those un-air-conditioned days.

In the countryside all the wheat and the rye, the barley and the beans, had been slashed to pieces in the battle. It wasn't until Beirut in 1976 and 1982 that I saw nature so molested again, burned to the bone; and found out that the bone of pines and firs was black.

I've read that there are nearly always vestiges at the scene of a crime that can act as clues. In 1972, in a little Circassian village on the Golan Heights, after six years of Israeli occupation, I picked up three scraps of letters. They were written in Arabic, and had all been sent from Damascus by a Syrian soldier who'd fled and taken refuge there. They didn't have much in them apart from a lot of quotations from the Koran suggesting God had saved his life so that there might be one soldier praising His mercy. In any case, either the family they were addressed to were dead, or the letters hadn't been delivered. Israeli soldiers had been the first to read them, and they'd just left them there.

The hamlet consisted of four little houses with green shutters and red-tiled roofs. They were all deserted, their doors and windows hanging open. There were villages like that in Normandy after the landing at Avranches. Looted by the Yanks.

What was strange at Ajloun was that they hadn't been able to take away the holes in the ground. I could still see the three little shelters where I'd slept with the fedayeen. The walls and ceilings were black with smoke. A few bits of brown blanket lay strewn about with the dead. I could tell where the latter were from a stone propping up a piece of paper, or a plastic-coated identity card. I recognized the oblong blue-green cards at once, each with a photograph of the fedayee who owned it in the top right-hand corner, and his assumed name written in Arabic.

As I went through the village I noticed the silence had gone even before I saw the peasants and their wives. The air was full of rustling and cackling, whinnying and chatter. No one returned my greeting, but no one did or said anything unfriendly either. I'd returned from among the Palestinian enemy like one rising from the dead.

When I got to Amman the whole Palestinian resistance was in complete disarray. The semblance of unity that the PLO lent it shortly afterwards was still lacking, and the eleven different groups were riven with dissension and resentment amounting almost to hatred. Only Fatah, though it too suffered from internal carpings and rivalries, showed a united front, if only in condemning all the other groups.

I'm still surprised at what happened after July 1971, that is after the fighting at Ajloun, Jerash and Irbid. A kind of bitterness entered into relations between the fedayeen. There were two I knew who were about twenty years old. They'd been friends at the same base on the Jordan, but one had remained a fedayee while the other had been promoted to a slightly higher rank. One day at Baqa I heard the fedayee asking for leave to go and see his wife, who was ill in Amman twenty kilometres away. This was the dialogue as I remember it:

"*Salam Allah alikoum.*"

"*. . . koum salam.*"

"Ali, can I have twenty-four hours' leave? My wife's pregnant."

"So is mine, but I'm staying here. You're on duty tonight."

"I'll get someone to take my place."

"Who's supposed to be on duty, you or him?"

"I've got two or three mates ready to replace me."

"No."

The more the one pleaded, the more the other, as if by a normal and necessary mutation, spoke like a petty tyrant. It wasn't a mere matter of discipline and security—it was the routine antagonism between officers and ordinary ranks. Two males confronting one another while fighting for a common homeland still a long way out of sight.

I've found out since that the hatred born between them that day is still very much alive. Now, it seems, they both speak excellent English, and you can hear echoes of their untiring hostility in their exchanges in English and American newspapers.

Is hatred there from the start, needing two friends to make its way?

Anything from or to do with Palestine disappeared, at first via Syria. I think it was about then, at the end of 1971, that the second wave of Palestinian fedayeen began to infiltrate Lebanon. Others, perhaps more wisely, managed through a Jordanian father- or brother-in-law to buy some land in the neighbourhood of Amman. They're said to be the richest men in Jordan.

When you're alone with them you find they still retain some

words from the real revolutionary period—1968 to 1971—just as a peasant who rises to be a managing director in Paris may still use an occasional phrase from the dialect of his childhood. But they sense you used to be on the same side as they were then, and a thin veil comes down over their blushes lest this should no longer be the case. Without waiting to be asked, they tell you how much it cost them to buy their house in Jebel Amman.

It took me several years to realize how some of the leaders—well-known ones whose names are mentioned in Western newspapers—became dollar millionaires. It was tacitly known or half-known that the seas of the Resistance had thrown up not a few bits of flotsam and jetsam but a whole strong-box in which each of them had one or more drawers containing proofs of his fortune in Switzerland or elsewhere. Each knew what the others had, too, because their fortunes were often the result of a division of the spoils.

The fighters knew all about it. Title deeds are easily hidden, but not a forest or a villa or a map. The high command knew, too. Perhaps they made use of it. Everyone in Fatah was familiar with Abu Hassan and his sports cars and pretty girls. I met him two or three times. The first occasion was rather embarrassing for him as I had to ask for his identity card in front of some amused fedayeen. Half amused himself but also half annoyed, he went through his pockets, and flushed when he drew from his windcheater the same green card as is carried by every fedayee. He was energetic and athletic, the all-powerful leader and organizer of Black September. I've been told Arafat exploited his vanity for the sake of the PLO. When I heard of his and Boudia's death when his car was blown up, it was like learning of a defeat.

But slowly and surely I came to see the real meaning of it all.

My conclusion was more or less this. It's natural that soldiers' eyes should light up with desire for possession when they break into some luxurious place, and even more natural that some of their leaders should be corrupted through handling kilos of unused greenbacks. When a revolutionary movement meets with success, such things become proof that one was in on it from the start. It's difficult to distinguish total devotion to a cause from a quest for position, ambition for money or power.

It's bound to be one or the other, especially when the aspirant has let it be known that he "offers himself up body and soul in the service of the revolution and of the common good."

This last is a literal translation of what I heard a leader say in July 1984 to justify his wealth.

The latecomers—revolutionaries of the thirteenth hour, who come running when the revolution is already a state—they have to fight barehanded against those who learned to savour the sweet taste of power during the Long March.

When Zuhayr Muhsin, supreme chief of the Saïka, was assassinated in a luxury hotel in Cannes, I was struck by such a flash of enlightenment I was afraid I might actually glow—a visual sign of how he'd embezzled funds intended to provide arms and food for the fedayeen. It happened so suddenly that I thought, briefly, I was the only person who'd found out. But some PLO leaders in Rome and Paris added to my confusion by laughing and saying, as they smoked their exclusive cigars:

"But we all knew about that. We used to call him the Bottomless Pits."

If they all knew, what did Muhsin himself know that kept everyone quiet while he was still alive?

Re-reading what I've written, I see I've already started to make judgements. I'm a long way past the stage of pretending to drown when I'm only up to the chin in water.

Hitler's first, inexorable duty every morning when he woke up was to look the same: the almost horizontal toothbrush moustache, every whisker sprouting from his nostrils, everything had to remain the same. The black forelock was no more allowed to switch to the wrong side of the shiny forehead than the arms of the swastika were allowed to turn towards the left. And so with the gleam in the eye, angry or ingratiating as required, with the famous voice, and with other things that can't be said. What would the dignitaries of the Reich and the Axis ambassadors have done if they'd seen a clean-shaven blond young Finn leap out of bed?

It must have been like that whenever someone has become a

symbol: take the Negus, from his built-up soles to his solar topi, from his socks to his sunshade; take Marlene, from her gold ankle-chain to her cigarette-holder. Imagine Churchill without a cigar! Or a cigar without Churchill! Can a keffiyeh be wound round anybody else's head than Arafat's? He made me, like everyone else, a present of a brand new one, with the usual "Do this in remembrance of me." He couldn't give away signed photographs like an actor, so he gave away a piece of himself. For Westerners he remains a keffiyeh with a stubble.

I was very surprised when I met him. From in front he looked as I'd expected, but when he turned his head to answer me and showed his left profile I saw a different man. The right profile was grim and harsh, the left very mild, with an almost feminine smile underlined by his nervous habit of tossing back his black and white keffiyeh. Its fringes and bobbles would fall over his shoulders, sometimes over his eyes, like the hair of an angry youth.

He was affable, and stared into space when he wasn't drinking coffee, but when I saw him from only a few feet away I realized what an effort you had to make—blindly, so to speak, in the darkness of the body—in order to look always the same to others and to yourself. What if a frog went to sleep and woke up a bullfinch? Would Arafat thinking be Arafat changing? It wasn't only to him the fedayeen owed the days of quiet, almost of rejoicing, that I've tried to describe. Not only to him. But it was he alone who was responsible for the defeat.

Was his lack of action thought, and so a continuation of action? That great spider, silently and imperceptibly spinning out his shimmering web as he drank coffee after coffee, gazing into the distance and letting me talk without listening to what I said—had he really got his eye on the other big spider, Golda Meir, weaving her real toils? He proffered a few words, wary as a fly picking its way over the web. Was that what he really was? Or was he playing the same game as Marshal Tlass in Syria?

"To begin with, all the flowers in Syria, from the humble forget-me-not to the edelweiss, then strange blooms he called Assadia and Talarnia; then eighteen unattainable women—Caroline of Monaco, Lady Di, Miss World '83, Louise Brooks, Lulu, etc., with a poem about each, published by his own publishing house."

That's what the Palestinians say about Marshal Tlass. One of the leaders told me, smiling, that despite the enormous rings he wears, he masturbates as he reads *Playboy*.

Descriptions of a few PLO leaders.

I can say nothing, or almost nothing, about Abu Ali Iyad. His photograph, like Arafat's, is all over the walls of the PLO offices and the Palestinians' houses. In June 1971 he was in command of the Jerash area. The Palestinians were surrounded, and under fire from the Jordanian army. Then a cease-fire was agreed, and Abu Ali Iyad was informed of it through Arafat. Because he was half blind and could only walk with a stick, and even then with difficulty, Hussein offered to spare his life if he would leave his companions-in-arms, the fedayeen. He stayed where he was, and everyone was killed.

Orientals, and even some Westerners, have never heard of Bayard. It isn't enough just to die. All the Palestinians revere Abu Ali Iyad, but perhaps when Arafat chose to embrace Hussein he remembered just another trap that Hussein had set for the Palestinians. His offer to save Abu Ali Iyad's life had really meant, "I offer you the chance to be a coward. Take it, so that I can shame all the Palestinians, both in their future and in their past."

Abu Ali Iyad's rejection was bound to be implacable.

When someone dies for a cause we sometimes wonder if the values involved should be regarded as immortal. But ought we really to speak of dying if through death the values in question are not merely handed on but also give birth to new reasons for living?

For this evening, my answer is no. Conventional heroism is pointless. But it's all right to die to disobey an order or to spurn a temptation.

That's all I'm going to say about Abu Ali Iyad.

Was it intellectual laziness on the part of the French, or a liking for the ring of the word "million," or a feeling that the old currency was descended from the original franc and the *louis* and *sols* of the *ancien régime*, that made the new, "heavy" franc take such a long time to enter into the everyday calculations of the people? It was the younger generation that first adopted the new franc.

Was it tradition? Inertia? Perhaps they're the same.

Before 1968–69 neither Fatah nor any other Palestinian organization was taken seriously. Even the name was unknown. For many French people, Palestine was the name of a country of industrious Jews who had lived there since the Creation.

The Jews had been "there from the days of Abraham and the Pharaohs." But Fatah's dynamism; the strength of its presence in the camps; the hope it gave to the Palestinians; the resistance it offered to Hussein and the people of Jordan; Nasser's backing; the wholehearted help of King Faisal of Arabia and the timid support of the other Arab countries; the personalities of its leaders—all these turned the PLO and the Palestinians into a political factor just as important as some territorially established member of the Arab League. And the PLO soon became a member of the League.

Setting aside the rumours of arguments, disputes and factions that beset all resistance movements, the PLO may be said to have ranged itself on the side of the Soviet Union from the beginning. And Israel did, said and wrote all it could to make the PLO seem an emanation, almost a direct dependant of the USSR. This interpretation chimed well with American—and European—Manichaeism. It also suited Soviet pragmatism. Somebody ought to write a book about it.

As mentioning names is impossible and fiction intolerable, this will be only a brief digression.

Self-sacrifice for a cause strikes us as something sacred because it's far away, sublimated to such an extent that we can't relate it to our everyday doings in the "rear." The "rear" isn't only the area remote from the military "front"—that safe distance from which reporters entertain us with words and images of massacres written up in embassy press offices, shot in studios, or photographed through telescopic lenses.

The "rear" is also the place from which you watch without fear, not ashamed to take your time as you turn from the newspaper article on Asia to the page on the Stock Exchange, then twiddle a knob on the radio, then go back to the article. Taking your time is also getting a kick. But the soldier who'll die if he leaves his shell-hole, the man holding his breath trying to escape notice as he lies among the dead, the man who's killing someone—they have no connection with the "rear." They are cut off from choice; they can't take their time. If you can dream, calculate, feel pity at the thought of dead or dying heroes, if you can even identify with them, it's because you've got time and are comfortable enough to do so. "Delight me with the sacred cause for which someone else will die."

Self-sacrifice is very complex. Once and for all, the heroism of the Palestinians is admirable. But it's sometimes the result of a quite trivial mechanism, an inextricable tangle of calculations in which death is avoided by what could be called either a miss or a mile, so crucial is the act involved—the cape eluding the horns, the edging along a precipice, the attack with sabres drawn. And it happens so close that the hero can see death.

It's in the form of a huge safe containing millions of dollars. The combination of the lock is suddenly revealed to him, and when the safe is opened its contents turn into jewels, furs and cigars, Mercedes, Maseratis, Marilyns, in that order. The hero, though he hasn't got the glory of Abu Ali Iyad or of Kawasmeh, has got gold, and the desire for more.

"Since I've got neither glory nor death, why should I deny myself their equivalent to make up for it?"

"However rich someone may be in castles and jewellery . . ."

"Give me two or three names."

"I know lots more. So do you. Say them."

"Name just one."

"He was just going to drop Arafat when Syria . . ."

"His name?"

"No."

It's difficult to understand how vulgar desires and orgiastic dreams were transformed into sublime devotion. And how proud deeds changed men who were strong, handsome and decisive into monsters of avarice slobbering with greed over a marble colonnade. Take anyone you like; sound his heart and liver and lights and excrement (we have to get used to it, to familiarize our sight and smell and delicate touch)—that's where our freedom by the Jordan came from. We owed our magical days and nights to the wheeling and dealing and spite of the leaders. In what inner sewers must they have fought for their own interests, on which Ajloun's freedom depended?

One day, in 1968 I think it was, the king, attended by his ministers, went through the main streets of Amman proclaiming, with the spontaneity of a young monarch:

"Long live the fedayeen! I am the first fedayee!"

The spontaneity and the demagogy were both perfectly useless. In December 1984 Kawasmeh was assassinated.

We can see through its thin skin that the resistance has lost blood. The veins through which mud flowed are growing clearer. Those which held clear liquid are growing murky. Strange to say, the purest ones are those that death destroys. It wasn't a real hell, any more than the shanty town was.

Arafat wasn't taking much of a risk in November 1970 when he gave me letters allowing me to visit PLO camps and bases. He probably knew the "Potemkin" bases had already been seen for what they were by even the dimmest Eastern and Western journalists. The details were the great give-away, and the most obvious ones were those that bolstered up the Palestinians the most.

The trouble they went to—the students from Montpellier, Oxford, Stuttgart, Leghorn, Barcelona, Louvain, Utrecht, Gothenberg and Osaka—to persuade people that the Palestinians were in the right in their war against the Hashemite régime. The correspondents knew it. Above all they could see the Palestinians knew nothing about making a sham base look like a real one. The fedayeen had no tradition of fake—of imitation marble passed off as real, of sham pathos mimicking pain, of any kind of play-acting.

There was nothing here like Bourguiba's famous rows of palm

trees—the tubs that hordes of policemen dressed as gardeners used to move around in the dark. Thus the president could make a solemn entry into every town he visited, and drive in an open car along a shady avenue which had sprung up in one (rainless) night. The following night, after Bourguiba had duly been received by the local dignitaries, the palms were moved on to the next stop on the dictator's journey south. He knew the importance of deception. He called out the name of every tree as he passed:

"Hallo, Rocroi! Hallo, Waterloo! . . . Fashoda! . . ."

On the Palestinian bases the students were glib in English, German, French and Spanish. They were always ready to pose for a flashlight photograph and hold the same forced smile over and over for the same paper; willing to affect joy or anger and choose a cliché suitable for a particular journal. But it was all a waste of time. The reporters, photographers and cameramen had already noticed the details that showed the base to be a sham, identified the youths who could talk but not fight.

Should the students be sent to war to learn the trade? The ancient debate revived: "Homer puts out his own eyes because he's not Achilles. Which is better, a quick death or to sing for ever?"

The journalists knew the difference between braving the fumes of smoke-bombs and going down to the Jordan amid a hail of machine-gun fire. So did the fedayeen, and the young lions.

Despite their Korean—North Korean—restraint, the Black Panthers couldn't throw off their mutual attraction. Their movement consisted of magnetized bodies magnetizing one another.

The fedayeen observed a smiling rigour. But the eroticism was palpable. I could sense its vibrations, though I wasn't bothered by it.

Does anyone remember the three rows of tanks surrounding the camp at Baqa, and how the Palestinian women decided to leave and walk home with their children to Palestine? Their object was to cover the escape of a Christian monk, a Frenchman.

That victory annoyed the Bedouin troops. Their dancing was a riposte to the political and military leaders of the PLO. But it's difficult to prove one's manhood, and even more difficult to escape it. And perhaps one should just let it be. The Bedouin's dancing was perfect, primordial, their choreography preserved from corruption by the barren sands that had protected it for thousands of years. But it looked young and fresh and beautiful to the eyes of the dejected fedayeen. Perhaps they regretted having challenged a tradition so old yet so unscathed it made the new world seem wrinkled and tired.

Three months later one of the PLO leaders got married. I was invited, not to the wedding itself but to a meal afterwards: the bridegroom had accepted the offer of a dinner party at Abu Omar's, at which I was present together with a few fedayeen in civilian clothes.

"Is your wife going to be a nurse?"

"Not on your life. She's a virgin."

"So you're determined to preserve her virginity?"

There was some laughter, but his face remained stiff and severe.

"I mean to have a real marriage. So my wife's not going to be a nurse."

"So you're against nurses?"

"Not if they're foreign. But my wife's a Muslim."

It was an old joke, but they told it again:

"Trust the desert to give us back our sources."

But I wonder if this strange saying oughtn't to be extended:

"Study Marx for the causes and failures of the English Industrial Revolution, and let the desert preserve our sources."

Perhaps the sand preserves the Arab world with its tents, caravans and camels, just as it preserves its manly, wild and tender dances.

WESTERN DREAM OF THE EAST	BEDOUIN'S DREAM
Tent	Air-conditioning
Travel	Ease
Camel	Mercedes
Dancing	Their old folks break-dancing
Virility	Farid el-Atrach

For part of 1970 and almost all of 1971, their indifference to international politics made the Palestinians, with the exception of their political leaders, think they were independent. Remember what Yasser Arafat said to a fedayee belonging to Fatah who asked:

"Why bother about whether the Russians or the Americans agree? Five years ago we went wherever we liked and did whatever we wanted, including the revolution, without asking anyone else's opinion."

"No one thought about us then. But now we're a problem, and problems are made to be solved—they can't be allowed to wander about at their own sweet will."

In 1910 and 1917 the Palestinians were unwittingly the dream or day-dream of Polish and Ukrainian Jews who probably knew little about Palestine except that it was the promised land, the land of milk and honey—though as yet the idea of evicting its inhabitants hadn't occurred to anyone. It was a place of dream, where everything still had to be built, and the Jews of 1910 dreamed of it as empty, or at worst peopled by insubstantial shadows who didn't really exist as individuals. But none of the Palestinians knew his garden was an empty space dreamed of far away and destined to be turned into a laboratory, while its owner was only a passing shadow.

But how were the buds to be nipped, the eggs to be crushed?

Swarms of amphora factories appeared, like so many lice, so many lice eggs. Did more and more Norwegians spend their holidays in Arab countries? The exchange rates favoured Scandinavian currencies in Algeria, Morocco, Tunisia, Egypt, Lebanon, Syria and Jordan, and tiny workshops reproduced the amphoras of thousands of years ago.

It was much the same in 1970–71: the "refugees" were not even the subject of dreams, but seen merely in terms of aid allocated annually and distributed by UNRRA (United Nations Relief and Rehabilitation Administration) in some camps somewhere to an undifferentiated mass in which no one had a name. But in 1970 an old word that had disappeared from political vocabularies was heard again: the word Palestinian. Neither masculine nor feminine, singular nor plural, it didn't denote men or women. It was armed; all the super-powers knew was that it represented a revolution; they didn't know yet whether they ought to keep an eye on it or destroy it. From 1966 on, the Palestinians, anarchic but apparently free, may have haunted a few political consciences, but for a long time they were the subject of dreams rather than thought.

The gypsy caravans used to gather at the entrance to—or, if you prefer, the way out of—the village, preferably by a rubbish dump, a mass of empty tins, old mattresses and broken plates where the barefoot children from the camp would deposit some things and take others away. The women in their flowing dresses of artificial taffeta used to go about telling fortunes, while the men wove baskets, their brown hands small, lazy and agile. Chicken thieves never ventured on to the farms, but the women and kids went into the villages to beg and steal and lie, nimble compendia of all the vices, a mixture of heaven and hell, whom ordinary folk just watched arrive and depart.

The fedayeen weren't outlaws, but like the gypsies they seemed to be playing to some kind of audience. The world? God? Themselves? Were they trying to appear the opposite of what they really were?

The last gypsy camp I saw was in Serbia, naturally at the entrance to or the way out of the village of Ujitse-Pojega, near a rubbish tip. The caravans were still made of wood painted in many colours and drawn by horses which had been taken out of the shafts that morning. The almost naked children saw me and ran to tell the women, who told the greasy-haired men. Each of the latter then showed a quarter of his face and one whole eye, enough to see me but no more than was necessary. Then the bits of faces disappeared, and soon afterwards two good-looking young women of about sixteen appeared and came towards me. Their indirect, apparently nonchalant approach was really as bold and studied as the swaying of their hips. When, sheltered by the wall of a house, they finally confronted me, their attitude was openly provocative.

Now at some distance from the camp, though its inhabitants must still have been watching them, they slowly raised their full skirts—one was green, the other black with red flowers—and showed me their unshaven private parts.

Palestine itself was an irregular satellite moving around within the Arab universe. And a pseudo-tribe, a sub-satellite of Palestine, revolved around Palestine without ever crashing into it.

This vestige of tribalism was still in orbit, just as the gypsy camps used to be in Serbia. The Serbs held aloof from them because of their customs or morals. Perhaps they themselves chose to be outcasts: it was their recipe for survival.

It seems to me that social as well as cosmic order calls for suns with stars revolving round them, and every sun keeping its distance. But although the social cosmogony of Palestine is so ancient, many accidents may perturb it: marriages of convenience, romantic love affairs, the victory of one tiny dynasty over another, an unlucky speculation by the Lazard bank. All these have their effect on the gyrations of both earthly and heavenly bodies, and for a moment made one see the Palestine revolution in a different perspective.

Israel was the sun that claimed to be the most remarkable in the universe, if not the brightest or most distant—the first to come into existence out of the original big bang.

When Syria became a Turkish province it saw itself as the mother of Palestine, which was part of the Ottoman Empire. But it was also the sphere in which the Leading Families moved. They were all more or less under the influence of the Sublime Porte, but each sought to elbow the others aside.

In September 1982, when the Israeli army moved from East to West Beirut, Nabila Nashashibi was afraid her Palestinian accent and appearance would expose her to rough treatment: she was the doctor in charge of the Akka hospital on the outskirts of Chatila. So she and her husband took refuge in a flat belonging to Leila, one of the last descendants of the Husseini family.

I asked Nabila to tell me about Palestine under the Ottomans. We were in Leila's mother's luxurious sitting-room.

"There were two famous families," she began. "The Husseinis and the Nashashibis. They were always fighting. Palestine was their arena."

She looked around her at the embroidered cushions, the rich materials, the objets d'art, the jewels, the people.

"Can you take me to the French Embassy? I don't feel comfortable here. It's not safe."

At once allies and rivals, the ancient families owed their prestige on the one hand to their common descent, through Ali and Fatima, from the Prophet Muhammad, and on the other hand to their openness to the West. The latter, rare in a Muslim country, was due to the fact that their children went to European schools in Lebanon or Palestine. I sensed that Fatah, and especially Arafat, had been making devious use of these families. But I also suspected that the families made use of him.

How did it come about, through what interplay of love and money, that two families—I can't mention their names—who used to be opposed to each other in everything, now came to be connected by marriage?

I mention all this because it's a good thing that the reader should bear in mind, at least while he's reading this book, that Palestine has had a complex history, with many contenders for power. It wasn't just an empty space. Now the leading families, especially the landed proprietors, have been dispossessed by Israel; but their peasants still revere them for being descended from the Prophet.

Long before they were fedayeen the people were Palestinians. The nation arose out of the remains of a forest—a couple of dozen family trees that wouldn't die, and whose last branches were still green. The most ancient family trees were at least fifteen hundred years old, perhaps more. They had been Christian and Monophysite under Byzantium; Jewish before that; Muslim since.

These very old families were used to cynicism, cheating and deception, and could cope with the world's upheavals. But immediately below them was a class that couldn't help being appalled. I learned about them in Beirut, where a newspaper editor told me fearfully, as if he felt he himself was on the slippery slope:

"My son has come home several times with fruit fresh off the trees. The first time I wouldn't eat any—I didn't know where he'd got it from. The second time I did eat some—I was so hungry. After that I used to wait for him to bring fruit home, and finally I became his instructor in theft. But stealing fruit or paraffin or flour is nothing. Lying is much worse, and that's what we've come to. The invasion has made us into common criminals, but above all it's turned us into liars. First our morals were eclipsed; now they've completely collapsed."

Listening to him, I seemed to see Dr. Mahjoub's frayed future.

A middle class that still believed in the virtues taught at St. Joseph's School was bound to suffer. The Leading Families, socially just above them, were a casual martial aristocracy protected from excessive scruple. Like all aristocrats, they could smile and say: "Theft is just moving something from one place to another."

Strangely enough, not far from Amman, the Hashemite government and the revolts in the camps, there was a small pseudo-tribe of about five hundred people who lived in tents even more patched than those of the Palestinians. They moved from valley to valley, living mostly off petty theft and even pettier alms.

Here is their story, if they didn't lie to me.

One day Dr. Alfredo came and asked me what we could do for this little band of vagabonds unknown to the official "travellers." In 1970 they numbered 563. Not only did they consist of just one family, but having been driven from one camp, village and district to another, they had no territory or land of any kind. Whenever they could they camped on barley fields that had just been harvested. The United Nations didn't recognize them even as "displaced persons," so it offered them no protection or help, and they were reduced to stealing and begging in order to live. They weren't qualified for any kind of job, and I got the impression they didn't like work anyway.

But this mini-pseudo-tribe had its own hierarchy, with the women at the bottom, followed by the little girls, then the male children, the various active men, and finally sixteen old greybeards headed by a chief. I saw but didn't meet the latter. He seemed to be, if not the oldest member of the tribe, at least the one who wielded the most power, and he therefore had the mildest and the most distant manners.

I was told the Arabic they spoke was that used in the area round the Syrian port of Latakia. Perhaps that was where they were making for: none of them gave the same answer about this, though they seemed to have started out in 1948, driven out of Palestine by Israel. Then they vanished into the Negev, where they stayed for more than a year. After that they went to Sinai, re-entering Palestine, now called Israel, and thence to Jordan through the various passes of Petra. They pressed on from place to place towards the north and east, never settling anywhere and apparently never making friends or trusting anybody. They had reached the region of Amman when we met them—Alfredo, Nabila Nashashibi and I. The population of this almost endogamous group hadn't varied since the Exodus. It had perpetuated itself through a practice severely frowned on by the Church. Incest.

All four of us went to see them—Alfredo, Nabila, a fedayee called Shiran, and me. Our first object was to count them; our second to find out what they needed. Shiran translated.

"We'll come the day after tomorrow. We've counted twenty-three tents. We'll bring eight blankets for each tent. Also matches. Cartons of cigarettes. Soap. A hundred tins of corned beef. Two hundred tins of sardines."

Almost all the people crowded round us. They were visibly disappointed that we weren't giving them anything right away. They greeted what we said with a huge shrug. They lived from moment to moment, and apparently couldn't imagine a future stretching from today to the day after tomorrow. Also, I didn't know quite why, it seemed to me we were dealing with a group that had deliberately opted out—perhaps banished by the Palestinians who still remained on the right side of the law—rather than the remains of a tribe that had dwindled away through wandering, death, weariness and want. If this unfortunate group had really been part of the community it wouldn't have been abandoned, however low it had sunk. Or so we thought.

What bothered us was that despite all Nabila's and Shiran's efforts, no one would give us his own name or that of the pseudo-tribe itself. This meant that when we tried to tell the Palestinian officials about their plight, it was as if we were talking about the hunger and cold of mere ghosts. If ever they did give any help they did so laughing, especially at us.

So we got some blankets and tinned goods from two or three stores in Baqa camp, where the people in charge were neither hardhearted nor particularly touched, but simply amused, and went back as promised two days later with a truck full of gifts.

In Jordan the camel is still a symbol of prosperity, so the tribe had a camel, four horses and a flock of goats. They all belonged to the head of the tribe, whom none of us had yet seen.

The men and women of the tribe may not actually have believed we wouldn't come back the day after next, or ever, but our return seemed as distant to them as that of a comet, calculated with difficulty by later generations with only a mythical memory of its last appearance. In a way our return made them seem their own descendants. A reappearance after an interval of two thousand years, and with heaps of gifts, called for a celebration.

A huge tent, narrow but very long, was put up, and the whole population swarmed round it. We left the truck nearby, guarded by a couple of fedayeen. An almost complete silence reigned, except for the greetings exchanged between Nabila and some of the women. Then a flap of the tent was raised and we were inside. The sixteen lords and elders were squatting on blankets at one end of the tent; we sat down on blankets at the other. Women served everyone with tea, the lords first. When the tea dispensers came to us, they served me first because of my age. The only sound was the considerable one of lips drinking boiling hot tea, a loud slurping which the English regard as unseemly but which is thought to be pleasing among the beards and the sands.

Then the lords' part of the tent rose up, and the Lord of the sixteen lords and of all the rest appeared. We had got to our feet with the sixteen, and we all stood motionless as the Lord gave the first of the sixteen lords sixteen kisses on his right cheek, the second fifteen—real smackers, which I thought indicated special favour— the third fourteen not very loud ones, the fourth thirteen, and so on to the eighth, after which he paused to get his breath and his saliva back.

He was bearded and of very noble mien. If he'd prostrated himself or had a boy attendant bearing the train of his black woollen robes, I'd have known beyond further doubt that this pseudo-tribe, like the Vatican, was pursuing the same ritual as that of the Court at Byzantium.

The chief resumed his labours. The ninth lord received eight kisses on the cheek, the tenth seven, the eleventh six, the twelfth five, the thirteenth four, the fourteenth three, the fifteenth two, and the sixteenth one—the last.

As soon as the chief had, almost surreptitiously, revealed to us the rites of his tribe, he turned his back on us without so much as a glance, and left the tent. One of his sixteen lords came over and told us very politely in Arabic that the chief accepted our gift, and that he, the lord, would take delivery.

What was the origin of those kisses handed out so sparely and with such discrimination? Never before, in Islam or anywhere else, had I seen a dignitary embracing anyone with that restrained emotion, as if sticking on stamps or pinning a different row of medals on each cheek. Lips and cheeks, as they met and parted, made the same noise as mouths sipping hot tea. Where did the custom come from? What was it in aid of? Was it just a ceremony designed to differentiate this pseudo-tribe from others? A new hierarchy had involved a new order of precedence. Would their children in ages to come still observe it, thinking it the oldest in the world?

Nabila, Shiran, Alfredo, the two other fedayeen and I exchanged glances. We'd either hand out the contents of the truck ourselves or else drive away with it full. The sixteen elders neither smiled nor objected, and withdrew. We took a look at the camp: instead of twenty-three tents there were eighty-seven. Each consisted of a piece of canvas supported by a branch and inhabited by one woman or a little boy. The most populous contained a little boy and his sister and one slightly older girl, all with runny noses. As we'd promised eight blankets to every tent it was agreed, as a compromise, that we'd go and fetch another four hundred.

By the evening of the following day the women of the pseudo-tribe were at the entrance to the camp at Gaza, trying to sell some four hundred blankets or barter them for more tins of sardines.

"In their place I'd do the same," said Alfredo.

"So would I," said Nabila.

"Me too," said I.

But we all thought it was a bit much to do it to us.

That was in the winter of 1970–71. Whenever I visited the Ajloun bases Dr. Mahjoub, ever thinner and paler under his tan, his hair always longer and with a few more streaks of grey, used to greet me with a smile. Because of a serious complaint of the spine he had to walk with a stick, and each time I saw him he looked older and more bent.

"If only we get through the winter!" he said to me in December.

And in January:

"The cold is a trial. Especially the wind and the snow. But it'll be all right when the bad weather's over."

In February he said:

"I wish the people in Amman would try harder to send food. We could run out. Look at the fedayeen—they're getting weaker and weaker. A lot of them have coughs. It's a shame. But when the sun comes back everything will be all right."

If he could have seen the rude health of the Jordanian army, in their nice warm barracks, fed on mutton and chicken!

In March he was optimistic.

"The sun will soon be back, Jean. Another rather chilly month and everything will be better. Thank goodness. We're almost out of medicines."

Mahjoub knew what had happened at Zarka: a few kilometres away a hospital had been built with money from Iraq, but the International Red Cross doctor and nurses, who'd been looking after a few fedayeen there, had to leave in two or three days when the hospital was taken over by the Jordanian government.

I think the idea for what we did, and its execution, were due to Dr. Alfredo. Anyway, it was he who mentioned it to me.

"Are you coming with us? We're going to see what's happening at the Iraqi hospital. Nabila will be there. Ferraj is driving the truck. One of his pals is coming too."

Just a few words about Alfredo. He was brought up in Cuba,

where he studied medicine. He was very devoted to the Palestinians. He spoke Spanish, of course; also English and French. He was Cuban by nationality, though born in Spain to a Castilian countess, and already very critical of Castro's policies.

He distrusted the Red Cross, which had refused to help the Palestinian Red Crescent during the fighting in Amman. As a doctor and a Cuban he knew all about the chicaneries of Western medicine. Was he joking when he said:

"Which would you choose, Palestine or Kathmandu? I haven't made up my mind."

The armed guard at the Iraqi hospital let us in. The entrance hall was full of packing-cases, all nailed up and labelled ready to go, together with cases of drugs and surgical instruments donated by Nationalist China, Taiwan, and various European countries. But there was no one about except the sentry, who incidentally was smoking while on duty.

No one on the first floor either. It had a balcony, and Nabila, Alfredo, Ferraj and I went out on it. A handsome fair-haired youth, completely naked, lay stretched out on some towels, fondling a blonde as naked as himself. Neither paid any attention to the disc that was playing on a turntable not far away. Our arrival gave them a shock. Ferraj and the fedayee withdrew, and the Swedish doctor and Dutch nurse put their clothes on.

"Bawl them out in French," Alfredo told me. "Nabila will translate it into English. Take your time, while I go and have a look at the wounded."

As a Palestinian doctor herself, Nabila Nashashibi was indignant, but like me she could hardly help laughing. However, we put on a good show of being really angry.

"There are about twenty wounded on the first floor with no one looking after them," Alfredo told us. He too had a go at the doctor and nurse, who seemed quite intimidated. Then he spoke to me in French.

"Keep them occupied a bit longer."

Nabila translated my sham reproaches to the now rather sheepish Swedish doctor. Then Alfredo came back: "Leave them now. We're off."

Two hours later every infirmary in the Palestinian camps was sharing out the contents of the packing-cases. Ferraj and his fe-dayee friend had loaded them on to the truck while the Swede and the Dutch nurse were receiving their rocket.

The next day, for reasons that had nothing to do with the robbery, we—an Italian doctor, Nabila, Alfredo and I—were ar-rested by the Jordanian army near Amman, and sent under police guard to prison. We were soon released, but Abu Omar, when he heard I'd been in jail, insisted on my going to stay on the Jordan, with and under the protection of the fedayeen. I wasn't allowed to go to Amman. He was afraid I'd be arrested. At Ajloun I met the Sudanese officer, Lieutenant Mubarak, again.

I could see Maurice Chevalier, with his boater tipped over one eye.

It's years now since you heard a real working-class accent in Belleville, Ménilmontant or Pantin. The old defence works, once the resort of criminals, have become suburbs where the French that's spoken is as grammatical and pure as the speech you hear on television or the radio.

But in 1943 I heard a plasterer with his cap over one eye correct a cop who might have been from Poitou about how to say "It looks like rain."

Now, though unfortunately they come these days without the Parisian accent or the forceful poetic slang with its whiff of pant seats and flies, you may still hear some of the words that were coined in my youth. If you want to rediscover swift repar-tee you need to wander round Rouen, Le Havre, the Grand- or Petit- Quevilly in Beauvais, Sens, Joigny or Troyes—where per-haps the prison stimulates inventiveness in the young. But the one with the gift of the gab is unlikely now to be a kid in hand-me-down trousers. More likely an Archbishop of Paris with the kid's working-class accent but without his stylish gestures.

Here's an example of the quickness I mean.

In about 1950 I hailed a Paris taxi and said where I wanted to go. The driver, a man of about sixty with a big grey moustache, hesitated a moment, looked me over, and then said:

"All right. I'm just going off duty and it's on my way to the garage."

I got in the back remarking, "In that case, I suppose you'll pay the fare?"

He looked round slowly, eyed me, then said, almost indulgently, over his shoulder:

"Right away, mate. And as usual, with love."

It was all there: the exaggerated Paris accent, the swift repartee, the wry sizing up and unerring choice of the appropriate mild tone. I'd been made a present of a small if somewhat mannered masterpiece at 1 A.M. in Paris in the place de la République.

But that sort of gift seemed to have been carried away in suburban trains from the five main stations of Paris to temporary terminuses elsewhere.

Men and women standing in the aisles in second-class coaches and sent flying at the bends in the rails, used to exchange pleasantries. And at stations like Deuil or Meulan the still shy half-Senegalese, quarter-Arabs and complete Guadeloupians used to step over beds of French geraniums without hurting a single one. Then suddenly the crescent moon emerged from the clouds and the station at Deuil became as international as Karachi Airport.

The jeans tightly outlining the men's thighs and hips were at the same time erotic and chaste, so well did the beauty of their lines suit the darkness. Everyone was naked.

But as soon as people said "Ciao" in every possible accent, all was silent again. Shadows strode along mute. Slang was unfashionable now.

No Frenchman would have risked using slang in Jordan. It was as out of place as farting, which the Arabs hated. In the past, the first two or three syllables of a word would be used in place of the whole. As anglers economize by cutting worms up into seven or eight pieces with their fingernails, so speech at the time I'm speaking of would be made up of scraps intelligible only to the initiate.

The two Frenchmen called Guy would never have spoken like that with Arabs present—they told me themselves it was crummy. I admired their delicacy. It was only later that I learned the real reason.

"It would be like speaking a secret language. You can be shot for less," Guy II told me.

"We work with the rank and file," said Guy I.

He opened his mouth to go on, but Guy II spoke again.

"Every man to his trade."

Guy I dotted the i's.

"The labourer is worthy of his hire."

"The Palestinians are human, just like us," said Guy II.

"Why wouldn't we help them? They've got a right to a country."

The last word seemed uncomfortable, left hanging in the air.

"They want a democracy," added Guy I. "It's in their manifesto."

"If Pompidou had stopped me coming I'd have told him to get knotted," said Guy II, throwing me a cool glance, as they say in the papers.

"I don't see why we shouldn't all be brothers," said Guy I.

"We don't want them to be annexed by America or Russia. France ought to give them a hand. And Hussein's a fascist. Why not get rid of him?"

They were Parisians, of course, but they didn't have working-class accents. More likely they came out of some métro station in the place de la Bastille. The Palestinians who were with the three Frenchmen and two Frenchwomen in the room in Amman just looked on without speaking. They didn't know that there on foreign soil they were watching a French battle that might have been taking place in a Paris bar.

No doubt it was magnanimous of the two twenty-year-olds to have hitch-hiked through Italy, Yugoslavia, Greece, Turkey and Syria to help the people of Wahadat to build new walls, not knowing whether walls and builders alike mightn't be laid low by Hussein's Bedouin. I think I've given a fair account of their dialogue. We were only throwing the fedayeen some scraps.

Magnanimity couldn't be the whole explanation. I wondered what thirst for adventure had made them travel through so many countries to get here. They didn't seem to have been inspired by any literary longings for the magic of the East; it wasn't Loti that made them retrace the steps of Marco Polo. They might have come because of a sudden impulse as mysterious as the original big bang, of which we don't know the consequences or even if it happened at all; but that phenomenon couldn't have had any precedent, whereas the journey of the two Guys had plenty. Had they set out for Kathmandu after May '68, and come upon the Palestinian camps on the way? Had they flicked through a left-wing leaflet and been fascinated by the word "fedayeen"? Why *had* they come? That they stayed was understandable: the situation had its charms. But why had they set out in the first place, and did they know what routes to take, what risks they ran, and above all what they were letting themselves in for? Maybe they were surprised to find themselves builder's mates, not knowing it was the last but one stage of their journey. After that came dying in action.

"We are all brothers."

I recognized the universal French bounty: we brought the others everything—how to build concrete walls, manners, women's lib, rock music, the art of the fugue, fraternity. And in the universal French bounty I saw myself occupying a position that was small, perhaps, but sure.

"If they go on like this my theory about France will be shattered."

But I said nothing.

Because they were French, they'd needed visas for only two of the countries they'd come through—Syria and Jordan.

They were both called Guy, but they spoke to one another like this:

"Hey!"

"Yes—what?"

"Did you call me?"

"No. Did you call me?"

"Ditto."

Guy I laughed, then Guy II, then the two women. For them and their girl-friends Europe didn't exist as a geographical concept, but France had a long history in which Jeanne d'Arc chatted with Mendès France. They brought the Palestinians the echo of a generosity born on the banks of the Seine. Through Omar, Monsieur Mustapha's son, who was acting as interpreter, the fedayeen came to understand May '68 and its discovery of exploited peoples, especially exotic ones. They smiled, but with the yawns of those who are hungry.

The room—an annexe of the Fatah office—made me think of the 1913 Russian Ballet: with five Parisian stage-hands standing by, several Nijinskys in striped costumes flecked with moss and dead leaves waited to leap on stage in *Le Prélude à l'après-midi d'un faune.*

Because they worked with the rank and file and thought dirt a sign of plebeian nobility and virtue, the four seemed proud of their grubby necks, faces, wrists and clothes. Guy stunned me by saying:

"A bit dressed up, aren't you, to fight for revolution in the developing world?—with your white silk shirt and cashmere scarf!"

We exchanged a few more words. Except for the Palestinians, everyone thought I was making fun of the revolutionaries when I said I'd stopped over for twenty-four hours in Cairo to go and see the Pyramids at sunrise, pink above the mists of the Nile.

"You came through Istanbul. Didn't any of you go to see Santa Sophia?"

"The girls did."

Somehow, when they spoke, the two Frenchmen made the word "Arab" begin with a small letter. Though their language didn't always pass muster, their manners were better. They greeted the Arabs as Louis XIV did his grooms, so anxious were they to annoy Pompidou. And they learned to eat very gracefully with their fingers, far better than I ever did.

This long passage about the Frenchmen is probably because I was afraid I might never hear again the Paris accent that once so delighted me. The passengers on suburban trains still speak with it, but I don't often go to the suburbs now.

Throughout their journey, and perhaps while they were getting ready for it, they'd worn youthful but ample beards and moustaches, under the impression that all the men did the same where they were going. They'd probably seen old copies of *L'Illustration* published in France in the days of Abdul Hamid. But all the Palestinians wore was a trim little moustache. The only beards the Frenchmen met with in the streets—rarely in Fatah—belonged to members of the Muslim Brotherhood. So the two Guys had to shave off their beards. Omar told it like this:

"When they first came here they had big heads, but after they'd been to the barber's they had such tiny little baby faces I felt like offering them my nipple."

"Canaille have, Jean!" *

His colour, his nakedness, the smoothness of his skin, his muscles, his litheness, the sweet, almost painfully sweet curves of his face despite the tribal scars that made him look like a branded animal, fabulous but one of a herd, a beast to be bought and sold—all this would have been nothing were it not for the sadness emanating from him. It seemed to swathe him in invisible shadows, not merely when he was alone but also if he fell silent in your presence. When you asked him a question, he answered. The answer would be precise, often complex, but clear, as it he'd already thought about it before he was asked.

But where did Mubarak's voice come from? Before, I'd foolishly thought that since Africa had more to do with imagination than with hard-and-fast geography, its inhabitants would naturally be strange, and their voices more like squealing than articulate language. But the slave trade, man-hunting, buying and trafficking and transportation had been—and still were—real events, involving bankers as well as traders, the rate of the florin as well as the crack of the whip, and itemized as minutely as dealings in uranium, copper, tungsten and gold are today. And not only was the French he spoke comprehensible and grammatically perfect, but he made a point of clothing it in the working-class accent I'd been looking for for so long that I'd come to think it had vanished, perhaps died. As languages can.

It made me smile to think that a negro from the Sudan—formerly the Anglo-Egyptian Sudan—had become a kind of Georges Dumézil, guardian of an accent as Dumézil had been the guardian of certain dying languages. Mubarak's rôle was even the more remarkable of the two, since an accent is more volatile than a language and vanishes faster.

It was like that time in Damascus when I got a French

* Literally, pale bastard.

programme from Tel Aviv on my radio and heard a reporter speaking in the cheeky accents of the Paris suburbs.

Mubarak smiled at me and said, in English, naturally enough, "Can I have?", and I understood him to say *Canaille have*.

So he could banish his sadness at a stroke. But it seemed to me he couldn't tell when it would come back.

He told me that when he was about fifteen he'd been in love with Maurice Chevalier, though he'd heard only two of his records, "Prosper" and "Valentine." He liked the accent, a parody of the accent of Ménilmontant, and adopted it. He was enchanted when I told him the popular name for Ménilmontant was Ménilmuche.*

All the other African Blacks I knew of about Mubarak's age were very cheerful even when alone. So I thought he must have some serious inner wound so well hidden I'd never know what it was or whether it was physical or spiritual. It seemed to me to add to his natural charm the tender appeal often found in young Blacks. Some boys' voices are so quiet you have to strain your ears to hear what they say, or tell them to say it again. And their faces, for no reason known even to them, are sad.

They are in mourning, each one a twin surviving a brother who died at two or three weeks old.

"*Canaille . . .*"

He smiled at my astonishment. I sometimes wonder if it was out of snobbishness that he mixed English with French.

"I'm the whole Jet Set rolled into one."

Then he vanished into his darkness, whence I heard him say in one of his languages what tired fedayeen were always saying: "We'll have all eternity to rest in."

It was one of those sayings of uncertain origin that the fighters attributed to Abd el-Kadr, Abd el-Krim, Lumumba, Mao Tse-tung or Guevara. I thought it sounded familiar, and said so.

He flashed me a sardonic look.

"It must have been invented by a Frenchman, since you French created the whole world."

---

* *Muche* is slang for hiding-place.

" 'Eternity didn't seem too long for me to rest in,' " I murmured.

"That's better," he said. "Who wrote it?"

"Benjamin Constant. *Cécile*. Or *The Red Notebook*—I forget."

He was almost taken aback.

"Another one who was impotent."

A recoil into himself that left him no more than a spaniel at my heels.

"You see, Jean, I'm an African in Asia. The Palestinians puzzle me."

"But Palestine's the country closest to Africa."

"For me Asia starts at the Pyramids. Pharaoh, Nebuchadnezzar, David, Solomon, Tamburlaine, Palmyra, Zoroaster, Jesus, Buddha, Muhammad—there's nothing African about them."

"Who are your people, then?"

"Napoleon, Isabella of Castile, Elizabeth I, Hitler . . . Territory and space are a misuse of language, perpetrated out of vanity."

It was much later, after his death, I think, that I found out he never slept with people in the usual way. Never with a man, either. His sperm seemed to be transmitted through the guttural tones of his voice to the person who heard it, male or female. Not that he told erotic stories—he seemed to avoid such details—but the warmth of that voice had the shy yet imperious sureness of an erect penis stroking a beloved cheek. In that too I saw him as obvious heir to the boys of the old Paris suburbs.

Did he put on the working-class accent deliberately? There was never any lapse to give me proof of it.

There are plenty of examples of accents being handed down by chance to faces that didn't go with them. After a one-night stand in Dijon a pilot from Martinique left a girl with a child who was typically Burgundian except for his fuzzy hair. A German girl from Hamburg dotted her otherwise elegant French with phrases like "and all of a sudden he dropped me in the shit," or "I was a silly cunt, he did me good and proper"—all uttered without a blush. A worker from the Vosges had been her lover for three years when he was a prisoner of war. He'd communicated with her as best he could, unaware how incongruous such words were in the circumstances, and above all how far they were from ordinary French. Perhaps an NCO from Pantin had met Mubarak in Djibouti when he was young, and left him that fine accent as a keepsake.

Mubarak never talked to me about it, except to say he'd listened to "Prosper" and "Valentine" a hundred times on the gramophone, and adored Maurice Chevalier's scratchy voice.

The harmony of the blue sky, the green palms and the ochre fields, of the whole landscape as it appeared to me in the dusk, reminded me that the Palestinians were part of the harmony too. The unconscious harmony of sky, palms, fields and fighters.

The only noises I heard for over a year were gunfire and the hum of a plane or helicopter: it wasn't until after the battle of Ajloun, when I heard them again, that I realized the hens had never stopped clucking or the cows lowing.

The last few lines were an attempt to put off asking the following question: would the Palestinian revolution have exercised such a strong fascination on me if it hadn't been fought against what seemed to me the darkest of peoples?—a people whose beginning claimed to be *the* Beginning, who claimed that they were, and meant to remain, the Beginning, who said they belonged to the Dawn of Time? To ask the question is, I think, to answer it. Taking place against the background of the Dawn of Beginnings, the Palestinian revolution was no ordinary battle to recover stolen land: it was a metaphysical struggle. Israel, imposing its morals and myths on the whole world, saw itself as identical with Power. It was Power. The mere sight of the fedayeen's meagre guns showed the immeasurable distance there was between the two forces: on the one hand just a few dead and wounded; on the other annihilation, accepted and even desired by Europe and the Arab countries.

The long rhapsodies about Israel; the congratulations on being the only democracy in the Middle East; tales of how the desert had been irrigated, fertilized and planted and each apple and birch tree given a name; the polite but implacable struggles between Ashkenazis and Sephardis; Israel's scientific, archaeological and biological discoveries—all these we only heard of in 1970 through the Occupied Territories. That is, via a kind of censorship that showed us only the distorted image the Jewish State wished us to see. Israel never spoke to us, we never heard about Israel, directly: it was the occupied Arabs who told us about it.

The State of Israel is a bruise, a contusion that lingers on the shoulder of Islam not only because of the last bite—in '67—but because soon afterwards it allowed Elie Cohen to be arrested and hanged, and because every Palestinian, every Arab even, felt threatened by Jewish espionage. Infiltration was not only possible, it was certain. A few days ago (1985), J. told me Mossad was supplying young people in southern Lebanon with opium and hashish.

"The American police have been accused of supplying drugs to young Blacks."

"I know. Mossad has training courses in the USA. The object may be different because the situation's not the same, but the methods are the same. Mossad hopes that while they're in a state of euphoria the young people will reveal the whereabouts of the fedayeen and their caches of arms. Through the radio and the press, and by a discreet but efficient whispering campaign, the Israelis have talked up their intelligence service to such an extent that the Arabs are still panic-stricken and disoriented.

"Several people have met the man I'm going to tell you about now. In the part of the city that was to become West Beirut—the Muslim part, almost entirely pro-Palestinian—a man appeared. No one remembers his coming. He was just suddenly there. He spoke Arabic with a Palestinian accent, and like the gods when they choose to live on earth for a while incognito, he was famous for his crazy goings-on. The kids who made fun of him and the parents who pitied him all called him the Madman. Madness has always been ubiquitous. It was natural enough that it should appear there like everywhere else; everyone has a touch of it.

"This harmless eccentric went in for tricks like appearing out of the dark and shining an electric torch in people's faces, singing some unintelligible chant the while.

" 'It's only the Madman,' people would say, with an indulgent shrug and a smile.

"No one went too near him, for he stank all over—feet, mouth (horribly), hands, backside, private parts.

"He'd sleep anywhere so long as it was out of the wind, wrapped up in a single blanket. He begged, and when he swore he said a lot of nasty things about the Israelis.

"Early on 15 September 1982, Israeli tanks entered West Beirut. I saw the first of them pass by the French Embassy. I wasn't surprised to see Israeli soldiers enter the city; but the people of Beirut were surprised to see the Madman in the leading tank. This time his face was grim and he didn't sing. He wore the uniform of a colonel in the Israeli army.

"I don't know anything more about him, but I'm sure his stench was a ruse, a clever device to stop anyone approaching him suddenly."

But in that period, between 1970 and the time when Sadat crossed the Suez Canal in 1973, Israel ceased to exist: all that reached us were shouts and laments, epics rather than cries, from the Occupied Territories. These noises didn't bother the camps or the bases too much. If anyone died or was ill on the other side of the Jordan, these were only family troubles or bereavements. But everyone realized that the war with Hussein benefited Israel by prolonging the occupation of Jordan, and that the diplomatic comings and goings showed the importance of places where we were of no importance at all.

Sometimes, towards evening, an Arab in a gallabiya would approach the camp. He would drink tea or coffee with us, eat a bit of rice, bid us a gentle farewell and go away.

"Do you know why he didn't sit down?" Ferraj asked me. "He couldn't. He had his gun strapped on to his leg under his gallabiya. He's on his way to Israel. If he has time he'll fire all his bullets, and perhaps, about midnight or in the morning, one Israeli will die."

What comes next is meant to show the difference between camps and bases. Of course it's intended for Europeans. Arabs know about it already. The two mentalities were very different.

Until 1972 the bases facing the Jordan kept watch over the Occupied Territories and the part of Palestine to which the UN had given the name Israel.

They were quite small military units of twenty or thirty Palestinian soldiers, all sleeping in tents and armed at first with ordinary rifles and later with a machine-gun or two.

There were bases at several levels. Some were right on the edge of the cliff overlooking the Jordan. These were supported by others a few hundred metres away, both kinds being on constant alert. Around the second semi-circle was another, and then a fourth. I had the impression they were stationed at intervals on four sets of heights. The area by the Jordan was rather exposed because the river bank was fairly smooth and open, but it was less dangerous than the area towards the Jerash–Amman or "asphalt" road.

The Palestinian positions were kept under observation by the Jordanian army, which itself had more or less secret relations with the people in the Jordanian villages close to the bases. But it was quite easy to move about in the whole of the strip from the "asphalt" to the Jordan.

The women never went to the bases except to bring or collect letters, and then they didn't wander about but just waited on the grass outside the guardroom.

So what psychological state were the fedayeen in? They had to keep watch over what was their own territory, traversed by enemies who thought or pretended to think they were free, though in fact a bullet lurked for them at every bend in the road. From Allenby to Damia Bridge—the name makes me think of the realist singer, Maryse Damia, and her song, "Immoral Prayer," in which a sailor's wife prays to the Virgin to let him be shipwrecked rather than captured by mermaids—the fedayeen in Jordan were facing Israeli soldiers scattered among the Palestinian people, a people who were the prisoners of Jewish garrisons and a Jewish administration. This meant there could be no random shooting across the Jordan. Only expert marksmen were sent to keep watch over the Occupied Territories.

With the passage of time the expression has lost its original force—an almost sacred force, comparable to that of "Alsace-Lorraine" in France. But now as then I'm fascinated by the comedy of hatred and the comedy of friendship, both of them often feigned, which still govern the drawing up of frontiers. A frontier is an ideal line that mustn't be tampered with except with the agreement of both the peoples concerned. Yet both sides keep a fierce watch over the boundary and the crossing of it. Hence the comedy of frontier agreements, where the negotiators' faces range from the darkly threatening to the charmingly meek.

A border is where human personality expresses itself most fully, whether in harmony or in contradiction with itself. If I'd had to be someone other than myself—a difficult choice—I'd have been a native of Alsace-Lorraine. It's quite different from being either German or French. Whatever they may say, anyone approaching a frontier stops being a Jacobin and becomes a Machiavelli. It might be a good thing to extend border areas indefinitely—without, of course, destroying the centres, since it's they that make the borders possible . . .

The Israeli occupation of West Beirut in 1982 gave rise to many stories. Here's one. Some kids led a group of Lebanese through a network of underground alleys to a workshop which the Palestinians had just left. All the Lebanese found were some very convincing forgeries of American dollars, which they stuffed into their pockets. It so happened that they were all lorry drivers.

At the time the military patrols wouldn't let Lebanese trucks through to the north—to Beirut, for example. Only Israeli trucks loaded up in Israel were allowed to pass. And so the fun began. A Lebanese truck driver would show the soldier on duty a bundle of dollars, the soldier would say a firm "no," the driver doubled the bundle, the soldier narrowed his eyes more slowly, snatched the dollars and pocketed them, then turned his back so as not to see the truck drive off. So thousands of forged dollars crossed the frontier, to the delight of the soldiers, the lorry drivers, and the people of Beirut, who were very pleased to eat fruit that hadn't come from Tel Aviv. First one lorry got through. Then ten. Then all of them. The imitation dollars went into the real pockets of real Israeli soldiers, who wound up either as prosperous civilians or in prison.

I was told in Beirut that this story was true. It was plausible enough. The enemy allowed a certain amount of collusion. It wasn't anything positive. It was a lull in which each party thought it had got the better of the other.

After the attack was launched in June, many Palestinian officers, NCOs and men who deserted from Hussein's army were able to escape because their erstwhile brothers-in-arms—Jordanians—apparently turned a blind eye. I've never heard of "rank and file" Israelis and Palestinians indulging in such courtesies. But border politics are so delicate, complex and confused that anyone trying to get to the bottom of them risks both his life and his eyesight.

In November 1970 there were a few young men on the bases—on the bases, not in the camps—with long untidy hair and bangs on their foreheads as thick as those worn by Sicilians and head waiters. And they could be heard joking in Hebrew. The older fedayeen were both shocked and fascinated by this ambiguity in their midst. We knew the fedayeen were taught a bit of Hebrew, too. When the fast was over the young men would eat here just like Arabs, wiping their fingers on the thighs of their trousers. Maybe, in Tel Aviv, they ate like Jews.

A chicken, boat, bird, dart or aeroplane such as schoolboys make out of bits of paper—if you unfold them carefully they become a page from a newspaper or a blank sheet of paper again. For a long time I'd been vaguely uneasy, but I was amazed when I realized that my life—I mean the events of my life, spread out flat in front of me—was nothing but a blank sheet of paper which I'd managed to fold into something different. Perhaps I was the only one who could see it in three dimensions, as a mountain, a precipice, a murder or a fatal accident.

What might have seemed a heroic deed was only a pretence, a good or bad imitation that unobservant eyes took for the thing itself. Such eyes, seeing the scar of a self-inflicted flesh wound on my arm, transform it into the evidence of some romantic adventure, complete with a seduced wife and a jealous husband. If I don't mention his name it only shows my integrity, my respect for the beloved, and my magnanimity in sparing the wronged husband's pride.

My whole life was made up of unimportant trifles cleverly blown up into acts of daring.

When I saw that my life was a sort of intaglio or relief in reverse, its hollows became as terrible as abysses. In the process known as damascening the patterns are engraved on a steel plate and inlaid with gold. In me there is no gold.

Being abandoned and left to be brought up as an orphan was a birth that was different from but not any worse than most. Childhood among the peasants whose cows I tended was much the same as any other childhood. My youth as a thief and prostitute was like that of all who steal or prostitute themselves, either in fact or in dream. My visible life was nothing but carefully masked pretences. Prisons I found rather motherly—more so than the dangerous streets of Amsterdam, Paris, Berlin and Barcelona. In jail I ran no risk of getting killed or dying of hunger; and the corridors were at once the most erotic and the most restful places I've ever known.

The few months I spent in the United States with the Black Panthers are another example of how my life and my books have been misinterpreted. The Panthers saw me as a rebel—unless there was a parallel between us that none of us suspected. For their movement was a shifting dream about the doings of Whites, a poetical revolt, an "act," rather than a real attempt at radical change.

Once these thoughts were admitted, others followed. If my life was really hollow although it was seen in relief; if the Black Movement was regarded as a sort of impersonation both by America and by me; and if I entered into it as simply and naïvely as I've described and was accepted without demur—then it was because I was recognized as a natural sham.

And when the Palestinians invited me to go and stay in Palestine, in other words in a fiction, weren't they too more or less openly recognizing me as a natural sham? Even if I risked annihilation by being present at actions of theirs which were only shams, wasn't I already non-existent because of my own hollow non-life?

I thought about this, sure that America and Israel were in no danger from a sham, from defeats presented as victories, withdrawals as advances—in short, from a shifting dream floating over the Arab world, capable only of such unsubtle acts as killing a plane-load of passengers. By agreeing to go first with the Panthers and then with the Palestinians, playing my rôle as a dreamer inside a dream, wasn't I just one more factor of unreality inside both movements? Wasn't I a European saying to a dream, "You are a dream—don't wake the sleeper!"

Scarcely had this thought occurred to me than I saw Bonaparte trembling on the bridge at Arcola; the Five Hundred outlawing him; Bonaparte passing out. What marshal was it who was really behind the victory at Austerlitz? I saw David painting Napoleon's mother at his coronation though she wasn't there. And wasn't he forced to crown himself because the Pope wouldn't knuckle under? Aren't the memoirs written on St. Helena one great hollow portrayed as a relief?

But from these thoughts there emerged another: all that we know of men, whether famous or not, may only have been invented to hide the abysses of which life is made up. In that case the Palestinians were right to set up the Potemkin camps, the camps of the young lions—though their wretched guns served to reveal rather than conceal them. Is the event that shows someone for what he is a sort of epic eruption, a fleeting upsurge of depths, of hollows that people as well as individuals shrink from admitting?

Perhaps the abjectness of the natural sham lifts him high enough to be seen permanently sticking up out of the lava. Another freak of nature.

Not only seeing oneself, but also touching, hearing and smelling oneself is part of the horror—and under it the joy—of becoming a freak. Escape from the world at last! Changing sex doesn't consist merely in subjecting one's body to a few surgical adjustments: it means teaching the whole world, forcing upon it, a change of syntax. Wherever you go people will address you as "Madame" or "Mademoiselle"; they'll stand aside to let you go first, the driver will hand you out of your cab; when you hear "Women and children first!" you'll know that you'll be put in a lifeboat while the male passengers of the *Titanic* will go to the bottom. You see yourself in the mirror with your hair in a chignon or an Eton crop—your fingers will touch it. Your first fragile high heels will break and leave you aghast. (The adjectives describing you in French ought henceforth to be feminine.) Your still unadjusted right hand will move to hide an erection no longer possible.

Not everyone will really be surprised by the various changes—hormonal, surgical or of habit—but all will inwardly salute your successful metamorphosis. Or in other words your heroism in having made the attempt, been ready to brave scandal and see it through till you die. Transsexuals are heroines. In our devotions they speak familiarly with saints, martyrs and criminals of both sexes, and with heroes and heroines. And the haloes of heroes are as surprising as those of transsexuals. If he doesn't die, anyone who becomes a hero carries a lighted candle around on his head for the rest of his life, night and day.

Our transsexuals come in all sizes. Madame Meilland was small compared with Mata Hari. A lot of fedayeen are heroes.

Mubarak walked along beside me as muscular, black, scarred and obscure as ever, but said nothing. Without putting it into so many words, Abu Omar had told me what my rôle was to be here.

"Your job will be a difficult one: don't do anything."

I'd understood this to mean I was to be there, listen but say nothing, look on, agree or seem not to understand. With the fedayeen I was to play the old codger; with the Palestinians someone from the north. And everyone else was as tactful as I was. It was here that I first used the word "mole" in the sense of someone infiltrated to supply intelligence to the enemy.

On various occasions fedayeen passing through Ajloun asked me such pointed questions I wondered if they thought I was a mole. It sometimes struck me they feared so, but my embarrassment was short lived. Even if the chiefs did have doubts about me, they sent me such handsome and agreeable young fedayeen I looked on it as a sort of tribute, a gift labelled "Look at this face for a couple of hours and be happy."

Mubarak went straight to the point.

"You're going to write a book, but you'll have trouble getting it published. The French aren't interested in the Arabs. Maybe a bit in the Palestinians, because they accuse us of continuing the genocide of the Jews in southern Lebanon. But secretly your country and England, the two most anti-Semitic countries in the world, approve of us. Only in secret, though. So you've got just a faint chance of being read—if your style is urgent and swift. I'll give you a simile. A puny child is supposed to take cod-liver oil. The sound of his mother's voice can make him smile and swallow spoonful after spoonful of the horrible stuff—empty the whole bottle. If you become their mother your readers will go along with you. Speak in a voice that's sweet but inexorable."

"An iron voice in a velvet glove?"

"It's natural enough you shouldn't understand the Arabs. But you ought to be able to get round the French . . ."

He suggested I write a film for him to direct.

"Are you an Arab or a Negro?"

"You're right—I'd need a point of view, and I haven't got one."

Between 1970 and 1982 I only went to the cinema once. I forgot the film and its images straight away, but I remember the evening itself as like one a tourist might spend in Bangkok in the hands of a masseur.

I was received by a cross between an armchair and a bed, with a back that sank deliciously as the seat rose to meet my elbows. I felt myself falling, horrified, into a voluptuous trap. Someone switched off the lights. My body was being buried in a bed of ashes that turned it into that of a *nouveau riche*, perhaps an emir—I fleetingly remembered being told as a schoolboy how St. Louis, out of humility, insisted on dying on a bed of ashes. My eyes, too, were regaled. The camera-cameriera leapt up cliffs and down precipices to show me among my cinders the eggs and nest of an ordinary blue swallow. It ought to have been a treat for someone poor, but I shot up and went to sit on some steps, hoping that at least my backside would be reminded of the rough school bench.

But even the steps were soft, and my eyes, used to exploring the whole of a still photo at their own pace, were having the details thrust upon them. I got up and left.

The magic screen with its zooms and its cranes would enchant the audience with the death of the Palestinians. But there were other reasons for their defeat than the fedayeen's desire to show the West a good profile.

Mubarak listened to me.

"What do you think of *The Bridge on the River Kwai*?"

"No one who didn't see the British fighting the Japanese after they were defeated can make comparisons with extras picked up in Soho."

"What about art?"

"No opinions on the subject."

"The starving have pleasures you'll never know. Fancy dying of hunger to provide you lot with photographs. But photos can be very useful. They can reflect you when you're too ugly in the glass. Have you ever wondered what your reflection thinks of you when your back's turned?"

"Do you want me to start disliking myself?"

"You used to be in the audience, and now you're backstage. That's why you came from Paris. But you'll never be an actor."

The isotope that had been walking beside me must have died. I couldn't feel any more radiations.

I don't know whether I was going to say that I couldn't wait, or that I couldn't bear, to see.

But Mubarak was gone.

Famous landscapes—the Pyramids, the Alhambra, Delphi, the desert—are supposed to be marked by the contemplation of all who have admired them. Lieutenant Mubarak's ways seemed marked by his having been too much admired.

Perhaps I was the only one who saw it that way, but he struck me as introducing into those chaste and modest bases a flirtatiousness aimed at everyone and everything. He deployed all his powers to charm young or old. But none of the fedayeen was susceptible to his studied presentation of his own form and features —eyes, smile, teeth, hair—perhaps because they all possessed the same advantages, modestly unexercised. So he knew I was the only one who was disturbed—slightly—by his presence. Especially when we got lost in the woods.

He was well aware of this, and when he sat down on the grass he did so in such a way as to show off his thighs. As we walked along he would turn aside, still talking, unbutton his flies, urinate, button up again, and hold out his hand and offer me a cigarette. The Palestinians might well, as they said in Arabic, have "let water" in the bushes, but not one of them would ever have offered anyone a cigarette with the same hand that had just taken out his penis, held it, and tucked it away again.

Mubarak was so obviously both a pimp—a barracks or red-light district ponce—and a whore that I could never make out what he was doing among the fedayeen or why he'd ever left the Sudan. Like many another he had been a student at Montpellier.

"Were you just having me on when you blamed me for the Pompidou government?"

A suave smile.

"When I see a new face, especially a white one, I can't help trying to make an impression."

He could hardly have passed unnoticed with his tribal scars and his face as black and shiny as patent-leather shoes.

Then for two or three months he was nowhere to be seen.

Perhaps he'd gone back to being one of Numeiri's officers. I hoped so. His desire to charm prevented him from being sufficiently implacable.

So here's how I first met Hamza.

Irbid near the Syrian frontier put up a better resistance than places like Amman, and the Palestinian camp on its outskirts fought better and longer than any other in Jordan. This was thought to be due to its geographical position near the border, which made the supply of arms, ammunition and food easier. A plausible but only a partial explanation.

After Israel occupied Golan the dangers to which the people on the border were exposed made them go in for more egotism and less solidarity. The notion of patriotism came in very convenient here.

"After all, we're Syrians, not Jordanians or Palestinians. And our country's threatened not only by Tsahal but also by Pan-Arabism in Damascus, Cairo and Baghdad. We must be on our guard. In other words, neutral."

Perhaps this common sense approach was behind Hafez

el-Assad's policy of "humbling the pride of the Palestinians and re-creating a Greater Syria."

How does a country, a homeland, come into being? For a long while Flanders was independent, then it became a Burgundian, Batavian or French province, and finally a sovereign kingdom that produced a new type of person: the Belgian. But what does it mean to be a Belgian? Or a Jordanian? Or a Palestinian? Or even a Syrian, after twenty-five years under a French mandate and five hundred years of Turkish occupation?

As for the people of Irbid, the explanation of their endurance was their courage, the layout of their defences, and above all the shrewdness of the Palestinian leaders, who knew better and faster than their counterparts in Amman and Jerash the day if not the hour when Hussein's Circassians and Bedouin would attack. And they'd built up such ample stocks of water, flour and oil that some provisions even survived the entry of the Bedouin troops.

I was shown an English translation of the order the Bedouin were given: Attack at four in the morning at the Maxime round-about. I was told the order came from the Palace.

You can't deny the bravery of the men and women of Irbid, or the defensive genius of their leaders. But if you apply such words to Irbid you have to deny them to Amman, which surrendered much sooner.

Lack of imagination on the part of the leaders, panic and indis-cipline on the part of the resistance and the population—these are mere words, the same as bravery and defensive genius. They all carry the emotional charge that invests our language whenever we try to describe something that really concerns us: we forget that what gave the words the weight they have today is the very past against which we are rebelling. We also forget that we'll al-ways need words whose meaning is shaky and uncertain.

The Palestinians will never escape the paradox that as the years and the centuries go by, words become charged with emo-tion, self-interest, scandal, contradictory events, events with dif-ferent facets. Just as capital acquires interest, so words, too, grow richer. How hard it is to bring about a revolution if you can't move those for whom you're fighting! But when you have to move them with words charged with the past—a past on the brink of tears, of tears that fascinate—then you've got your work cut out!

There were plenty of signs that the Bedouin were on their way.

But even when you know all resistance will finally be in vain, you have to resist.

One of the signs was the stream of people, dishevelled, dusty and dehydrated, fleeing along the roads from the camps at Amman, Baqa and Gaza on mules, in lorries or on foot. There was chaos in whatever administration was left: chaos both in the customs and in the police. Some Palestinian and Jordanian cops rushed to their posts, while others deliberately joined Fatah.

Some of the leaders, especially Khaled Abu Khaled, thought I wasn't safe at the Abu Bakr hotel. So they sent for a young man, who came towards us smiling.

Can anyone who's been to see *The Battleship Potemkin* fifteen or twenty times say it wasn't ever just in hopes of spotting that friendly peaceful face by the gun turret?—the face of the Russian sailor handsome enough to make the soldiers swarming down the steps halt in their tracks?

This soldier was carrying a Kalashnikov, of course, but that was so common I didn't notice. All I saw of him—or of anything, almost—was his pleasant face and black hair.

It was more than pleasant, illuminated by the certainty that the resistance at Irbid was his life's whole purpose. He was twenty, with black hair, a keffiyeh, and a just nascent moustache. He was pale—sallow, rather—despite his tan and the dust.

"Has your mother got a room free?"

"Mine."

"Tonight?"

"Tonight I'm fighting. He can have my bed."

"Take him there, then. And God protect him—he's a friend."

Abu Khaled, the Palestinian poet, shook hands with me. I never saw him again.

We could hear the sound of heavy artillery, but it was still some distance away. The guns must have been at Jerash, which in 1970 was a very small village of adobe houses near a Roman site with some columns still standing and others lying on the ground. "Roman site" says it all. Hamza insisted on carrying my bag. At first I didn't notice anything about him that I wouldn't have seen in other fedayeen: he had the same smile and cheerfulness, a voice so soft it was almost sinister, a kind of casualness and then a sudden gravity. And, like the others, he wasn't at all boastful.

"My name's Hamza."

"Mine's . . ."

"I know. Khaled told me."

"He told me your name too."

He'd gathered I knew a few words of North African Arabic, and he used them with me.

It was about noon, towards the middle of the month of Ramadan, when Muslims don't eat or drink or smoke or make love until after sunset. According to the Prophet it's with joy, not vexation or reluctance, that people should offer up a month of fasting from dawn to dusk, alleviated by nocturnal feasting. A layer of calm, almost as visible as a snowfall, covered the whole of Irbid and its Palestinian camp. Men, women and things all had a kind of detachment suggesting great peace—or a determination so steely the slightest shock might shatter it.

The material vagrancy of Islam and Islamic society, its nomadic wanderings through space and time in obedience to who knows what impulses, have been reflected in the nomadic nature of their calendar, with its changing dates for the fasting, prayer and feasting of Ramadan. Unless of course these changes symbolize some cosmic wandering we don't understand. Instead of the rigidity of Catholicism, Islam offers patterns that are always changing, on earth as in heaven.

The tension you felt near the road faded as you penetrated further into the town and the camp.

Men and women, whatever their age, were going about certain in the knowledge of where they were and what they were doing. Every act had its own value and importance, neither increased nor diminished by the proximity of the heavy artillery or of the Syrian frontier—that escape route, or trap, for fleeing Palestinians. No one knew if the frontier was open or closed. You might think it was open when it had been closed five minutes before. And vice versa.

It was October 1971, and I can vouch for the fact that the man in the street in Irbid, as well as the shopkeepers and hotel managers, were already quite obviously hostile towards the Palestinians.

"I'll find a taxi, and tomorrow you'll be in Deraa. And the day after that in Damascus."

A lot of people in the camp, probably all of them, knew Hamza. They greeted him with a word, a smile or a wink as they went by. He smiled back.

"What's your religion?"

"Haven't got one. Catholic, if you insist. And you?"

"I don't know. Muslim perhaps, but I don't know yet. At present I'm a fighter. Tonight I'll kill one or two Jordanians—fellow-Muslims, in short. Or they'll kill me."

He smiled at me as he said all this, not knowingly or with self-satisfaction at the smartness of his reply, but with shining eyes and teeth. The noise of the guns and shells was so constant it seemed part of the temperature. We went along a street where huge fellows with slight moustaches leaned against the walls with rifles in their hands. Their hair came down to their shoulders and ranged in colour from light brown to ginger. It was also curly, or rather worn in ringlets in the so-called English style. Trying to find an ever-shrinking sliver of noonday shade, they made themselves paper thin and merged into the thickness of the walls. Hamza exchanged greetings with all of them.

"They're fedayeen belonging to Saïka,* " he said.

Saïka was the name of a Palestinian organization entirely dominated by Syria. The word, uttered in the presence of those massive musketeers in their leopard-spotted uniforms and silent crêpe-soled shoes, sounded to me outrageously like "Païva."

The association, and the idea to which it gave rise in that stifling street, made me chuckle quietly. Hamza noticed.

"What are you laughing at?"

I was so surprised by the question and by my own laughter that I said:

"The heat."

It seemed to me, and to him, a satisfactory answer.

---

*An elite commando force.

Hamza, whose own haircut was conventional, didn't say much about the soldiers, except to tell me briefly of their bravery. He must have known the difference between bravery and valour. The Saïka soldiers were valiant in war, and brave to fight with their hair in long ringlets. I couldn't help imagining them waking up and drinking tea as they crimped one another's hair with curling-tongs.

But I also thought: "When they have to prove their courage in battle they'll be lions."

In 1976, at Tal-el Zaatar, they showed the other beasts they were more terrible than lions. But their victims then were the Palestinians of Fatah.

Here I shall speak of the deaths of Kamal Udwan, Kamal Nasir and Muhammad Yusif al-Najjar, three leading members of Fatah. Kamal Nasir, whom I met, was the one I liked best. The one I liked least was Kamal Udwan: his blunt questioning got on my nerves. They all did their utmost to remain anonymous, but finally their prudence almost completely relaxed.

They used to meet their friends and the newspapermen at the Strand Hotel in Beirut. I passed them several times in the street on the way to the Algerian Embassy, and they never had any escort or bodyguard. They smoked as they walked along, apparently without a care in the world.

I believe it was in the sixties that the fashion started, timidly at first and then boldly, for young men to wear their hair down to their shoulders. Any style would do, apparently: long; medium length; with a fringe; straight, black and greasy; flowing; all over the place, brown and frizzy; blonde and curly. But the femininity of the hairstyle had to be counteracted by a very manly physical stance, with as much muscle as possible both visible and latent.

This fashion, carried to extremes and even beyond in England, was born in California and grew out of the American army's reverses in Vietnam. I believe there was a sort of world flowering or spring: defeats in North Vietnam burgeoned in long hair, unisex jeans, single diamond ear-rings, Berber bracelets and necklaces, bare feet, Afro haircuts, boys with long hair and beards kissing one another in the street, marijuana and LSD smoked in public, one joint between nine or ten people, with long coils of smoke passing from one person's stomach to the open mouth of his lover and scarcely diminishing from mouth to mouth and stomach to stomach.

But here the youthful flowering was no spring: it took place in a Middle East where it was already summer, nearly autumn, and heading for a hard winter.

The security services of the PLO had stationed pairs of feda-yeen as bodyguards at the foot of the stairs and by the doors of the three leaders I'm telling you about. This is what Daoud told me:

"After dark two English-speaking hippies with fair curly hair appeared with their arms round one another's necks, laughing and exchanging kisses. They staggered up to the two guards on duty at the foot of Kamal Udwan's stairs. The guards shouted insults at the two shocking queers, who promptly showed the excellence of their training by whipping out revolvers, shooting the guards, rush-ing up the stairs and killing Kamal. Much the same thing happened at the same time to Kamal Nasir and Muhammad Yusif."

It's because of this act that Murder may be considered as one of the Fine Arts. And like all works carried out under the aegis of the Beaux-Arts, Murder deserves a medal or two.

I imagine six chests were duly decorated. Legend and circum-stantial evidence has it that six fair-haired youths were chosen for the task, and that may have been the most difficult thing about it. Not that there weren't plenty of young men with fair hair, but you had to wait for it to grow long enough to be arranged in ringlets. The part that tended to get in their eyes was cut in a fringe.

Of course some commentators claim they all had their heads shaved like parachutists, and wore wigs. Anyway, they all agreed to undergo the necessary training. To make their caresses plausi-ble, each couple had to get used to kissing and being kissed on the mouth. The muscles of their arms and legs, their agility, the inno-cence and hairlessness of their faces—all had to be brought to perfection. Above all, their voices had to sound feminine and not falsetto. Only when they were completely plausible did their navy land them silently and by night on one of the Beirut beaches.

During their training they had acquired a perfect knowledge of

Arabic, with a Palestinian or Lebanese accent, and in particular a long list of the slang words used in the foreplay of desire.

We know what happened to the three PLO leaders and one of their wives.

The six Israelis, after putting their revolvers back in their holsters, tore off their wigs (if I adopt that theory) and joined up to return, at the easy pace they'd learned from the Phalangists, to the beach. There a boat with a quiet motor would pick them up and take them back to Haifa. I can't actually describe them, but I imagine the six athletes, all curls a few minutes ago and now close shaven, proudly showing the crew how they kissed one another on the lips to shock the bodyguards into thinking they were just shameless, giggling Arab pansies. And how easily they then went ahead and killed the three Palestinian leaders.

Was theirs the pride of being Jewish—pride in not being as other men are? Newspapers all over the world described the assassination, but none of them called it terrorism on another country's sovereign territory. No, it was considered as one of the Fine Arts, deserving the relevant Order and receiving it.

There was no shortage of blonds; lots of young Sabras were of Ashkenazi origin.

Instead of having me baptized, the orphanage, even though it didn't know whether my mother was Jewish, might have had my body marked with the "shallow slandered stream." If I'd been brought up in the Talmudic faith I'd be an elderly rabbi now, all prayers and tears, slipping damp notes between the stones of the Wailing Wall. My son would be a major spy in Mossad, working in the Israeli Embassy in Paris, and my grandson would be a Mirage pilot, smiling as he dropped his bombs on West Beirut.

A stupid thought, for in that case I wouldn't be writing this book or even this page. I'd be someone else, with different thoughts and a different religion, and I'd look for my ancestors among the furriers. I'd have curls down to my chest. I'm sorry to have missed that.

The commando force sailed back to Israel. Earlier the same night, fashionably dressed, they'd come and sought out their victims' houses—probably described by other Jewish observers with Belgian passports. Divided up into three couples they'd given perfect performances as queers in love, then suddenly switched from acting to action, made their escape covered by seemingly neutral colleagues, jumped into their inflatable boat and sailed back to Haifa under the dark sky.

Why did I have to write about the murder after describing the Saïka soldiers' long hair?

As he related the episode, which he knew about only by hearsay, Daoud showed a certain admiration for its audacity and style. Such perfect execution implied the hand of a single great artist; unless it was the work of a very clever organization for whom this operation was one among many. It seemed to me that as well as admiring it he was amazed that such a swift and violent deed could be accomplished almost playfully by slaughterers with long fair corkscrew curls.

You may suppose that Israel praised the exploit in the newspapers in Jerusalem and other cities. It probably does the same thing now when it stops and sinks Palestinian boats at sea.

Six curly blonde wigs, a bit of red on the lips and black round the eyes are not much to have brought such unsuspected dismay to the streets of Beirut. The inward laughter of transvestites who never ceased feeling like men may have echoed the terror of real transvestites, afraid of being found out through their voices and gestures and using all their efforts to disguise them. But the six Israelis couldn't afford to forget for an instant that they were men, trained to kill and with muscles meant for fighting.

The strangeness of their situation lay in the gentle feminine delicacy of their movements, and their transformation from one moment to the next into the precise gestures of murderers—not murderesses. They knew how to kiss tongue on tongue, heads on one side, and penis on penis; but all that was easy and obvious. What was more difficult and took longer to learn was how to lift a hair very lightly off the beloved's brow, or flick a ladybird off his shoulder.

The rehearsals, in a street in Israel, must have taken some time. The youths had to be able to arrange the fold of a scarf and give a high-pitched laugh, then whip off the glad rags and become warriors whose one object was to kill. Really kill. Not as in the last act of a play, to applause, but for real, with dead bodies.

186 · JEAN GENET

I wonder if it isn't comparatively easy and pleasant to slip into tender femininity, and hard to throw it off to commit a crime. But heroism was involved there too. As with Charles V, abandoning his empire, his kingdoms and his oceans for the monastery at Yuste.

It took us about an hour to walk to Hamza's place. We were already starting to get used to our own brand of gibberish, which I shan't attempt to reproduce here, and were even then linked together through a code we might almost have worked out in a previous existence. We seemed to comprehend one another better than if we'd actually understood all the words we exchanged. Mistakes were neither here nor there.

The streets became more and more deserted. I thought the people were probably having lunch or taking an afternoon nap. I found out they were watching. Through the windows, from the roofs. And cleaning and oiling their guns. Getting ready.

Two men of about sixty who were squatting in a sort of barn beckoned us over to sit beside them. They held out their hands politely. Each had a Lebel rifle. Without hostility, they asked Hamza if he knew who I was.

"A friend. I've got orders to protect him."

No more questions were asked about me. I asked one of the Palestinians if I could hold his gun. Both immediately started to hand over their rifles, then, simultaneously, both drew back and first unloaded them. We all burst out laughing. I told Hamza that the name Lebel, the Handsome One, augured well for our friendship. I wrote it down, he read it first from right to left and then from left to right, then held out his hand as all Arabs do as a sign of understanding and co-operation. I took aim at a branch but didn't pull the trigger, then handed back his treasure to the man who'd lent it to me.

Both Palestinians were peasants, but those old-fashioned guns rejuvenated them, took them away from fields and harvests and back to adventure, blood and death.

They weren't imitating other people, either. Unlike their leaders, who just when they ought to have thought of some original way of marking an occasion, happy or sad, only aped the West.

The monument to the martyrs—the dead—in the camp at Beirut, made out of wood and cheesecloth and one little light bulb always burning, struck me as moving in its poverty. But Alfredo, the Cuban doctor, was sent to Europe not only to raise money but also to find some marble or perhaps granite hard enough to make a statue like a First World War memorial in France.

"I'm hungry," I said to Hamza after we'd left the two men. "Aren't you?"

"Wait a while."

"I could buy a tin of something."

"Wait."

We were walking in the sun again. The camp was below, and the road sloped downward. When we came to a little white wall with a white-painted door in it, Hamza took a key out of his pocket and let us into a small courtyard, locking the door again afterwards.

Outside the room which I later found out was her bedroom stood a Palestinian woman dressed in the sort of gown she'd have worn back in Haifa. She was smiling, and she had a gun. She must have been about forty. The gun slung over her shoulder was the same as Hamza's. He greeted his mother in Arabic. She went on smiling, and wearing her gun. Her introduced me, still in Arabic.

"A friend."

She brushed my hand with her fingertips.

"A friend, but a Christian."

She had withdrawn her hand, but went on looking at me, smiling still as if amused.

"A friend. A Christian. But he doesn't believe in God."

Hamza had spoken gravely but very gently. She let her smile play—actively—over both our faces, then turned to her son and, still with a smile which seemed the faint echo and only visible sign of a great peal of laughter filling her whole being, said:

"Well, if he doesn't believe in God I'd better give him something to eat."

She went into her room and Hamza took me into his. The family had fled from Haifa after it was bombed, and eventually found refuge in Irbid. In 1949 the camp still consisted of patched-up tents. Then it became a shanty town, with walls and roofs made of sheets of aluminium, corrugated iron and bits of cardboard, just as wretched as the camp at Baqa.

No sooner had I written and read over the above than I realized it portrays only one aspect of the truth about Baqa. For where else would you find such cheerfulness as gathered together on clear days on the slopes of that pitiless mountain, almost silent but for the children? If I looked closely at the weak points in the fabric of the tents, I could see some of them were reinforced with very strange materials—perhaps a strip torn from a blouse from Limoges which had reached here via Beirut or Irbid or Amman. Clumsy shapes shuffled about among the tents, their shoes probably still unlaced.

Half or three-quarters of an hour's work in the little infirmary donated to Baqa by a popular charity in France, and the whole newly awakened camp would laugh. Fruit and vegetables would be spread out, and real—not plastic—flowers. The red, pink, green and yellow of the fruit and vegetables, their colours and their substance, were rich and real there. The sun was rising in the sky, the kids were starting to play. The slightest thing would make them burst out laughing, the same as in Lisbon.

It's true, what I said just now about sadness in the camps. No Palestinian, falling asleep, saw his own poverty: just before he switched out the light he counted up his mandarins and aubergines. By the time he woke up he'd thought of a new way of arranging them: the colours would look better in alternate bands rather than in pyramids. Every misfortune was soon cancelled out in this mental catalogue: the dreary atmosphere disappeared from the camp, and the sadness from the people's faces. And gradually, as the families there worked at any jobs they could get wherever they could get them, scrap metal was replaced by concrete.

Hamza showed me his bed, where I was to sleep that night.

"I'll be on duty. I'm a junior officer." (I seem to remember he was in charge of about ten or twelve fedayeen.)

He showed me a hole in the floor by the head of the bed.

"If Hussein's artillery and machine-guns get too close, get my mother and sister and take them down into the shelter. We keep three guns there."

His mother came in and put a tray on the little table. Two plates heaped with pancakes, together with a few lettuce leaves, some quartered tomatoes, four sardines and, I think, three hard-boiled eggs.

They ate them, Hamza and the godless Christian, at about three in the afternoon in the month of Ramadan, when the sun had scarcely started to sink in the sky.

I can still see the sky-blue of the little table and its black and yellow flowers, just as I can the details of everything else my eyes and those of the fedayeen once rested on: rocks, trees, fields, the fabric of tents from close to or far away, fir trees, still water, running water, water dark and stagnant. From the twinge of melancholy I feel if ever it leaves me, I know this emotion will never cease to exist. Even if I myself am shot dead it will still go on, felt by someone there, and after him by another, and so on.

Unless, of course, they flood the whole place. Then the eye will rest only on a lake or a dam and Israeli fishermen.

Hamza and his mother would never see Haifa again.

After lunch, Hamza took me into the school yard. The classrooms were empty. All the children were in the playground, groups of Palestinian kids talking about the approach of the Jordanian artillery without either boasting or fear. They all had one or two pairs of grenades slung over their shoulders or tied to their belts, and an Algerian teacher who spoke French told me that none of the boys would sleep that night. They'd be waiting for the moment to take the pins out of their grenades and toss them at the Bedouin soldiers.

In this book and in other places I've often spoken of the simple bravery of the Palestinians. Certainly there were fears, tremblings, shrinkings from death. Certainly there were weaknesses: legs often wilted at the sight of heaps of gold or the sound of new banknotes, like the click of 1920s court shoes. The desire for power is so great that it takes great courage to resist it. But I witnessed only one failure.

A little while back I spoke of courage with reference to the physical struggle of the Palestinians, applying the word to mental effort and energy. But the word bravery is more suitable for physical defiance of death and danger. The Palestinians, by challenging the contempt implied in the words terrorism and terrorist, and by their indifference to the fact of being cast as the devil, showed both courage and bravery.

How can one accuse the fedayeen of being afraid? Apart from the night of panic I've attempted to describe and explain—only attempted, for I wasn't there—it was all like a kind of game. You saw death—for it was visible then—hovering over you and the enemy, uncertain which to choose. Revolution became quite an amusing sport. A fight to the death, yours or the other's, for land either here or there. If when you lose the game you lose your life, is it such a serious matter, since when you lose you have to pay up with a smile?

But do people get themselves killed to win land, or only to gain victory?

In the great Gallery in Milan, where two covered passages meet, there's a mosaic floor. One small part of the simple pattern has been worn away. It depicts the testicles of a horse, Colleone's horse—the name means "The Well-Hung," more or less. No pair of citizens strolling there ever forgets you have to grind your heel on that part of the mosaic in order to acquire some of the stallion's virility. Three or four men, arm in arm, doing this, remind you of a minuet. No woman has ever been allowed to do it.

The school yard had become a sort of fair-ground where every boy showed off the double or quadruple monstrous testicles he carried at his waist or over his shoulder. But what was at once obscene and innocent was their metallic nakedness.

My hands were attracted by their roundness. The boys, already bold fighters, talked of nothing but war, in accents much more grandiose than those of the fedayeen.

Did the fedayeen think of something else, something precise? Of a woman's thighs, for instance? Or of other places chosen regardless of reason?—hair, eyes, breasts, private parts, buttocks. Or were they lost in a mist of diffused desire, and each pure as an angel? Could you be so close to death and have no desire to transmit life, or to enjoy what you still have but what a moment from now will be no more? The apparent absence of sexual desire was quite out of keeping with the ordinary life of strong young males.

You sometimes read, in romantic contexts, of heroes betrothed to death. Orgasm is a very masculine noun in French, but it's scuppered by such feminine nouns as death-agony, death, woman and war. They have the last word.

Between the verticals of the letter H, between the carved uprights of the Arc de Triomphe, the straddled legs of the fedayeen and the downstrokes of Hamza's name, there ought to be a parade of victorious battalions, followed by guns and tanks.

Hamza and I were in his mother's house. That seems to suggest that his mother was the head of the family. But having seen her with her son, and remembering the looks they constantly exchanged, I can guess now what their then imperceptible communications really meant. She was a widow, but very strong; a mother armed exactly like her son; and in fact the head of the family. But every microsecond she smilingly delegated her powers to Hamza. And he, while taking orders from Fatah, left her in command and was secretly guided by her.

Remember the Black Virgin of Montserrat, showing her son as greater than herself, as taking precedence of her so that she might exist, and of the child so that he might live for ever.

This wasn't—and I realized it as soon as my hand felt the weight and shape of the first bullet—just any old thing, like filling a basket with aubergines. Loading Hamza's and his brother-in-law's gun meant that for the first time I was taking part in the mysteries of the resistance. That night the bullets I'd put in the cartridge clips would be in guns aimed at Bedouin soldiers.

A sliver of moon appeared, heralding the end of Ramadan. The white courtyard was dark. Hamza and his brother-in-law left me alone with the two women. He didn't mind trusting me in this way, perhaps because he had confidence in Khaled's assurance that I was a friend. Or perhaps he was concentrating all his attention on what lay in front of him: defending Irbid. Or—but it was probably the same thing—risking his life.

I've been told here (in Beirut) that the CIA and Mossad, sometimes allies and sometimes rivals, are good at cajoling and even winning over captured fedayeen. This suggests that both the CIA and Mossad have some sensitive agents. The fighters refuse at first to say anything, and are even ready to die under torture. But when things are explained to them artistically, poetically, they eventually speak. They ought to be warned against Israel's poetry and charm.

The fact that the Virgin Mary is called the Mother of God makes you wonder, since the chronological order is the same for parenthood human and divine, by what prodigy or by what mathematics the mother came after her Son but preceded her own Father. The order becomes less mysterious when you think of Hamza.

The sound of guns and mortars had got nearer, answered by bursts of machine-gun fire and odd rifle-shots from the fedayeen in Irbid.

I lay fully dressed on Hamza's bed, listening to the noise of battle. It grew less regular but remained just as deafening and apparently close.

Then in the midst of this aural chaos two little reports from nearby seemed to hurl the din of destruction back. I suddenly realized they were two peaceful taps at the door of my room. While iron and steel exploded in the distance, a knuckle was banging on wood a few feet away. I didn't answer, partly because I didn't know how to say "Come in" in Arabic yet. But mainly because, as I said, I'd only just realized what had happened.

The door opened, light from the starry sky came into the room, and behind it I could see a tall shadow. I half-closed my eyes, pretending I was asleep, but through my lashes I could see everything. The mother had just come in. Was she taken in by my pretence? Had she come out of the now ear-splitting darkness, or out of the icy night I carry about with me everywhere? She was carrying a tray, which she put down on the little blue table with yellow and black flowers, already mentioned. She moved the table near the head of the bed, where I could reach it. Her movements were as precise as a blind man's in daylight. Without making a sound she went out and shut the door. The starry sky was gone, I could open my eyes. On the tray were a cup of Turkish coffee and a glass of water. I drank them, shut my eyes and waited, hoping I hadn't made any noise.

Another two little taps at the door, just like the first two. In the light of the stars and the waning moon the same long shadow appeared, as familiar now as if it had come into my room at the same time every night of my life before I went to sleep. Or rather so familiar that it was inside rather than outside me, coming into me with a cup of Turkish coffee every night since I was born. Through my lashes I saw her move the little table silently back to its place and, still with the assurance of someone born blind, pick up the tray and go out, closing the door.

My one fear was that my politeness might not be up to hers—that some movement of my hands or legs might have betrayed my pretence. It all happened so smoothly that I realized the mother came every night with a cup of coffee and a glass of water for Hamza. Without a sound, except for four little taps at the door, and in the distance, as in a picture by Detaille, gunfire against a background of stars.

Because he was fighting that night, I'd taken the son's place and perhaps played his part in his room and his bed. For one night and for the duration of one simple but oft-repeated act, a man older than she was herself became the mother's son. For "before she was made, I was." Though younger than I, during that familiar act she was my mother as well as Hamza's. It was in my own personal and portable darkness that the door of my room opened and closed. I fell asleep.

In 1970, and again in 1984, the population of Jordan presented amusing disparities. The largest and most downtrodden element were and still are the Palestinians. Then, more powerful but fewer, came the Bedouin community, the tribes and families of soldiers devoted to King Hussein. Last and above all the rest, the Circassians, almost entirely made up of generals and senior officers, leading government officials, ambassadors and advisers to the king. And these three orders were of course crowned by the royal family itself, with the king, who claimed to be directly descended from the Prophet, just about managing to control an ill-assorted household in which the official wives were in turn either Egyptian, English, Palestinian, or half Jordanian and half American, with broods of children enough to puzzle the shrewdest genealogist.

There are some fifty thousand Circassians in the kingdom. They obey and also rule the king. They are a gang of which Hussein is not the boss.

"To whom could we owe greater loyalty than to King Hussein, a direct descendant of the Prophet?" the head of a leading Circassian family said to me once. He showed me his village in Jordan, one of the well-watered sites chosen by the Benedictines in the Middle Ages to build their cloisters and cultivate the land.

"We fled from the Tsars," he said, "because they wanted to convert us to the Christianity they have the cheek to call Orthodox. Sultan Abdul Hamid took us in, and we're still grateful to him for all the land he granted us. It wasn't poverty or love of adventure that drove us out of Russia and our mountains. We still have our riches—our material wealth and our language. I could show you our saddles embroidered with vermilion and gold thread, our gold and silver stirrups and spurs, our gold-brocaded boots."

He didn't show me them, but he gave me a detailed description.

His was a peaceful people, he told me.

"But what about your language? It's so different from Arabic. It's said you use it as a secret language."

"Secret?"

"The Circassians are the only ones who speak it, among all the Arabic and modern European languages. That makes your people a band of confederates."

"We are a peaceful people."

"Which people nowadays say they aren't peaceful?"

"Yes, peace is fashionable at the moment."

"In 1860, adventure was in fashion, and cavalcades, and the famous Circassian dancing."

"Yes, we were quite in the fashion then, too."

But there was something amiss with the peaceful picture he drew for me: the ardour, the weapons and the war, the horses, the music and dancing and singing, the courtly love and the reserve towards women that made it impossible for a man to so much as touch the cap or apron of one of the opposite sex in public. The mother-in-law, especially, was put on such a pedestal she sounded to me like the most inaccessible of Beloveds.

But the description was so eloquent and minute it struck me as invented and mechanical. That was all anyone was supposed to know about the Circassians, and with the same official certainty with which we know Richelieu was a cardinal.

The paterfamilias referred several times to all the wealth they were supposed to have left behind—he actually made this slip—in the Caucasus. I got the impression that the Circassians went over to Abdul Hamid in quest of land and easy conquests, and perhaps in order to be able to settle permanently and tame or subdue the Bedouin tribes.

"How was it it took you such a short time to dominate the region, establish your authority and get strategic control?"

He smiled kindly, and I noticed how well his trim white moustache went with his straight white hair.

"Because we're the best," he said.

"You haven't been very good to the Palestinians."

"Savages! Mere savages who wanted to seize power!"

"But you've got the power and you're holding on to it. You came from Russia by choice when the Palestinians were driven from their homes."

"Let them fight against Israel! You talk about them like a Frenchman of the left. Jordan wants to be left in peace."

If anyone had dared utter the word treachery they'd probably have been so outraged they'd have killed him. But that's the word I use. After they left Russia the Circassians went over to the enemy, the Ottoman Empire. And when the last Caliph went into exile and the Empire shrank within the limits of Turkey, they offered their services first to Glubb Pasha and then to Hussein. I can't feel any sympathy for them: they always offered themselves to whoever was in power. They were driven by the need to dominate, and the brazenness of their actions repelled me and filled me with a kind of disgust. I'll come back to them again later.

"What about the Sursok family?"

"Friends. Not all of them, of course—there are a few black sheep. But although they're Christians they're our friends. They're rich."

"The way they got rich wasn't very edifying."

"You mean selling their villages to the Jews? Every land-owner's done it."

Hamza returned at dawn, covered in dust, weary eyed, smiling happily. He stowed his gun away in the shelter by the bed.

"Congratulations, kid," he said, addressing a military salute to the entrance to the cellar. "You shot well tonight. I appoint you gun of the first class."

He laughed. The two friends who were with him remained serious. He lay down and probably fell straight asleep.

I went into the mother's room, intending just to drop in and say goodbye. She smiled. She was crouching on the floor, knead-ing the dough for that evening's bread, but rose and made me some tea. Water hadn't been rationed that night. The town had put up a good defence. The people were obviously proud of them-selves. Unlike Paris in 1940, Irbid had held out.

"The Syrian frontier's open."

Everyone in Irbid knew at once. I decided to leave as soon as the first collective taxi was ready. Meanwhile I spent two or three hours walking through the as yet undamaged streets.

The face of the town changed in just a few minutes: it seemed to me its pride disappeared with the rising of the sun. As the light grew stronger, so did the anxiety on people's faces. They looked at each other in silence, almost with hostility, suspicion. From being a town that was happy and proud of itself, Irbid became a gloomy place where the leaders bossed their subordinates about. It was rumoured that Israeli spies were moving about freely there, some of them women.

A young woman journalist, a Swiss, asked to be driven near the battle zone, and her driver found she had a medal in the form of a Star of David among her things. Before he could accuse her, she accused him. The police found out the truth: the journalist really was Swiss, and a Christian, and the driver was an agent provoca-teur. They roughed him up a bit and smuggled the girl across the Syrian frontier. But there were other reports of spies.

The nervousness was probably fuelled by the fact that the

town was encircled: the Bedouin were approaching under the command of the Circassians, and there was an increasingly convincing rumour that the customs post was in the hands of the Jordanians.

There was a great commotion among the Palestinian leaders. I was there long enough to see military chiefs replaced by political officials, of the same age and with the same manners as European politicians. They were self-important, sure of the orders they were about to give and thus of their own intelligence. They were convinced they were the best and shrewdest of negotiators. They drove up to HQ sitting on the right of their drivers, wearing hastily knotted ties (but still wearing ties) and leapt out of their seats almost before their cars drew to a stop. Then they drove their way through the fedayeen and shot straight up to the senior officers.

Does every revolution have some grey beards and white hair in reserve to deal with a setback? From the light on the ancients' eyes I could see that the "flower of youth" were going to be saved at last by the old men, who would accept compromises where the young men wanted to fight.

I don't know if it was because of the distance or rather the strangeness of the Muslim world, but when I was in the midst of it during the desert of Ramadan, when cigarettes had disappeared from men's mouths and smiles with them, surrounded and jostled as I was by Islamic ill-humour waiting for night, I kept remembering parables from the New Testament. But I interpreted them in my own way.

The Catholic Church is the incarnation of authority and Biblical morality, and any representative of those superpowers was my enemy. In the story of the tribute money the Church, contrary to the spirit of the Gospel, has interpreted "Render unto Caesar the things that are Caesar's, and unto God the things that are God's" as "Submit to the political powers that be."

But what the young joker who made fun of the poor fig-tree really said to the apostle was this: "Don't play the fool and attract the attention of the cops. We'll pray, and my Father will soon do the necessary. Just pay the official his money and make tracks."

The great thing was not to attract attention, to make my trip to the Middle East seem quite ordinary, just a rather lengthy visit. I'm talking about the trip I made in July 1984. To try, very discreetly, to find Hamza's mother.

So I'd take a bath, or at least wash my feet, shave and put on a clean shirt, imparting some seriousness to the journey instead of coming and going like Jesus with his layabout's vocabulary: "Behold, I come as a thief."

It wasn't out of modesty or delicacy that I dressed conventionally, but in the hope of domesticating to some extent the dread Failure. I admit I was superstitious. Would I have dared to walk under a ladder? But I believed in the punitive power of the ladder, not in that of God.

Near the travel agent's office some very young men in civilian clothes, without any visible signs of belonging to the forces, were putting their names down to go to Deraa or Damascus. They were paying for a seat in the first taxi to leave.

General Hafez el-Assad had just brought off his *coup d'état* in Syria. Tanks said to have come from Damascus to help the Palestinians held back from crossing the Syrian frontier, despite the fact that it wasn't effectively defended.

The Iraqi army was bolder. One day it crossed the frontier in the morning and crossed back again at another point in the evening, without making it clear who was being threatened: the Syrians, the Jordanians, the Palestinians or the inaccessible Israelis.

The Palestinians were now on their own. Three Arab countries had just let them down flat. Sinai, the Golan Heights and the West Bank of the Jordan were occupied by Israel, and the only countries who showed the least loyalty to them were the Gulf States and above all King Faisal.

And it wasn't much comfort to hear that members of the Palestinian resistance, including Dr. Habash, were still being held in Syrian prisons.

The so far safe territory of Jordan was shrinking literally by the hour. I heard Mafraq had fallen. Hamza, in bed but awake, threw me a smile. I believe it was then I realized he smiled through his teeth rather than his eyes.

"You'll have to leave this morning."

It was nearly eleven o'clock. I said goodbye to his mother and sister. They were getting food ready for the coming evening and night, one for her son and the other for her husband.

And as it's part of my memories of 1970, I must add that it was in the toilet in that little Palestinian house that I learned to do without paper and clean myself with the bottle of water provided. As I'd already eaten and drunk there, I was now really one of its inmates.

Hamza had no identification on him except, in his pocket, the little rounded blue-green card that every fedayee carried. There was one seat left in the front of the taxi—next to the door, not the driver—and Hamza took it for me. He insisted on paying my fare to Damascus.

We said goodbye. Counting it up exactly, we'd been together and talked for almost exactly seven hours. Khaled Abu Khaled had given me into his care the previous day about noon, and this morning I was parting from him at about eleven.

The taxi drove out of Irbid. I couldn't see the road for a white patch that came between me and it: the back of a coloured photograph of King Hussein fixed to the windscreen with four bits of sticking plaster. The driver had taken it out of the glove compartment and stuck it on to the curved glass. The faint transparency of the king's thin moustache and self-satisfied smile got on my nerves.

"The Palestinians accept the Americans' victory without turning a hair."

As no one in the taxi showed any sign of surprise I must have said it to myself. The driver's face wasn't visible, but under his black and white keffiyeh you could see the glint of his black moustache, eyebrows and glasses.

At that stage of the resistance it was already being said that Hussein was being helped by the American menace. I was filled with rage when I read something he'd said or was supposed to have said in a French-language newspaper:

"I'm the biggest loser in this [1967] war. A third of my kingdom is occupied by Israel, and I may never get it back."

He probably said it as if it stood to reason: Jordan was his property. The Bedouin king owned a huge garden stretching from the Red Sea to the Syrian frontier, and a gang of good-for-nothing Palestinians had broken in to steal his cherries and oranges. They had to be driven out with their backsides full of lead.

Without checking to see if there was any truth in the story, the Palestinians went round telling everyone they'd seen a photograph of Hussein taken with Golda Meir.

"Where?"

"On her yacht."

"Where's the photo?"

"Top secret."

"One of Mossad's practical jokes. If the photo really existed it would have been reproduced all over the world."

Think of the publicity the two accomplices, Begin and Sharon, gave Bechir Gemayel when he was foolish enough to have dinner with them both.

The king's career was only what you'd expect. His great-grandfather was the Emir of Mecca, showered with gold by the English. His grandfather was king of Transjordan (later Jordan), and was assassinated by a Palestinian member of the Husseini family as he left the El Aqsa mosque in Jerusalem. His father, Talal, an enemy of Glubb and the British, is said to have died insane in a nursing home in Switzerland.

"So I've got to be driven by this chap, a coward because he seems to be running away, but bold enough to flaunt a picture of the king at passengers who hate him."

So I must have thought, forgetting that the picture also served as a *laissez-passer* for us all.

The American music on the radio faded down slightly behind an announcement that Irbid had just surrendered.

We were approaching the frontier post held by the Jordanian customs and police.

The people and fedayeen of Irbid had put up a "gallant resistance," but shown "more courage than tactical skill."

One of the other passengers translated this tribute into English for me from the glib Arabic of a Circassian general.

But honour does not necessarily reside in death, nor dishonour in flight. The Prophet himself pretended to leave Mecca via the south in order to mislead his pursuers, then suddenly turned north towards Medina. The holy trick gave its name to an era which is already fifteen hundred years old: Hegira, the Flight.

Some of the fedayeen hid their weapons in Irbid and went to Syria, while others took refuge in the Golan, neither Syrian nor Israeli for a few more years. But none of these escapes, however closely examined, could be said to have had any effect on the war, though taken all together they constitute a stain on the resistance.

It was a painful episode, and the Palestinians were jeered at in the French and Israeli press and the Western press in general.

The passengers in the taxi sat in embarrassed silence all the way from Irbid to the frontier. No one was detained at the customs, not one case was opened. The policeman and customs officers struck me as even exaggeratedly polite, and none of them showed any surprise at my French passport.

The taxi driver set off again, then suddenly stopped in the neutral zone, about a hundred metres wide, between the two countries. He took the photograph of King Hussein, still smiling, down off the windscreen, opened the glove compartment and put it inside, then took out a coloured photograph of Yasser Arafat and stuck it up on the windscreen with the same four bits of sticking plaster. Neither he nor any of the passengers batted an eyelid.

"There's probably an informer among us," I thought.

I'm no expert on medieval or Renaissance art, but I do know that the earlier *pietà* were carved out of hard, knotty wood, which was supposed not to rot. When the group was finished the artist would paint it, just as prisoners in French jails still paint lead soldiers. Similar figures were later hewn out of blocks of marble: a gaunt naked corpse with pierced hands and feet and its head and chest resting on the knees of a woman. All you could see of her was her hands and the oval of her face; all the rest was covered with draperies, more or less skilfully and pleasingly disposed according to the artist and the period.

Such groups, painted or carved, may be said to have invaded

Christendom between, say, the Carolingians and Michelangelo. While the face of the corpse in these compositions is usually quite calm—though sometimes it may seem shadowed by the memory of the suffering on the cross—the face of the woman shows great sorrow, with eyes bent down over the dead man and deep furrows on either side of the drooping mouth. The woman, the Virgin Mary, usually looks older than the man whose body rests almost entirely on her knees, but some groups show her as a virgin mother younger than her dead son. Occasionally this youthfulness is the result of the long and ardent kisses bestowed on it by generations of believers. The kisses have smoothed away the wrinkles from the face of bronze, copper, silver, marble or ivory, thus producing four hundred years ago a miracle of rejuvenation now performed by plastic surgery.

The taxi took the road to Deraa. Apparently without being touched, the car radio stopped giving out pop music, and what we heard now was so different in its rhythms and played on such different instruments that I was forced to listen. At first I didn't recognize it; then suddenly, almost before I remembered the name itself, I found myself thinking: Rimsky-Korsakov. That was it.

I'd left Jordan a country under surveillance. The Syria I was entering was the same.

As soon as we were out of Jordan the image of Hamza and his mother started to haunt me. It was strange: I saw Hamza alone, gun in hand, tousled and smiling, just as he'd looked when Khaled Abu Khaled introduced us. But instead of standing out against the sky or the fronts of houses, he seemed to be framed by a huge dark shadow lowering like a storm cloud, the contours—or as painters would say the values—of which suggested the vast and ponderous shape of his mother.

But if I thought of the mother herself, for example when she opened the door of my room, her son was always there too, enormous, watching over her with his gun in his hand. In the end I never imagined just one image on its own: there was always a couple, one of them seen in ordinary attitudes and realistic dimensions while the other was a gigantic presence of mythological substance and proportions. It might be summed up as an apparition of a colossal couple, one human and the other fabulous.

Of course what I've just said is an inadequate account of what happened: the images were always changing. Hamza appeared alone at first, and his hair stirred not because of the wind or because he moved his head, but so that his mother, or rather a sort of mountain resembling his mother, might suddenly appear behind him, coming neither from left nor right, above nor below.

Amid that world, that language, that people, those faces, those animals, plants and lands all exuding the spirit of Islam, what preoccupied me was a group embodying the image of the *mater dolorosa*. The mother and son, but not as Christian artists have depicted them, painted or sculptured in marble or wood, with the dead son lying across the knees of a mother younger than the son de-crucified, but one of them always protecting the other.

And that symbolic image, where one figure as soon as it came to mind inevitably summoned up the other, always hovered over its counterpart, the image still of human proportions. I'd seen Hamza and his mother for too short a time—real, chronometric time—to be sure it was always their true faces I remembered during the fourteen years I thought about them. But I did remember truly, I think, my feelings when I met them—Hamza and his mother, with her gun. Each was the armour of the other, who otherwise would have been too weak, too human.

What archetypal image was it that painters and sculptors really followed for so long, when, apparently inspired by the Gospels, they took the grief or motherhood as their subject? And above all why was it the image of that group that haunted me for fourteen years as persistently as an enigma? And lastly, why did I undertake a journey, not to find out the meaning of the enigma, but to see if it existed, and if so in what terms?

Which came first, the group often known as a *Pietà*, depicting the Virgin Mary and her divine Son, or some other image farther back in time and in some place other than Europe, Judea or Palestine? In India, perhaps. Or perhaps rather in every man.

And should so many precautions be taken against incest if it was committed, unknown to the Father, in the intermingled dreams of mother and son?

Perhaps it's not very important, but it is very strange, that for me the seal, the emblem of the Palestinian Revolution was never a Palestinian hero or a victory like Karameh, but that almost incongruous apparition: Hamza and his mother. That was the couple I needed, for in a way I'd cut it out to suit myself, cut it out from a continuum that included time, space, and all connections with country, family and kin.

I'd made a good job of detaching it from the universe to which it naturally belonged, selecting just the two elements I could assimilate—the mother and one of the sons—and imperiously discarding the two other sons, the daughter, the son-in-law, and probably also a family, a tribe, perhaps a whole people. For, as to the latter, I'm not sure I feel as strongly now about the nights of the Revolution as I did in 1970. But perhaps even then I was looking for the Revolution's emblem and seal, as in the seal of the Prophets in the Koran.

But why had this oft-repeated, profoundly Christian couple, symbolizing the inconsolable grief of a mother whose son was God, appeared to me like a bolt from the blue as a symbol of the Palestinian resistance? And not only that. That was understandable enough. But why did it also strike me that the Revolution took place in order that this couple should haunt me?

I haven't been back to Deraa since 1973, but it's probably still a little frontier town, now in Syria.

I went through it one evening in 1970 on my way from Damascus to Amman. What I remember about it best are two hands beating out an improvised rhythm, continually interrupted by another, on a couple of planks. It was in a house that Fatah had bought and converted into a little hospital-cum-infirmary containing eight beds.

Two fedayeen who looked like giants to me stood bareheaded in the leopard-spotted uniforms I always saw them in later, leaning over two deal boxes piled on top of one another in the passage, near the door. Their thin but tough fingers conjured a complicated but cheerful rhythm out of the wood. They were talking and laughing in voices which, though guttural and grating, gave off a certain sweetness and languor. The syllables, and especially the consonants, seemed to stick in their throats, but then to be softened as they fell out of their mouths and into the darkness.

Muhammad el-Hamchari called me.

"Our neighbours have invited us to tea."

On my way to join him I passed the two fedayeen and saw their profiles. They were beating out more and more skilful and difficult rhythms on two new deal coffins which their long thin fingers transformed into drums. A third coffin which I hadn't seen before was propped up, open, against the wall. I especially noticed the knots in the wood, perhaps so that the lugubrious atmosphere underlined by the ever merrier rhythms thumped out on the coffins should be fixed in my memory.

As we drank tea in the house next door Muhammad said:

"I brought you here because the corpses have arrived and they're just going to nail up the coffins for the funeral."

And he put down his china cup.

The first two fedayeen were so handsome I was surprised at myself for not feeling any desire for them. And it was the same the more Palestinian soldiers I met, decked with guns, in leopard-spotted uniforms and red berets tilted over their eyes, each not merely a transfiguration but also a materialization of my fantasies. And apparently at my disposal.

Perhaps that was the explanation: I wrote and perhaps thought the word "decked," but those guns weren't ornaments, they were used in earnest. The fedayeen didn't do as I told them, they didn't appear and disappear to suit my convenience. What for a long time I took to be a kind of limpidity, a total lack of eroticism, might have been due to the fact that each individual was completely autonomous. I can best express it briefly—but I shall have to come back to it—by using the word prostitution. Prostitution was absent, and so was desire.

The only thing that disturbed me was the thought that this lack of desire coincided with the "materialization" of my own amorous desires—unless, as I said, the outward reality made the inner one superfluous. That's how it had been with the Black Panthers in the United States.

"The more Palestinian soldiers I met" . . . I substituted this phrase for "The deeper I penetrated . . ." I mention the change, the avoidance of *double entendre*, to show the kind of self-censorship that hovers over me whenever I write about the Palestinians.

The sudden appearance of a flock of living, laughing, independent infantrymen left me on the brink of purity. They were like a cloud, a barricade of angels come down to keep me from the edge of an abyss: for I realized at once, with joy, that I was going to be living in a vast barracks.

My obedience to my former daydreams, rising up within as if to complement me, really was subjection. The youngest, most uncouth, most malleable of the fedayeen would have burst out laughing if he'd found out he could be desired, or in other words chosen to play at soldiers.

Perhaps, when you're lonely, when you're near death, when you risk nothing because all is lost . . . ? But it wasn't certain. Perhaps among the Palestinian soldiers I found the exact opposite of the shanty town I described above.

Have I said what happened at Ajloun, among the fedayeen? Without the battle being either known or named, we fought. We piled up slogans, questions, answers, arguments crude and subtle, but it was not like the sort of barricade you make with cobble-stones and old mattresses. (The word "barricade" conjures up a mixture of strong things, to resist, like bricks and rocks, and softer things to act as shock absorbers, like cushions and old armchairs, boxes and broken prams.) We heaped up trivialities to build our own kind of rampart—to fend off what adversary there at the back of beyond? The Devil? And all the time the feeling grew more strong that the barricade was too weak.

You have to understand that the people you call terrorists know without needing to be told that they, their persons and their ideas, will only be brief flashes against a world wrapped up in its own smartness. Saint-Just was dazzling, and knew his own brightness. The Black Panthers knew their own brilliance, and that they would disappear. Baader and his friends heralded the death of the Shah of Iran. And the fedayeen, too, are tracer bullets, knowing their traces vanish in the twinkling of an eye.

I mention these truncated lives because I see in them a joy I think I also see in the final rush of Nasser's funeral, in the ever more complicated and lively transports of the hands that drummed on the coffins, in the almost joyful passage in the "Kyrie" of Mozart's *Requiem*. As if so great a sorrow can only express, and at the same time hide itself, in its opposite. As if the sound of utmost mirth and exultation can do away with pain and cauterize its cause.

Perhaps having built a barricade when you're sixteen provides you with a sort of safety rail. If you've once taken part in building one, even inadvertently, doesn't its usually latent image reappear like a warning signal whenever you're tempted to join the police, or support any manifestation of Law and Order?

No sooner do I write these words than I remember: a few days after the last massacres in Amman, when it was certain the fedayeen had been beaten by Hussein's Bedouin, a policeman of Palestinian origin who had not only left the Jordanian police but also fought against it, joined up again. I remember seeing him the day he did it, and I remember what he became: Sorrow personified. Might he, if he'd been a bit younger and more intelligent, have become a really good cop, perhaps even a really good man?

In a little while I'll tell about Ali, the young Shiite who if anything went wrong wanted to have my bones so that they could be buried some day in Palestine. In 1971, talking about the dangers from Israel, he said:

"Don't forget a lot of tobacco fields have been bought on the quiet by Israelis, right up to the mouth of the Litani."

I'm writing this on 20 January 1985, the day chosen by the Israeli government to withdraw its army from the banks of the Awali. Perhaps from Sidon, from south of Sidon up to the Litani.

I mentioned what Ali had said to Daoud Thalami, one of the leaders of Naief Hawatmeh's PFLP.* Daoud smiled.

"Israel doesn't need to use men of straw to buy land," he said. "Whenever it wants to it can cross the border, annex part of Lebanon, and build kibbutzim and Israeli colonies there."

---

*Popular Democratic Front for the Liberation of Palestine.

But Ali was right. Fear in the border region had grown so great it had materialized in buying and selling.

Daoud was right too. All Tsahal had to do was shell Beirut on the pretext of driving out the Palestinians, appear to give Europe a guarantee of good faith by means of staged withdrawals, then halt at the Litani and leave a military force in possession between it and the official frontier. After that it would be child's play to adjust the map in Israel's favour.

One of the things I couldn't go along with in the Palestinians was their optimism. Like all revolutionaries they confused liberty, independence and the possibility of becoming oneself with that of becoming more comfortable, whereas rebellion calls for rigour and intelligence. But despite all this I felt enormous friendship and admiration for them.

But from Deraa on, the Syrians made no bones about criticizing the fedayeen, often in crude and aggressive terms.

(Only now do I remember that Deraa was where Colonel Lawrence was raped by a pasha in the Turkish Army. I didn't remember it once while I was there.)

The taxi driver who took me as his only passenger to Damascus regarded them as trouble-makers who'd caused the loss of the Golan in 1967 and brought the Israeli borders closer to Damascus. I might have understood the Syrians' fear, but what really lay behind their arguments was the cowardice of shopkeepers who'd already knuckled under to the authoritarian Hafez el-Assad.

"Do you know the camps?"

"There are some in Syria. Hussein ought to have had more guts. He put up with a state within a state for too long. Here in Syria the fedayeen are in the Saïka, under the thumb of Zouher Mohsen, who's under the thumb of the Syrian general staff."

The taxi's radio was now playing Scriabin instead of Rimsky-Korsakov.

"Anyway, if you want to be left in peace in Damascus, keep quiet. We like Palestinians when they're civilized."

A rebellion or revolution may not be so much a matter of conquering or winning back land as a deep breath on the part of a people who've suffered for fifty years from that kind of stereotyping.

In July 1984, on the way back from visiting Abu Hicham's fifty *dunums* (less than five hectares) at Ajloun, I drove over one of the two hills where the fedayeen had traded songs back and forth, and looked for the stream I'd heard there one night. It was still there, but channelled now through three pipes, and completely silent. It was being used to irrigate beds of lettuces and cauliflowers. Everything was becoming fixed in time; only the birds were new.

The stream speaks no more, even at night.

The Ajloun chickens cackle and crow.

In the Palestinian camps the floors, the walls, everything is made of concrete.

The road from Deraa to Akaba is tarred and wide.

My eyes can distinguish fields of barley from fields of wheat, rye and beans. The landscape is no longer grey and gold.

In 1970, '71 and '72 every fighter could catch echoes of the struggle taking place within the central committee of the PLO. I paid no attention to the dissension among the leaders of the various elements. I was interested in the fedayeen themselves, not their party loyalties, and I sometimes upset everyone just when I thought I was reconciling their differences.

A Damascus newspaper had announced that I was staying in Syria for a week, and it gave the name of my hotel. Two young men of about twenty came to see me, and while they were having lunch with me I suddenly noticed their anxiety not to be seen by the other guests. These were all Bulgarians, all men, all utterly silent, and they went about in fours.

"It would be better for us not to be seen with you. The Fatah office is in this hotel."

I showed them the letter from Arafat giving me permission to meet the leaders of all the movements.

"So you're with Fatah just by chance."

They belonged to the PFLP, whose leader was Naief Hawatmeh. The group's physical presence during the fighting—Georges Habash was in North Korea—and the courage, devotion and tactical skill of all its members had won them Arafat's respect, if not his friendship.

"Our movement is different from Fatah. We have even less ideology, and we want to be an independent group within the PLO. Even if we're not in the majority we carry some weight. You might have phoned to let us know you were coming."

I told them my trip to Damascus, and to anywhere else, was of no importance.

In the face of the enemy—Jordan or Israel—they united so quickly it made me see their previous discord as a sort of oriental game, like draughts or chess, whisked out of sight at the mere suspicion of danger.

Later on I realized that the rivalry between the eleven groups that then made up the PLO was changing, thanks to male aggression, into hostility. The struggle for pure power—pure in the chemical sense—worked against the desire for money and the power money could bring.

I thought I could distinguish two kinds of power. The first was American, aiming at wealth and display. Its opposite was the Russian idea of power for its own sake, purged, perhaps mystical, but proud and absolute, and sometimes vested in a puny personage always soaking in a hip-bath.

One day the still youthful leaders of the PFLP insisted on taking me to the Golan.

"But it's occupied by Israel."

"We want to take you there."

"We'd have to pass several Syrian road-blocks, and they won't usually let anyone through without permission."

"Don't worry. We're going tomorrow."

We left Damascus by car at about three in the afternoon. There were nine of us—eight fedayeen and me. The fedayeen had brought keffiyehs and black glasses for everyone. Perhaps they believed in Poe's theory in *The Purloined Letter*, and our bowling through like clowns in broad daylight was supposed to make us invisible. Or perhaps they thought the soldiers would weep with laughter at our cheek, so that all they could see through their tears was a drunken mirage. Or that they'd let us through because they were so doubled up they couldn't speak.

"It's Lieutenant Ali," said one of the fedayeen in Arabic to a Syrian soldier. He was examining a pass with several stamps on it.

"This army's like a sieve," I thought to myself. "Any Golda Meir could drive straight through it."

We drove on to the farm where we were to spend the night before continuing on foot to the Israeli-occupied Golan Heights. We were there, drinking tea, when I heard footsteps in the next room, the sound of doors opening and shutting, and an argument conducted in Arabic with a Syrian accent. Then someone opened the door behind me and said in French:

"Good evening, monsieur. I've been sent by the captain to see if the French gentleman needs anything for the night."

I said no thanks. The Syrian NCO said, "Are you sure?" I said, "Quite sure—I'm fine."

The NCO: "I can go, then."

Me: "Yes."

Him: "OK."

He gave me a military salute and went out without a glance at anyone. Everyone was embarrassed except the farmer and his wife and son.

"Let's go to bed," said Farid suddenly. He was one of the leaders, aged about twenty-three.

The brusque appearance of the NCO was an obvious reaction to our psychedelic penetration of the Syrian army. There could no longer be any doubt: I was being treated to some sort of play-acting—but where would it end? But I wasn't worried. It was very amusing. Unless the fedayeen's sudden embarrassment was put on, and the Syrian corporal was an actor trained in a Damascus drama school.

I went to bed.

We set out on foot through an icy morning before the sun was up, and after two hours' walk on the slopes of the Golan (pronounced "Jolan" here, in Syrian Arabic) reached a little deserted Circassian village. On the top of the nearest foothill I saw a small fort that had been put up in haste by the Israelis. In the still heavy mist you could only just make out the original Syrian construction, built—like Soueda, the capital of the Syrian Druses—of alternate and equal slabs of white marble and black basalt. According to our leader, the garrison had a swift and efficient radar warning system. All was quite silent and still.

"We'll go up another three or four hundred metres. I've located five or six cork-oaks on the slopes. As soon as anyone hears a plane we all choose a tree and take shelter."

The sun was getting hot.

"Are you tired?"

"No."

"We'll stop and have something to eat first. We've made good progress and we're pretty safe spaced out like this. But we need some food."

Around us there was nothing but a stretch of yellowish grass, a few trees, and of course some basalt rocks. We had the sort of light snack that commandos eat when they're in action. It was then that the son of a Gulf prince, a lad of about eighteen, speaking the French he'd learned in a luxurious Swiss boarding school, said:

"Tell us frankly what you think of us. Are we real revolutionaries, or intellectuals playing at revolution?"

Maybe not all Naief Hawatmeh's group were the sons of Leading Families, but all the members of this commando were more or less "sherif," that is to say descended from Ali and therefore noble. One was a prince's son, another the son of an eminent Palestinian doctor, another was a business lawyer, another a rather distant member of the Nashashibi family.

There they all were, full of expectation, except the prince's son. His father intended to disinherit him. He'd left his Swiss school for two reasons: he was a romantic and he was homesick for the Mediterranean. It was difficult not to think that however magnanimous these kids were, their relatives would be better off if they died in a Marxist cause.

"Since you ask the question," I said, "it *is* one that presents itself."

The Arabic translation rang out. I thought I saw a shadow pass over the eight faces. But the leader of the commando made an instant decision.

"The Frenchman understands. No point in going up any further."

As we went down from the Golan—I wasn't sure I'd actually been there—they improvised a song like the one I've already described, a sort of round in which each stanza interrupted and overlapped the preceding one, and eventually merged with it. This time they didn't mention Munich; instead they made fun of Golda.

Before we separated—that is, before I went back to Damascus—we stopped at the farm where we'd spent the previous night. The farmer gave me back my passport and my money, which the fedayeen had advised me to leave with him.

"We still have to help the peasants finish the harvest. Have some tea and wait for us."

When they came back they said:

"You see—as Mao said in his Red Book, although we're intellectuals it's our duty to help the peasants with their work."

"You only helped for half an hour."

With no questions asked, without any difficulty or disguise, we crossed back through the Syrian army twenty-four hours after we'd passed through in the opposite direction.

Back in Damascus I went to the French Institute. I knew an expert in geography there. He produced some staff maps on which I could trace our route from Damascus, the path leading through the basalt rocks to the farm, the farm itself, the little Circassian village and the hill. He pointed out the recently built Israeli fort.

"They took you to the Golan all right. But why?"

I thought they'd wanted to demonstrate how daring they were, and also the way, as good Marxists, they helped the peasants— much more than Fatah, with whom I still was. They must have thought I'd write it all down. What they didn't know was what my friend at the Institute told me.

"You went to the Golan sure enough, but to the more or less neutral zone. The Palestinians are allowed to go through there for two or three hours every day, because anyone shooting at them might hit the Syrian peasants herding their cows and sheep. What's more, it's near the Jebel Druse, where Israeli-based Druses often take it into their heads to go. And no one wants any incidents!"

He smiled.

"Yesterday morning you just went for a little constitutional. Tiring, but not dangerous."

Thanks to a box of Havana cigars I bought in Damascus and gave to the commanding officer at a Jordanian customs post, I managed to take the French-speaking fedayee—the prince's son—with me into Jordan. In Amman he met some of his friends in the PFLP, and came with me to the Fatah office. My arrival was announced to Abu Omar, who embraced me. But when I asked where the fedayeen would find Naief's office, he answered:

"I don't know. He'll have to look."

The prince's son was in Damascus two days later.

I'd seen a different facet of Abu Omar's personality: the spirit of faction had got the better of simple comradeship and even of politeness. Later on he himself referred to the matter.

When he'd got Arafat to give me a pass and a friendly recommendation, he may have thought I might use it to go and see movements other than Fatah. But he hadn't really thought I'd dare. Not wanting to vent his annoyance on me, he directed it against the PFLP.

Soon afterwards he revealed the sort of inner conflict that often made him irritable.

One day on the heights of Ashrafieh in Amman, he pointed out the water tower to me, the places where there'd been fighting, the gutted houses and some private arms caches. But he wouldn't tell me where the light artillery was.

He took me round the camp. The guns were trained on the entrance to the royal palace. Then he went over to a wall, raised the corner of a grey blanket, called me over and showed me the first Katyushka I'd seen.

"They're all pointed in the direction of the palace."

He smiled. I thought he looked relieved.

"But you oughtn't to be showing them to me."

"No, I know. We won't say any more about it."

His need to be truthful was almost as imperative as his need to lie.

Perhaps this book has come out of me in a way that's beyond my control. It flows too jerkily, and probably shows what a relief it is to open the floodgates and release pent-up memories. After fifteen years, despite my silence and attempts at reserve, what has been repressed leaks out through the cracks. But Abu Omar needn't have worried. In those days of great love I knew how to keep secrets.

Almost as soon as I arrived in Jordan, and after I'd told him why Muhommad el-Hamchari had brought me, I'd been surprised and even annoyed by one of Abu Omar's decisions.

His plan to drive me across Jordan from Amman to Irbid, five kilometres from the Syrian frontier, and to introduce me to groups other than Fatah, suited me very well. On the way, in the car, I asked him about the relations between the Palestinian peasants and what might be called the Jordanian Bedouin. Excellent, he said. I knew this trip was a propaganda exercise: my going to talk to the organization of Palestinian women was supposed to prove that a Frenchman, and through me France as a whole, was interested in Palestine. Why shouldn't I play along?

When we got to Irbid it so happened that the poet Khaled Abu Khaled was there, and as soon as he heard of our arrival he was intrigued and came to meet us. He spoke French, and when I told him we were going to see the Palestinian Women's Union, and that Abu Omar had said the two populations got on well together, he flew into a kind of rage.

"Why do you bring him here and tell him lies?" he said to Abu Omar.

And to me:

"The Palestinians and the Jordanians get on very badly. The Jordanians hate us. No doubt it's the result of government propaganda, but it's a fact. The people mistrust our teachers, our officials, our doctors. The people of Jordan are at war with us, and he tells you everything's fine! He's lying. The Palestinian women know it, but they won't say anything in front of you."

Abu Omar had gone pale, but couldn't stop him. I was disturbed by Khaled's vehemence and by the fact that Abu Omar had concealed the truth from me, so I decided to go back to Amman, calm down, and try to sort things out in my own mind.

It was a gloomy drive back. When we were stopped at Jordanian road-blocks Abu Omar, who had no identity card—he was a high-ranking fedayee, but still a fedayee—suggested I show my French passport, as that would cover both of us.

What worried me then and worries me still was this: I found that when Khaled went back to Damascus he wasn't allowed to broadcast on Radio Damascus any more. The officials told me the change was at his own request: he wanted a rest. The word madness was never mentioned, but even more disagreeable words were: psychological and intellectual fatigue; nervous breakdown. The tactfulness of these expressions struck me as more insulting than frankness.

But it was strange that Khaled's madness—for he must have had an attack that day in Irbid—should have given him the lucidity, courage or recklessness to tell me that I, the naïve newcomer, was having the wool pulled over my eyes. He was trying to do two things: to tell me of the danger his people were in, and to say it loudly to prevent my being taken in.

Do you remember my conversation with an Algerian officer, linked in my memory to the spring of 1971 and my astonishment as I watched long lines of processionary caterpillars? I can recall the beginning of our dialogue.

"Who are you, really?"

"A friend of the Palestinians. Of the people and of the fedayeen. Who are you?"

"An Algerian officer. How long do you think this war between Israel and the Arabs is going to last?"

"I don't know. Perhaps another five years."

"You could say a hundred and fifty."

When I arrived, to an enthusiastic welcome from the fedayeen, I probably wasn't clear-headed enough to evaluate the opposing forces or make out the divisions within the Arab world. I ought to have seen sooner that aid to the Palestinians was an illusion. Whether it came from the Gulf or from North Africa it was ostentatious and declamatory, but flimsy.

Gradually my feelings changed, especially after the 1973 war. I was still charmed, but I wasn't convinced; I was attracted but not blinded. I behaved like a prisoner of love.

I thought three years of passionate love was inevitable. Five years perhaps. But after that there'd come the typical lover's weariness.

In a hundred and fifty years' time, in the world as a whole and in this part of it in particular, my death and other upheavals and all thought would be as if still-born.

And a hundred and fifty years was what I got, when I'd naïvely foreseen five in which I went from victory to victory.

So much love to start with was bound to grow less.

The faces of the old Palestinian women; the prettifying of the houses; the new-fangled objects made in Japan like those you see among the Altiplano Indians; the tons of solid cement designed to hide the poverty of the earth—all went to show that every revolution would deteriorate, would capitulate before the invasion of stultifying comfort.

No one watching the television programme I mentioned at the beginning of this book actually saw Nasser's funeral, though they may have agreed to say they did. The chanting of the Koran, the close-ups of fists and eyes, and such long shots as the screen allowed, would have made up a scene our memories could have done nothing with if it hadn't been for the title at the beginning: "Funeral of the Rais, Gamal Abdel Nasser."

A seething tangle of arms and legs and skirts (all men's); were they the people? And amid all the puffing and blowing, not a breath about the Palestinian revolt.

Arafat's prediction was fulfilled: " 'They' " (this was the same lack of differentiation as Arafat was fighting against)—" 'They' take photographs of us, they film us, they write about us, and thanks to them we exist. And then suddenly they may stop, and for the West and all the rest of the world the Palestinian problem will be solved simply because no one sees its picture any more."

Anyone in Europe could put an end to that picturesque funeral by turning a knob of his black and white TV. But meanwhile the trees were full of urchins and old men who'd used their last strength to perch up in the branches. And when in September '82 Arafat and his men set sail for Greece, we saw the same thing: a funeral ceremony on foreign ships and urchins cheering in the branches of the trees. All the Arabs seemed to have realized that the death of Pharaoh meant the death of the Umma.

The people who seemed to me nearest to the earth, to the clay, and of the same colour, the ones whose palms and fingers came into closest physical contact with things, also struck me as the vaguest and most non-existent. Their deeds were mere rudiments of deeds.

A fedayee's first gesture on arriving in Israel—kissing the soil of Palestine—was made a mockery of by a white-robed Pope stepping out of his luxury cabin after enduring air pockets and their terrors. The fedayee's presence was already known, even in the dark, to all the alarm systems—electric, electro-magnetic, phosphorescent and infrared; and to others still secret. But instead of being on his guard and taking aim, shooting and dying like a killer, he was frozen for ever a burst of Israeli gunfire in the same position as a Pope prostrating himself to kiss the earth.

But sometimes, when the heroes set out for the Jordan in the evening, I seemed to see them returning as local councillors, mayors and members of parliament, though they were setting out to proclaim their heroism through death on the cliffs. *They* didn't kiss the earth. They came up from the Jordan like statues on steeds of iron.

The Phalangists could march like the Sabras, and they had the same swank, the same look.

It's now September 1982, and we're in Beirut.

The fedayeen have disbanded.

The women pretend.

I was told the narrow-gauge Damascus-to-Hejaz railway, which goes through Deraa and which Lawrence so often blew up, had been re-opened. The wife of the British ambassador was said to have made the inaugural trip from Amman to Mecca.

However agile I or rather my transport—planes, trains, ships, cars, helicopters—might be, and no matter how easily the money for the journeys was found, inside me lay the corpse I'd been for a long while. What surprises me is how still it lay, despite air pockets, sudden starts, high seas, bumps and broken propellers. Everything jolted along, and me with it, a parcel and at the same time a human being, a name and a tomb, a parcel and a corpse, eating, looking, laughing, whistling and loving left, right and centre. It seemed to me the world changed around me while I stayed inside myself, certain only of having been.

Perhaps the memories I record are mere draperies with which my corpse is still being decked. Perhaps what I write is no use to anyone. But the cadaver of myself, most certainly killed by the Catholic Church, will receive quiet homage from paganism.

"What's the point of talking about this revolution?" It too is like a long-drawn-out funeral, with me occasionally joining in the procession.

I did some quite long stints close together in 1970, '71 and '72, in Jordan.

At the age of sixty my hands and feet grew light again, my fingers capable of clutching a tuft of grass at the top of a slope and balancing my would-be weightless body on the precarious stone on which I stood. I could hoist myself up just because the tuft of grass itself was so weak! I could climb as fast as the fedayeen, and I declined their hands outstretched to help me as I reached the now treeless plateau from which you could see Jericho.

"Quick, come and look—the lights of Jericho!"

Abu X——, who had climbed up faster than I, pointed across the gorge through which the Jordan flowed. Some of the lights were moving.

"That's where I was born."

He was so moved I owed it to him to be silent. I found out later that the only lights you could see at night from Ajloun were those of Nablus.

Do you remember Omar, the young fedayee who translated into French the sort of pro-Palestinian lecture the farmer's wife gave me at Ajloun? He was the son of the former Turkish officer belonging to the Naboulsi family. I met him again in Deraa.

Rather impolitely, I asked him for news of Ferraj, not of his father.

"I don't think he's so much of a Marxist now he's married."

"Is his wife a Palestinian?"

"Of course. He used to be an internationalist on the subject of women, but when it came to choosing a wife to give him sons he's like the rest of us—guided by a morbid, because Arab, patriotism."

But do you still remember Ferraj, the fedayee leader whom I liked talking to best when I first arrived in Ajloun? When I saw Omar I didn't think about Ferraj any more even when I was talking about him. I thought about the black sergeant—Palestinian but black—who had dinner served to me before the Ramadan fast was over and gave my leavings to a couple of fighters. He and his behaviour had left me with a feeling of uneasiness, a sick feeling of aversion which I couldn't throw off. I told Omar what had happened.

"Abu Taleb is dead. Killed by a Jordanian bullet, probably. It's to stop his sort of attitude being handed down that we're going to bring about the revolution."

"I don't see the connection."

"He was the grandson or great-grandson of a Sudanese slave. Fatah made him a staff sergeant, but he was still a practising Muslim and wasn't supposed to eat until after the moon had risen. For him—the descendant of a slave even though he'd been made an officer—you were a guest. You had to be served first. After you the mere fedayeen could share the leavings."

"He regarded the fedayeen as servants?"

"That was part of it. They were servants because they were under his orders. But though you didn't know it, that tiny event had repercussions all over the base. The two fedayeen who ate after you understood your embarrassment, and pushed him around a bit. He said they were racists."

"Is there racism, then, in Fatah?"

"Not in that particular form. In theory there's no distinction of colour, religion or class among us fedayeen—but what about the education we received in the past? My father sees himself as an aristocrat, and so does my brother in Germany."

It was then I realized my discourtesy.

"How is your father?"

"Quite well for an old man. Still living in a world of his own."

"What do you mean?"

"As you saw the night of his birthday, he thinks of himself as belonging to the old France—a representative at the court of the Grand Turk of France, the Torch of the World. His world."

"He likes Loti. I wasn't supposed to know anything about his wives, but he mentioned them so often I got the impression he used them as a sort of shield or bullet-proof vest. He couldn't have been afraid he'd be shot, but through trying so hard to hide his wound he attracted my attention to it."

"That was typical of a member of his generation, and especially of a naval officer. He knew Ataturk, Inonu, Hitler, Ribbentrop, Franchet d'Esperey and Lyautey. He'll die still believing in his pet slogans. You must have noticed some of them. 'The ladders of the Levant,' 'The Christian West,' 'The Virtue of the Simple'—he applies that to waiters and means the virtue of the simple-minded. 'The School of Alexandria,' 'The Silk Road,' and 'The Sword of Islam'—meaning Napoleon."

"In short you think your father's a joke."

"Absolutely. But when we met you asked me about Ferraj and Abu Taleb, not my old man. I knew you were interested in Ferraj, but Abu Taleb?"

"What did you know about Ferraj?"

"That first evening you spoke only to him and for him. He told me so himself."

"He was joking, I suppose?"

Omar hesitated, then looked me straight in the eye.

"To a certain extent. But he was moved, too. You have to do everything fast when death is at your heels. You loved one another all one night, exchanging only looks and funny stories. He'd remember it for ever."

Omar's rather simplistic explanation of how racism might have existed in Fatah, subtly and sublimely hidden by extreme delicacy, temporarily drove away my uneasiness when I thought about that dinner.

I suddenly saw the word racism in a new light. It literally

appeared to me—at once harmless and lethal. The more harmless the more lethal.

Mme. G—— is a wealthy woman who still lives in the avenue Foch in Paris. During the Algerian war she was a stout defender of the Algerians. She even felt sorry for the terrorists.

"The worst thing we do to them is regard them as different from us because they have different customs. But even the English drive on the opposite side of the road from us French."

She never forgot to mention she was French.

Another lady, more provincial than the first, thought she was going further as well.

"I'm Jewish and I know what racism is. In spite of the solemn decisions taken at Vatican II, the Christians still regard us as deicides. And Christianity will never forgive Islam for competing with it, especially in Africa and Asia. All racism is wrong."

But genuine ladies probably prefer the word "Asian." This seems to suggest they've read Montesquieu, so that a whiff of aristocracy bears them up into the ageless realms of the intellect. At the same time it suggests the conquest of the Huns, the Golden Horde, and even rickshaws.

Mlle. de B—— used to say "Asian."

"Islam is nothing yet, but the Asians gave us Buddha five centuries before Christ. How can one call them barbarians? How can one accept racism, or even the concept of racism?"

Now Mme. G—— happens to be married to a big French landowner who was driven out of Algeria, while the father of the provincial lady had been a major-general in the colonies. Mlle. de B——'s family owned thousands of hectares in Indochina before Vietnam became independent. And she was really very sweet to everyone from the Third World: she very democratically treated an Indian servant and a Maharajah exactly the same.

The three ladies didn't know each other, but when they defined racism they all left out one factor: contempt, and what it implies.

When I told Omar about them he said:

"I'm not surprised. Here . . ."—Deraa is in Syria, but he meant Jordan— "Here the Jordanians, the poor and the millionaires alike, use the Portuguese word, *compradores*, the go-betweens who do the West's dirty work. Everyone blames the woes of the Arab world not on the compradores themselves—we're all that—but on the word, which we all deflect from ourselves on to some undefined others. Your French ladies have all produced a definition of racism that omits contempt. Otherwise the consequences for themselves would be too painful. But racism applies to anyone who sees the enslaved as subhuman, to be despised—and he'll always despise them more in order to exploit them more, and exploit them more in order to despise and enslave them more, and so on ad infinitum."

Omar was killed by the Syrians at Tal-el-Zaatar. His last words to me were more or less as follows:

"Without knowing each other your three French ladies all studied one question that's really quite simple but that it was convenient for them to misunderstand. That's the link between them, despite the difference in their ages: their refusal to pronounce the forbidden word."

If someone's attracted to someone, an offhand attitude won't disguise it. Whenever I saw Mubarak I could cold-shoulder him as much as I liked—even when he was standing up he wallowed in my discomfiture. His chuckle reminded me of Samia Solh trying to attract attention to her necklace of Venus.

"I know about French literature too. Even the Surrealists: Baudelaire, Vigny, Musset, to mention just a few."

Such cheek didn't bother me. I was enchanted to discover the lout underneath the officer. I still wonder if he didn't pass his exams through the mere outrageousness of his mistakes. But he was bound to know a few secrets.

"Would you say there's any racism among the Palestinians? As a Black . . ."

"Of course."

"Of course what?"

"Of course there's racism. And I may be black, but I'm clean. My fingernails are pink, for example. Yours are black, never cleaned—in mourning you call it—but they're not the same black as my face.

"This is how the racism works. Most Palestinian officers are sure the art of war was invented by them. But obviously I must have learned about it in Europe, because for them Africa's completely uncivilized. Except North Africa, of course. I'm really supposed to fight by sinking my bare teeth in live flesh."

"Have you been a Muslim for long?"

"From birth. I was circumcised. Want to have a look? But one of my great-grandfathers was a spirit-worshipper. My family can be divided into three: Muslims, spirit-worshippers and Christians. Each religion despises the others."

"Are they all as black as you?"

"Just about."

I told him about the dinner Abu Taleb gave me. He thought for a bit, but not long.

"Have you ever wondered why I've sought you out and tried to talk to you so often?"

"No."

"Because I get under your skin. And you're the only one here I have that effect on. The other officers are suspicious of me, and for the fedayeen I'm just a negro."

"But none of them despises you?"

"For them I scarcely exist. Would you'd like to hear a confession? We can't exist through our intelligence. We can only tell we exist by getting under other people's skins. You're one of 'them.' You know what the feeling is."

"I never noticed it in Abu Taleb."

"If he'd been Sudanese he might have been sensitive, too. By singling you out for special treatment he thought he was thanking you, but really he was revenging himself for the petty cruelties the fedayeen inflicted on him. But don't talk to me about my colour. It's through that and my muscles that I disturb people, and that's fine. But I'd rather not talk about it. Are you glad to be with the Palestinians?"

"Very."

"The Israeli soldiers are young. Would you be glad to be with them? I expect they'd be very nice to you."

"Even if you see me as white, I'm like you—I'd rather not talk about it."

We often got near, but never quite reached, such simple and obvious revelations, just as you can just miss a precipice in the dark and be amazed when you see it at sunrise.

One day, near the Palestinian Research Bureau in Amman, I saw a fedayee cupping his hand round a flower that a Frenchman had stuck behind his ear, as a joke. It came to me as a revelation: the Palestinians' struggle meant protecting a fantasy, and that wasn't going to do them any good. It wasn't a question of weakness or strength—I just knew at that moment that everything would come to grief.

Earlier, in Nepal, the folds of a sari had awakened me to a truth. But I saw it only through a veil until one day, in a steam bath in Karachi, a Pakistani unfurled a long, very white strip of linen, and I realized what until then I had merely glimpsed: this was the robe, the seamless robe of Christ that I'd heard so much about.

I'd been thinking only of my own solitude, but now Mubarak's suddenly struck me. If he wore his colour and his ritual scars arrogantly, it was because they were the symbol of his uniqueness here, and of a loneliness that abated a little only when he was with me.

"You can't imagine how sick they make me, with their revolution that's supposed to give them back their little houses and gardens, their little pots of flowers and cemeteries. Which have already been ground to dust by Israeli bulldozers anyway."

I haven't transcribed my conversations with Omar and Mubarak literally. I've tried to use some notes, and even more my memory, to reproduce their tone of voice and the general outline of what they said. But I can't tell if the men I'm trying to describe speak to you now as they spoke to me then.

A memory. A young Arab nurse was on call at the tiny hospital at Gaza Camp. There was one room for both patients and doctor. It held eight beds. Dr. Dieter had one bed, a German male nurse another, and a third was for unexpected patients or visitors passing through. I often slept in it. Sometimes Nabila occupied the next bed to mine. They were field-hospital beds, of course; more like stretchers.

The other beds, occupied by three or four men who were seriously wounded, were in a row opposite. And at the end of the room there was a large alcove enclosed by three blankets sewn together. A fourth blanket formed the roof.

It was the custom for people to address one another familiarly in the second person singular, except of course when speaking English. But when I was there Nabila, Dr. Dieter, the German male nurse, the German female nurse and Alfredo all spoke French. Every so often a remark would be added in German, English or Arabic.

The German woman was learning Arabic. She'd come to Jordan in about 1969. She was always the first up in the morning, handing out aspirin, cough medicine, ointments and other harmless remedies to patients from the camp. Then Dr. Dieter would come and hold his surgery. With some difficulty he got the fedayeen and their officers to agree that seriously ill civilians should be seen before fighters who were only slightly wounded.

This is how we slept. Men and women alike, we took our shoes off but kept our clothes on to lie down on camp beds with one or two blankets. Except for the German woman, the nurse. Every evening after she'd done her washing up and closed her Arabic book, she said goodnight to us in German and retired into the alcove. No one asked any questions, probably because everyone except me had guessed the explanation.

"Why this performance and why that contraption?" I asked Dieter.

He answered in a whisper.

"So that she can say her prayers. She's a nun, with a special dispensation not to wear the habit of her order. She only puts it on to sleep and to pray."

In my mind I compared these strange practices to those of the chief kissing the notables of his pseudo-tribe.

"So that she can say her prayers?"

"You weren't here ten days ago. In the middle of the night she let out a frightful shriek. She said that while she was still awake, with one hand trailing out of the bed—the beds are very low, as you know—she felt a sort of ball of hair that moved. So she screamed."

"Had she been dreaming?"

"It was the head of one of the patients, crawling on all fours."

"Trying to rape her?"

"Every evening she brings two bottles of surgical spirit back here from the infirmary. Before, she used to lock them up, but the patients would always manage to open the cupboard, and next morning they'd be in a stupor. So then she started keeping the bottles in her bedroom—what she calls her bedroom."

"So what's happened since the screaming?"

"The political officer of the camp takes charge of the two bottles every night. He's a strict Muslim and doesn't drink."

The nun was not only devoted in her ordinary duties; she also went with Dr. Dieter to look after Palestinians beaten up by the Jordanian police in Baqa camp. She had to endure insults and blows because she was serving the Palestinian people, and eventually she was put in prison in Amman. The West German ambassador managed to get her sent back to her convent in Munich.

No one thought the Resistance was fatally wounded, but we could tell from certain signs that it had lost a lot of blood. Long queues of patients without anything visibly wrong with them came to the hospital just to prove to themselves that all they needed was a tablet to turn into conquerors again. A word of advice from Dieter was sometimes all that was needed:

"Don't spend too much time lying down. Move about."

The only symptom they exhibited was profound depression.

"I saw the same thing before I left Biafra," Dieter told me.

One morning before I left, the German nun told me, roaring with laughter:

"Do you know how they used to wangle it? First they stole my thimble, then they filled it with surgical spirit, and each one had a thimbleful. Egalitarian as ever. And in the morning they were all blind drunk!"

She was still laughing.

"Does your order allow you to wear only certain materials and colours?"

"We're advised to wear black and dark colours. But the only thing that's compulsory is flat heels. And quite right. In flat heels we are truly servants."

"Have you ever worn high heels?"

"Of course."

"When?"

"*Ach, mein Gott!* In the convent, when the bishop came. I was Mary Magdalen in a play, and my heels were so high I felt giddy. I couldn't move or speak. But fortunately Jesus saw my difficulty and provided me with a chair. Thank goodness—I thought I was going to die!"

Nothing definite is known about Abu Omar's death except what follows, and that's not really certain. He and eight other soldiers hired a boat to go to Tripoli. But according to one version, when they were somewhere out at sea they were captured by a Syrian patrol boat, taken to prison in Damascus and shot. Another version says the boat was sunk by a Syrian shell and they all drowned. Alternatively the Syrians took them prisoner and handed them over to the Phalangists, and the Phalangists killed them.

There are several surprising things about all this: the number of different accounts, the absence of any evidence, and the silence that enshrouds it all. It seemed to me the leaders were embarrassed about it, too. Eight men and Abu Omar: that makes nine. And Abu Omar's real name was known: it was Hannah.

While the name of the Cid is remembered, that of the Leper is for ever forgotten, though he's accorded a capital letter. That was all he got for giving the Campeador, the Champion, the chance to show his magnanimity with a kiss that resounds through history, classical drama, poetry and the novel right down to the school-boys of today.

The Palestinian revolution is full of anonymous heroes who helped to bring it about, but because we can't talk to them any more we forget their faces and banished names, and no longer talk about what they did. But some of their deeds remain, though it's not impossible they will one day be attributed to others. The decision to go from Beirut to Tripoli by sea, by night and in the middle of a war, and then being machine-gunned to death—all that may one day embellish the end of some soldier who lived twenty years ago or who will die thirty years hence.

Here's how I met Abu Omar. I phoned to say I was driving to Amman from Deraa, and he said I was welcome and made an appointment for us to meet the next day in the lounge of the Jordan Hotel.

He was just coming downs from his room when I arrived.

"Come and have a coffee."

The bar was closed.

"I'd forgotten—this morning is the beginning of Ramadan. Where shall we go for coffee?"

His surprise told me he was a Christian. A Palestinian Christian. The order of the two words ought never to be reversed. The last thing I remember him saying is:

"When the Syrians invaded Lebanon it was us, the Palestinians, who resisted them."

When the Syrians, with great difficulty, took Tal-el-Zaatar, it was thought they had Israeli experts as advisers or at least observers. The progress of the Syrian army in Lebanon was slowed down but not halted. It reached Sidon, and it was there that Abu Omar was seen for the last time in broad daylight. Perhaps he—and other leaders too, including Arafat—had seen what the Syrians were up to.

Mubarak told me, after his first long conversation with him:

"All his revolutionary activity consists in examining the reasons for becoming a revolutionary and what one's attitude should be afterwards. He makes me feel I'm just a temporary receptacle for his ideas. But that's only one aspect of him, probably not all that important. Another is his involvement with Arafat and other CCOLP* leaders."

I've been told it was he—or, according to others, Abu Musa alone—who said the Syrian tanks should be greeted politely in Sidon and allowed to proceed to the barracks. So the tanks and their crews, surprised but delighted with their welcome from the fedayeen, were conducted to the barracks. Then, when about thirty-six tanks were drawn up in the barrack square and their crews about to climb out of their turrets, the tanks blew up and their crews with them.

---

*Central Committee of the Organization for the Liberation of Palestine.

"Splendid isolation," the expression that defines and describes the United Kingdom so admirably, was a phrase that came to mind to describe the Palestinian revolution in the years from 1970 to 1973 and after.

What one got from the papers and the radio were bombastic, funny or cynical accounts designed to boost Israel, Hussein or western democracy, but rarely the PLO. Some attention was paid to it, or rather it attracted attention from a few readers, but the revolution itself, the living body, evolved all on its own, despite the limited aid of the Soviet Union, China, Boumedienne's Algeria, and an appearance of support from the Arab states. I make an exception of the devotion of doctors from all over the world, as well as of nurses and lawyers, mostly working on a shoe-string. But I also remember consignments of medicine too old to be effective, powders stale and worthless, gifts not only useless but even dangerous dumped by cynical manufacturers on the Palestinian Red Crescent.

In the midst of this confusion the revolution remained isolated, a body with its internal organs almost invisible, a body not made up of the bodies of individual Palestinians, but rather the result of events. Its circulation was slow, in battle after battle, military defeat after military defeat which the European papers ironically called political or diplomatic successes. But they were real defeats, of a body extending from Jordan to the West Bank and vice versa, crossing Syria to Lebanon, staggering under the Syrian invasion of Lebanon, yet not dead despite Beirut and Chatila, and not yet buried even in Asian Tripoli.

In the midst of all those enemies trying to kill it, the body still stands. There's an archaeology of the Resistance, which became a Revolution in the thirties. It was young then. It was quite easy to help the revolutionaries, but impossible to become a Palestinian. Isolation was splendid because it was the very nature of the revolution. America, with the help of the Arab countries, tried to uproot it.

A few sentences back I mentioned the Syrian invasion of Lebanon in 1976. But who remembers it? Who remembers Tal-el-

Zaatar? The armies of Hafez el-Assad, the Alawite Muslim who asked favours of the Christian Pierre Gemayel, came down from Damascus to the slopes of Anti-Lebanon and swept on to Sidon, which fortunately was defended by a Palestinian colonel.

His plan of action was submitted to the leadership of the PLO. Several roads from the north and the east converged on Sidon. All of them were blocked except one, and that was the one taken by the Syrian tanks. They made straight for the barracks, halted, and just as the last tank arrived the whole lot exploded. It's said there were between thirty-two and thirty-six of them. Abu Omar conveyed the Sidon defence plan to the PLO, but it was Colonel Abu Musa who drew it up. Now he's the leader of the Fatah dissidents, a friend of Hafez el-Assad. Against Arafat.

Muhammad el-Hamchari came from Damascus the day of Hafez el-Assad's coup, and we thought the Palestinian tanks would go into Jordan to help the fedayeen. I found out later that some Iraqi tanks had crossed the Iraqi frontier and then crossed back again the next day without having done anything. The explanation Damascus and Baghdad now give of their aggressive stance one day and their withdrawal the next is that they were obeying orders from the Soviet Union. Just as Hussein now explains his battles against the fedayeen by saying that without them Israel would have occupied Jordan.

Only a few days ago I asked one of King Hussein's friends about it:

"Yes," he said, "The king got a threatening letter from Golda Meir."

I put the same question to a diplomat who'd been stationed in Amman at the time.

"Not on your life!" said he. "The order to fight the Palestinians came from Washington and London."

It's a three- or four-hour drive from Amman to Damascus via Deraa. I needed to do some research at the French Institute in Damascus, but only got in after being questioned and looked coldly in the eye by relays of cops, and passing through solid banks of bewhiskered cavalrymen mounted on diminutive horses.

They were from the mountains near Aleppo, and all long-time

supporters of Hafez el-Assad. I can still see their wide stirrups and the green flags of Islam.

The house of the new President of the Republic was next door to the French Institute, and Assad must have been making a speech. The director of the Institute invited me to stay for lunch, and we sat on for quite a long time chatting and drinking coffee. When I came out, all but a few of the mounted soldiers had gone, but I brushed by a couple who for some strange reason had ridden their horses up on to the pavement.

"What are you doing? Are you mad?"

"Hallo, you speak French? So do we. We're keeping our horses out of the traffic. They've never seen so many cars, and they're frightened."

"Where are you from?"

"A village some way from Aleppo, but in that direction."

"And you speak French?"

"I was a French NCO. I took part in the revolt against the Druses, against Sultan Attrach."

"And you've come down from the mountains to support Assad?"

"Of course. He's an Alawite, like us. At least he'll rid us of the revolutionaries."

"Which ones?"

"The Palestinians."

I was caught. A sort of nostalgia made me sympathize with these two, who were about my age or a few years older. Their dilapidated stirrups were close to my shoulder, the horses they rode were small, they wore baggy Turkish trousers. One of them asked me what I was doing in Damascus, and I told him, in Arabic, that I'd been a soldier in Syria when I was eighteen, and that I knew Aleppo. In one bound they both leaped to the ground and threw their arms round me.

I'd already been put in the picture in Deraa by a Syrian taxi driver who hated the Palestinians, though he hadn't leapt off a horse to kiss me.

Not all the Syrians showed such open hatred of the Palestinians, but whether it was in Damascus, Latakia or Homs, I never heard anyone come to their defence. Saïka, of course, which came under direct orders from the Syrian generals, was exempt from criticism.

I was more comfortable, much more comfortable, in Syria than in Jordan. Affable Turkish manners were still prevalent there in 1971. I could talk for hours to an old bootblack who hadn't forgotten his French. From him, sitting on the little box while I sat on my chair, I heard the history of the last thirty years of Syrian politics—the history of the series of *coups d'état*. I felt a long way from straightlaced Jordan, even though it was full of Palestinians.

Looking at the faces of all those armed peasants I saw that what made them peasants was the fact that they owned lots of horses. Everything about them showed they were chiefs back home in the mountains. The way they held their reins in one hand and their guns ready to fire into the air on any pretext, their white beards and moustaches, only reinforced the impression. Perhaps these bandits wondered how I managed to exist without a horse or a gun.

It may have been something in their expression when they relaxed, but I saw them as minor chieftains rather than fighters.

Fatah was the group that had most members like them: youths who delighted in scrapping and looting and guns. At twenty they're more hooligans than heroes. After the Palestinians signed an agreement that allowed them to stay in Lebanon, a lot of these lads used to come from southern Lebanon to spend a few days in Beirut. Their berets were usually trimmed with braid, and they wore black leather jackets, jeans and trainers. Their moustaches were so frail and new I was amazed they didn't all have sticks of kohl in their kits. When they greeted me their left arms stayed down stiffly at their sides, and only the right hand was raised, palm outward. Some of them left Arafat for Abu Musa in 1982.

This was how Abu Musa and Abu Omar prepared the barrack square. As soon as they knew the Syrians were coming, Abu Omar got his men to bury mines in the sand, with detonators attached to wires just beneath the surface. The surface area of the square taken together with the number of tanks made it possible to place each mine so that every tank would be completely annihilated—steel, iron, watches, watch-straps, muscles, cartilages and all.

I tell the story as it was told to me. Professor Abu Omar was Kissinger's pupil at Stanford, and proved an able tactician. He thought up the plan. Abu Musa carried it out.

The outside of Mubarak's knuckles, the part you hit with, showed little cracks or wrinkles where the skin was slightly paler than on the hand itself. These mauvish fissures seemed to me to let through a humanity as anxious as the heart of a frightened hare. It disturbed me far more than any dreary notions of fraternity or racism could.

Whenever, almost inadvertently, through awkwardness or a secret need to declare myself, I talked to him about how I'd been abandoned as a child, his fists, already clenched, would tighten even further. All the cracks disappeared from the knuckles, and the skin was left smooth and black without any trace of mauve. Had he been moved by the words "orphanage" and "public assistance"?

I was looking at his fingers, not his face. Mubarak told me I reminded him of a distant relative of his who lived in exile in Djibouti.

This is the story.

"In our country, when a young negress belonging to one of our tribes has a child who hasn't got a father, the tribe takes charge of it. But when your Vietnamese, Madagascan or French soldiers—but especially the Madagascans, who were quite light skinned though bronzed under their greasy straight hair—used to rape our girls, the tribes used to throw both the girls and the babies out. You fathered so many children that France there and England here [he meant the Sudan] set up a much-detested organization to deal with them, a kind of public assistance for bastards doubly or triply beyond the pale. They were bastards, black, and the children of girls put in the family way by NCOs—sons of whores from every point of view. But they got a good education. They learned English, French, German and Arabic. And I found out I had a cousin like that, living in exile with his mother in Djibouti."

I learned later that Mubarak didn't suspect I realized he was really talking about himself. The misfortune he spoke of was his own and that of his mother. If he suspected his father was a Madagascan it was primarily because his hair wasn't woolly, because sometimes his skin looked coppery rather than black, and because he was subjected to insults that were addressed only to Betsibokas. The exodus was his own, though in the opposite direction from that of the cousin in the story: hence his excellent French. Because of his mother's recklessness, Khartoum meant death, and it was tantamount to suicide for him to enter the Sudanese army.

I mention all this because many of those who fought in the cause of the Palestinians—those card-players without cards— were regarded in Europe as outcasts without any real identity, without any legitimate link with a recognized country, and above all without a territory belonging to them and to which they belonged, with the usual proofs of existence: cemeteries, war memorials, family trees, legends and, as I was to find out later, strategists and ideologues.

What am I doing here? If chance exists then there's no God, and I owe my happiness on the banks of the Jordan to chance. But though I may be here through the famous throw of the dice, isn't every Palestinian here by chance too? I was brought here by a series of extraordinary events, and it was equally strange that I should choose to exult in it.

Shall I ever see Hamza again? Is it necessary *for me* to see him again?

His mother was bound to be so diaphanous as to be almost invisible. But was it necessary *for me* to see more in her than the ruins of a life? Hadn't their love, hers and her son's, and my love for them, told me all there was to tell about myself? They'd lived through the Palestinian revolution—what more was needed? It had naturally worn them out. And since I, the author of this account, don't need them any more, their death won't affect me much, if I find out they *are* dead.

Abu Omar's doomed voyage didn't upset me despite its tragic end: it was too long ago, too formally recited, and finally too over-written. And so with the physical disappearance of Ferraj, Mahjub, Mubarak and Nabila—about all of them I know nothing and never shall know anything, except that they existed when I saw them and as long as they saw me and talked to me. But now they are too far away, too far away or too dead. In any case, gone.

The present is always grim, and the future is supposed to be worse. The past and that which is absent are wonderful. But we live in the present, and into the world lived in the present the Palestinian revolution brought a sweetness that seemed to belong to the past, to that which is far and perhaps also to that which is absent. For the adjectives that describe it are these: quixotic, fragile, brave, heroic, romantic, serious, wily, smart. In Europe people talk only in figures. In *Le Monde* on 31 October 1985 there are three pages of financial news. The fedayeen didn't even count their dead.

It matters how long a revolution lasts. For the Palestinians, the misery of being driven out of their country in 1948 with few belongings and many children was followed by the cool reception given them by the Lebanese, the Syrians and the Jordanians, and the reluctance of the Arab countries to use enough force to make Israel withdraw, or at least to bring about a fairer partition than that drawn up by the UN in 1947. There were several reasons for this reluctance: the rebels were a threat to wealth, and countries like Saudi Arabia, the Emirates, Lebanon and Syria were hand in glove with America and Europe. Israel, moreover, was demonstrating a military and political strength that made it seem wise to treat her as an equal, even if only on the sly. And where was the advantage in supporting a people who'd never been a real country, only a province of Rome, Syria or Turkey, or a mandated dependency of Britain.

Meanwhile the territory that should have been Palestinian according to the thunderbolt of 1948 remained Israeli territory, and the Palestinian people were steered into what were first called "transit" and then "refugee" camps, under the surveillance of the Arab police of the three countries that had agreed to accept them.

I can't explain how the resistance arose. But it's clear a few hundred years aren't enough to crush a people out of existence.

The source of the revolt may be hidden as dark and as deep as that of the Amazon. Where is it? What geographer will go in search of it? But the water that flows from it is new, and may be fruitful.

Some English lady readers still love romance. And in addition to everything else, the Palestinian Revolution seems to have provided the world with a living example of knight errantry. One reason why people went to Jordan was that they hoped to meet a Paladin.

The various hazards that have allowed me to survive in the world don't allow me to change it, so all I shall do is observe, decipher and describe it. And every phase of my life will just consist in the undemanding labour of writing down each episode—choosing the words, crossing them out, reading them the wrong way round. They won't be set down truthfully, as some transcendental eye might see them, but as I myself select, interpret and classify them. As I'm not an archivist or a historian or anything like it, I'll only have spoken of my life in order to tell the story, a story, of the Palestinians.

The strangeness of my position, then, appears to me now either in three-quarter or half-profile or from the back. Never from the front, with my age and stature apparent. I calculate my dimensions from the scope of my movements and those of the fedayeen—reconstruct my size and position in the group from the pattern of a cigarette moved downwards, a lighter upward.

We're told the desert is advancing in Africa and a desert of ingenious cutlery was advancing over the whole world. Maybe it was designed to ward off death-dealing missiles; but there was the spark, the triangle of light on the edge of the blade, and the blade's descent through the wooden grooves of justice. The fascinating dawn ceremony of the guillotine.

I've read novels in which men have died because of the fascination of a woman's eyes. There's a shop in Châtellerault where I once saw a knife as small as a penknife with blades that opened slowly one after the other and then gently shut again, after having threatened the town in all directions. For it revolved, and as it did so it threw out a challenge north, west, south and east, menacing first the street where I stood, next to a baker's stall, and a few seconds later the cutlery shop itself.

Every blade or similar device had its own special function, from the lethal spike capable of piercing a grown man's heart through the chest or the back, to a corkscrew for opening a celebratory bottle of red wine. The handle was shiny and made of horn, and when the knife was closed it looked harmless. But, open, this small provincial masterpiece swelled up until its forty-seven blades resembled a porcupine at bay or the Palestinian revolution. That too was a miniature threatening in all directions: Israel, America, the Arab kingdoms. Like the penknife in the window it turned on its own axis and no one wanted to buy it. But now it seems all the parts have gone rusty, except the toothpick. Perhaps other weapons are ready to take its place.

As long as it was alive and bloody, a new multi-purpose penknife presenting either the lethal blade or the corkscrew, the Palestinian revolution drew me away from Europe and France. It was a success. I want its success to be permanent. But what will become of it? For the moment it has escaped the smug self-satisfaction of the FLN.* Algeria may have dreamed of turning the whole Islamic world upside down, but it has only produced one more provincialism. The Palestinian leaders seem weary. And those who have any energy left often apply it to following the fluctuations of their fortunes on the Stock Exchange.

When I went back to Irbid in July 1984 the revelation of the town, the camp, the house and the mother, all Hamza's glorious past, were things of the past. No pride or happiness was left in the mother's voice or eyes. I gazed at the withered skin, finely hatched with microscopic but visible wrinkles; at the veiled eyes, if veil is the word for what made the eyes like glass marbles scratched by sand, two marbles that looked at but didn't see me; at the blotches and marks on the skin and the henna clinging to the dandruff in the white hair. And I looked at the shoddy pseudo-

* National Liberation Front.

modern equipment, apparently made in Japan, that only made the house seem poorer than it was before.

The past fifteen years had seen Jordan invaded by Japanese products, the poor quality of which was revealed by how quickly they broke, and the worthlessness of the bits. Radio and television sets, electric cookers, machine-made lace doilies, refrigerators, air conditioning—they'd all been imported from Tokyo or Osaka, but three months after they were bought, none of them worked. They only made the place look neglected, whereas before it had been cheerful with only its whitewashed walls and blue and yellow table.

Every Palestinian camp has its young men, but their eyes no longer light up at the thought of conquering Jerusalem: instead they're interested in dreary tales told by their fathers, who left Amman to free Jerusalem via Amsterdam, Oslo and Bangkok, and grew older through absence than through any exploits.

If one Palestinian feared he was going to be forgotten, he feared the same thing for all of them. Already the Islamic Jihad, the Sunnis and the Shiites were outdoing them and stealing the Arabic and European headlines. Once the word Palestinian in a headline was enough to make people buy the paper, hoping to read of fresh deeds of daring. Now, when they see it, people hope to learn of Palestinian reverses. The public may take pride in its heroes; that doesn't stop it enjoying their downfall.

If one watchword was the reconquest of Palestine, its complement was revolution throughout the Arab world and the overthrow of all reactionary régimes. The leaders managed to persuade the people in the camps to go without food to buy arms for an all-out war. But where were the arms? When did the battles against presidential or royal monarchies take place? What became of the money? These and similar questions are being asked so loudly in the Palestinian camps they drown every other sound.

"The rebellion was young and so were we. And too trusting. We set out our goals too fast and too clearly. Brecht was right when he said revolutionaries shouldn't neglect guile."

That was the answer I got one day from Abu Marouan, PLO representative in Rabat.

Neither Hamza alone, nor his sister and her husband alone, nor the mother alone, could have become symbols of the revolution. I see quite clearly that there had to be Hamza, his mother, the night of battle and the firework display of the nearby guns.

And now it's all disappeared.

When someone leaned out of the window of a departing train it used to be the custom, apparently, for his friends to run alongside waving their handkerchiefs. But the custom has probably died out, just as the piece of cloth has been replaced by a neat square of paper. You used to know the train would take good care of the traveller, and you expected him to send you a postcard. If someone set out on a journey on foot, his friends would wait until he or even his shadow disappeared. But even in his absence he was still with them, and if they heard he'd died or was in danger or trouble, they felt for him.

Here's what a Fatah dissident said to me.

"The Palestinians wanted to be an entity—wanted to leave an image of themselves as a single whole, historically, geographically and politically. Even when they were scattered to the four winds they wanted to form an indivisible and unchanging block in the midst of the Muslim universe and of the universe itself.

"Historically they saw themselves as descendants of the Palestinians, 'The People from the Sea'—in other words from nowhere.

"Bounded as they were geographically, on one side by the sea and on the other by the desert, for a long time they hated the nomads: they got their livelihood from the earth, and they were attached to it. Perhaps they were good at accepting things. They were Christian under the last of the Romans, but apparently accepted Islam without too much trouble. And after that came the Ottoman conquest. But they wouldn't accept Israel. So there they were, caught between two greater and two lesser forces: America and the USSR on the one hand, and Israel and Syria on the other.

"Politically they wanted to be themselves, independent on their own territory. But the revolution led by Arafat and the PLO has failed. Israel is protected by America, partly because of the American Jews, but perhaps also because of Israel's position, which fitted in so well with America's policy in the east.

"If the Palestinians, after rashly embracing Maoism, are now supported by the USSR, it's not because they can really bring anything to the relationship—it's because they have a situation and a movement that can be exploited.

"Then there's Syria. Palestine, like the Basque country of France and Spain, was once a province proud of itself, of its originality, its tradition and its legend. It rejected complete integration. But today Palestine's only hope is in Syria, partly because of the skill of Hafez el-Assad—he himself belongs to the Alawite minority—who can treat with Israel. For the possibility that Syria could come out on top might make the USSR take Syria's strategic and military support seriously."

"You're suggesting Hafez el-Assad as the man of destiny?"

"Neither the expression nor the idea is fashionable at the moment."

The dissident went on politely.

"What a lot two or three words can contain, and conceal! Bitterness may nourish ambition, and ambition the will to conquer. The latter almost always leads the conqueror to ruin, death or shame, though the conquest itself may survive. Then the cards are dealt out differently—a metaphor stolen from the Arab chronicles by your orientalists, and from them by your journalists."

"You mean Assad's ambitious enough to conquer Israel?"

"The USSR might be ready to support him if he seems a real ally. That'll finish him off, but not the USSR. Then the game can start again without him."

"That means perpetual war."

"I know. And the Palestinians are tired. But if you see life as anything else but endless war . . ."

"What the Palestinians prize most is their originality, and if all they've got left to fight for it with is their fatigue and their passiveness, they'll fight for it with them."

"Those are Jewish weapons!"

Most Palestinian fighters still seemed to me to reflect the flamboyance of the Leading Families. They were ceremonious in victory—or rather, victories being rare, in the way they congratulated one another after battle. Bravery under fire was still a chivalrous ideal, at once "old hat" and primordial, as much Muslim as Christian. Everyone whether of noble or plebeian origin seemed to vie with the rest in distinction, in those forests where no one was vulgar. Was it the nearness of death? The Greeks had an expression: "May the earth be light on you." You could say that before he died a fedayee was light on the earth.

It might have been a mere fossil or archaism, a survival from a dead language or cult of honour. But that didn't seem to matter. The quasi-religious respect and authority vested in the leading families, and now become almost natural, didn't only act as a brake on the boldness of the fedayeen while allowing every kind of audacity to the families themselves and their descendants. It wouldn't have been true in present-day Europe, but there, in that place and at that time, a few leading Palestinian families were facilitators of the bold and the new.

"I'm frightened when I see the sons of martyrs made much of. Not every martyr dies a hero. And the virtues of the father, even if he did die a hero, are not easily passed on to the son when he's educated to privilege, preferential treatment and easy success. That doesn't create a hereditary nobility—it produces a gang of heirs who exploit, squander and ruin the name they bear."

And yet joy was all round me. Far away, but all round me. I was on the edge of a lake of it. At its centre was a group of laughing Israeli pilots with fair curly hair, just landed from their planes.

"We Jews, we super-males, have just laid our eggs over West Beirut."

Perhaps I was the only person among the ruins who could understand the relief not only of an army but even of an arm, a weapon, that has just been used. Think how sad bombs must be, buried in their silos—bombs that will never be used, at once terrible and worthless. A knife ought to cut. A shell ought to be fired. Both ought to be at once the murderer and the victim.

Tsahal had killed. A sign had probably been enough for the people to understand and fall silent, as if praying or listening, to hear the first drone of the Jewish squadron. Then at last it was there, dropping its bombs with relief and going on its way, in a curve over the blue sea and in the blue sky, back to the peals of laughter on the Israeli bases.

"Yes, weapons are terrible. They kill people. Arabs. But if they hadn't been born we wouldn't have had to kill them when they were ten or fifteen."

Adding, rather sadly:

"All those missiles lying unused in the silos!"

Sad but detached:

"They're American, though. But there's still gold left in the rocks, oil in the sand, diamonds in the ore. And, as we love a thrill, why don't we invent the future?—find out what hasn't yet been exploited, weigh our brains and see how many Jewish grey cells it takes to achieve what can only be expressed in the form of equations, symbols and geometries as yet unknown."

Waking began before you raised your eyelids. A few moments' sloth and light was on the threshold, and the eye knew it was in action as the last images of dream mingled with the first of the ferns of Ajloun. Everything in the world was waiting for me to wake up to the world, to wake up here where my every wait was rewarded with wonder.

"You would not seek me unless you had already found me"— an aphorism of Christ's, but useful nonetheless.

The papers, that is the journalists, describing the Palestinians as they were not, made use of slogans instead. I lived with the Palestinians, and my amused astonishment arose from the clash between the two visions. They were so opposite to what they were said to be that their radiance, their very existence, derived from that negation. Every negative detail in the newspaper, from the slightest to the boldest, had a positive counterpart in reality.

I might as well admit that by staying with them I was stay-ing—I don't know how, how else, to put it—in my own memory. By that rather childish expression I don't mean I lived and remem-bered previous lives. I'm saying as clearly as I can that the Palestinian revolt was among my oldest memories. "The Koran is eternal, uncreated, consubstantial with God." Setting aside the word "God," their revolt was eternal, uncreated, consubstantial with me.

Is that enough to show how important I think memories are?

The peremptory way Mubarak gave orders both amused and irritated me, and one evening at Baqa camp I tried to imitate him.

"Je-han! Je-han! Come in!" I shouted—he preferred to give orders in English. I pointed my finger as I'd seen him do. As no one ventured to laugh I realized I hadn't been funny. He was silent for a moment, thinking; then, emerging with difficulty from a long sleep or well simulated meditation, he said:

"Now I'll imitate Jean imitating me."

Seeing yourself in the glass, once you realize the left is on the right, is nothing. Nothing beside seeing yourself there under the trees, without a mirror, talking and walking about, and so cruelly depicted by the voice of the Sudanese and the movements of his whole body, including the position of his feet, that everyone but me burst out laughing.

What really hurt was that the laughter was rather patronizing. Not mine, though—I had too much admiration for the performance.

He imitated me going up and down some mud steps. Thanks to him I saw myself as a huge figure outlined against an almost black sky, descending in the distance, though nearby, a bit stooped with the weariness of age and from marching up and down hills as high to me as the clouds over Nablus, and limping at the end of the day. The limp was simplified and exaggerated, but just like the way I walked.

I realized I was looking at myself for the first time, not in a so-called Psyche mirror or cheval glass but through eyes that had found me out, not only hill by hill but step by step. Everyone had seen and recognized me. It was only later that I realized how much cruelty there was in that little performance.

Mubarak quite often used a Toyota to transport supplies. In addition to the black NCO who gave my leavings to the fedayeen there was also an elderly Egyptian who I was told came from a tribe near Fezzan. At that time, in 1971, the Rolling Stones, though not yet world famous, were already well known, and the Toyota had a radio in the dashboard that also played cassettes.

The truck was standing still, the pop music going full tilt, and I watched without being seen. Mubarak, barefoot and wearing only his trousers, was dancing. He needn't have been ashamed, either, for he danced very well, mixing rock style with Sudanese, while the elderly Black, with his greying fuzzy hair, strummed without looking at it at a non-existent guitar, his right hand working where you pluck the strings, his left coming and going on an imaginary neck.

"Terrific!"

Without a word Mubarak put on his vest and shirt and soft-soled shoes, stumbling and nearly falling, or perhaps nearly killing me, in the process. Then he got back into the Toyota with his friend beside him and they shot off, leaving me enveloped in a cloud of black exhaust fumes and a deliberately offensive racket.

I don't think he ever forgave me for catching him dancing as if in Africa. I was rather annoyed myself at his rushing off like that, and my attempt to imitate him was the result of my resentment.

The music of the Rolling Stones was real, but the guitar was not, and its absence reminded me of the game of cards played with non-cards.

Everything seemed more and more disjointed.

In white America the Blacks are the characters in which history is written. They are the ink that gives the white page a meaning. If they ever disappear the United States will be nothing but itself to me, and not a struggle growing more and more dramatic.

The heirs, the descendants, are descending further and further into negation, sinking and fading uncontrollably into drugs. The heirs who were supposed to be the foundation on which white America stands are collapsing. Principles and laws totter before their grace, together with the skyscrapers that were their proof and justification. In Chicago, in San Francisco, where despite all the pregnant women there was a dearth of youth—a few faded flowers. In New York, where grime is a sign that the world toiled for by the legendary pioneers is renounced by their sons and grandsons, mingling with yet separate from the flowery ones.

But a rough black movement, strict when need be, was trying to understand this world, this rejected world, in order to build another. The negation was denied and transformed by the pleasure of being. The Black Panthers' Party, faced with that dive into the void, braced itself, used every means, deliberately gave its own life if necessary, and raised this necessity around itself to endow the black race with form. The hippies, covered in flowers and vague ornaments, made love and got stoned and sank; the Panthers rejected the white world.

They built the black race on a white America that was splitting, together with its police, its Churches, its pimps and its judges. But the hippies were already luxuriant, blades of wheat cracking the block that was America. The Panthers got guns. Though it wasn't yet clear, they were like the hippies in one respect: they hated that Hell.

The Black Panthers' Party wasn't an isolated phenomenon. It was one of many revolutionary outcrops. What made it stand out in white America was its black skin, its frizzy hair and, despite a kind of uniform black leather jacket, an extravagant but elegant way of dressing. They wore multicoloured caps only just resting on their springy hair; scraggy moustaches, sometimes beards; blue or pink or gold trousers made of satin or velvet, and cut so that even the most shortsighted passer-by couldn't miss their manly vigour.

To the image of the black race as a kind of writing I add another: a dark piece of smelted ore, and in the middle a streak of shining metal: the Party.

The Black Panthers' women wore men's trousers, and often boots as well. They were the same age as the men, and tried to conceal their seriousness.

The above are a few hasty points about the appearance of a group of people who instead of hiding showed themselves off. The Black Panthers attacked first by sight. They were immediately recognizable by the tousled visible signs I've described. They were consciously linked to every people that had ever been oppressed, emasculated, beaten, robbed of its history and its legends. Linked too to what only a short time ago had rejected the West, rejected an exhausted but still noxious Christianity. Around them, around us, there feebly flaps a lingering evangelical morality that is on its way out, but which once existed. It was to throw this off as quickly as possible that the Black world, and its surest sword, the Party, was struggling. It shattered worn-out angels and precepts with the help of the very precepts the Christian churches had forced upon it.

True, there was a kind of mad fertility about it all. That hair, those beards and whiskers, those gestures and shouts were like a great profusion of ferns. The Blacks made you think of ferns or tree-ferns, without flowers or fruit, propagated by spores. True, disorder brought more disorder. Nothing seemed sure. Neither direction, directions nor directives were sure, either for the peaceful or pacified Blacks, or for the Whites. True, these flames and their sparks could consume those who kindled them. True that the vortex seemed to be master, not the men. That their admissions had been those of madmen and their ruses the ruses of animal predators. That, as the Gospel of John says, referring to John the Baptist: "He must increase, but I must decrease."

I put it like this: "He must increase *in order that* I may decrease."

True, for those who did not experience them, their violent acts seemed anarchic. They smelled of sweat, for they didn't wash much and they ate fatty food. True, the Panthers made incursions into white territory and then took refuge in the ghetto, as if in a protected shack; but for them everything was a challenge to which they had to rise. Nothing can be as it was before. Up to 1793 the king = the king. After 21 January the king = the guillotine, and the princesse de Lamballe = a head on a pike, sovereignty = tyranny. And so on. Letters, words, a whole dictionary changed.

The Panther movement, whose behaviour at first seemed quite crazy, was to become quite commonplace, even to some Whites. People = noble, and Black = beautiful.

Except on the fedayeen bases in Jordan, I'll never have been so much among the dead—so long as I go along with the myth that says the activities of the dead are different from ours. The colour of the Panthers' skin had something to do with it, but that wasn't the only thing. The way the police hunted them down meant they belonged to an animal world. In order to escape they sometimes resorted to sudden temporary invisibility. Even their office furniture was funereal, and so were their meals.

One of the causes of this was probably the danger they ran of real, cadaverous death, which led to a kind of deification of the dead, of prisoners and of everyone, by means of photographs, photomontages and uplifting poems. All of which were funereal without being lugubrious.

And so I wrote the above. But now I'd like to add a correction: it's the whole black American people that belongs to the dead, through its way of carrying on, the converse of that of the Whites. Despite the peals of laughter, the singing and dancing, the whole black race is enveloped in despair.

As a privileged witness to a mystery, I was no longer fair skinned, no longer one of the Whites. When David Hilliard held out his hand and smiled at me for the first time in the car—it was being followed by a police car—I was quite happy to descend into the world of darkness. Body warmth, sweat and breath seemed not to exist. The Panthers are dry: they move about in an atmosphere where Whites couldn't long survive.

Emerging from a press conference in a luxurious villa belonging to a White, David said it was the first time in his life—he was twenty-nine—that he'd set foot in such a place.

"What were your impressions?"

He laughed.

"I was very uneasy. Too many Whites together. I was afraid of being accused."

"What of?"

"Of being so black."

He roared with laughter.

When Bobby Seale spoke on television from a prison cell in San Francisco, I didn't understand. At first. It seemed so far-fetched that a man accused of murder could have made the speech being broadcast that evening. Here's how it came about.

Bobby was in prison in San Quentin, and the governor, no doubt with the consent of the legal authorities, allowed a black television cameraman to interview him. The photographer was a young Black who was more of an Uncle Tom than a Panther, but he wore multicoloured clothes and his hair, beard and moustache were phosphorescent. He was rather stupid when it came to discussion, but brilliant with the camera. A warder brought Seale into a cell where the equipment was already set up, and stayed during the shooting, but he didn't intervene. Bobby sat on a chair and talked.

At first there was such disagreement between him and the multicoloured cameraman with his Afro haircut that they nearly came to blows. Then the shooting was done in several sessions, and the film was put in the can.

Maybe the authorities disagreed as to whether or not it ought to go out on TV. I don't really know. Bobby Seale was extradited from California to New Haven in Connecticut. He was still liable to be put to death, but in a different manner. In California they used the gas chamber; in New Haven it was the electric chair.

Who'll ever know what made the Californian authorities decide to let the film be shown? Bobby had told his story to the camera, and put up a fight, in a cell in San Quentin; he was now in solitary confinement in New Haven; and I saw and heard him in San Francisco.

I was shattered. In answer to the multicoloured man's first question, about food, Bobby talked about his mother's and his wife's cooking and the things he used to cook for himself when he was still free. He went into great detail about his favourite dish. He talked about the spices that ought to be put in it, how long it took to cook, and how it should be eaten: the revolutionary leader was talking like a chef.

Suddenly, and it *was* suddenly, I understood. Seale was talking not to me but to the ghetto. Familiarly, easily, he spoke of his wife, smiling as he said that now, unfortunately, he had to make do with masturbating, which was some consolation, but disappointing.

Then suddenly—and it *was* suddenly, again—both his face and his voice hardened. And to all the Blacks listening in the ghetto he addressed revolutionary slogans all the more open and uncompromising because the sauces recommended at the outset had been so smooth. The political message was brief. Bobby had won. So much so that the television channel had to give the film a second showing.

A prisoner who sees himself as outside the law because he's been put where he is, is proud rather than resentful. He may desire freedom, but he likes prison, too, because he's managed to fix himself up with freedom there.

Freedom in freedom; freedom in constraint. The first is given, the second wrested from yourself. Because people go for what's easy, and asceticism is exhausting, they prefer the freedom that's given. But they may also secretly value the proscription that makes you find liberty within yourself. The unbolting of the prison door is a wrench as well as a release.

People love the ghetto. With a love that's also hatred, no doubt. But it's something that the Blacks, excluded from the white world, have succeeded in managing their misery. It's much more that they've found, brought to light and built up a freedom indistinguishable from pride.

David and Geronimo took me to a barber in the ghetto for a shave, and the barber was a black woman of about fifty with mauve hair. She's never shaved a White before. The men—black, of course—who were waiting their turn talked to me about Bobby Seale, whom they'd watched on TV the night before. They didn't seem particularly excited about it: he was just one of their own people saying what needed to be said to the Blacks and what the Whites needed to be made to understand. As a spokesman he'd done his work well: hair-splitting might have been resented.

"Did you come from France to listen to him or to help him?"

"It's up to the Blacks to get him out."

"It mustn't be the Whites who do it. That would be another victory for them over us."

I asked if they agreed with what he'd said.

"The warder was white. The Whites had given permission. From prison he could only say what he did. But we understood on a higher level."

So what Bobby said had been in code. And the code had been

deciphered. Bobby had used the same kind of stratagem the slaves had used on the plantations. To pass signals for escape or revolt they'd used the African music that later became jazz.

Some morning or evening, in various flowing rhythms, they would announce in a language only they understood a rendezvous by a river, which they meant to cross and flee to the north. They'd have chosen voices, men's or women's, that were fleshly and erotically warm, able to attract as surely as males on heat. The object was flight, to give help to other escaping negroes, to kindle fire and war; but the appeal was made in a voice in which Blacks recognized the promise of fun.

And so, with humour and gravity both, telling men still at liberty about recipes for dishes he'd dreamed of in his cell or jams and jellies that survived in his memory, talking of his wife and his nights without women, Bobby Seale was sending out a call. And the Blacks who were listening had got the message.

When the armed Black Panthers marched to occupy the Capitol in Sacramento; when their athletes stood on the podium in Mexico and defied the American flags and national anthem; when their hair, moustaches and beards grew with insolent vigour, President Johnson was in power. Johnson bombed Vietnam, while in California a group of black men and women, through every possible act, sign and gesture, made sure that nothing would ever be the same again.

The black words on the white American page are sometimes crossed out or erased. The best disappear, but it's they that make the poem, or rather the poem of the poem. If the Whites are the page, the Blacks are the writing that conveys a meaning—not of the page, or not of the page alone. The abundance of Whites is what the writing is set down on, and it forms the margin too. But the poem is written by the absent Blacks—the dead, if you like—the nameless absent Blacks who wrote the poem, of which the meaning escapes me but not the reality.

Let the absence of invisibility of the Blacks we call dead be well understood. They are still active. Radioactive.

When the Panthers' Afro haircuts hit the Whites in the eye, the ear, the nostril and the neck, and even got under their tongues, they were panic-stricken. How could they defend themselves in the subway, the bus, the office and the lift against all this vegetation, this springing, electric, elastic growth like an extension of pubic hair? The laughing Panthers wore a dense furry sex on their heads. The Whites could only have replied with non-existent laws of politeness. Where could they have found insults fierce enough to smooth all those hairy, sweaty black faces, when every curly whisker on each black chin had been nurtured and cherished for dear life?

A well-known dramatic theme in the ghettos of Alabama: one day or night, in a deserted square, a Black sees a White emerge from the shade of a sycamore tree, then another, and another, and another. Their fair hair is cut short, and the way they swing their shoulders is different from the way the Blacks swing their hips. Idly perhaps, they move towards the Black. Then they surround him. He'd like to run, but his legs fail him; to shout, but no sound comes out of his mouth. The Whites roar with laughter and walk away. The negro who dared to go out alone has been "put in his place."

At Yale University, when the seven Panthers who'd been invited to speak about the arrest of Bobby Seale walked in, the three thousand whites in the audience were three thousand assailants. They encircled the Panthers, but instead of fists they thrust at them arguments cast in Europe and polished by a thousand years of Christianity.

But the Panthers wouldn't play by the rules.

"We answer your arguments primarily with the opposite arguments, but also with sneers and insults. You are fierce quarrellers, and your metal theologians have broken both bodies and spirits. Ours. We are going to outrage you first, and only then will we talk to you. When you've been beaten and crushed, we'll tell you our arguments calmly. Calmly and regally."

Another Black said:

"It's not that a new theory is 'truer' than the old ones, but by destroying or even just displacing them the new one produces the cheerfulness you feel when someone who's lived a long time dies. When everything's tottering, even verified verities, it makes you laugh. So we're going to laugh! Revolution is the happiest time of our lives."

Ringlets, Afro hairdo's, beards, whiskers, moustaches, laughter, shouting, steely looks—all the tropical exuberances they amused themselves with also asserted, and prevented others from denying, their existence.

"We've decided to be like this, and you'll see us as we want to be seen, hear us as we want to be heard. The eye comes before the ear. In the beginning there was the colour black, then our ornaments, and only after that the American language as we have adapted it, as much for a joke as to annoy you. Nothing will be said except in terms of black."

"We're going to try to cover the old truths with new ones. You'll see how strange that is."

It would be rash to say Sankt Pauli was beautiful even when the night-club quarter was rebuilt. But I didn't really feel any disgust, unless it was swamped by astonishment. Round the dance floor there were tables and chairs and customers. On the dance floor, five donkeys with men and sometimes a woman on their backs—five frightened donkeys drunk on beer. Another detail: the dance floor was covered with a fairly thick layer of mud. Every tipsy animal was trying to throw its (usually German) rider, who would be toppled into the mud amid roars of mirth and swillings of wine torrential as adolescent pee. No, I don't think disgust ever managed to get through surprise.

I wanted to describe that quarter, but especially the part of Hamburg between Sankt Pauli and the statue of Bismarck, going towards the city and the old police headquarters. That's where the ruins began. The upraised hands of the caryatids—naked men twenty metres tall, made of pink marble or granite—supported only the sky or, if you prefer, nothing. Bullets and shell splinters had left the muscles of their thighs and chests unscathed. Beside my memory of them, the twenty-storey blocks in Beirut looked like cardboard or plywood.

I was reminded of the pink granite of Hamburg when I saw the shoddiness of the materials used in Beirut, where nothing was ever left of the houses but iron girders sticking out of what must have been very flimsy concrete walls. The sight of Beirut and my memories of Berlin and Hamburg in 1947 convinced me of two things: that Israeli airmen were as good as the RAF, and that Lebanese building was specially designed to make it easy to clear away the ruins.

The ruins of the three cities were not identical, nor even alike, but what was left of them proved that two contrasting civilizations had been consumed. Yet there seemed to be a kinship between the RAF and the pilots of Israel: both had the same pin-point precision, perhaps both used the same intelligence methods.

I've said above (or will say below), that the expression *entre chien et loup* [literally, between dog and wolf, that is dusk, when the two can't be distinguished from each another] suggests a lot of other things besides the time of day. The colour grey, for instance, and the hour when night approaches as inexorably as sleep, whether daily or eternal. The hour when street lamps are lit in the city, and which children try to drag out so that they can go on playing, though their eyes, suddenly active, are closing in spite of themselves. The hour in which—and it's a space rather than a time—every being becomes his own shadow, and thus something other than himself. The hour of metamorphoses, when people half hope, half fear that a dog will become a wolf. The hour that comes down to us from at least as far back as the early Middle Ages, when country people believed that transformation might happen at any moment.

In order to record the next phase of the story, probably a rather tedious one, perhaps I ought to draw back at first and take a run at it. It was a simple matter, but the mere thought of it, let drop inadvertently in passing, brought howls, almost shrieks of protest from the PLO officials who heard me.

And what was it?

What I feared most were logical conclusions: for example, an invisible transformation of the fedayeen into Shiites or members of the Muslim Brotherhood. None of the people around me thought such a thing possible, perhaps rightly if it were a matter of a simple, external, visible change. But since every man is born and grows up with his own inner, hidden doubts and conflicts, it wasn't utterly out of the question that a fedayee might secretly harbour a potential Muslim Brother within himself.

For me in particular, in that particular place, the expression *entre chien et loup*, instead of connoting twilight, described any, perhaps all, of the moments of a fedayee's life.

For us the expression has a certain faded charm because we know that in our countryside all the wolves have been killed, caught by the leg in the famous wolf traps or shot in wolf hunts. Even the word wolf itself crops up very rarely, surviving mostly in a few old sayings. In short, we don't know much about wolves now, and no one believes any more that a dog might turn into one.

But in the Middle East there was still a danger that a Palestinian might turn into a Brother, as a dog used to turn into a wolf.

But as one of their leaders told me today, 8 September 1984, that such a thing was impossible, let's pretend this digression was never either written or read.

The same thing happened with the Black Panthers in the United States. Not that the whole of the party was contaminated by Nixon's police, but the FBI increasingly made use of internal black rivalries—between both men and women—to try to make the Panthers vanish for ever, eaten up like bacteria by white corpuscles. And that's what appeared to happen.

At the time I've spoken about at such length, in 1982, the streets, and especially the alleys, of Beirut were full of bronzed young men, part of whose faces, the part above the upper lip, was white. That was how you recognized a Palestinian. He'd thought to pass unnoticed by shaving off his moustache, but the pallor of the skin was a give-away.

In the United States the Blacks were the characters inscribed on the whiteness of America, giving meaning to that wan continent.

In Jordan it was as if revolts and revolutions were each a kind of holiday, longer or shorter, more or less bloody, as the case might be, and ending when everyone got too tired.

I could have disappeared from the quadrilateral of Ajloun without anyone knowing. There were so many gaps in that army, no one noticed them. We seemed to come and go without let or hindrance. The guards relied on family characteristics of face or gesture to tell one soldier from another, rather than on uniforms, the famous camouflage suits, which any enemy Bedouin could have bought from the American army surplus. All the fedayeen—therefore everyone—wore camouflage except me, with my white hair, my age, my corduroy trousers, and above all the way I was obviously part of the bark and the leaves anyway.

The officials were told in advance on the two or three occasions I left the bases to go to Damascus, Beirut or Paris, but I know that if one day I'd just disappeared, no one would have worried or been surprised.

No one, nothing, no narrative technique can ever tell what they were like—those six months the fedayeen went through in the mountains of Jerash and Ajloun. Especially the first few weeks, before it got really windy and cold. I could give an account of events, indicate times and dates, describe the fedayeen's successes and mistakes, the weather, the colour of the sky and the earth and the trees. I could do all that, but I could never convey the faint intoxication; the feeling of walking on but not touching the dust and dead leaves; the shining eyes; the complete openness of the relations not only between the fedayeen themselves but also between them and their leaders.

They were imprisoned inside an area sixty kilometres long and forty wide, but their bearing reminded you of the young knights you see in tapestries. They were prisoners, but to look at them you'd think they were prisoners on parole. There under the trees everything and everyone was quivering, laughing, filled with wonder at a life so new to them, and to me too. Yet in the quivering there was something strangely still, alert, reserved, hidden, as in someone silently on the watch. Everyone belonged to everyone else, yet each was alone in himself. *Seul* [alone] but not *saoul* [drunk]. Or perhaps . . . ? Anyway, both smiling and strained.

The part of Jordan they'd fallen back on—I use the words retreat or fall back according to the date—was wooded. And they were so happy there under the trees that in the eyes of the privileged of the Arab world the Palestinian revolution was really a kind of picnic.

In addition to the trees the area contained some small Jordanian villages where all you saw were a few rather barren-looking fields and two or three farmers' wives who quickly whisked out of sight. When I examined the soil I saw it was good and rich, but very thinly and inefficiently ploughed and inexpertly sown. The oats and rye were sparse in one patch and overcrowded a few yards away.

The young soldiers looked after their weapons with almost amorous devotion. The grease they used was so transparent it was hard not to think of vaseline. They might have been in love with their guns. To have one was a sign of virility triumphant, but strangely it also banished aggression.

When we were having tea, or in the evening, they would ask me to tell them about America and the skyscrapers. They must have been prepared to hear anything, however wild, because they showed no surprise when I told them that American cities with their vertical houses crapped where they stood. Not at regular intervals, like healthy human beings, but all the time, day and night, through several arse-holes at a time, emitting waves of shit into the streets. The skyscrapers in New York, with storeys of people in their intestines, emptied themselves violently, and then felt relieved, as after an attack of constipation. Until the eternal colic began again.

"Did it smell?"

"Not much. Americans' excrement is pale and odourless."

"But," said Khaled Abu Khaled, "you told me America used to be covered with forests. And that they've got very powerful machines. So why, instead of putting up skyscrapers, turning out all that crap like orange-squeezers, didn't they build the same sort of thing underground? Then they could have left the trees as they were and gone down in lifts."

"Like miners, only with galleries made of pink marble?"

"Perhaps."

"And live like the negroes in South Africa?"

"Is the electric chair a real chair?"

"More like a throne. The condemned man sits in it with his hands and arms on the rests."

"Why don't they kill him lying down?"

"Or standing up?"

"So it's on a throne. And who else is present?"

Revolutionaries often die young. They're not in a position to invent New York. They cross the sea, the sky, gardens. At night they go into rooms and kill or hide, bumping against the furniture. Their most peaceful movement is like a flash of lighting. The world below, our world, for which they'll all be killed, lives from day to day. It cooks its meals, goes to bed. But supermen stay awake and eat anything that comes to hand, at any old time. Even when they're serious, revolutionaries are only playing, hatching schemes to be worked out properly later. It's all a question of style.

Mubarak, in his camouflage overalls, appeared and disappeared. If he wasn't at Ajloun was he on one of the other bases, or in a camp? If so, which, and what was he doing there?

In all my life I've seen only one bit of radium, and that was Abu Kassem. I soon came within the influence of his radiation, which I can only describe as a constant bombardment of particles. There was also something erotic about it, but belonging to the past—perhaps a lack of discharge experienced actually as a discharge or explosion.

For some time I thought or pretended to think he was a present to me from the leaders. Or rather that, even before I heard his arguments, his presence was supposed to convince me of the seriousness of the resistance. (At the time we couldn't make up our minds which word to use: Palestine liberation, resistance, or revolution.)

He was the first to come and greet me, with another fedayee who could speak French. His physical beauty disturbed me not so much because of the attractiveness of his face and eyes and what I guessed about his body, but because each element, imperfect in itself, combined into a harmony that made him seem a pent-up force.

"Salam Allah alikoum!"

"Alikoum Salam!"

"Are you from France? What part?"

I suddenly felt as if I'd been caught in a velvet trap. It was the first time I'd been addressed like that: instead of the ordinary *salam alikoum* the ceremonious *Salam Allah alikoum*.

"Paris."

"I've seen you walking. You limp slightly."

"A small wound in the heel. I had a fall in England."

"Is it cold in England?"

While I was hanging my jacket up on a nail, Abu Kassem disappeared. His fedayee companion seemed as surprised as I was.

"Where's your friend?"

"Gone out. He had to have a crap."

We looked out at the bushes.

"What does he want?"

"I don't know him. I met him on the road. He pointed at you and said, 'That's the Frenchman.' And then came over."

Abu Kassem reappeared beside us, silently but with a hint of a smile.

"That'll help you walk."

"Thanks."

I took the branch which he'd stripped of leaves and knots and even bark with his penknife.

"Translate," he said to the fedayee. Then: "How old are you? The same age as my father, or as my father's father? You haven't got much time left to make a revolution in France."

Abu Kassem was insufferable. He gravely instructed me in Leninism, with emphasis on its serious side. He'd learned passages of Lenin's works by heart when he was seventeen, and now he recited them to me in the evenings with the fervour of a *faqih* reciting the Koran. While his French-speaking friend was translating, he used the interval either to think up the next phrase, or preferably injunction, from Lenin, or to take a comb out of his pocket and tidy his hair.

In every fighter proud of being solid as iron, I should have detected the tremors of a man more afraid of the light than of the dark.

"What about your leaders?"

"What leaders?"

"Yours. You obey your leaders. Why?"

"Someone has to give orders. They obey Kosygin in the Soviet

Union, don't they? You don't understand—you're French. Why did the French betray de Gaulle?"

"Betray?"

"Replacing him with Pompidou. De Gaulle had to retire."

"My name's Rashid," said the interpreter, interrupting my answer. "Don't be too hard on Kassem—he's very young. At that age people believe in loyalty to one man, silly idiots. And they go on believing in it till they're forty or fifty years old. I'll explain things to him quietly in Arabic. You get some sleep."

"Sardina, sardina—always sardina!"

The fedayee on kitchen duty brought in the tins of tuna and opened them. For all the fighters, and for Abu Kassem in particular, every kind of tinned fish was sardines. He was born near Mafraq and had never seen the sea. Everyone contributed a drop of water as we tried to describe it to him. First of all we told him it was blue.

"Blue water!"

Then we drew some fish for him in the sand, quite different in size and shape from those out of tins.

"What sort of noise do they make?"

No one felt equal to imitating the voice of a fish.

"We ought to save some for Mubarak," I said.

Then all the rest noticed he wasn't there.

"You've told us about the apparitions of Mary, Jesus's wife," said Abu Kassem, half sarcastic and half intrigued.

"Not wife. Mother."

"Mother? You made her sound young. So when she speaks, what language does she use? The same as the sardines?"

"When she appears you know where she is, but where is she when she's not there? Do you know? And where's Mubarak?"

Kassem said no more.

It wasn't a serious conversation. Each of them was thinking of his own disappearance on the other side of the Jordan.

I wasn't the only one to realize Abu Kassem's radioactive properties. His muscular body smiled at everyone, but if a word or a gesture referred to his attractions his body showed its teeth. Like many of the other fedayeen, he was marked out for the Jordan, and he seemed to go there quite peacefully, aware of his beauty and the glory surrounding it, and aware of the glory that would surround his death. Did his beauty help him to die?

To examine the question in full, here's the other side of it: When ordered down to the Jordan and so to his death, could an unattractive fedayee—if there was such a thing—see himself as anything but a victim? Or, to cancel out the humbleness of his life so far, would he try to be a hero, the terror of the Jews?

Once, when my taxi was being held up by a Syrian army patrol near the Lebanese frontier, a keffiyeh above a face with a stubble of beard came out of a nearby house and I thought I recognized Arafat. But he walked right through the fedayeen without anyone getting up. It wasn't him. But when his car went by quite close to my taxi, and I saw his other profile, it was him. Yet my newspaper had a photograph of him in Algiers.

He spent his time showing one or the other of his profiles all over the place. Some queens do the same thing, travelling through their countries dressed in out-of-date clothes from department stores, and riding on a donkey to give photographers time to record the acclamations of the peasants.

It was like this. The Rolls parked by a donkey; the queen got out . . . And so on.

Arafat disappeared in the crowd, then got into the car. So many of the people there looked as if they had scrofula, it would have been a crime to take anyone's place and deprive him of the chance of being cured.

After his sensational appearance at the United Nations, Arafat seemed to be slipping towards nothingness. The Palestinians got nervous. Depression was in their faces, their bodies and their words. What had kept the fedayeen and the Palestinians as a whole going from 1965 to 1975 was the fear of being forgotten. Had the time come when Arafat's warning turned out to be a premonition?

He'd said: "Europe and the rest of the world talk about us,

photograph us, and so enable us to exist. But if the photographers stop coming, and radio and television and the newspapers stop talking about us, Europe and the rest of the world will think, 'The Palestinian Revolution is over. America and Israel have settled the matter between them.' "

I think most of the PLO longed to create an image that would inspire respect.

But in Jordan in 1970–71 I saw fedayeen glad to be able to pilfer cars, cameras, discs, books and trousers with impunity. As an excuse they told themselves and others they were revolutionaries. The revolution, the highest possible authority, not only protected them but even encouraged them to steal. Not to pilfer might have made them look timid and "non-revolutionary." After all, Revolution began with the sacking or confiscation of rich people's wealth.

The slogans of the Palestinian revolt named three enemies: Israel, America and the Arab police states.

And it was because of the third that the youth of the world saw the fedayeen as moving in a halo of light. But, not having equalled the heroism of Leila Khaled throwing a grenade in an El Al plane, they were basking in an image they hadn't earned.

I can quite believe there were always sharks among the leaders who instead of hijacking aircraft hijacked the Resistance's funds. Some Palestinians, very ordinary people, cited evidence to me, named names, and were full of contempt for Arafat's entourage.

And the leaders, like the ordinary fedayeen, excused themselves in their own eyes, and perhaps in their consciences too, by appealing to the supreme criterion: "It's for the ultimate victory of the revolution." The fedayeen were even more aware than I was that enormous sums were falling into the hands of officials and their wives and children.

A great fuss was made of the sons of "famous martyrs." Generations of heirs came into being, fraught from infancy with new rivalries—rivalries between clans, towns, villages, families, clients and alliances.

I wonder, as a matter of fact, whether all the money from the Gulf countries, all the aid from the Arab League, wasn't thrown at the leaders for the express purpose of tempting and eventually corrupting them.

Families of historic or perhaps legendary origin, dating anywhere from mythical times to the days of Lawrence, and hailing from Mecca, Medina, Damascus (home of the first Ommeyads), Jerusalem in the days of Titus or some village in Galilee before Jesus was born, surrounded Arafat with a kind of dateless history. The best of them, the Leading Families, even supplied the revolution with such ardent heroines as Nabila and Leila, and many others whose names are unknown.

The "wets," whom I shan't deign to name, fly by Concorde from London to Rio, from Los Angeles to Rome, and live in the avenue Foch or on Monte Parioli.

I only saw Abu Omar angry once; but I remember how furious he was. His pink face went suddenly white, changed from smiles to gravity, from round to long. He was in such a hurry to take off his glasses he seemed to snatch them off his nose.

I'd said, "If you take God as a postulate . . ."

After a few seconds' silence, his anger shot up like a thermometer in boiling water.

"God isn't a postulate! He's . . ."

"What?"

"The First Fact, Uncreated."

"And the Second?"

"The Revolution."

God, Creator and Fact Number One, Eternal and Uncreated, was for him self-evident. But his angry rejection of the insipid but harmless word postulate; his affirmation of his God and his categories; his anger—these went about as far as Islam allowed. Abu Omar had known for a long time about my unbelief, my lack of deference towards a divine Being. So was his fury caused by my clumsy words, which might have made him my accomplice if he hadn't objected to them? But I think there was something else in his look, his pallor, his quivering voice. What? As well as anger, fear. What if God could be given and taken away? What if he were not unmoving?

Sometimes a pupil remembers doing what the teacher told him—remembers having taken the sponge on its string and passed it back and forth over the letters chalked on the blackboard and wiped them out. A similar movement of a fedayee's hand, a slow gesture of farewell and obliteration, accompanied by a spoken goodbye, was so efficient that the faces of friends ordered to go down to the Jordan disappeared for ever.

But like a schoolboy seeing the words he's sure he rubbed out reappear on the blackboard, the fedayee refuses at first to recognize the face he's certain he erased, but which now belongs to a "martyr," leaning against a tree and smiling. He may have the wit to feign delight to hide his amazement, for a man doesn't rise up again unscathed from the realms of the devil unless he's signed a pact with him. A man doesn't return from Israel. I've often noticed that gesture of farewell wiping out a face and a body. And seen the face and body appear again the next day. I don't know why, but the camp took on a mischievous air then. But Abu Kassem never came back from the Jordan. He was twenty years old.

In our conversations both Abu Omar and I avoided the slightest allusion to his brief rush of emotion.

Wherever I went in Jordan he translated smiling but accurately the theological brushes I was forced to enter into with convinced Muslims. He brought great courage and intelligence to whatever he did.

Through him I came to understand the narrow lives of the Palestinian women in the camps. Their age-old memory is as if made up of the stitches in their ancient embroidered gowns: the sum of many brief, tiny memories laid end to end, so that the women know when to buy thread, to sew on a few buttons, patch the seat of a pair of trousers or go back to the shop for some salt. How long to endure the forgetting of past sufferings, and when to add to the memories, to the salt, to the thread, to buttons, to the memory of the dead and of the fighters, to the eggs, to the tea. All that continuous life! And on top of all that, how to remain dignified, noble, when left a widow with thirteen children.

He was really grieved when he said to me one day:

"Jean, I tremble sometimes, but I've really trembled, especially in my right hand, since I heard Arafat was going to see Frangié. To think of his shaking hands with a man who called himself a Christian on the very day he murdered seventeen peasants! And in a church that was his as well as theirs."

I know these are the words of a drowned man, or rather the words I make him speak. He saw the Revolution as an adequate solution to a difficult problem, as an Absolute Art made up not of day-dreams but on the real mental activities—certainties, hesitations and despairs—of one who'd given himself to the cause. Every day, several times a day, he had to pretend to approve when hare-brained or wrong-headed fedayeen laughed and told him of victories won over the Bedouin through acts he himself regarded as brutish or criminal.

"How many dead?"

"At Ashrafieh? Five at least. The Bedouin's head was completely severed from his body. It bounced from top to bottom of the steps."

At that time the fedayeen controlled the heights of Amman near the water tower, directly overlooking the Royal Palace.

"The head bounced down the steps?"

He pretended to be amused because he thought that, as an intellectual, he ought to harden himself. An enemy's head bouncing down the steps was certainly more comical than a water-melon would have been: a water-melon wouldn't have been covered with real blood. I wasn't really saddened by his affection of mirth, but I did ask him if he'd laugh as heartily if my hands were dripping with gore after decapitating a Jordanian with a sword, and we could still hear his head bouncing down the steps.

"What a horrible idea!"

And his face, especially his eyes and mouth, really did express revulsion.

"But you're amused when a fedayee tells you the same thing."

"I'm not used to slaughter, or accounts of it. It's time I toughened up."

We both knew—he better than I—an official who'd lost an eye opening a parcel bomb.

"Which eye was it?"

Abu Omar thought for a bit, then admitted: "I forget. The left, I think."

"When did you last see him?"

"Yesterday morning."

"And you've forgotten?"

"Yes—I'm not very observant. Is it important?"

"Which eye has Dayan still got?"

"Do you want to compare them? Supposing the Palestinian still has his left eye and the Israeli still has his right? You're not going to put it in your book? It would be amusing, but . . . what about Arafat?"

"He wouldn't let me."

"He'd understand one thing: you take an interest in some very funny things."

"Are you sorry for the official who lost an eye?"

"Of course."

"And for Dayan?"

"Of course not."

He laughed again, but not heartily. Then suddenly stopped, and to my surprise:

"We really ought to wait for the Salt meeting," he said.

"Why Salt?" I asked.

Salt was the little village in Jordan that I described earlier. It was a Christian village that still had a Turkish look about it; it used to be the capital of Transjordan. There was a sort of cellar there used as a shop, with Romanesque vaulting and round pillars with the stones showing. It also had some elegant little white marble columns with worn sculptured capitals softened by time and damp. The columns looked all the more elegant for being protected by the hefty great pillars, which tried to look as small as possible. On the right was a heap of water-melons, on the left a pile of aubergines. At the back, oranges. It struck me that the fruit and vegetables were worthy of the Byzantine architecture.

But Abu Omar was really answering a question I'd asked before—"Arafat's invited to Moscow—when's he going?'—and by Salt he meant the Strategic Arms Limitation Talks.

When he realized the misunderstanding he started to laugh again with such abandon that he had to take off his glasses and dry his tears with his sleeve. Now that he's dead I'll never know whether his mirth was caused by the Bedouin's head bouncing down the steps or by our cross-purposes. At the time I thought I detected a shrill note in his polite laughter, the beginning of hysteria. Perhaps he hoped the laugh over the mistake might cover up and make me forget the other one.

Beneath the painful hilarity at the image of the victim, beneath the deliberately simulated cruelty and childish, strident laughter —you can hear the same from tipsy Englishmen in pubs of an evening—there lurked a quick and serious intelligence, a mind on the alert, endlessly pondering the current upheavals. And, if you looked closely, you could see a total devotion. Five years before his death Abu Omar was already drowned in the revolution.

Have I told you before that he was a good man?

Like all the other leaders, neither more nor less ostentatiously, he stood up the instant a fedayee came into Arafat's office. Such an obvious and funereal tribute was like a frill round the legs of a piano, or a hastily buttoned fly. The fighter bringing in a telegram, a cup of coffee or a packet of cigarettes was bound to know what it meant: that is you're a hero, therefore you're as good as dead, and so we render you the honours due to a martyr and weep for you in advance. We've got springs under our seats and as soon as a hero comes in we're ejected into mourning.

Where did the custom come from? And how long will it last? An ordinary fedayee had only to enter and all the officials, male and female, would stand up. And the dead man bringing in the newspaper would see his own open grave with the officials standing all round it, proud both of the hero and of themselves and pointing him into the beyond.

Abu Omar used to laugh at this ceremony. He'd accepted it innocently at first, but afterwards he wearied of it.

Of course it was just a military ritual, like holding the little finger in line with the seam of the trousers. But if fedayeen being honoured enjoyed a couple of seconds' glory, it was the glory of the grave. (I wrote "gravestone" at first, but crossed it out because a granite or marble gravestone has words carved on it, and the grave I'm talking about is deep but non-existent and bears no date or name.)

He slapped his thigh, like someone who's heard a good joke.

He even said to me once, serious and ironical at the same time:

"I was very middle-class this morning."

"How do you mean?"

"I went to my aunt's house to have a shower. She's a Palestinian, but a monarchist too."

"Taking a shower isn't middle-class any more. It isn't revolutionary either. There are showers in every football stadium. A bath might be a different matter..."

"I didn't like to say so, but actually I did have a hot bath... Horribly bourgeois, wasn't it?" He laughed.

"So why did you do it?"

"For the last four months I haven't been able to stomach my own smell. It was the first time for ages I'd felt water on my skin. The only time the fedayeen feel water on their skin is when it rains."

Like the word France, the word Palestine means different things to different people—peasants, aristocrats, financiers, the fedayeen, the Leading Families and the new bourgeoisie. None of these groups or individuals seems to suspect that these differences exist, and that they may eventually lead to conflicts. The word Palestine will one day no longer mean what it seems to do now, namely a common accord. Instead it could stand for a fierce class struggle.

"Mountains are so beautiful!"

Setting aside the understandable exaggerations of geologists, mountains provide climbers with a test, mountain-dwellers with a yodel, Cézanne with something else again, and others with heaven knows what. But basically mountains have a kind of personality to which everyone relates in a special way, and anyone who speaks of them speaks only for himself.

Abu Omar's aunt belonged to the respectable Christian bourgeoisie, for whom a bathroom was not a luxury nor even just a bit of plumbing, but an obvious underpinning of the word Palestine. She had a profound contempt for the fedayeen.

She might have accepted them if it hadn't been for the fatal influence of the phrase "Your Majesty": the only language she deigned to speak was English, together with a few bits of low Arab dialect, including some coarse Palestinian oaths. But she was much more impressed by the Queen of Jordan than by any revolution, especially one that sprang up out of soil in the form of a beggars' revolt. All she did for her nephew, from the time he joined the PLO until he died, was to let him use her bathroom once every three months.

Abu Omar called upon the resources of his university education, but instead of making his life easier they only added to his uncertainties. Now both his life and the revolution seemed unreal.

Some insects that live on the branches of trees are invisible. When I was a kid I sometimes crushed some green or brown bug without realizing it, until the smell told me I'd killed a creature whose only defences were its ability to freeze on the spot, the fact that it was indistinguishable from the branch it was on, and perhaps the vengeance contained in the fart-like stench it left on my hand.

A young fedayee told us the following anecdote for the second time. When the Jordanian tanks left their barracks and headed for the hospital, he hid among the patients, intending to avoid being taken prisoner by passing himself off as a serious casualty. But when they got there the soldiers fired at everybody. They were said to have killed between thirty and forty people: ordinary patients, army casualties, nurses and doctors. Some took refuge in an annexe, but all of them were killed.

The fedayee who told the story said both times that as soon as he'd heard firing he'd got into bed with his gun beside him. He then feigned death till he got drowsy, or maybe even fell asleep, amid the smell of blood and death.

But was he telling the truth?

An old Palestinian woman said to me: "To have been dangerous for a thousandth of a second, to have been handsome for a thousandth of a thousandth of a second, to have been that, or happy or something, and then to rest—what more can one want? Did we stay for a few minutes in Oslo? Maybe. If we'd stayed there for sixteen years we'd have frozen the world. But we were sensible. And dangerous for only a few seconds."

When the fedayee woke up it was dark, he said—as in his first telling of the story. Not a sound in the ward. By the crushing weight on top of him he realized he'd fallen asleep for a moment under a pile of dead bodies. He plucked up his courage and opened his eyes. Some Bedouin soldiers were having a quiet smoke and taking hardly any notice of the victims of their handiwork.

Had he got the presence of mind to act like the insect? Could he, despite some irresistible itch or pins and needles in one foot, lie stiff as a corpse, keeping people away for fear of the imminent stench? Did he feel safe, hidden under defences more reliable than an armed camp?

He had his gun beside him. He aimed at one of the Bedouin and shot him dead.

The Bedouin's companions didn't know where the shot had come from. Though they were terrified, they tried to find out, but the fedayee was still protected by the corpses and managed to claim four more victims.

"Five dead in all."

Abu Omar looked at me with a thoughtful frown.

"Five? Yesterday he said four." Kissinger's former pupil was upset by the mistake in arithmetic.

I answered in French.

"He's only young. It's his first exploit and he's told the story often. It's natural he should add details and claim a bigger bag—he livens things up so as not to bore himself with repetition. Hunters and fishermen always do it. Even French ones. The fedayee hides under the details as he says he did under the dead bodies."

I could see Abu Omar was even more sceptical of my explanation than of the fedayee's claim to have been asleep with one eye open.

He told us he managed to get out of the hospital without trouble.

"Because it was night I lived to tell the tale of the day."

Abu Omar pretended to believe the story, and to be pleased by it, as he did with others. The fedayeen were never ruffianly or case hardened: they had a kind of smiling serenity and elegance which prevented that.

Abu Omar was never coarse for an instant, either, though a sensitive man, especially an intellectual, may try to conceal what he fears is an effeminate delicacy beneath an affectation of brutality. But he overdid it. As I've heard friends say of an actor, "He did his nut."

What remains in men's minds, what they deliberately erase, and what disappears of its own accord, may be either subject, cause, occasion or circumstance. It's hard to say who or what creates a glory or an echo, what somehow sets memory in motion when you read, aloud or to yourself, the story of the Kiss bestowed on the Leper.

The leper in his cowl yields himself the Cid. Similarly, out of courtesy, a dead man is replaced by Antigone, a wounded man by the stretcher-bearer, a drowning man by the lifeguard, the wolfhound by Hitler. What am I saying?—by Hitler's hand, by just his little finger stroking it. But the dog has vanished, and all that's left suspended in mid-air is the caress, the eternal caress that is at once a proof of the magnanimity and the means by which it will go on existing for ever.

And so, in the Palestinian revolution, masses of corpses were swallowed up and their limbs scattered in order that a few winged details, absurd but heroic, might survive to be remembered by two or three generations.

You'll never know anything about the beggar into whose hand I dropped a couple of dirhams—neither his name, nor his past, nor his future. All we know about the Cid is that he kissed the leper—apart from a tragedy famous for several centuries. What do we know about Hitler, except that he burned Jews or caused them to be burned, and that he stroked a wolfhound? I've forgotten all about the beggar this morning except for the two dirhams. And what's a wolfhound doing here, biting the legs of a Greek shepherd?

There must be another story struggling to get out from beneath the one I've been telling. There are still two or three hospitals where they look after lepers. But do they really look after them? Perhaps the experts inject people with the virus so that future Cids can show what heroism and Christian charity an Arab's capable of. Through leprosy, which conferred another sort of obliteration, he overcame oblivion.

TWO

I'D ALREADY been told the Palestinian Revolution might be summed up in the apocryphal phrase, "to have been dangerous for a thousandth of a second."

The first time I went to Amman I drove there from Deraa and arrived in the pink mist of dawn; it was like entering Haroun el-Rashid's Baghdad in about AD 800. Yet at the same time an obstinate notion lurked inside me that I was really strolling about in Saint-Ouen or thereabouts in the 1920s.

When after some difficulty the Palestinians got to Ashrafieh, the highest point in Amman, they used to joke that they'd got frostbitten fingers from the snow at those Himalayan altitudes. The walls of the houses round about Ashrafieh were built of rubble, but though they were sometimes dilapidated or singed they were never bloodstained—in short, they were as ordinary as the suburbs of a European capital. The main mosque, in the eternal, universal Arab-Colonial style, was built of three hundred and forty different kinds of marble.

After living in one of those houses for a few days I realized what life was like in the camps. In Baqa camp the people sang and danced and fired off real bullets to greet the plumbers and their pipes when they came for a few weeks to instal water-taps at every level. When a family needed water in the winter of 1970, the wives and daughters, even the little girls, had had to queue up at the camp's one tap and take it in turns to fill up a couple of green or red or yellow plastic buckets, each with a different picture of Mickey Mouse painted on the side.

In many a poor village in the Muslim countries there's only one brass water tap, and all the women, married and single, enjoy going there to exchange insults and gibes and what exiles from the circus call horrors. Every woman sets down her bucket, full or empty, to keep her place while she launches into a lengthy tirade about the inadequacies of her husband throughout the previous night, sometimes stopping with her hands on her hips to wait for the other women's laughter or cries of indignation.

But the Palestinian women were always silent, too worn out to speak or even to want to. Their way of getting hold of the handle and carrying the bucket was always exactly identical, because it had been repeated three or four times a day, three hundred and sixty-five days a year. The position of the arm was just right: the woman knew the weight of every drop of water.

They were granted only one distraction: once a month a Jordanian came from Amman with a horse-drawn cart, selling plastic utensils. Then the women, and sometimes a few happily inspired men, would ponder long over the choice between bright green, bottle green, reddish brown, dark red, deep black, an almost pornographic scarlet, and one, two, three, four, five ... ten different blues. And always, on every bucket, a stencilled Mickey Mouse. And near the line of buckets there was the sound of the water.

That was all. And that too was what the camp lived by.

When I said above that "Every woman sets down her bucket," I didn't mean that every single woman went to the tap, as they used to go to the well, to make fun of her husband. That paragraph was just to underline the soberness of the Palestinian women. For *they* weren't sure their husbands would be back.

Re-reading what I've written, I see I've forgotten to mention the scarves they wear over their hair, covering it up completely, or all except a few roots.

Another amendment. Not every woman in the camps has either the time or the inclination to embroider the famous Palestinian robes, or the cushions now so rare that the ladies of the Leading Families wring their hands. If the husband dies the wife will take up a gun instead of a needle. So no more tapestry cushions, except machine-made ones.

The little road that led from Salt to the fedayeen base near the Jordan, now properly surfaced, went past a hill with a white villa on top. It attracted attention even from the road, for the hill, a truncated cone, was covered with close-cut grass like an English lawn, and the green slope itself, from the house down to the road, was always covered with long silver ringlets of barbed wire. At the foot of the hill there were more rolls of barbed wire between the surrounding wall and the road, and Bedouin soldiers, sentries without sentry-boxes, stood guard there with their guns, undoubtedly loaded and ready, trained on the road.

The barbed wire behind them looked as soft as the corkscrew curls I've described falling down to the shoulders of the Saïka soldiers in Irbid. Other sentries were also on the watch, reacting nervously whenever a horse and cart or a car or a local man or woman came along.

The wall surrounding the villa on the side towards the road looked like a blockhouse. It had openings or loopholes through which a light machine-gun or the famous Katyushka had a very wide angle of fire on the road and the countryside opposite. Behind all this the villa itself was invisible and possibly quite comfortable. Every weekend it sheltered the head of the Jordan police. It was very close to the fedayeen base. Was that why its chief, Dr. Mahjoub, took such precautions?

We arrived at the little base at Malijoub after dark. As soon as Nabila entered the room, Dr. Mahjoub looked as if a stone had just hit him between the eyes. I believe he actually blushed. Perhaps it was the first time he'd ever done so in his whole life, this tall man of thirty-seven, deeply tanned by the desert winds and the sun, with the shoulders of an athlete slightly bowed over a stick steel tipped like an ice-pick.

Nabila was very beautiful. Perhaps she's even more beautiful now, at fifty, than she was then. In the summer of 1982, during the three months' siege and shelling of Beirut, she was head of preventive medicine in Lebanon.

All of us except Nabila shook Dr. Mahjoub's outstretched hand.

She and I were sitting next to one another. She warned me gently that I mustn't be surprised at what was going to happen: it was only to be expected.

"You can't understand. You're French."

Even after fourteen years I still don't understand Mahjoub's character or his fear of women. He soon made up his mind. As soon as we'd had something to eat, Nabila was to be taken back to Salt, which we'd just come from.

It was very dark by now. Watching her go, I thought of Iphigenia and Mata Hari, all the women led off to execution on the orders of a gentle man obeying orders rather than mercy, and decreeing death as the only solution. Nabila left between two armed fedayeen.

As a doctor herself, but also a Muslim, etymologically owing obedience, she may not have felt it as acutely as I did—the ferocity not of Mahjoub but of the law which said that a woman alone (though what did the word mean in our situation?) could not sleep among soldiers. The danger wasn't to her but to them: if they slept near her they'd be on the edge of an abyss.

Was Nabila less alone between the two armed soldiers? She wasn't their prisoner. All three of them were prisoners of the darkness. And yet no one was invisible because of all the sentries, fedayeen and Bedouin coming and going through it. The part of the road that passed below the villa fortress was very brightly lit, and guarded by men who were sentries, a word that's feminine in French though it refers to the opposite sex, as is very easily recognized. So on that road where the cars were guarded by armed soldiers, themselves in the line of fire of invisible Palestinian sentries, Nabila was alone.

"No one must be able to say a woman's spent the night on a base," said Mahjoub in French, loud enough for me to hear.

Two hours later the two fedayeen came back. Nabila was going to spend the night with a woman dentist in Salt.

"A Palestinian?"

"What does it matter so long as it's a woman?" answered Mahjoub. "We'll send someone to fetch her tomorrow morning."

She came, not smiling but apparently without resentment, and insisted on going straight to Mahjoub's office. He smiled and held out his hand with a friendly smile. I hadn't seen that gentleness on his face the evening before: he'd looked severe and disturbed. But I saw it again now, as I did whenever I saw him. I see it again now as I write.

"Would it have been so difficult, then, to explain to the fedayeen that a Palestinian lady doctor had to sleep here because it was dangerous to drive back to Salt in the dark?"

"They'll have understood my decision. The Palestinian people as well as the Palestinian middle class would have agreed with me. If the Bedouin had found out there'd have been a scandal—people would have said we ran a brothel. Nabila is well aware of all that."

In 1984 some Jordanian tribes living near the desert still remember him in spite of his name (Mahjoub means "hidden"). He was a doctor. He came from the prisons of Egypt. He was tall, handsome and apparently strong, though in fact his body was already ill. He became a legend.

As a healer he was able to influence the desert dwellers, to undermine the alliances of some of the more timorous leading tribes and make them exchange their allegiance to Hussein for agreements with the Palestinians. But the results were not too dependable. The tribes had given their word to the descendant of the Prophet: they looked down on the Palestinians, who'd been driven out of their own lands and were too peaceful and fond of gardens. Mahjoub had a lot of trouble, but luck was on his side. The son of one of the sheikhs fell ill, and Mahjoub made a good diagnosis and cured him. To show his gratitude, the father hid Mahjoub and his men, who were wanted by the desert police, and they were able to escape to a secret base.

Those are the main outlines of the legend, or perhaps its point of departure. Other legends were grafted on to it, and other miracles, though the first of the latter succeeded thanks to a pinch of antibiotics. Just in time. Royalist army doctors were starting to produce so many miracle cures among the tribes they were almost commonplace. Penicillin was becoming the desert's staple food.

We left Salt for Ajloun, and I stayed there from October 1970 until May 1971. Mahjoub, another Palestinian and I slept underground in a sort of shelter or burrow under the trees. Revolutionary as everyone was, there was a strict unwritten law of the blind eye, a sort of politeness about one's own body and other people's which decreed that they were all invisible. Perhaps it was what's called modesty.

It was one night when we were walking from one point to another around Ajloun that Mahjoub told me card-playing was forbidden. He referred to it as if it were some terrible thing that never happened. He was as unreasonable about cards as he'd been about Nabila, making her run the gauntlet of a night fuller of enemies than of men.

"The enemy would say every base turned into a dive at sunset. And card-playing, I don't know why, causes quarrels. Knives are drawn. Sometimes blood."

I found the manners of almost all the ordinary Palestinians, men and women, delightful. But their leaders were a pain in the neck.

Most of them surrounded themselves with a ceremonial that needed no help from marble and chandeliers. The main object was to stretch out to infinity the distance between the door and the official the visitor wanted to see. Before you got to him with a simple problem that he could have solved with a couple of minutes' thought and a few words, you first had to explain your errand at length to the sentries. Then:

"Wait here. I'll go and see."

The sentry would saunter off, and after an interval return at an equally leisurely pace.

"Come this way."

This gave you the chance to see what an ordinary fedayee, charming, smiling, always ready for a joke, could turn into in a few hours, and what he would remain for a few hours more. Yesterday he was a boy throwing stones and trying to kill birds who were cleverer than he. He would even pick a flower, smell it, then give it to me. But today, because he was on duty, he marched along in front of me like a zombie.

Next I'd be ushered in to a second official who before anything else insisted on hearing the whole story over again, though he had no authority whatsoever to deal with it. He'd have me taken to a third official, then to a fourth, and so on in a kind of snakes and ladders that at long last brought me to the official I'd come to see.

He was speaking into a field telephone. What was he saying to the Unseen?

"If God wills . . . His tooth-ache will be quite better tomorrow, I assure you . . . If God wills . . . No, don't worry, it's not contagious . . . At least I don't think so . . . Of course . . . If God wills."

He put down the receiver.

"Oh, I wasn't expecting you. How are you? Good news from France? Are they writing about us in *Le Figaro*?"

"I'd like . . ."

"Coffee or tea?"

(To the soldier: "A couple of coffees, please. Jean and I have a lot to say to each other.")

"The kids are stealing tablets from the dispensary. Probably just for fun. But the tablets are dangerous. We ought to have a sentry on duty."

"It's difficult to stop kids larking about."

"The pills could be fatal if they take too many of them. I lock the door, but they prise it open in the daytime, let alone at night. Could you please detail a fedayee to stand guard?"

The official took a piece of paper, wrote down the order and handed it to the sentry. When I got to the dispensary there was already a fedayee guarding the door. It had taken me rather more than three-quarters of an hour to reach the official, and he had kept me two minutes.

But the ones who made you run an obstacle race weren't the most dangerous. The worst were the ones whose heads were full of neat but crude slogans that they unloaded on you like a ton of bricks. The one I dreaded most was Thalami, who I believe meant to turn me into a perfect Marxist-Leninist. The Koran had a surat for every occasion: David Thalami had a quotation from Lenin. And he wasn't the only one. In the early days I told myself the revolutionaries were only young after all.

One superior youth suddenly came out with a sentence in German.

"What's that?"

"Lukács. What's your answer?"

The pains in the neck really were awful.

Mahjoub was as delicate as a girl, but not so difficult.

After the massacres at Sabra and Chatila in September 1982 some of the Palestinians asked me to write my memoirs. For six months I hesitated. The problem was Arafat's situation in Tripoli and in the PLO itself. When I was in Vienna I met some other Palestinians who hoped I'd publish my recollections.

"Put down exactly what you saw and heard. Try to explain why you stayed with us so long. Why you came. You intended to stay for a week. Why did you stay for two years?"

I started writing in August 1983, went right back to the 1970s, and found my memories carrying me on to 1983. I plunged in, helped by the many people who took part in or witnessed the events I recorded. Being abroad helped me see things afresh: France seemed far away, and shrunk very small. One fedayee's little finger seemed bigger than the whole of Europe, and France just a distant recollection of my childhood.

I'm not at all sure that when the Congress at Basle, after considering Argentina and Uganda, finally decided that the Jews should settle in Palestine, the choice was divinely inspired. After all, what the Jews call the Promised Land was promised first of all to one vagabond who'd walked all the way from Chaldea and another who'd come from Egypt. But the country known as the Holy Land is famous because of the events recorded in the New Testament. The Jews ought to hate it rather than love it. It gave birth to those who became their worst enemies, starting with St. Paul. Without him and Jesus, who would remember Jerusalem, Nazareth and the carpenter, Bethlehem or the Sea of Galilee? The Gospels are full of them.

"The English Protestants knew the place from the Old Testament too."

"Have you ever had a good look at stuffed animals? The geography of the Old Testament is stuffed. Nature plays hardly any part in Jewish history. Except for the bits about the exiles. They mention Nineveh and Ur, Egypt and Sinai. But they never come alive like the Sea of Galilee, or even Golgotha."

Monsieur Mustapha, whom I'd met in a café, was so eloquent in his hatred of England I wondered if he was really thinking of his straitlaced youth and regretting not having dared to touch the gold coins in the open packing cases. So many Turkish officers must have had all that wealth dangled under their noses! Nowadays they seem very virtuous not to have stolen any.

Monsieur Mustapha always talked to me in such old-fashioned language that the Ottoman Empire appeared a country of fable, steeped in sperm and blood. In short, just how the novelists describe it, except for one detail that struck me as quite plausible: the beautiful slaves were indeed the enormous females with the sort of breasts and thighs Caliphs adored, but it took so much jewellery to cover those vast expanses of flesh that the ornaments of one favourite had to be taken back to deck her successor the following night.

"It was because of the tinkle," said Monsieur Mustapha.

When I passed this remark on to Omar as a joke he said:

"The sound of that English gold is still ringing in his ears. Short of piercing his own eardrums he'll never get rid of it."

When I saw the Syrians playing cards in secret I was fascinated by a card called the Wheel and another called the Swords—in fact, by the whole pack. Just as under the arbour in Ajloun in the Arab style, or in Spain in the Spanish, so in Damascus they had their own way of folding the pack lengthwise, so that when a card was thrown down it fell on the crease in an unstable equilibrium. It might topple to one side and lie like an open boat drawn up on a beach: even if it was a Knave of Hearts it might be one moment a female offering herself and the next a male taking her, even if it was a Queen of Clubs. Compared with the nice clean pack people use for a game of bridge, it made for a sort of erotic game.

Mahjoub's "I don't know why" about card-playing, offered almost as an explanation, makes me wonder if he didn't fear Nabila's presence on his own account. The mere sight of a face might have been enough to make him go all weak and unable to think. The subject of card-playing might have affected him in the same way. But I don't see any connection between the two. Except something like this, but it's so personal I'll have to wrap it up a bit: when Manon Lescaut went to the Havre de Grâce to join the Chevalier des Grieux, she left behind in Paris a beloved brother who made his living cheating at cards.

Everything—the place, Manon, Mahjoub the Hidden, the Cheat, the Queen, the Kings, the Knaves, the Swords—it all swirls about still inside me. Only Mahjoub himself is uncontaminated. Each image arises out of the others, or is its own and their double. But Nabila too stands out bright and clear and alone.

I'm still the battleground for a struggle which Muslim theologians could probably explain. Can such a solitary God (He is called the One, the Alone) coexist with chance? Or is what is called chance willed by God? Is the outcome of a game of cards something divine?

One evening when we were alone, Mahjoub smiled, as he always did, with a sweetness close to affection, and offered me a Gitane. He despised the Virginia cigarettes donated by the Emirates.

"I was once in love, madly in love, with a little girl eight years old," he said.

I didn't think he'd chosen that moment in advance. Perhaps it just seemed a suitable opportunity.

"I used to go miles out of my way to look at her. I never did her any harm, but she did a lot of harm to me."

"How?"

"She wouldn't take my presents, for one thing. And she sulked. I think she sensed her power. Hurting me was a game to her."

"At eight years old?"

"Sometimes she behaved like a woman of forty. Her village was quite a long way from Cairo, and she knew I made the journey just to look at her. Just for that."

"And did it last?"

"She got to be nine, ten, eleven. When she was twelve she was a woman. But I wasn't interested any more."

"You were well out of it."

"No. I was in pain when I loved her, but I was very happy."

A silence fell between us. We seemed much farther apart than before. Or much closer—but I don't think so, because that would have embarrassed me. I felt as if there was a yawning gap.

"Don't be sad," he said, walking away from the hummock where we'd been sitting.

I stayed and finished my Gitane. I wondered why he'd told me. And why then.

"Jean, I've forgotten the name of that church, but I don't think it was Notre-Dame-des-Fleurs."

L'Orient le Jour (*The Eastern Daily*), a French-language Lebanese paper, had been sarcastic about my being with Fatah on the banks of the Jordan, where John the Baptist had lived. But the only time anyone mentioned it to me was one day when Ferraj said, "The only thing that matters is that you're with us."

It seemed to me that all that interested the fedayeen was how the party was going to end. For it was a party, the Palestinian revolt on the banks of the Jordan.

A party that lasted nine months. To get an idea of what it was like, anyone who tasted the freedom that reigned in Paris in May 1968 has only to add physical elegance and universal courtesy. But the fedayeen were armed.

One day in March Mahjoub suddenly appeared beside me, though I hadn't heard him approach. His presence was a kind of inner silence, so imposing that I believe I used to lower my voice when he was there. Perhaps it was his moral attitude, reminiscent of Saint-Just, that made him so impressive. Writing about him, I feel as if I'm adding a page to the Golden Legend.

"Have you seen the buds?"

"They were a long time coming but they're here now. They're all sticky still, and I get covered with pollen when I shake the branches. The almond flowers will soon open, and the leaves unfold."

"The sun's hotter and the fedayeen are more cheerful. March and April are fairly easy months. If we get through them, if we hold out that long, the revolution will have won."

"I didn't think much of the arrangements at the minor bases— the ones in the forest."

"I think they'll be all right. Tactics aren't my business, but the comrades in charge aren't worried."

"You're like Naief Hawatmeh."

"How?"

"He talks of nothing but science—scientific tactics, scientific socialism . . ."

He laughed. But another leader had come up, and now spoke to him rapidly in Arabic. Sometimes he pointed to me. Then he went off in a hurry, without saying goodbye.

"He wants me to tell you he's the new officer in command of this sector. And you've passed him twice without acknowledgement."

"So what?"

Mahjoub smiled.

"He was trained at Sandhurst, and he wants everyone to know he's the boss. Even you. He knows Arafat's given you permission to come and go as you like, but he wants the authorization to come from him as well. But forget about him—go on as you have been doing. The fedayeen are getting their colour back, they're putting on weight and muscle, and starting to sing and whistle again."

During the two years in which we used to meet quite often, Mahjoub used to range from emotional outbursts to the most silent helpfulness, from the extremest caution to the most extravagant boldness. But once he'd staked out an area with those long legs of his, any feminine presence there was sacrilege. He was one of the best-loved of the leaders. And when you think about it, his rather childish and conventional moral judgements were as acute as the judgement of Solomon, inconvenient though they might have been for the child who was cut in half.

He came in, and you were delighted to see him. He went out, and you were aghast. Though he himself was sensitive and uncertain, he gave others a great sense of security.

Certain Christian priests who work in South America, though they themselves were brought up according to the most conventional morals, find themselves in sympathy with the guerrillas. If he hadn't been a Muslim, Mahjoub might have been one of them.

He brought out one argument after another to convince me

that card-playing suggested some disreputable joint, and would soon be sniffed out by the elderly puritans in their houses or tents. When I refused to agree, he tried to prove that card-playing was bad for the health. He was a doctor; he should know.

But one day he told me all the army chiefs played cards.

"Well, then?"

"I've got used to it."

As our first image let us take the hand. The arm is lifted high with the hand palm upward, then the hand is turned over and the fingers, still stiff and compressed from being clenched, suddenly open. Like a bird swept along on its back by a squall, the hand turns over, opens, and drops the dice on to the marble table.

There are plenty of literary descriptions in which an eagle hovers and wheels over a lamb grazing unaware. Or soars over Delphi and drops the omphalos, Jupiter's umbilical cord, from its beak. Sometimes it's carrying Ganymede, astounded but tipsy already, off to Olympus, where it lets him fall on to an eiderdown of clouds.

And so the hand of the dice player, raised up high, hovers a moment then turns over and spills the numbers on to the marble, spills fate on to the café table. The dice make a terrible noise as they fall, urgent as the beat of a drum. But now that fate has spoken the gambler's fingers relax and come back to rest on the table.

And with cards it's the same as with dice. The players try to be clever and conceal their hands from one another. But it's Zeus who decides.

"Let not God play at dice with the world." Translated, the saying doesn't mean much: if God is, He is by definition Everything, the game of dice along with all the rest. So hey presto, chance's name is Providence. When the Koran declares games of chance sinful, the prohibition sounds like a makeshift attempt, a perversion of words, to stop the gamblers asking the lurking question: If God decides the result of the game, then if I win it's because he's chosen me, but why me? It's only natural I should be appalled . . . Or if it was chance and not God that made me win, is chance swifter than God? Did God come to exist by chance?

Mahjoub never mentioned the size of the stakes, but I found out they were sometimes thirty times as much as the players earned. But the officers were artful and perhaps, mistrusting his frankness and naïvety, they played for matchsticks or beans when he was there.

He moved about in a mixture of anguish and innocence. Perhaps all he needed to become the local contemporary saint was to have stigmata and be resurrected. But he isn't dead yet. He's still alive, in Cairo.

He lacked faith and therefore wonder, but maybe he had them in their secular form—for the beauty and goodness of the world. His innocence didn't seem to bring him actual happiness, but it let him express it so ardently it seemed quite natural and spontaneous.

"Look at how soft the yellow of the buds is! Think how strong the leaves will be!"

But it seemed to me such reactions to the vigour and hope of nature were designed to put me off the scent. Even in the sunlight, the darkness around him was deep.

The sons of peasants sometimes try, vainly, to conceal their origins by using a sophisticated vocabulary. In the same way the shallowness of those who'd had a wealthy upbringing showed through despite their vaguely revolutionary activities.

No one seemed to suspect that mere commonplace swindles had led to the opulence which even today has devastating effects. Wealth makes vulgar manners seem charming. And so with the profound shallowness of the fighting, which was often treated as some kind of hobby.

Right back as far as you can go there were alliances with Crusaders; new kings; brigands among the younger sons of the minor nobility; improper solicitation of legacies; brutal plunder legalized by forged seals of golden or bull's-blood wax. As for the Crusaders themselves, they created new sovereigns, overlords and privileges; they married the daughters of descendants of the Prophet, inherited the wealth of Byzantium, tolerated slavery under the Ottomans.

I omit a lot of important details: all the concatenations of baseness and arrogance, bravado and abjection, from Clovis to Weygand, from the Prophet to Hussein.

Time, and above all the prestige that comes from occupying the same offices for centuries, have naturally lent lustre to the Leading Families. And their children follow the same tradition, making matrimonial alliances with the feudal families of Lebanon, Syria, Jordan and Kuwait. In other words, they marry large fortunes. What ought they to feel—remorse, regret or repentance? Repentance lasts the longest.

This book will never be translated into Arabic, nor will it ever be read by the French or any other Europeans. But since I'm writing it anyway . . . who is it for?

That elegant eighteenth-century edifice, the library of the harem in Istanbul, keeps its doors and windows shut. And the highest dignitaries of the countries that almost unwittingly made up the Ottoman Empire do their best to keep them shut. Documents in every language are kept in solitary confinement. But even when they're locked up they frighten all the Leading Families, whether Greek, Illyrian, Bulgarian, Jewish, Syrian, Montenegran or even French.

If I say "darkness spread over all the world," I mean that at a certain moment everything seemed to coincide so closely with everything else that I briefly experienced what might be called cosmic unity. But it wasn't long before the split between things and living beings was suddenly borne in on me again.

The Ottoman Empire melted away at a snap of the fingers, amid the kind of ridicule that's almost a relief. What survived was the shrill lament of the Eunuch trying to console the Shadow of God on earth, the caliph of all believers, on the deck of the British cruiser carrying him into exile.

That cry might have been my own. I didn't hear it myself, but perhaps the Palestinians thought they heard it not only from my lips but from my whole being all the time I was with them. Over a year.

The harem library must be kept shut. The slightest crack and a plague would be unleashed on Istanbul and sully all Turkey. What is written in those books, in the same characters as those in the uncreated Koran, is the evil, corruption, treachery and prostitution perpetrated by the great families of the Ottoman Empire.

Sometimes the price paid to obtain the office of Grand Vizier was a couple of testicles. Hence all the whispered orders—so that the receiving ear would be less likely to detect the tell-tale soprano. Hence, even today, the fact that a bass or baritone voice is regarded as proof of manliness. Hence too the way some Turkish officials, speaking on the radio to state informers, address them as "Dear spies." What family, Turkish or otherwise, hasn't included at least one eunuch, one emir's or elderly sultan's concubine?

But everything, including the plague, is safe under lock and key.

For one people to exaggerate the inhumanity of another race that has persecuted them—well, anyone can understand that. But when the persecuted people develop a resemblance to the persecutor, that strikes me as an almost superhuman challenge to the rest of the world. What is called for is either an almost impossible heroism or a tolerance of all too human nature.

Which is it? Sublime challenge or spinelessness?

Last night a Palestinian woman—perhaps she bore a grudge about something—told me that the oldest families in Palestine, all able to prove they're related to the Prophet, are still influential in the revolution.

Say there was a very noble Palestinian family rivalling the Husseinis, and a distant branch produced Yasser Arafat, what effect would that have on the other descendants? Scandals among the nobility give offence in the West. Not here.

One part of Nabila's family produced court officials, their excuse being loyalty to the direct descendant of the Prophet. But what about her? She was certainly the most beautiful girl in the kingdom before the war against Hussein, when the fedayeen bases threatened only Israel.

Like children playing kings and queens, the Leading Families used to war among themselves, quarrelling over and sharing out the country's power and resources under the cold eye of the Ottomans. They produced offspring who were rebellious, but rarely against privilege. It's worth noting that no *ashraf* family—that is

one descended from the Prophet—paid taxes, though wealthy plebeian families did. Whether it consisted of office, land or money,
no heir ever refused a legacy, however shameless its origin—not
even if it derived from the most blatant imposture.

The descendants were furious when "their" peasants, now
become fighters, got themselves massacred by men they didn't belong to—the Jews, or Hussein's Bedouin. But we must distinguish
between the emotion due to sheer magnanimity, and that which
appeared when the revolution established a new nobility, the aristocracy of arms.

Circumstances like to produce ironies. One day I heard an
Arab, not particularly rich, say to another:

"What do you mean by talking to my caretaker like that!
I'm his master, and if he's done anything you don't like it's for me
to tell him off, not you."

The Leading Families took umbrage when their farmers were
injured by the Jews, perhaps out of patriotism, perhaps out of pity,
perhaps with a premonition. But chiefly because a stranger had
interfered with something that was theirs.

As well as being descendants of Muhammad, these families
were also, if not more, at the base of all nobility. In Morocco I
once saw two family trees belonging to one chief. One genealogy
went back to Muhammad, whose name was dusted with gold at
the top of the parchment, while the other traced a pedigree back
to Abraham: his name was in mauve ink, also dusted with gold.

The great families had been living as Muslims in Palestine for
a long time when they were suddenly confronted by the Frankish Crusaders. The Palestine aristocracy saw the Lusignans as
a vile gang of Poitevin brigands whose only women were camp-
followers. Arab princesses compare them to the whores who
served the lords of the desert and slept several to a tent with cups
and saucepans and teapots hooked to their gilded belts.

Nabila had never heard of the Lusignans, still less of their
strange disappearance in the form of a winged serpent. Was Guy
de Lusignan's wife one of de Nerval's *Chimères*?

But the Frankish gang became a royal dynasty overseas, ruling
Jerusalem and Cyprus for two centuries. They had relations of interest and of love with Muslim dignitaries and their daughters.

The Palestinians, according to whether they were dark or fair, would smile and say they were descended from Ali and Fatima, or from Frederick II Hohenstaufen and Guy de Lusignan. This was so much in keeping with legend, that is, with history, that it would be foolish not to make use of it. In Palestine and Lebanon, some people's descent runs from the Normans to the sons of Saladin, whose mingled Jewish and Persian blood flows on without interruption.

Nabila was born to a Muslim family. I didn't go to see them when I was in Amman in July 1984: I hope she's still all right. Her parents' house was old but very pretty, and stood in a big garden near the middle of the city. It was there, at her mother's, that I met her in September 1970.

She was a qualified doctor in Washington when she heard about the massacres on the American radio. She caught a plane at once and came to join the Red Crescent, to which she still belongs.

When I was starting to write this part of the book I tried to find out if the families I've been talking about still had important positions in the Palestinian resistance.

Here's what Leila, Madame Shahid's daughter, told me:

"They haven't got the prestige or the arrogance the old chiefs used to have. But Arafat gives posts to members of the best-known families to underline the continuity of the struggle against an occupying power. That's all Arafat asks of them. He wouldn't let them do anything more."

There used to be a music-hall number in which a dancer in a crinoline down to the ground glided to the front of the stage with such small steps that her knees never stirred her skirt and the audience thought she must be on roller-skates. Then, when she smiled and took her bow, she lifted her skirt and revealed the very roller-skates whose existence the spectators had both suspected and feared.

German television showed us Mitterrand at Sadat's funeral. His four solid groups of bodyguards surrounded him so closely, and he moved so swiftly in his armour, they seemed to be carry-

ing rather than protecting him. Or instead of walking he might
have been going along on roller-skates or a skateboard. But if it was
the latter, the swiftness and elegance of the kids who perfected
the sport had been replaced by a solemn and comical slowness.

In television pictures of first-class funerals you sometimes
see the gun-carriage bearing some royal remains being drawn by
horses wearing black petticoats down to the ground. Like an already exhausted filly, the French President approached on wheels
into close-up.

But that carnival image conjured up another, and instead of
its entering into me I entered into it. The image was of the long
sateen skirts of marionettes, into which puppeteers put their fore-
arms. They then make the little creatures move about on the tiny
stage, accompanying them with a voice of thunder.

The President was like a marionette with the lower though
sexless part of its body hidden under a huge sateen cuff. His head
stood out above the bodyguards or policemen who were carrying
him, and it was from the police that he derived his strength. But I
couldn't hear the voice: it must have been drowned by the drums.

But better than any theory this image showed that might came
before right. Having seen it proved on television I felt reassured.
Might came before right, the second proceeding from the first via
sateen sleeves.

Through the dead Abu Omar, hanged, shot or drowned, but
moving about still because of my sateen sleeves and speaking
with my voice, I issue words with which he himself might well
have disagreed. And I do so without qualms, knowing that my
readers' capacity for humbug will match my own.

Through what I make him say, Abu Omar comes back to life.

Daoud Thalami worked at the Palestinian Research Centre in
Beirut. From a letter he wrote me in Paris in 1972 I learned that
Hamza had been imprisoned in a camp at Zarka, near where three
Swissair planes had been forced to land.

Daoud had found out about it, he wrote, from Khaled Abu
Khaled, the poet. It was after the massacres at Ajloun and Irbid,
and Hamza had been tortured by the Jordanian army to make him

admit to being the leader of a group of fedayeen. His legs had been injured. Though I had a vague idea of what torture meant, I couldn't imagine the details. But the Palestinians had told me of the Bedouin's and Circassians' hatred and resentment, and of the depravity of the king.

Who were Hamza's jailers? What suffering was being inflicted on him?

Thinking of Hamza and his family, and of the mother–son relationship that might have been just a figment of my imagination, maintained a kind of double life in me, as indispensable as a vital organ that I mustn't allow to decay or be removed. Whether this presence within me was necessary if I was to remain faithful to the resistance, I wasn't quite sure. I'm not quite sure of the contrary, either. But that the relationship between Hamza and his mother, or rather the triangle formed by their mother–son responsibility, should have come to live a life of its own inside me, independent as an extra organ or a developing fibroid, seemed to me as natural as similar phenomena in the animal kingdom or in tropical vegetation. It didn't worry me that this pair's destiny should continue within me in this way, because their fate symbolized the resistance, at least as it had come to seem to me in my thoughts.

Those two, whom I'd known for only an evening and half a day, brought together and crystallized the whole of the resistance, while at the same time remaining their own strange couple, Hamza-and-his-Mother. As I read Daoud's letter, each of the elements in the couple was being tortured separately and in different ways.

The monarchy was getting stronger, thanks to American arms. The imitation crowns stuck up all over the streets and squares of Amman, once made of aluminium sheeting so thin it looked only two dimensional, were now made of silver- or even gold-plated metal, or took the form of cupolas with five-pointed stars on top. The king, formerly as thin and flat as a blank page, was gradually acquiring weight, substance and a third, perhaps even a fourth, dimension, and finally became writing and meaning.

The following digression will be quickly begun and quickly finished. The behaviour of some adult Palestinian men sometimes made me think of a maternal rather than a purely military attitude. One leader in charge of twenty fedayeen, married and with a wife in Syria, never went to bed himself until he'd seen the blankets shared out among his men. Another went round all the posts as far as the Jordan valley to take the fedayeen their mail. Certain motherly, though I wouldn't call them specifically feminine, duties made the leaders look on the young soldiers, with their downy moustaches like smears of ash, as sons or dear ones rather than subordinates, as is still the way in the West.

"Virile" might apply to some of the things Hamza's mother stood for, but it's not the right word for her. She brought Hamza up, and it might be said a man alone knows what's right for a man alone. But women alone in the camps showed themselves to be such good strategists that the word almost deserves to be feminine. When the male youth of America was bombing Hanoi and North Vietnam, it was said that only feminine imagination prevented the worst.

Too much or too marked an affection between two youths up there in the mountains forbidden to women seemed the sign of an almost amorous understanding. How could a smooth skin fail to disturb a slightly rough one when all around, at every point of the compass, steel guns bristled, trained on them ready to fire? Death was lurking, rendering insignificant every authority but itself. How can one condemn a sudden desire that's really a sort of extreme unction?

What had happened at Zarka? And what sort of a life was Hamza living, if he was still alive? The imagination alone, though good at inventing the actual tortures, is unequal to conjuring up the witches' sabbath that goes on between torturers and victims. Can instruments of torture, so specifically shaped, discover how the destruction and humiliation of body and spirit can be made to yield pleasure? And was the mind of man capable of inventing those shapes on his own? One suspects that wars of liberation involve pleasure, often sexual pleasure, as well as naked suffering. One suspects but doesn't know, and one is sometimes mistaken. Better stay silent, since we know nothing of the complexity and complicity of some gentle torturers, or of the artistic groans of some victims.

Television advertising expanded in the 1980s, and though no one dared make fun too openly of the East or of the Arabs, there were plenty of mocking images based on myths about Islam, Iran and Egypt. One cartoon showed a caravan of camels each with five humps; every camel lost a hump whenever it dropped some dung, and each dropping opened to reveal a huge packet of Camel cigarettes. In another example, four sheikhs sitting on four carpets took off on a wild flight over towns and minarets to a funeral; when they got there, the least skilful sheikh won his carpet at bingo. That sort of stunt is easily faked on film, and can be light and amusing, but when I saw it on television I was disturbed. What if all those fantasies were projections of something we couldn't face up to in ourselves?

But what bothered me most was the strength of the Hamza–Mother image, linked to that of the Pietà and Christ. The uncovering of my unease, like the delicious lancing of a whitlow, led me to undertake my last journey from Paris to Amman. I'd once believed the desert to be an infinite wilderness empty of life; a place of mirages and apparitions ranging from djinns to Father de Foucauld;* a drier up of throat and spirit.

I thought I undertook that last journey in obedience to an external reality, but in fact I was haunted by an inner dream dating from when I was five years old. Unless, at the approach of death, I just wanted to write another, a last, volume about my travels.

I'd written the first volume borne aloft on the gaze of two fedayeen, whom I'd seen banging on a couple of deal coffins destined for two newly dead bodies on their way to their final hole. Thus borne aloft, I'd gone on from one dazzling fedayee to another until they but not I were all used up. Like the sheikhs in the television advertisement I'd flown on magic carpets—on eyes, on teeth, on legs. Like a sheikh crouched down on my mat I'd arrived at the end of my journey exhausted. And only now do I ask myself, had I really stayed in the same place all the time?

---

*Charles de Foucauld (1856–1916) was a French Trappist priest, missionary and explorer, murdered in Tamanrasset in the Algerian Sahara.

It seems to me nothing out of the way happened on my first journey from Paris to Beirut, and that I felt only minor surprise when Muhammad el-Hamchari took me to Deraa. I was annoyed when a young lion greeted me almost ceremonially, standing at attention and giving an English salute with his hand level with his eyebrows. Then he showed me the first martyrs' memorial in Chatila, unknown at that time and certainly not expecting to become as famous as Oradour. Both villages struck poses. Which would become famous?

But the whole more than eighteen months' trip was carried along on a ray from the eyes of the two fedayeen drummers, smiling and beating out ever new rhythms on the coffins. Throughout that journey, whenever I realized how tired I was, a twenty-year-old fedayee handed me a cloth; diced for my bones; listened to me, and I to him, all night; stood before me taller than a minaret; smiled as we shared a sardine. And always the ray from his eyes took over from the ray from the eyes of the two fedayeen who smiled as they drummed on the coffins in Deraa. All those rays transported me, and I still wonder whether a large part of my happiness didn't derive from the fact that I was being carried along in a sort of mobile barracks.

Rainbow fringes: the young Blacks hesitated between revolt and Uncle Tom. Soon many of them carried appearance to excess: hair ever longer and more vertical; corduroy trousers ranging from raspberry and periwinkle to lilac and cherry; gold leather boots; savage-style beards and moustaches; sequin waistcoats; silk caps perched on the four or five hairs that stuck up out of the mass; private parts deliberately outlined by the crotch of the trousers; outrageous words and phrases designed to hurt as much as impress the Whites. They were merely the rainbow fringe of the Panthers, whose verbiage and insolence they copied though they lacked their guts and their austere devotion to the black race.

I'd got a certain idea of the Panthers just from the newspapers, modified by a few corrections of my own, but there was such a difference between the idea and the reality that I soon realized the flamboyant youngsters were just a fringe. They were frauds, working as clerks or the like for a few hours a day and doing their act in their spare time. But if out of foolhardiness or by mistake one of them went into a White district, he had only to see a few shapes emerge from under the sycamores in the square and his eyes and legs and whole body would know the terror David referred to when he said "There are still too many trees." Far away as they were from the Panthers, they were still much closer to them than I was: they were haunted by fears and fantasies I'd never know except in ironical translation.

If the Panthers had been nothing more than a gang of young Blacks playing havoc with the preserves of the Whites, thieves dreaming only—only!—of cars and women, bars and drugs, would I have put myself out to be with them?

Though they read Marx and threatened to attack free enterprise with his philosophy, they hadn't lost their desire for exclusion. They were antisocial and apolitical, but sincere both in their temptations and in their attempts to create a society whose implications, idealistic or real, they contemplated without unduly high hopes. They were haunted by negatives—"anti"-forces—and all the time I lived among them I sensed a terrifying tension: a rejection of every kind of marginality striving with an equally strong attraction to marginality and its strange ecstasies.

Revolutionaries are in danger of getting lost in a hall of mirrors. But they are necessary, those intervals of sacking and looting that skirt and sometimes briefly fall into fascism, that break free of it only to return with even more abandon. Such intervals were not exactly avant-garde, but they were forerunners: the product of young adolescent Blacks driven more by a frantic sexuality than by the ideas they professed. And perhaps, even more than by sexuality, they were haunted by the idea of death, which they translated into looting.

The real Black Panthers were like this for a time. Their violence was almost violence in the raw, but as a response to white violence it had a meaning beyond itself. The Panthers had to open breaches, make gashes, in order to make contact with the world: hence marches in which arms were carried openly, murders of policemen, bank hold-ups. Their coming into the world caused fear and admiration. At the beginning of 1970 the Party still had both the suppleness and the rigidity of a male sex organ: and it preferred erections to elections.

If sexual images keep cropping up it's because they're unavoidable, and because the sexual or erectile significance of the Party is self-evident. Not so much because it was made up of young men, great screwers who would just as soon shoot their load with their women in the daytime as at night, but rather because their ideas, even if they seemed rather basic, were so many sprightly rapes committed against a very old and dim but tenacious Victorian morality—an American projection, a century later, of a morality that had its source in England, in London, at the Court of St. James. In a way the Party was also Jack the Ripper.

No? No. Because Jack the Ripper fathered children. Every witticism provoked peals of laughter. "Black was beautiful" because it brought a kind of liberty. But for the Whites whatever the Panthers did threw a halo of darkness round them, even in the daytime.

But there's this too: when they appeared in the ghetto they cast a light that did something to disperse the fog of drugs. As they uttered a few foul oaths screwing the Whites, the young Blacks wore a faint smile that made them momentarily forget their need for a fix.

They laughed later on when I said to David, who'd insisted on calling a doctor when I had the flu:

"You're a mother to me."

They often amused themselves by mixing up the sexes and catching grammar out in sexism, but their whole block and tackle, perfectly moulded, was much in evidence through their trousers.

It was a long time before the sculpture was exploited. I mean as power. The Blacks' natural, though to the Whites excessive, virility was seen as an exhibitionism quite different from that of the profusion of white bosoms at the parties given for the Panthers. The previous period had been one of extreme, though Victorian rather than socialist, prudery. Even the famous theory calling for eroticism, scatology, obscenity and extravagant, protuberant couplings, remained chaste, a stereotype to be used only against the devil: in other words Nixon and white imperialism.

At all events, trousers were cut in an almost Florentine style, and the doctrine was expounded in an ostentatious manner.

Logically enough, the Blacks had moved on from line-engraving to sculpture in the round.

The first time I met David Hilliard was when I lectured to the students at the University of Connecticut. After the lecture the black students invited us to their chalet on the campus. I got there after David. He was sitting down, talking, in the midst of all the black boys and girls. I was struck by the mute inquiry on their black faces, those middle-class faces turned towards a for-mer truck driver only slightly older than they were. He was the patriarch speaking to his descendants and explaining the reasons for the struggle and the tactics by which it was to be waged. The links between them all were political, but that was not the expla-nation of their solidarity: also present was a very subtle but very strong eroticism. It was so strong, so evident yet so discreet, that while I never desired any particular person, I was all desire for the group as a whole. But my desire was satisfied by the fact that they existed.

What did it mean, my pink and white presence among them? This: for two months I was to be David's son. I had a black father thirty years younger than myself. Because of my ignorance of America's problems, perhaps also because I was naïve and not very strong, I had to use David as a point of reference. But he was very careful with me, as if my weakness had somehow made me dear.

If it's hard to speak of the physical attraction and eroticism of the revolutionaries, it's even harder to describe the physical repulsion and disgust inspired by boys and girls apparently devoid of grace. It can happen, and it's unbearable.

Among the fedayeen, Adnan made me feel like that. (He was killed by the Israelis.) And he must have been repelled by my homosexuality.

Sex, even before it emerges into consciousness, is probably the most widespread phenomenon in the living world. Perhaps it has still to be proved that it's the direct and sole cause of the will to power, but power, though not necessarily connected with will, seems to be present even in the vegetable kingdom. Another, perhaps less universal, function is the desire, more or less conscious in every man, to produce an image of himself and propagate it beyond death so that it may wield a power, or rather an unforceful radiance at once sweet and strong. The image created is quite detached from the man concerned and from any group or act. This makes it exemplary in the special and paradoxical sense that it's unique, and will not serve as an example. It's a kind of ironical order: "Whatever you do, don't detract from my oneness."

This widespread function, being perhaps connected with death, desires fulfilment while the person concerned is still alive; he gets hung up on the image of himself. But this can't be: the desire prevents its own fulfilment. A young man having his photograph taken adjusts his appearance a little, making it more studied or more relaxed—in any case, different. He adopts a pose, for this chance image may be the last.

But it's not enough just to write down a few anecdotes. What one has to do is create and develop an image or profusion of images. And it's about time to examine their function, too.

Words like mythomania, waking dream and megalomania apply to someone who can't project his image of himself properly. It should live a life of its own, though it may be affected by what the man himself does while he's alive and by his exploits—or miracles—after he's dead.

But one can't really explain the social function of these images and of people's attempts to make them exemplary: that is separate and unique, though joined together they make up both memory and history. There's probably no man in existence who wouldn't like to be a legend on a large or small scale. Who wouldn't like to be a world hero—exemplary, unique and influential not because he's powerful but just because he exists.

From Greece to the Panthers, history has been made out of man's need to detach and project fabulous images, to send them as delegates into the future, to act in the very long term, after death. The real influence of Hellenism began after Athens was dead. Christ ticks Peter off for trying to prevent him from realizing his image: from the very beginning of his public life Christ does all he can to attract attention. Saint-Just could have escaped after he'd been condemned to death by Fouquier-Tinville, but:

"I despise the dust of which I am made and which speaks to you now, but no one can ever take away the independent life I have won in history and in heaven."

When a man invents an image that he wants to propagate, that he may even want to substitute for himself, he starts by experimenting, making mistakes, sketching out freaks and other nonviable monsters that he has to tear up unless they disintegrate of their own accord. But the operative image is the one that's left after the person dies or withdraws from the world, as in the case of Socrates, Christ, Saladin, Saint-Just and so on. They succeeded in projecting an image around themselves and into the future. It doesn't matter whether or not the image corresponds to what they were really like: they managed to wrest a powerful image from that reality.

An image isn't exemplary (that is, unique) and active as a source of imitations, but as a starting point for actions which, though they'll be thought to be through and for it, will in fact be against it. But above all it's the only message from the past that's managed to get itself projected into the present. Historians' discoveries of new sources and new interpretations make no difference. They try to replace so-called archetypal images with others. But are they truer? Neither truer nor less true, since they're all images from the past. Historians may demolish a legendary hero whose image, accurate or not, fascinates us still. But they'll only be able to replace it if they provide facts and explanations that we can sympathize with and assimilate, if they create new images that give us something we can talk about.

The theatre may disappear in its present form. It may already be threatened. The essence of theatre is the need to create not merely signs but complete and compact images masking a reality that may consist in absence of being. The void. To create the ultimate image he desires to project into a future no less absent than the present, every man is capable of supreme acts that will topple him into nothingness.

Ferraj had all the appearance of what's called a healthy man and a sound fighter. When I met him he was twenty-three years old. He was the one whose body, face and mind, so vivacious and full of life, attracted me the first night I spent with the fedayeen, a night that lasted until dawn. It was to see him I went back there among the trees.

He emerged from a shelter with another, younger fedayee. He looked ill at ease when he saw me. He hadn't been able to conceal the fact that he'd just tugged his pullover down and his trousers up, which others might have seen only as an attempt to tidy himself up. But their faces were too eloquent. Ferraj's face was red; the young fedayee was flushed with triumph.

What was it that had swooped down like a hawk on that dynamic and magnanimous leader, reducing him to nothing but desire for this lad?

Where was the perversity? In Ferraj, all of a sudden? In the boy's knowing look? In the clear sky, where desire hovered ready to swoop? Or in me, who saw or thought I saw all this?

What rôle was there for me under those golden leaves?

My only importance, but it was a great importance, was this: because of me the fedayeen used to gather together, tired but cheerful, usually in the evening. I think the first assembly was organized by Ferraj: I'd mentioned that my white hair was too long.

"A fedayee can turn his hand to anything. Sit down on this stone and I'll turn you into a hippie."

He said it very ingeniously, the French words for "hair" and "stone" entwined with others in English and classical Arabic.

We at once attracted a group of ten or twelve fedayeen, smoking their everlasting Virginia cigarettes and appreciatively following the flicker of Ferraj's scissors around my head.

"Why did you say you're going to turn me into a hippie?" I asked him, used the same language as he had.

"Because now your hair will be down on your shoulders every month."

They all laughed. And not only my shoulders but my knees as well were covered with snippets of white hair.

The first stars came out, timidly at first, then in droves all over the still purple sky. It was all more beautiful than I can say. And Jordan is only the Middle East!

By now my hair was coming down to my feet.

Was the relationship between Hamza and his mother peculiar to them, or were they both obeying a general law among the Palestinians whereby a widowed mother and a beloved son became one? By now the couple, carried and nurtured inside me for so long, contained an almost incestuous element.

My hatred for Hussein and his Bedouin and Circassians focused less and less on their massacring of the Palestinians and the fedayeen. Hamza's torture-blackened legs, nothing but two huge wounds, were enough for me, though I'd never seen them and knew they belonged more to the Palestinian people than to me.

The moment of decision always comes, but it hasn't yet come for me. The time to examine myself about the Palestinian resistance and its repercussions inside me; about watching revolutions from plush and gilt stage boxes. What other place are we to watch from if the revolutions are first and foremost wars of liberation? From whom are they trying to free themselves?

Did Mahjoub tell me everything about the eight-year-old girl he was once in love with? I seem to remember he mentioned muslin, the colour of her dresses, the materials they were made of, and how they only showed the tips of her toes. What became of her? He only remembered her as a child. Was she dead? Was he living with a dead woman and hiding the corpse? Perhaps walking with Mahjoub was accompanying a funeral procession. But if the little sweetheart was cold, what about the woman? Was he speaking to me in metaphors?

Though today it looks like a meadow where Norman cows might graze, Tal-el-Zaatar ("the hill of thyme") used to be the biggest Palestinian camp in Beirut. Ali lived there, with other members of Fatah. He'd never been up in a plane. Whenever one crashed he used to laugh and sing and dance about.

Their country exists: dispossession brings depression, depression anguish. A gulf accompanied all Palestine, every Palestinian everywhere. Homeland and health were lacking.

"Are you leaving an hour from now?"

"Yes."

"By air?"

"Yes."

"What if the plane crashes?"

There were often pieces in the paper about planes crashing into mountains or the sea. Or disappearing over the North Pole so that the injured passengers had to eat the dead ones. Ali was twenty and could speak French.

"No point in thinking about that now. If there's going to be an accident . . ."

"But we want your bones."

No one knew in advance where he would bury his dead: the Palestinians were almost as short of cemeteries as they were of farmland.

"What's your name?"

"Ali."

"No—I mean the name your grandfather gave you."

Now a Fatah official tells me:

"Ali died at Tal-el-Zaatar. There aren't many individual graves. We buried them a barrack-room at a time. No soldier can have a hole to himself, even one only a few inches deep. We had to trample them down four at a time, all pointing towards Mecca. But why do you ask? Do you mean to mourn just one person? What's the point of mentioning him in your book? Did you meet him often?"

"Three times."

"That all? You can't mourn just one fedayee. I'll bring you the records—they've got thousands of names in. You can order yourself a few kilometres of crêpe."

Palestine was no longer a country—it was an age. Youth and Palestine were synonymous.

Ali, in 1970:

"Why don't you mind talking to me? Elderly people—sorry—usually talk among themselves. We're just the ones they give orders to. They know about things young people aren't supposed to know about until they're crippled with rheumatism. In the old days, when an old man acquired wisdom he took to wearing a turban, the one being a sign that he'd earned the other. Just look around you."

"Don't the leaders ever ask you questions?"

"No. They know everything already."

The idea of accepting some territory, however small, where the Palestinians would have a government, a capital, mosques, churches, cemeteries, town halls, war memorials, racecourses, and airfields where soldiers would present arms twice a day to foreign heads of state—the idea was such heresy that even to entertain it as a hypothesis was a mortal sin, a betrayal of the revolution.

Ali—and all the other fedayeen were the same—would accept nothing but a great firework display of a revolution, a conflagration leaping from bank to bank, opera house to opera house, prison to lawcourt, sparing only the oil wells. They belonged to the Arab people.

"You're sixty years old. You're not completely finished yet, but you're not strong. In the presence of an old man a Muslim holds his breath and stays his arm. So no one here would finish you off. But I'm twenty—I can kill and be killed. What if you were twenty—would you be with us? Physically? With a gun? Do you know if I've ever killed anyone? I don't know myself—I know I've fired a gun and aimed to kill. But even though you're weak and can't see well enough to aim, you've got enough strength to pull a trigger. So will you? You came here, but you're protected by your age. But you could waive that for a moment."

My answer was of so little interest I keep it to myself. Age and weakness had given me immunity; Ali had reminded me of it.

"I'm saying all this because I know that when I die it won't be for the young, it'll be for the old fogies. Or for three-month-old babies who'll never know anything about either my life or my death."

It doesn't trouble me to set down the words of one who died young—if Ali died at Tal-el-Zaatar, in 1976, he must have been twenty-six—and whose flesh and bones have mouldered away into those of at least three other fedayeen. Ali isn't even a voice, unless he's a faint pale voice concealed in mine.

"At Tal-el-Zaatar the chiefs talk to one another in whispers. Or else very loud, as if we're incapable of understanding what they say. They even go in for high-flown speculation, sprinkled with references to Spinoza, despite his origins. To Lenin too.

And the Code of Hammurabi. We simple soldiers just stay quiet and wait for our orders: 'Make some mint tea.' 'Bring some Turkish coffee.' "

"What would you do with my bones? Where would you put them? You haven't got any cemeteries."

"It wouldn't take long to scrape off the meat and gristle—you haven't got any fat or muscle. Then we'd divide the bones up into little heaps, and each of us would carry some in our kitbags. And we'd throw them into the Jordan."

He gave a mirthless laugh.

But then he smiled again, a charming way of covering up the joke we'd shared.

"And when the war's over, with a bit of luck we'll fish them up again out of the Dead Sea."

I couldn't be in love with Ali. The beauty of his body and face, and especially the fineness of his skin, disturbed me. But how can you make a comrade of an ideology?

He knew I loved him, but it didn't make him the slightest bit arrogant. It awakened his kindness, but no affectation of laxity. And yet he knew I liked boys.

One night in the tent I was awakened at two in the morning by shouting and laughter. The fedayeen were drinking, smoking and eating like horses after fasting all day for Ramadan. I asked for a drink and a cigarette. Laughing at my drowsiness, Abu Hassan questioned me on the subject that had caused the raised voices.

"What do they say in Paris about sexual freedom?"

"I don't know."

"What about Brigitte Bardot?"

"I don't know."

I must have yawned as I said it.

"What do you think?"

"I'm a pederast."

He translated. Everyone laughed. Abu Hassan said calmly:

"So you haven't got any problems."

I went back to sleep. They were expecting to be ordered to the Jordan from one minute to the next, so they were likely to dwell on the subject for one minute rather than two.

Was I ever in love with Ali? Or with Ferraj? I don't think so; I never had time to dream about them. And the presence of any one fedayee was enough to eclipse the shades of absent favourites.

Every barber knows what a cowlick is—a recalcitrant tuft of hair that will lie in any direction except the one it ought to. Imagine a head of hair made up entirely of cowlicks, with a beard of the same composition, not fuzzy or frizzy but spreading out like rays. Whiskers and hair like that look as if they're laughing to start with. If you add yet more rays shooting out in all directions you get a face that's beaming because it knows God made it like that, in his image, and that you have to laugh about it in his honour.

People are too ready to talk about apes when they see someone hairy. This chap made you think of a very distinguished English-woman, especially when he was eating. With his fingers, of course. Though he sometimes trimmed his moustache when it grew into his mouth, he never touched his eyebrows, hair or beard. But the trimming of the beard revealed a surprise: his smile.

In the midst of that mass of laughing hair were two grave black eyes which sometimes burst out laughing themselves, two pink lips opening wide in a smile, then a laugh, that showed teeth and a shy pink tongue. His body remained a secret. God, creator of men, might have amused himself with this one and made him hairless under his clothes. I don't think anyone ever found out.

"Who's that? He seems to be following me about."

I was sitting out of doors with some fedayeen, round a table set with three or four enormous dishes into which everyone dipped.

I'd scarcely asked myself the question when recognition must have shown in my eyes, and the hair and intractable beard came over and two arms were thrown around me. It was the Syrian Muslim who'd embraced me in the tent and discussed theology with me. He told me he'd run all the way from Ajloun to Irbid pursued by a hail of bullets that never managed to hit him. We shared a few bits of chicken and some fruit, and then he went away again.

Fire came down from the sky.

Beirut was divided in two, each part steadily doing its own thing. One half endeavoured to eat, the other half wiggled its belly and buttocks on polished parquet. The two halves joined together somewhere to make up one Beirut, though I never knew where. But the organic link between the shanty towns and the palaces was obvious: it consisted of informers and whores. The juxtaposition of want and lucre must have delighted the gods. Bingeing knew all about need, and need knew all about fun. No one forgot anyone, any more than a palace forgets a shanty town or vice versa. But happiness didn't exist in either, only orgasm, its ecstasy born of the sight of ingots, themselves born out of others' pain.

No one can still be surprised by the pilot fish guiding the shark, the bird relieving the buffalo of its ticks, or the pike's belly containing a slightly smaller pike, and that pike containing another, and so on. The dimensions decrease but never the appetite and greed. It isn't cruel; just curious, experimental.

Was this the truth Abu Omar had discovered? Was this what made him laugh to hide his revulsion when a fedayee described the red dotted line left by the severed head as it bounced down the steps with its eyes still open? Had he thought you rode into revolution on a charger, galloping through a golden gate into a realm of knights errant?

At Petra, in the open space between the great rows of Romanesque-looking porticos hewn out of basalt, I saw two young people on horseback. They'd been married the day before or betrothed that morning. They didn't see me. I was too old, and riding a tired horse, and wisely their idyll blotted out the rest of the universe: the rocks, the two-thousand-year-old sculptures, the scum of Beirut, revolutions, and the devotion of a man for a child.

When light and shade, before they merged, hesitated a moment on the straight yet curving line of the horizon, the twilight line like a kiss on lowered lids, the young man and the American girl dismounted.

Perhaps I felt as the Palestinians did when they heard the first Hungarians and Poles in Palestine, in about 1910. The road signs between Beirut and Baabda were in Hebrew.

Vernacular Arabic sounds as if it ought to look like vermicelli when it's written down, and it *is* all twists and turns. The Lebanese refer to Hebrew script as "spare parts."

Arriving in Beirut from Damascus and seeing those signposts at the crossroads was as painful as seeing Gothic lettering in Paris during the German occupation. The trilingual road signs reminded you of the Rosetta Stone, but the languages were English, Arabic and Hebrew. Symbols had been added to convey their meaning—left, right, town centre, railway station, north, HQ. Few people read the writing.

The Hebrew characters, drawn rather than written and carved rather than drawn, induced a sense of unease, like a quiet herd of dinosaurs. Not only did this writing belong to the enemy—it was also an armed sentry standing over the people of Lebanon. I had a childhood memory of seeing these incomprehensible characters carved on two oblong stones joined together lengthwise and called the Tables of the Law. I say "carved" because the illusion of relief was given by alternations of light and shade. Most of the letters were squat and rectangular; they read from right to left in a broken horizontal line. One or two had a crane-like plume on top: three slim pistils bearing three stigmata and waiting for the bees who'd scatter their age-old, nay primeval, pollen all over the world. But the feathers—they belonged to a letter that sounded rather like *sh*—didn't add a touch of lightness. They expressed the cynical triumph of Tsahal, and had the slightly foolish grandeur of a peacock's head or of a dumb girl waiting to be serviced.

The tops of some bamboos look as though they're moving because they *are* moving. The Eiffel Tower sways. The downstrokes of those letters produced the same nausea because they didn't move. That writing hadn't only surged up from childhood. Though it had been presented to the world on top of a mountain, it came from the cave, dark and deep, in which God, Moses, Abraham, the Tables, the Torah and the Commandments had been imprisoned.

Now, back at this crossroads belonging to a prehistory before prehistory, and even if we didn't know much about Freud, we felt the enormous pressure which after two thousand years had brought about the Return of the Repressed.

But above all we were surprised and repelled by the terrifying discontinuity: the letters were separated by immeasurable spaces filled with several layers of time—a time as dead and incalculable as the space between a corpse and a living eye looking at it. In the space between each Hebrew letter, generations have been born and spread abroad, and its silence shattered us worse than bullets and bombs.

Ajloun, my favourite place, at peace again, was mine. Every sparrow there knew my name, the paths led me along of their own accord. The brambles, capricious to others, were courteous to me. All this may seem exaggerated, but it suggests how close a man and a place had become. Around Ajloun and quite near, I could hear rumours of war and political treason. I could tell the clouds were massing, black and full of flame. Yet despite or perhaps because of the dangers, these slopes enclosed a hollow of peace.

In the gestures and manners of the fedayeen, and in their assurance, I saw, despite the defeat, the sort of euphoria that exalts newly successful "stars" and makes them attractive. And it also seemed to me, though less certainly, that the loss of serenity surging through every angry man or people in revolt is really a more difficult and supreme kind of serenity; and that rebels deserve honours and not the opposite.

If I say the grace of the soldiers in arms was like theatre amid the greenery, I'm trying to make legible what was happening inside every fedayee. Without knowing exactly how far the rays of the revolution reached, he felt he was being seen, watched. And from a long way away; perhaps distorted, if distance alters the eye's habits. His brightness protected him, but worried the Arab régimes.

The same question may be asked not only of every nation there's ever been, but also of every political or religious movement. What was missing from the Middle East, from the Arab world, from nations, from rebellions? What was it the Arab world so urgently needed, that the Palestinian resistance should come into being? Only twenty years have gone by since 1967, so it's still very young for a movement that sees itself as much more than a superficial attempt to recover lost territory.

The resistance germinated and grew because it was provided

with oxygen. When you see how many pages European newspapers devote to it you realize how we'd miss it if the resistance stopped. At first it seemed as if people's interest might reflect some secret, well-concealed irritation with Israel. Nothing was said against that country. In forty years Europeans have learned to keep quiet: they know how touchy and sensitive Jewish skins are. The porcupine ought to be Begin's emblem as well as Louis XII's.

It's possible that the world—like France, between 1854 and 1873, producing a man who brought French prose to white-heat—willed the youthful revolts of the Palestinians (like what Rimbaud called "natural revolts") defying whatever tried to hold back their poetry.

A girl of sixteen—Austrian, of course—had the nerve to say to me and some Panthers, stealing the most appropriate description of their violence from under my very nose, that "the Black Panthers are very affectionate."

Remembering her, her resolute face and her tone of voice, I say: "The Palestinians are very affectionate," too. Perhaps I risk the expression so as to say in one word what made me stay with them. But why did I come in the first place? That's another story, more obscure and buried deeper inside me. But I'll try to dig it out, though the enigma is difficult and elusive, visible one minute and gone the next.

Anyone who's never experienced the pleasure of betrayal doesn't know what pleasure is.

Thinking of Hamza brought back his cheerfulness. Did he learn it from fighting? I'd also noted a physical magnanimity in him. His gestures were not as sweeping and emphatic as those of someone from the South of France or Lebanon, but they were broad and generous. Gunfire, whether near or far, couldn't increase his generosity but it did increase his gaiety. He was more than a hero; he was a kid.

In other days I think I'd have avoided words like heroes, martyrs, struggle, revolution, liberation, resistance, courage and suchlike. I probably *have* avoided the words homeland and fraternity, which still repel me. But there's no doubt that the Palestinians caused a kind of collapse in my vocabulary. I accept it in order to put first things first, but I know there's nothing behind such words. And precious little behind all the others.

I got used to the fedayeen, sure that they thirsted for justice and wanted a fairer life, as they still said. These reasons for rebellion still existed, but underneath them, unsaid (especially not to themselves) and much stronger than those hopes, illusory or otherwise, were orders received which never appeared in their books. Such imperatives included a love of fighting and physical confrontation, together with an underlying desire for self-slaughter, for glorious death if victory was impossible. Of course victory was pleasant to talk about: victory will come when the enemy is defeated, and will be followed some time later by a juster social order existing as yet only in official declarations. And behind all this was the phrase with which Arafat ended every letter, personal or official: victory or death.

Revolution seen as a sort of speleology, or an expedition up an unclimbed face of the Jungfrau.

"I can't make up my mind."

"What about?"

Dr. Alfredo, who mightn't yet have heard about the Cuban revolution, answered:

"Whether to carry on this revolution or spend the rest of my life rock-climbing."

I liked his brevity. For about a fortnight he'd been looking disconcerted, desperate even, because of Arafat's silence.

When the chairman of the PLO had asked him his nationality he'd answered in one word:

"Palestinian."

This was not well received. From the sudden silence that fell in Arafat's reception room I could tell he didn't like hearing others claim that distinction. He was too proud of his people to let anybody else, even his best friend, call himself one of them.

"You saw—he doesn't accept me as a Palestinian. So either I fly off in a rage, or I stay and fight till I die."

What made the fedayeen supermen was that they put the predicament of all before their own individual wishes. They would set out for victory or death, even though each still remained a man alone with his own sensibilities and desires. It must have been then that they were beset by the temptation to betray, though I think it was almost always resisted.

When I thought of the wealth accumulated by many of the Palestinian leaders it struck me that all that furniture, all those carpets and dresses were really a kind of glossy magazine, the kind with photographs of country houses and antique armchairs that people day-dream over. Is it treachery to flick through a magazine? Of course, it's more difficult to stroll through an apartment on paper than in three dimensions, but it uses up less energy. And what if you only do it a few times a year?

Is that worse than thinking yourself a fedayee when you're only one by your own choice, wearing the appropriate costume and keffiyeh and even soul for no more than a few hours in a lifetime? Isn't a Westerner amusing himself in that way much the same as a warrior taking his ease in a country mansion that to all intents and purposes exists only on glossy paper? To be a fedayee for a moment when you haven't had to endure a fedayee's woes is like wearing a forged medal.

What about those who misappropriate money in order to ward off the temptation to betray, while remaining in the revolution, with all its responsibilities and risks? Which is worse? The man who diverted money in order to divert the temptation to betray, or the one who chose wealth for its own sake?

It was Abu Omar, the one who laughed so awkwardly about the severed head, who told me how Fatah had suddenly and unexpectedly become important.

"In 1964 Fatah was only a little stream. Arafat, who'd been an engineer, resigned from his job to become a full-time revolutionary. The battle of Karameh was called a victory both by the Palestinians and by the Arab world as a whole. So many people joined Fatah it was five or six times as big as it had been before. Other organizations sprang up too, sometimes in opposition. The former refugee camps became training camps. Fatah developed mainly in Jordan, where many government officials supported it. All the people living in the occupied territories supported us too, and so did Palestinian students and teachers in Europe, America and Australia. We've got students in Melbourne, you know. The present king declared himself the first among the fedayeen. Even then he was the last. Fatah, an international ocean now, was only a little stream then.

"But the stream was free, and the ocean is patrolled by an American and Soviet fleet. We used to strike whenever and wherever necessary. We acted only in the name of the Organization itself: neither the leaders nor the fedayeen bothered about the great powers—the USA, the USSR, Britain and France. I was going to add China, but no—since 1948 China had been listening to what was going on in the rest of the world, and it had seen that our attempt to return to the territories we'd been driven out of was one of the great movements of History.

"Apart from Arafat and a few other officials, there was no one strong enough or shrewd enough to lead what had become a whole nation in turmoil. It might have all died down: plenty of independence movements have been forgotten. But we had the good fortune to discover our three enemies: the reactionary Arab régimes, America and Israel, in that order."

"You put Israel last?"

"I know you're making notes, even if you're not taking them down now. So I'm talking to someone who's going to write a book, and I prefer to tell the truth. You can check what I tell you and what you see here with what you can read in the papers in France or at the French Institute in Damascus. The reactionary Arab states, especially those in the Gulf, huff and puff about Israel, partly because it has attacked Arab territory but mainly for trivial reasons of religious ritual. But they're all faithful allies of America. And what about America? Does she support Israel, or just make use of her to extend American influence in the region and protect the Gulf oil wells east of Aden?

"In a way, Israel has helped us escape being choked to death. You know the facts. The Jews have been scattered all over the world without a country ever since the Romans drove them out of the land God promised to Abraham. It may have been promised, but in fact it was conquered by Joshua. Then, after two thousand years of wandering and suffering (mainly in Europe), they demand their Promised Land, our Palestine, back again, and without waiting for God to keep his word, chase out the current inhabitants because they're Muslims and Christians. That's roughly what happened. The details we see now are due to the English."

There was a longish silence, during which I pondered the question: "Who lived in Palestine after the destruction of the Temple and Titus's decision to expel the Jews? Was it the remainder of the Canaanites? Did any Jews stay on, and were they converted first to Christianity and then, around 650, to Islam?"

The reason I give so much space to what Abu Omar and Monsieur Mustapha said is that wherever I went in the Middle East—Jordan, Syria or Lebanon—the Palestinians were always puzzling about not only their rights to the land but also their own origins. One Palestinian woman told me:

"We were the real Jews. The ones who stayed on after AD 70 and were converted to Islam later on. So the persecution we suffer from now is inflicted on us by our stateless cousins."

Abu Omar went on: "The psychology of the Jews may have been formed by their wandering through the West, where they experienced, all at the same time, wealth, power, the contempt of the Christians, and science. The scientific intelligence. I sometimes think of Einstein as a German scientist of the Jewish faith, with the fears, the resentment and the nostalgia of the ghetto. This psychology led the Jews to resent the Palestinians, even before they openly turned against us. It was a great stroke of luck for us that Israel decided to be our advertising agency. What an echo chamber! If the Tamils had had one like that, where would the Batavians have been? Israel is so fond of propaganda it was certain from all eternity to become its own public relations man. Second only to France, of course. And the Church. That was very useful to us. But there was a risk, if we weren't careful, of ruining our movement by making it unreal.

"One evening Arafat told me about what was, and still is, one of his fears. 'For some months now our revolution has been fashionable. We owe this to Israel. The papers, the photographers, the television companies, all the cameramen in the world come to see us and produce romantic stories and pictures. But suppose they overdo it? The Palestinian Revolution will cease to exist because it doesn't produce any more stories and pictures.' "

"So Arafat's object—among others, of course—is to instigate

spectacular events in order to attract shoals of photographers, professional mourners and eulogists. Bards."

"Always joking, aren't you! I don't mind. It gives me the chance to smile a bit, even if you are making fun of the revolution."

"The highest form of art!"

"Yes. But let's be serious. As I was saying, the revolution's in danger of becoming unreal through rhetoric, images on screens, and metaphor and hyperbole in everyday speech. Our battles are in danger of turning into poses—they look heroic, but in fact they're performed. But what if our play were interrupted, forgotten, and ..."

He stopped in time, smiled, but then said it anyway.

"... thrown into the dustbin of history?"

"But aren't you in the revolution to get your land back?"

"I'll probably never live there. I'd like to tell you why the revolution, though it involves getting the land back, doesn't stop at that. Just a few more words about Israel. Israel has to exaggerate the dangers and troubles it claims to endure just because we live so close. By means of a well-placed network of amplifiers and loudspeakers it spreads its shrieks and laments all over what it calls the diaspora.

"Some other time I'll tell you why we're lucky to have America as an enemy. I'll tell you the day after tomorrow, if you feel like coming back to Ajloun. But will you come?" He smiled.

"Ferraj isn't here any more ... A PLO car will take you as far as Jerash. But have your French passport ready if you see a Jordanian roadblock."

It wasn't in Hamra, nor even in a fashionable street, but in an ordinary shopping street in Beirut, lined with parked cars. Suddenly the place was overrun. First by an expensive but ancient car, with two men with moustaches sitting in front and three behind. It drew up on the right, and the five men remained inside. Then came another car, the latest model Cadillac, almost as wide as the street, which stopped neither on the left nor on the right but in the middle of the road. Three women got out, two in Arab dress and one European. The driver stayed at the wheel but another man got out: he was about forty, with a black beard and moustache, obviously very strong and probably carrying a gun. Then came a tall and beautiful woman wearing a long black dress down to the ground and a small veil just covering her eyes. She smiled: princesses always smile at crowds, and a crowd had already gathered to accept her largesse.

She went into a shop that had a window display of verses from the Koran engraved in black on gold or gold on black lacquer. The man with the black beard blocked the doorway just by standing there, so I couldn't see what the princess was doing. She came out after a very short time, and her court formed a sort of guard of honour for her to walk back to the Cadillac. But one old woman in the crowd didn't get out of the way fast enough, and the bodyguard pulled her aside so roughly she knocked into some of the bystanders. No one protested, neither did anyone smile at the old woman's discomfiture.

The man with the beard gave an order in Arabic to the driver of the first car, which must have been full of policemen or more bodyguards. He told him to drive back to the embassy. The Cadillac followed. The street went back about its business.

"Who was that?"

That was all. The gesture—that of a bodyguard pushing an old woman into a crowd—had come all the way from Abu Dhabi to happen here, in an ordinary street in Beirut in Lebanon.

Here's what remains of what Monsieur Mustapha told me.

"Of course my family claims to go back to before the time it was converted to Islam, between what you would call AD 670 and 700. It belonged to an agricultural and trading community."

"What did it trade in?"

"From time immemorial in dyes, henna and lentils. The people lived off the land and the sea. I don't know much about the period between about 700 and 1450. After that, the Ottomans didn't really try to standardize all their empire, and if a few Leading Families hadn't fought one another, Palestine would have been at peace."

"How did a family get to be a Leading Family?"

"By genuinely descending from Ali, or by being clever enough to make people think so. Do you think Europe has a monopoly in sham genealogies? Our equivalents of your ducs de Lévis, descended from the Virgin Mary, wrought havoc throughout Islam. Our Leading Families made war, like yours, while the peasants . . ."

"Slaves!"

"That's where you're wrong. If the Prophet was chosen out by God—'I have chosen one among you'—it was so that one human voice might denounce slavery. That's what Muhammad did. He was a Congress of Vienna in himself. Anyway, slaves or not, the peasants worked for the lords, who were, or are supposed to have been, my ancestors."

"So it's not certain your descent is legitimate?"

"Oh, Monsieur Genet—fancy you talking to me about legitimacy! Who dare say any man's mother was faithful to her husband? After 1453, as they did with all of Syria and Arabia and part of Europe, but not Morocco, the Turks made Palestine into a colony, a subprovince of Syria. The Turkish conquest came after . . ."

"The Frankish kingdoms?"

"Forget Melusine and Bouillon, Lusignan and Foulques Nerra, and all the other adventures you think so important. Don't forget, though, that the story of Melusine may come from the 'Arabian Nights,' where a snake with a human voice has ideas about the Prophet although the Prophet wasn't going to preach Islam for another two hundred years. The snake spoke—in Arabic, of course, and very good Arabic too—before your Lusignans were born.

"The Ottoman officials were very tactful. They collected taxes twice a year, I think, but their Christian soldiers didn't disturb us much. The Turks fleeced us, but they had the effrontery to leave us free. Leading Families like ours had houses in Jerusalem, Hebron and Acre and palaces on the Bosporus, with light-fingered stewards whom we used to hang just to keep the custom from dying out. While they were still alive they looked after our lands, our mulberry trees and our silkworms."

His house consisted of just one floor led up to by a few steps. I seem to remember the inside as one huge room with a white marble floor that served as sitting-room, dining-room and kitchen all at once. Monsieur Mustapha lived, probably lives still, in the Turkish style. He smoked a hookah and loathed everything about himself that was Arab, especially his son Omar, the scientist and fedayee. The only thing he read was Turkish poetry—Djelal Eddin Roumi.

"And then after all that time, just as the people might start to think the land they'd lived and worked on for twelve hundred years was theirs, someone comes and pulls it away from under them, slowly at first, like drawing a carpet out of a room without upsetting the armchairs.

"Please excuse my French—I hope my Arabic is better. Could they have known in the fourteenth, fifteenth and sixteenth centuries—I still use your centuries, because your people colonized Time after they'd colonized Space, and because you tell me you're writing a book that's going to be read by Christians—could our Palestinian people have known that men speaking Russian, German, Polish, Croat, the Baltic languages, Serb and Hungarian would come and create the 'Lovers of Zion' here? Or that Zion was both the mystical and the geographical centre of a country men dreamed of in Kiev, Moscow, Cologne, Paris, Odessa, Buda, Cracow, Warsaw and London? Neither we, the masters, nor our peasants knew a plan had gradually taken shape in dreams so far away from our own nights, in which we dreamed other dreams. Things were growing, bones were hardening, all was hastening without our suspecting it towards our destruction. It wasn't until 1917 that we realized the plan was materializing in the rotting corpse and shipwreck of the Empire.

"We were surprised at first when that motley crew of men and women started to arrive, apparently at random and sad at having to leave the Carpathians and the rain and snow. The Jews in Europe had been dreaming of Zion, but no one here had dreamed their Zion was our El Kods!

"Mounts of olives, Solomon's Temple, the Song of Songs, suns, fields of wheat, grapes all the year round—bunches weighing five kilos; but also bankers' projects and violinists' day-dreams. The Palestinians, working at their oil-presses and ploughing their fields, didn't know they were being dreamed of and that a thousand snares were being laid around them and their country.

"When the young Ali you mentioned told you the Zionists had secretly bought up tobacco plantations between the present Israeli border and the Litani, in theory he was right. Our land registers were kept more efficiently in Warsaw than in Jerusalem. The Jewish violinists became hunters at once other-worldly and accurate: they may have had gypsy violins, but now had Israeli guns. My own family still didn't know they'd been under observation for two thousand years—for what else did 'If I forget thee, O Jerusalem' really amount to?—and that their life, which they thought they owed just to their own fidelity to the land they nurtured, was only lent them by Slav hunters just waiting for the right moment to sound the halloo and start the chase.

"The Palestinians, for their part, never dreamed about the European Jews, tormented by the pogroms, when the first victims arrived in the shape of socialistic farm workers better versed in theology than in cereals. The Palestinians hadn't dreamed of these people's promised land. It was only later, and gradually, that they saw they themselves were only characters in dreams, though they still didn't foresee the rude awakening that would take away both their lives and their living.

"All this prevented the Palestinians from seeming quite real. An Israeli, seeing them as a people of dream, of shadows rather than flesh and blood, may have thought that in fighting them he had only to deal with a pack of peasants and a non-existent army. But the fedayeen did exist, and I suspected their revolt was designed to prove both to themselves and to the Jewish Zionists that even though they were only Palestinians they really were turning into creatures of flesh and of spirit, who wouldn't just melt away when the Ashkenazi woke up.

"It seemed to me the distance between the two lots of recalcitrants was infinite—that it grew in proportion as we, the Palestinians, wanted to be free and independent of Zionist sleeps and awakenings. And the distance between the people of dreams and the real fedayeen was proof that a new element had come into the world, capable of changing the Middle East and all the Muslim peoples and their governments. The latter existed mainly to suit the West, which wanted the Arab world to remain a race of shadows. Our liberty increased as the distance increased between the shadows we used to be and the nuisances we were becoming. Our freedom and its riches were contained in that gap, which we went on widening. The real danger, though we didn't know it, had been a northern, orchestrated dream."

"Did your family serve the caliphs in Constantinople in the past?"

"Of course."

His brother-in-law entered. Monsieur Mustapha, a Muslim, had married first a German and then a Circassian. His Circassian brother-in-law was a French-speaking senior official with fair hair and a very white skin. Mustapha's complexion was not really dark, but the contrast made me realize how pale-skinned the Slavs were, and I was less surprised than before that Europeans sprang to the defence of Soviet dissidents more readily than to that of American Blacks. Unless the latter were dancers, singers, high-jumpers or jazz musicians—people on the fringes of society. It may be that his brother-in-law's presence made Monsieur Mustapha less scathing about Westerners.

"Of course we're Muslims first and foremost, and so are the rest, especially Syria. As a Turkish subject I'm Syrian too, you know. The Empire let both Syria and Palestine go on existing, just as your Provence and Narbonnaise were allowed to become provinces of Rome. Palestine's uniqueness was respected by the Ottomans. The Empire was about as manageable as a fifty-ton lorry on a mountain road, and it let the Greeks, Romans, Serbs, Slovenes, Syrians, Lebanese, Albanians and Palestinians keep their own characters. The Ottoman Empire's worst crime was not making the Arabs adopt Turkish cooking. But what it's criticized for most is its army of Christian mercenaries."

He couldn't say too much. The Circassians, formerly Russian, had come and settled in the Empire rather like the Christian mercenaries he'd just mentioned. And his brother-in-law, with his china-blue eyes, was listening.

"What about Israel?"

"Until the end of the last century we'd forgotten who we were. The Israeli invasions gave us back our soul... Your reaction to that word suggests you don't believe in the existence of the soul, but our soul leapt up so fiercely that to begin with we had more trouble with it than with the invaders.

"I wanted to explain how we came to be part of the Palestinian people. Will you be shocked if I use the example of a wet-nurse? When we're babies we make use of her milk, we love her the way you people love a Dutch cow, and we're quite capable of selling her or hiring her out. But if someone steals her we forget about the milk and remember her name, the black patches on her hide, her horns. We defend her. We sometimes treated the Palestinian peasants harshly even though they'd fed us. But Israel wants to deny Palestine and deprive it even of its name."

"But what *about* Israel?" I insisted. "How did Polish Jews think of the Palestinians? What name was Palestine known by in the Crimea when the world was still flat? How were its people supposed to be dressed? Did the Jews know when they started out that it was the beginning of an invasion?"

"If instead of coming to Jerusalem Israel had helped itself to a state in Sicily or Brittany, we'd have had a good laugh and Israel would probably have been our friend. I don't think they'd have had their present ingrained contempt for the Arabs—even stronger perhaps than their own sense of Jewishness. Imagine Brittany— Brest and Quimper—full of kibbutzim and speaking Hebrew! And the Bretons refugees in Wales, Ireland, Spanish Galicia and Galilee. You'd have laughed too. If it isn't certain the Palestinians are direct descendants of the Canaanites, it's even less sure Miss Golda Meir was the great-granddaughter of Moses, David and Solomon."

Monsieur Mustapha's account struck me as both vague and half hearted. When I saw him again we were alone, and I asked him to tell me more about the Norwegian Jews and their dream.

"What I said wasn't a true description. I haven't dreamed their dream, I didn't know I was the one they were dreaming of. Or rather that they had their eye on. From far away in space and time. The images in their dreams must have been quite vague. In the same way we Palestinians think the sea came to us in a dream.

"What did those who went back home from Jerusalem to Uppsala, Buda, Kiev or Warsaw say about it? What language had they spoken there? None of them knew Arabic. Greek and Latin, perhaps?"

"Copernicus wrote in Latin."

"He wasn't a Jew. What stories did people tell on the shores of the Baltic? Remember the fanciful maps in the fourteenth century—they were still covered with monsters, impossible men and beasts. Pilgrims and traders invented strange races and marvellous flora and fauna."

"Did your people ever dream of conquest?"

"What would have been the use of dreams or day-dreams?"

"I meant military conquests?"

"When you're thin and weak conquests can only be dreams. But take it I didn't say anything. For two thousand years someone had their eye on me and on my country. We didn't know. The eye was in the snow. From father to son for generations, snares were patiently set for me."

"It's the same with all weak countries. They know nothing about the predator over the sea."

"That's no consolation! The dreams never stop for a second. Sometimes I wonder if our brain's only purpose isn't just to dream our lives. You, Monsieur, have told me, and others have done the same, how marvellous it is to be with the fedayeen. I don't know anything about Tsahal. People talk about its democratic spirit, how its officers and men are equals. Would you be as happy with them?"

"If I were a Jew ..."

Four old Palestinian women, then a fifth, were squatting in a new patch of waste ground at Jebel Hussein. By "new" I mean that it had become waste recently, the day before or at most the day before that, as the result of a napalm fire. The old women, laughing, invited me to go and sit with them.

Indians in the Andes crouch down too, buttocks on heels, hands touching the ground so as to keep their balance and be ready to run away. All those who walk for days and nights, staff in hand, are waiting for the moment when they can squat down— the Moroccans, the Jerries, the Arabs and the Turks.

A family of Desert Princes—all men—came to pay their respects to Hussein after he narrowly escaped death in August 1972. I was in Amman, staying in the Jordan Hotel opposite. The family went like this: great-grandfather, grandfather, father, son and seven grandsons. They sat down on black divans, and for some time neither moved nor spoke. After five minutes the father had only one leg; it hung down to the ground while the other was tucked up under one buttock. Gradually the whole family were perched on the divans, legless, like men on the edge of a precipice in a Japanese drawing. They smoked and spat on the carpet.

We see from Khomeini that the Iranians adopt the same position, as do the Indians and Japanese—sitting on one buttock. All the different attitudes of rest, some of them near to flight, some of them reflecting immemorial weariness, produced what looked like a group of men transfixed in the epicentre of an earthquake. The comparison amuses me. I mention it because it reminds me of a young American who asked me:

"Why do you travel all round the world?"

"I want to make a chair that's never been made before, so I have to see all the chairs there are already."

The one who looked the oldest of the women had, despite her smile, the most imperious way with her.

"We're in my house."

The others smiled and nodded.

"What house?"

"Can't you see?"

Pointing a finger covered with rings, she showed me not the remains of her own house but four other little heaps of cold ashes, each surrounded by four blackened stones.

Who had ordered two French-speaking fedayeen to take me, three hours earlier, to a little villa standing unharmed in its own garden near Jebel Hussein?

"You'll meet an official personage there, the president of the Palestinian women in Amman. Be very polite. She's middle-class and needs careful handling."

"Is she delicate?"

"She's useful."

Wahadal and Jebel Hussein were the two Amman camps the

Bedouin soldiers made the best job of destroying. A pack of cards lay on a low table in the sitting-room, probably waiting for me to cut and deal. The lady president came in, shook hands with everyone, sat down, and asked us to do the same. Then she picked up the cards and smiled. And that smile ravaged her naturally chubby face. Unfortunately the faces of Dora Maar are made use of too often for me to make that comparison here. All her blood had rushed to her legs and feet; the face itself went suddenly livid. She looked straight at me and cruelly, crudely, mangled out an invisible text, forcing the arguments of the Palestinian resistance on me.

"We have our rights. UN Resolution 242 is quite categorical, and I'll never let Israel or Jordan either dictate UN resolutions or obstruct them."

I stood up.

"We know all that bullshit. You can keep it."

Unlike the fedayeen, she knew enough French to understand what I'd said.

"I'm telling the truth."

"If the leaders of Fatah appointed you they must be as stupid as you are."

The two fedayeen helped the lady president dry her tears, then escorted me out of the house. But they were so outraged they then left me.

"You behaved extremely badly. And we had so much trouble getting her to take that job."

Once rid of them, I was relieved to come upon those old women so cheerful in misfortune as they sat by the embers of their lives. The remnants of hearths that I saw—five times four smoke-blackened stones—symbolized the five houses that had burned like coals.

Although their scarves were arranged to conceal a few locks of white hair dyed with henna, none of the old women was veiled. They laughed—desperate, but elegantly so. What they said to me was interpreted by a Palestinian official just as old and just as cheerful as they. But I felt I understood them before I heard their words translated. They bared their solitude to the bone.

"Where are you from?"

"We ought to warm him up some tea!"

"Is France a long way away?"

"Is it draughty?"

In a style that was emphatic yet light and graceful, they told me how everything had been burned by the Bedouin soldiers and the napalm bombs.

"That's the stove, there—see?"

A thin brown finger pointed to four blackened stones and a little heap of ashes. The woman also showed me a cup made of very thin blue porcelain.

"I've been told it's from China. Look. Not a scratch. It fell on to the ashes: blue looks very nice on grey."

Trouble suits old women when they can be as funny and elegant as that. The sky was blue too. The sun was hot, and the fire burned even though it was out. As well as the cup that had survived bullets and flames intact, there was also a teapot, dented and black all over, but not more so than before. They insisted on making me some tea.

"It's going to be a cold night."

"But we're not alone. We all have relatives. Plenty of them. We go to one or another of them every night. We spend the days here, in our houses. At our age you like your own fireside."

Each of the old women had a house.

"Is Hussein going to last?"

"Are you crazy?"

They laughed and asked if I didn't want to take him and show him to the French.

"They'll never have seen anyone like him!"

"Did you know a revolution was like this before you came here?"

That was the first time the word was mentioned. Perhaps the lady president of the Palestinian women, alone and still weeping, was playing patience? Did she know that fifty yards away from her garden the Palestinian women themselves were playing a simpler kind of patience, resulting in the cheerfulness of those who have ceased to hope?

The sun curved onwards. An outheld arm or finger cast an ever thinner shadow, but on what soil? Jordan, according to a political fiction decreed by England, France, Turkey and America.

"Hussein dropped incendiary bombs. My husband was one of the first casualties."

"Where is he?"

"There!"

She started to lift her arm, but either to save energy or because she was tired, at her age, of having made the same sweeping gesture for three days, she let it fall again.

"He's there. On the other side of the wall. We all scratched away as well as we could to make the hole deeper, but there's no soil—it's all rock. They'll find him a proper cemetery some time this week. Fatah's promised us. The napalm sent him up in flames, my old husband. First his hair and his eyes. But the fire stopped in time. He's as clean now as a fish-bone."

All of them had perfectly hairless faces. Did they pluck their facial hair, just as young Arab women still remove their pubic hair?—under their black petticoats, more black petticoats, and more again, how many only their husbands know or knew. And where did the skirts and the scarves come from? Were they inherited, or received as gifts? I couldn't help imagining the thin bodies, never washed because the broken water-pipes were still not mended. The undesiring bodies, overtaxed by the cares of a broken-up family, by war and its useless precautions, were already the colour of compost. No place here for the bright adornments indulged in by the old ladies of the Leading Families.

As for the cemetery they spoke of, I could only imagine a mobile one, like the sort Ali had had in mind for my own bones, divided up among the fedayeen, until they could finally be buried in the Dead Sea. Probably a collapsible cemetery, a solemn symbol of graves never dug in the sand, where corpses were at the mercy of jackals. A kind of war memorial that had to be dismantled quickly, in wind, rain or sun and sometimes under the moon, and the parts carried away: gold paper wreaths, gold-lettered tributes, quotations from the Koran, simple poems, one or two light-bulbs run on a battery. Graves, tombs, cemeteries, monuments—all had to be collapsible and adapted to nomadic life.

"The Bedouin are good shots. They fired the napalm from bazookas."

Seventy years ago—if I'd been in a position to listen—I'd never have heard a woman, even a woman of the world, say anything as daring as "Have you got the bread?" Yet here was a toothless old Palestinian woman calmly talking about "bazookas," and her contemporaries mentioning "napalm" as if the word was not at all unusual. The modern military vocabulary suited them perfectly. I was surprised they didn't say anything about the Pentagon's "sophisticated weapons."

One advantage of age and emigration is that you can tell lies almost with impunity, since witnesses are either dead or unavailable. In 1918 all the capitals of Europe were suddenly full of taxi drivers who were Russian princes. Are the refugee camps full of families who've left treasures behind in Palestine and don't know what's become of them?

Those five old women, whose names I never knew, had no soil either above or below them. They were in a place without space, where any step must be a false one. Was even the ground firm under their ten bare feet? The land grew less and less solid as it approached Hebron in the distance, where their friends and relations still were. Everyone made himself as light as possible, wafting voluptuously about in the Arabic language.

The Palestinians had become insufferable. They were discovering mobility—how to walk, how to run, how to switch ideas about almost daily to produce a new game or another phase of the old one.

Ferraj was in a good temper, so he put on a cheerful air and spoke to me with his hands in his pockets and the two thumbs sticking out, his legs planted wide apart and his body tilted back. He'd seen one of James Dean's films and borrowed some of his not altogether tough arrogance. I asked him what made him become an atheist.

"Before I can answer that I have to go back to my natural position. Just a minute . . . All right. Atheist? I have to be one if I want the people to get the Gulf oil back. You see what I mean—I can tell from the look in your eyes."

"I don't see in the least."

"Oh well, I'm not surprised—with Pompidou in power the French are a bit behind the times. Muhammad did a good job fifteen hundred years ago. The emirs, the kings and the most wretched little 'sherifs' owe all their present prestige to their origins: they are, or say they are, and they can prove it thanks to the forgers, the descendants through Ali and Fatima of the Prophet—blessings upon him. But if the Palestinians could convince the Arabs Muhammad was only a fake, the Prophet would collapse in ruins, and so would the prestige of his descendants."

"But the Koran's printed in millions of copies. It's recited on every television set in the Muslim world. Your plan to destroy Islam will take a thousand years."

"So there's no time to lose."

He put his hands back in his pockets, straddled his thighs again, and lit up an American fag like a good little hood.

"Any other questions?"

I was on time for my appointment with Abu Omar at the PLO office, and told him about my session in the lady president's drawing-room, the pack of cards on the table, the UN resolutions, the Palestinians' rights, the consolation offered by the fedayeen and my abrupt departure.

"What a pity I wasn't there—it's not often we get a laugh. The committee were wondering how to get shot of that lazy bourgeois windbag."

He stopped laughing to wipe his glasses, which steamed up every time his emotions were the least bit stirred. The world must have looked blurred and vague to him, and I wondered if the revolution seemed a matter of urgency or more like an eye operation. He wiped his glasses. I thought resentfully, "He can laugh—he didn't have to endure the lady president's drawing-room."

One bombing is like another through their lighter side. Twelve years later a Palestinian friend told me how his house in Beirut had burned down, and all his books and notes stayed upright where they stood on the shelves. It was only when he went into the room that the displacement of the air made them all disintegrate. And there, unharmed on top of a soft heap of ashes, was a charming little porcelain cup. Just like the one at Jebel Hussein. A nod and a wink. From whom to whom?

"Let's talk about the effect on our people of the fortunate mishaps of Nixon's Americans. We knew we might be defeated. But Vietnam's victory gave us new heart. The fedayeen had a good laugh watching TV and seeing the American ambassador in Saigon fold up the embassy flag, run and throw it on to the marine helicopter waiting impatiently on the lawn, jump in after it, and finally slink off across the sea on an aircraft carrier. Perhaps it was when the people of the Third World saw the United States on their bended knees in Saigon that they dared hope the Palestinians would soon usher in the revolution.

"But we know how régimes make use first of one party and then of another to stay on top. The United States are Nixonian now. We can't use the same tricks as they do. We can't bomb New York."

"And they wouldn't dare come here with their bombs . . ."

"You never know. I think you may be wrong. If we get too friendly with the Russians . . ."*

"They'd protect you."

"No, they wouldn't. That I am sure of. The Russians may be our allies, but they'll make use of us, not we of them."

"You started off by talking about 'fortunate mishaps.' "

"The struggle between Israel and us is a struggle for survival, but a very local one. Setbacks seem absolute. The war between us and the Bedouin seemed almost like a step backward, with two tribes, even two clans, at loggerheads, and a great tribal chief, Nasser, ordering us to exchange the kiss of peace. And Arafat and Hussein obeyed. You're always against leaders, but even you must admit they're very good at kissing in public. I don't think America's very fond of kings—from Washington they look rather like witch-doctors—which is why Hussein affects simplicity, like a president.

"But Israel didn't want to see too many Jordanians siding with the PLO. They were afraid it might lead to the creation of a

---

*Abu Omar was speaking in 1972. He seems to have foreseen Beirut going up in flames in 1982, abandoned by everyone, the Arab countries among the rest.

Jordanian-Palestinian or a Palestinian-Jordanian republic—you remember the arguments about what to call a republic that had a name but was never born. With England's backing Israel persuaded the Americans to help Hussein. Hence his victory. And the Cairo agreement, the secret accords between Hussein and Golda, and above all the Zionist infiltrations into Lebanon and here in Amman. Don't forget that at the start of the first millennium we were Byzantines, and all schismatics to a greater or lesser extent."

"Who were your ancestors?"

"Probably Monophysite Christians. But in my family we're not sure of anything, least of all of the various religions we've belonged to at one time or another.

"But as I was saying. The American intervention turned us into real belligerents, at first on a Middle Eastern scale. We soon had the same political, though not territorial, status as the Philippines, Formosa, Israel, South Vietnam, South Korea, Guatemala, Honduras, Santo Domingo and so on. But dormant revolutions risk a rude awakening. If the UN comes into it, the rebel becomes an enemy of the United States. And then the Russians have to mix in too.

"America's aid to Hussein brought us out of the obscurity of tribal wars fought practically with clubs and bows and arrows. The flow of arms into Amman in the winter of 1970 made us one of the many enemies of international capitalism. You can see the result. It's gone to our heads and put us in danger. The cameras are on us too much. We must be careful not to overdose on limelight. If we keep making appearances, especially all dressed up for battle, we'll turn into showoffs of the revolution."

(The above fragment of conversation dates from 1972. Abu Omar was still trying to make me understand the relationship between the revolution and the kings and princes.)

Much as Abu Omar might talk to the greater glory of his master Arafat and the PLO in general, all too often I saw the fedayeen engage in operations without really knowing from start to finish what their objective was. A machine-gun, a rifle, twenty rifles might loose off here and now, while the target was pinpointed three days ago and the range decided the day after that, two hundred kilometres away.

Bullets landed after HQ had forgotten all about the order to fire them. Copies of the order would moulder in a heap of files while the men who'd just shot at shadows would never know till their dying day of the danger they'd been in two or three days before.

If they'd eavesdropped on some of their leaders the fedayeen would have known the price of a suite in the various Hiltons of Europe and Africa. It wasn't as expensive as now, but the men on the bases were beginning to talk. The fedayeen were beginning to get angry with leaders who were "servants of two masters."

But doesn't power always change into gold, and gold into power?

Weren't Napoleon's armies in Italy made up of veterans from the year II of the Revolution as well as young recruits? Five years went by between the popular uprising and the time Bonaparte was made a general. The troops who fought at Fleurus and Jemappes were probably the same as those who'd fought at Arcole. The enthusiasm that first made them defend their own country later turned them into champions of popular liberty. Everyone except the officers travelled on foot. The Murat family archives and their treasures give some idea of the looting that went on in Italy.

Victory only opened up careers to generals, but the ordinary soldier was able to satisfy the baser cravings that go with heroism. The field marshal's baton was safer in the hands of Lannes. The French Revolution, and especially the army of the Rhine, was full of the nobility of the Empire. Marshal Ney may have been dreaming of a coronet when his horse was shot from under him in the battle that made him Prince of the Moskova.

More dreams of gilt and velvet came true under Napoleon III. He and his court were born of the not very serious revolution of February 1848.

Since 1962, and right up until 1985, power, administration, the police and the law in Algeria have all remained under the influence of the FLN. The bourgeoisie and the diplomats in Algiers have converted the bare feet, the burning villages and the superb risks into their own alleged origins, in much the same way as the kings of Jerusalem and Cyprus claimed to have been born, one awkward night, of a serpent.

The fedayeen dreamed, and as they couldn't surround themselves with a luxury and prestige of which they knew nothing, they had to dream that too. One day a fedayee showed me a photograph of a part of the royal palace and said:

"All that just for one man."

Implying: "All I've got is an eighth of a shack, while that little king . . ."

Another remark by another fedayee, pointing to a picture of the queen:

"She's the one I'd really like to have it off with . . ."

A third fedayee, quoting from the Koran, the voice of God:

"I have chosen one out of you . . ."

Then he asked me:

"So he chose Muhammad the Prophet. Why Muhammad and not me?"

Amid all these bourgeois dreams, did the fedayee see himself as a hero? When fatigue, dust and boredom acted on him as hashish and opium sometimes do, did he see himself looting some emirate and climbing higher and higher until he had a state funeral and a statue erected in his memory?

What day-dreams make a man go to the sacrifice? Stereotypes.

"Do you want the king to give you his palace?"

"The only happiness that's acceptable is the happiness you give someone else. Giving to me would be too good for him. I wouldn't take it."

"So you fight the revolution for others."

He laughed.

"No one will take it. And they'll take it less and less. As you see."

He was twenty-three. Explain his confusion by his age: mine, three times his, hasn't managed to sort things out. So he dreamed of the destruction of gilt armchairs, and dreamed up the words to speak of it when asked.

———

A few days ago I looked on with sadness and amusement as a Palestinian poet, whose name naturally escapes me, was talking to the PLO representative in Rabat. Whereas in 1971 all the fedayeen and their leaders had thin legs, hollow cheeks and concave stomachs, the stomachs now were convex. The two sets of fly-buttons seemed to be sniffing each other like dogs. The real conversation was taking place between pot-belly and paunch. The faces were far away from each other.

Barley and rye, olives and beans, were what the Jordanian peasants lived on.

When I emerged, still drowsy, from the tent where we slept— about thirty soldiers and I—I saw that the fedayeen, still warm from their last erotic dreams, had piled their arms and were standing by the road, laughing at what they'd found when they turned out of their sleeping-bags.

They were aged between fourteen and twenty.

Opposite them stretched an almost ripe field, half barley and half rye, and frisking about amid the ears was a flock of goats, munching up the crop in a frenzy at their own good luck. A goatherd about ten years old was laying about him at random, trying to get them out. He hadn't got a dog: goats are not sheep. The boy's stick stung, so the goats fled to a corner of the field, like feathers in an eiderdown when you beat it. You couldn't tell where they'd run to next, but come what may they weren't going to leave their green and yellow paradise.

Green and yellow were the colours of the field, but I'd often seen them in this part of Jordan. Seen between the dark green of two palms, or between two trees yellowed by autumn, or between two light green towels hanging on a line, the sky was never the same blue. I'd got into the habit of looking at Ajloun, interpreting it, in terms of the primary colours, blue and yellow, and their product, green. An over-simplied symbolism, of course, but one that haunted me.

The fighters, themselves not much older than the goatherd, were much amused by the triumph of the goats. Perhaps they sided with them because they were doing as they pleased, but

336 · JEAN GENET

above all it was charming to see the ears of barley and rye sticking out of their mouths and their jaws moving from side to side. Each goat's Adam's apple bobbed up and down under its little beard every time it swallowed. The shameless nimble goats, unlike sheep, were the very image of freedom, rebellion, anarchy—just what the fedayeen themselves wanted to be, and thought they were.

The goats and kids bolted down the barley and rye without even stopping to belch between two tufts. The fedayeen, perhaps because distractions were so rare around here, took no notice of the goatherd's anger, which was plainly visible on his face and not far from despair. What must it be like to be a Shepherd of Nations, trying to guide them all towards common ends without being too hard on their individual whims!

The fedayeen were the ones who'd taken me to see the Jordanian farmer's wife a few days before, when they'd listened to her respectfully. It was her field that was being devastated now, and the boy was one of the Palestinians' few friends. For him the spoiling of the crop was due not only to the goats but also to his own inefficiency. So while the fedayeen's gibes had no effect on the goats, they did dishearten the young peasant.

The fighters had all been born in the desert or in some town in the Gulf, and all they knew about was guns. They'd learned a few slogans in Arabic from Marx or Lenin, very occasionally from Mao as well, but they didn't see any connection between the rye and barley bread they ate three times a day and these broken and trampled stalks, more thoroughly destroyed than they would have been by a seven-hour hailstorm.

When I told the leader of the fedayeen to help the little goatherd, he laughed louder than all his men put together.

I realized then the distance between the vagabond I still was and the guardian of law and order I might become if I succumbed to the temptation of law and order and the cosiness they can bring. Every so often I need to remind myself of the struggle that has to put up, not against the enticements of France—the French are such a prosaic nation there's no problem—but against the allurements of rebellions whose apparent poetry conceals invisible appeals to conformity.

The small-scale chaos in that field of rye, barley and goats, contained within four hedges, might be taken as a symbol of the Palestinians' depredations on the borders of southern Lebanon. But the Shiites' anger obviously has other causes than the pranks of the fedayeen. Why do I write "the Shiites' anger"? That's what the papers say. They never mention the wrath of the big citrus and tobacco growers of southern Lebanon. I'll go into that in more detail in a later volume.

Too much charm, especially when it seems effortless, is bound to make very beautiful women unbearable. Men who live at a distance and received only occasional glimpses of their charms can resist them better and longer. But when the seductive arts and their preparations are practised under our very noses we become like Molière's maidservant, on whom he's said to have tried out his plays as he wrote them. She knew his ideas would work triumphantly, because they'd be presented to an audience of strangers brilliantly lit and dripping with gold and jewellery, while she was just a servant there to take off the master's make-up and get his bath ready.

"Move it back at least three metres. I'll still be on the embankment but protected by the slope, and the servers can lie down and work under cover. The fedayeen will be more accurate and use up less energy if they feel safe. And the muzzle of the machine-gun itself will be clear of the tree and able to adjust more easily to the direction of enemy fire. So much for the first gun. Train the second to the right so that it covers the whole valley, including the hedge by the side of the road—the Bedouin could hide behind that."

Mubarak, the Sudanese lieutenant, was beside me in the midst of the fedayeen, acting as if he were on an official tour of inspection. The charmer I'd sought out, and whose presence both oppressed and exalted me, seemed to have taken in the defects of the set-up at a glance. None of the emplacements was flat, and if anything went wrong the servers would have been exposed and forced to act blindly. He's a born soldier, I thought. Not only by his skin but also by his military skill he belongs to brightest Africa. I said as much.

"What you're seeing is Sandhurst! I'm just applying the lessons of classical artillery. I once had to study Napoleon's strategy at the church of Saint-Roch."*

One day he said to me, probably as a joke:

"Look at me. I'm terrifying. As terrifying as an Englishman. I'm an African, and Africa has been an island, like England, since your de Lesseps, whose name rhymes with forceps, severed us from our Siamese twin sister, Asia. Thanks to that smart guy, Africa has given you the slip and drifted away. Look at me—aren't I in full sail?"

He was the sort of officer who can sum up any situation at a glance and knows immediately what to do.

"This is war. So we fight and win."

That was him in a nutshell.

There he was, suddenly plain and simple and stripped of all his paraphernalia. Not that his trappings were effeminate. On the contrary, they were almost childishly manly. But basically they were playthings, and seemed to have come out of a handbag. Then all at once nothing was left either of coquette or cocotte; only hunter or prey. It wasn't through his eyes but through the shape of his nose and the muscles in his neck that he sensed where danger threatened.

The fedayeen soon saw what was what. They stopped being children fascinated by a boy and his goats, and obeyed orders like soldiers. The new arrangement radiated intelligence. Even I, who knew nothing about defence, was pleased, or perhaps rather relieved at seeing the weaknesses corrected. So I must have been unconsciously aware of them before. The new arrangement made full use of our main resources, the machine-guns.

From then on I saw Mubarak in a new light.

He'd sat down in the grass beside the first machine-gun, and that's where I see him when I think of him now. He showed the group leader the target, right down to the half circle he could spray with bullets when the enemy were in position opposite. Then he

---

*Napoleon, newly appointed to command the Convention forces in Paris in 1794, defeated the insurgents by bringing in his artillery and attacking them outside the church of Saint-Roch.

lay down on his back, closed his eyes and smoked for a while. An African was lying down beside me. His colour, his partly bare body, his muscles, the contours of his face despite the tribal scars—all seemed to me to have been prepared back in Africa for battle, confrontation, guile or flight.

The husband of the woman who owned the field rode by on his mule.

"It wasn't a very good crop anyway. He'll claim compensation from Fatah. If I were really conscientious I'd tell him to multiply his claim by ten. Kuwait can afford to pay up."

"Is that your view?"

"Yes, but it's his, too. That's why I don't do anything."

I feel I must give a physical description of Mubarak the Fuzzywuzzy with straight hair. At twenty-five he was a champion athlete at an army cadet school in the Sudan. My dreams of the past are often in colour, and I see Mubarak as mauve, with Prussian blue predominating. His hands, neck and arms were very muscular. A butcher at la Villette, wrapping him up for you, would have said, "He looks heavier than he is." His moustache was straight, of course, and rather meagre, and he wore sideburns like the King of Morocco. He was sinewy and agile, but that mass of flesh and bone produced ideas as pure and soothing as music.

"A country is basically a collection of plots of earth, and earth has to be weeded. And weeding, whether it's your country or your garden, a city square or a little railway bank, is a badly paid job for a roadman or a labourer. The Palestinians don't realize what's in store for them, and how hard they'll have to work to get rid of the couch grass sown by the Israelis. The fedayeen are masters of the world because they're playing a deadly game."

I heard a little trill: a hummingbird was nesting in his bass voice.

"Aren't the fedayeen anxious?"

"Happy. So you said. Or were you out of your mind? They're happy because they're masters of destruction. Rebellion kills other people, but it gives life to the rebels themselves. Because they go all out, they live life to the full. They're on cloud nine. They're high on enthusiasm, heroism and patriotism. People sometimes have trips on aeroplanes!

"Do you think I'm talking like an ignorant negro . . . But what a bloody shame it'd be if when they got their country back they had to do what's called 'exploit' it! At the moment they're in a dream, the Palestinian dream, but how long will it last? Probably until the day on which... the day when... Which is correct, Jean?"

"Don't stop. Carry on regardless."

More hummingbirds.

"They'll continue in their Palestinian dream until the Soviet Union points its finger at a mountain somewhere and turns it into a 'star.' Then the revolution will still be Palestinian but it'll be called the Andean revolution. But it's better to be a revolutionary movement, a total one, even in a tiny little province, than to cultivate a garden."

"Why?"

"Because a revolutionary movement is eternal, and we have to believe in eternal recurrence. To be part of the Palestinian movement is to belong to the immortal Satan, who from all eternity has made and will make war on God. Although, as a movement, it's linked to time, the Palestinian movement mustn't be content with conquering a ridiculous morsel of space."

"That may be true for the fedayeen, if they think only of themselves. But what about the Palestinians in the camps, remembering their villages in Palestine?"

"Ideological folly. Ambition on the part of the so-called leaders."

"You came here with the Palestinians. You told me off in Jerash and accused me of supporting Pompidou. And now you play the artist."

He smiled. Irresistibly.

"So you agree!"

"About what?"

"That I'm a typical negro—all show. And note, because for a White you're not too much of an idiot, that what gets up everyone's nose, especially that of the Arabs, is that the Palestinians' dream is as powerful as their existence. Their revolt has given them something: the carbon dioxide inhaled by the pretenders, the king and emirs and the Whites of Europe is oxygen to the Palestinians. If they'd stayed in their cocoons and never got past the pupa stage they'd have been bearable. But they burst out of their cocoons, and now they're flying. And laying bombs."

Mubarak was joking. He took a breather and went and picked some milky nuts from the hedge.

"I don't like the Arabs."

"You speak their language well."

"As a negro I had to. But I'm an animist. The only boss I recognized is a Jew—Spinoza. The worst thing I accuse the Arabs of is drunkenness: they get drunk on wine, marijuana, singing, dancing, God, love. And when they wake up the exaltation has gone and all they've got left is a hangover. The Palestinians haven't woken up yet. They're still completely drunk. Still poets."

Then, inconsequently, as I thought:

"When someone makes a political choice, he ought to be quite clear. But when someone goes into a revolutionary trance, he ought to leave it vague. Above all he shouldn't try to understand. Negroes don't think. They dance."

"You think a lot."

"What do you make of me? I've filled myself with vices. If you do that and you're forced under torture to say who you are, you confess nothing, you just tell the torturer who you're not. But your powers of observation—"

Here his voice grew even more melodious. Not sweet or cloying, but clear and tender. I knew the sting in the tail would come any moment now.

"Your powers of observation aren't all that brilliant. You call me Mubarak the Fuzzywuzzy, but that applies to millions of men and women. And my hair may be oily, but its straight."

"People with fuzzy hair are going to rule the world."

"It's not certain. And anyway, what a fate! To rule the world just because the hairs on your head and the whiskers in your beard are like watch-springs. Your pallor makes us coloured and takes away our oomph."

"I once flew from Brasilia to Carolina, at the confluence of the Tocantins and the Amazon. It took from eleven in the morning till two A.M. the next day, on a little plane with about twenty or twenty-five seats. We flew over the mountains, and the plane kept dropping like a stone in the air pockets. All the passengers were Whites, mostly planters. One was a dealer in baby tigers the size of cats, and tiny panthers only a few months old. Probably there were a few plainclothes cops. And a doctor."

It's impossible to reconstruct the incident in what's called direct speech, so I'd better narrate it.

The sun was beating down on our old crate, which kept dropping one or two thousand metres, or perhaps only twenty-three—I don't know.

Fear. Not the fear of the mind and the imagination, but the mute fear of every organ in your body: liver, kidneys, intestines, heart, lungs, pituitary gland and stomach. So many silent beings suspended above the earth, waiting for the next touch-down in order to come to life again. My whole body was in the grip of fear.

The planters, each of whom owned at least five thousand hectares of land, spoke a few words to me but didn't smile. They wanted to be like their ancestors, the Portuguese from Europe, who remained pale by way of a challenge to the tropics and the equator. Each one wore a thin moustache and had a long thin face like Michel Leiris, but what they said to me was very commonplace.

"Who's he?"

I shrugged my shoulders.

"Who knows?"

(I'm still talking to Mubarak.)

"They weren't the slightest bit interested in me or the object of my journey, but every time we hit an air pocket I was afraid for them. On the ground their thousands of hectares worked by blacks would have kept me at a distance. But up in the sky, with the sun blazing down, they were just bundles of organs huddled up in the darkness of the body. That's the only time I've ever felt men were my brothers. If the plane had crashed and I'd survived, I'd have prayed for the repose of their souls. And this is what the whitest, the sternest and the richest of the planters said to me:

"We Europeans...(for I feel like an American from top to toe—from top to toe an American American, with the same feet, wasp waist, shoulders and head)...we've got nothing against negroes. And I drink a glass of Californian champagne like every-one else when King Pele scores a goal. And throw a party when he helps Brazil win the World Cup. You understand what I'm say-ing, don't you, *señor*, even though my French isn't very good? I learned it in China."

"Formosa?"

"Red China. Some time ago. I have a lot of respect for Pele, you know. Those three sitting behind us don't understand. They're Ger-man. Probably Jews. But we need to be careful with the negroes. We've been overrun by them."

"The Whites, overrun by the Blacks?"

"*Si señor*. The invasion started a long time ago. If you go to Carolina del Norde you'll see the negroes have kept to the banks of the river and the Americans to the hill. But go to Bahia and it's Africa."

As always in Brazil, we made a pretty rough landing. The plane stopped just long enough to put down the three Germans and the mail bag, and then we were off again.

"There's a lot of exaggerated talk about our natural resources," said the Brazilian. "Our wild animals that are caught and sent to zoos, our rubber and rare woods, the Sugarloaf Mountain in Rio, Copacabana Beach, our snakes. It's true a few Americans make a living out of them. But we ourselves are going to be smothered by negroes and mulattos."

We were coming in to land and circling over a little cabbage patch. As the plane homed in I could see the cabbages getting big-ger and bigger, their stems getting taller, and the field turning into a forest of royal palms.

I'm told most of the fields in that part of the country produced several harvests of marijuana, but I was concentrating on the palm trees and the buzzards and didn't notice anything. When the huge black birds alighted on a banana leaf it didn't even quiver; when they spread out their wings to fly away again, the whole tree bent with the effort. I don't think a B52 made such a stir taking off.

When I had to go back to Brasilia some friends took me to the Tocantins river to meet an Indian they knew—a handsome young man of twenty-seven with almond eyes, high cheekbones and straight hair. He greeted us warmly and introduced his "family": his wife, a negress, and four little boys, all with fuzzy hair. The only way I can convey his distress is to repeat his words. They were like a death certificate.

"Look at their colour and their hair. I live in the midst of strangers. They're all the family I have. It's to feed them I go fishing. When I was born there were about five hundred men in my tribe. Now there are fifty. I'm not growing old—I'm dying where I stand. Not by getting wrinkles and grey hair, but by taking up less and less space in my own family, by getting thinner and thinner and fading away, while all around me Indians give life to negroes. I watch over my tribe's death agonies while I'm still alive."

The nest of hummingbirds awoke in Mubarak's guffaw.

"Do you mean my mother ate Indians' flesh? It's true I ought to have curly whiskers, and my moustache is smooth. How well you know me! The hummingbirds in my laugh aren't singing. If your ears were really keen you'd realize they're sighing. When you told me about the Palestinian staff sergeant, the Black who served you your dinner all on your own and let the fedayeen gnaw the bones and lick the gravy off the plate, do you think I didn't recognize the danger hanging over us? We may still involuntarily respect the slave-trader, but what the staff sergeant gave away that evening was not your leavings but your equality."

"Get to the point."

"If we act in a way that perpetuates slavery it's because, secretly or otherwise, probably secretly, it's neither the time nor the place for cynicism. The negroes! You've no idea how much they respect musical notation . . ."

He made a pun involving black and white notes, sperm and homosexuals. I pretended to demur.

"I know. I'm very vulgar. I can just hear myself . . . Have I shown you my will?"

"No. People don't make wills at your age."

"Want to see it?"

He put his hand in his pocket.

"No."

"Just a glance."

From his khaki trousers he drew out something about the

size of a fingernail, held it in his pink palm for a moment, then unfolded it.

"Can you read Arabic?"

"Not very well. I can see it's signed and dated."

"I'll translate: 'A shroud will be enough. Don't waste money on four planks for a coffin. Once I'm dead let me rot fast.'"

He folded up the tiny will again.

"Where do you keep it?"

"By my left ball. A testicle testament. Hey, did you really love those Portuguese in the plane in Brazil?"

"Love's too strong a word. The plane in the air pocket was our whole universe. You down below were just survivors, or dead. You were less real to us than the plane's propeller. So we had to do the best we could with the universe we had. All that separated me from the owners of thousands of hectares worked by their negroes had evaporated. Inside that steel cabin they'd become as basic as I was myself."

"What about that idea of praying for them?"

"It was the only thing I could do for them. The same thought would have struck you in my place."

I can no longer hear his answer. The great mauve muscular mass was still visible, but it had become inaudible. It spoke to me with the distant voice of ants.

Remember I'm trying to describe what a man of twenty-five was like who's been dead a long time. Twelve years, I think. Readers may say I use a mouldy, dislocated old ass's jawbone to do it. But every memory is true. A whiff of cool air fleetingly revives a moment that's past and gone for ever. Though perhaps not as powerfully as a drop of perfume, every memory nevertheless brings back the dead moment; not in the living freshness of then, but throbbing with another kind of life.

But a book of reminiscences doesn't present the truth any more than a novel does. I can't bring Mubarak back to life. What he said to me that day and other days will never be reconstructed as it really was. I could write a description of Carolina del Norde. But how can you answer a dead man, except with rhetoric or silence?

This may apply to all words, but it's certainly true of words like sacrifice, self-sacrificing, abnegation, altruism. To write them down as a tribute to someone who dared to live them, and live them to the point of dying for them, is indecent. Like the war memorials covered with similar easy tributes.

Parachutists are said to see the earth approaching with a speed that accelerates with the rate of their fall. And when I'm about to use the sort of words I've just mentioned, I must be careful. Careful not to hide the naïvety or hypocrisy of the word "prayer" in particular—it's worse than any tribute. To write the word sacrifice is very different from actually making a sacrifice, above all the sacrifice of your own life: seeing the world annihilated as the earth approaches to annihilate the parachutist. A man who sacrifices the one life he'll ever have deserves a tombstone of quiet and absence. One that will swallow up both him and anyone capable of naming him or the heroic act that brought about the ultimate silence.

I remember a question Mubarak once asked me:

"Jean, a postilion used to be the man who rode the near horse of a pair drawing a coach. Why is the same word used in French for the drops of saliva in a splutter?"

A fortnight after Mubarak's overhaul of the position, the enemy—the army of Bedouin and Circassians—attacked not from in front or from the right, where their approach was covered by the guns, but from behind.

Several fedayeen were killed and the rest were first taken prisoner by the Bedouin and then sent to the camp at Zarka, in the desert. The Syrian Muslim with the spiky black hair and beard escaped on the way there, under cover of night. I heard about all this when I got back from Beirut.

In July 1984, twelve years later, I went back to Ajloun. The woman's farm was still there, but I was told there were other people living on it now. It would have been too difficult to explain to them how I'd come there in 1971.

I imagine the previous farmer and his wife, who were elderly and friends of the Palestinians, left everything and fled with the fedayeen, or else stayed and were killed, perhaps tortured, by their neighbours. Were they buried near their farm? Or far away? Unless, when I knew them, they were spies, as good at their job as the Israeli who pretended to be mad in Beirut and then came back wearing the uniforms of a Tsahal colonel.

Mubarak was living it up in Beirut, ignorant, perhaps, of the tragedy at Ajloun.

In France, in the winter, a child will marvel at how frost appears on the windowpane with its white ferns, then slowly but surely disappears, melted by the heat of the room or the child's own breath.

The sudden disappearance of some fedayeen one day in broad daylight, into a bush behind a heap of rocks, left me just as astonished as the ironic presence of a squirrel sitting on the moss, both eyes staring into mine. Then they rolled all round us, and the next moment there he sat again, mocking me from his comfortable perch on the flimsiest branch of a tree. Everything was laughing—the squirrel, his swiftness, his tail, the tree, the stones—and I was part of it.

Had the fedayeen played a trick on me?

It's only now I feel I'd like to have been a tree myself, so as to see how they really felt about me. What rôle did I really play amongst them?

If you put back the fourth wall of the stage the characters become people. When an actor's in front of me I can't see his back. An actress is carrying a bag on the screen; but what's in it? What's underneath or behind the handkerchief? Every play is cut off from every other. The fedayeen, the leaders, what they did, the Palestinian revolution—it was all a play: I could see the fedayeen when they were there, but as soon as they left my field of vision they ceased to exist. Evaporated would be a better word. Where had they gone to? When would they be back? Where from? What did they do when they were there?

The fact that they were like ghosts, appearing and disappearing, lent them a life more powerful than that of things that never evaporate and whose image is there all the time. Or rather the fedayeen's existence was so powerful it could afford those sudden, almost courteous evanescences, relieving me of too insistent and tiring a presence. For the fighters' rapid and constantly varying vibrations were too much for a sixty-year-old nervous system to cope with.

I've only to hear the phrase "Palestinian revolution" even now and I'm plunged into a great darkness in which luminous, highly coloured images succeed and seem to pursue one another.

One image: Ferraj came into the world at the age of twenty-three, and asked me, smiling, sitting on the grass, if I was a Marxist. And for a whole evening I was so obviously consumed by his existence that Abu Nasser, one of his friends, annoyed by the current passing between us almost as naturally as the circulation of the blood, looked at us and muttered:

"I could see right away those two were going to hit it off."

Ferraj and I never spoke of the bond between us either to one another or to anyone else. It was a secret only to us.

The person it vexed the most was Abu Nasser, who was excluded by it. That evening, though my words were addressed to everyone on the base, I was really talking only to Ferraj, and was only interested when I thought he was won over. And I believed he was really speaking just for my benefit, though he got some pleasure from his friends' irritation.

But Ferraj vanished when I left the base. That was his first disappearance. The person who emerges most clearly in his place is Abu Nasser, his opposite.

I feel, now, like a little black box projecting slides without captions. My times with the fighters seem to have consisted of abrupt appearances and disappearances. But all of them were vibrant.

I've never been to Israel. For me it was just a sort of rifle range interspersed with banks, computers, big hotels serving kosher food, traps everywhere, buses full of machine-gunned children, and tanks rumbling through the streets. The traffic was directed by beardless shortsighted young philosophers with forget-me-not eyes, bifocal glasses and thin hairy arms sticking out of short-sleeved shirts printed with patterns of mauve flowers. That's what the Tsahal infantrymen looked like to me when I arrived in Beirut on 15 September 1982; I saw them, to be precise, at the intersection on the road to Baabda.

Posters and magazine advertisements exhorting tourists to visit Israel are especially proud of the trees that have been planted in the desert. Eretz Israel is as good as Shakespeare at making forests move. One of them stopped at the village of Maaloul, near

Nazareth. The houses of the Palestinians were mined and blown up—the usual practice at the time—and the forest swept on. If you scratched the ground under the trees you'd find the cellars and foundations.

On every anniversary of what's known as the Liberation, Israel comes and sees how the trees are getting on. Each tree bears the name of the person who planted it. The former inhabitants of the village, or their Palestinian descendants, come here too, to picnic. The first, who were last, laugh and get drunk. The last, who were first, describe what they used to be like. For a few hours—much less time than the Obon dead are allowed in Japan—they do their best to bring the dead village to life again. They tell the young people about one detail after another. Thinking they're remembering, they actually improve on the facts and invent a village so cheerful and happy and far from their present sadness it only makes it worse. But gradually, as the imaginary village comes to life, the sadness disappears, and young and old make awkward attempts to dance their ancient dances.

They've brought pots of distemper with them, and on the ground, on trees and on strips of material they draw and paint a past reality, a present fantasy.

For the Palestinians of Maaloul the anniversary is a renaissance, a feast for the dead. For one day there's a village again—it may be only a lifeless facsimile but it's extremely vivid. Not just a thing of the past but a reincarnation, as New York is of York.

If you wanted to go into a house you went round a tree with a door painted on it. To go upstairs the young Palestinians climbed up into the branches. For a day the word resurrection really meant something, and so did nostalgia. This wasn't the sort of longing that precedes the struggle for a real return. But it reminded you how in Brittany and other Celtic regions the fairies, driven out first by the Romans and then by the Christian clergy, sprang up among the trees and by the springs. The fairies return every year for a celebration in a kind of makeshift village, and some humans are frightened by their singing, laughter and jests, of which they still understand a few words or even whole phrases. And so the very real state of Israel finds itself shadowed by a ghostly survival.

I was told of all this by Mademoiselle Shahid. A young Palestinian called Michel Khleifi has made a film about it.

The young fedayeen wouldn't mind my comparing the funeral of a Muslim leader to a rugby match where the ball is a coffin that may be empty. And I can't help saying their own struggle was a sort of lethal game that made Western spectators tremble.

"Those silly buggers'll set the whole planet on fire."

The game—pretending to be arsonists on a worldwide scale— was typical of kids who never had any toys. If it's amusing to destroy a six-inch-long tin warship, to stamp it to bits and skim the pieces over a nursery school pond, how much more entertaining it is to derail a high-speed train, bring down a real airliner. In short, to do the same as the kids in Beirut, with their steel-rimmed glasses and happy faces at last: sitting in Merkava tanks shooting at twenty-seven-storey blocks of flats; watching them double up like someone in fits of laughter; seeing that the cement, the steel girders, the balconies, the marble, all that had made the building's pride, were of the best possible quality. The block of flats turned into a white cloud slightly tinged with grey near the foundations, and the shortsighted faces lit up.

"Scarcely had the notion of firing crossed our mind or the rocket left the tube than the building was no longer static, but bent over with a bellyache. And we saw it with eyes grown pale poring over sacred texts and looking through magnifying glasses for diacritical marks."

To depict the Palestinian resistance as a game or a party doesn't mean one is taking it lightly. The Palestinians have been denied houses, land, passports, a country, a nation—everything! But who can deny laughter and a light in the eye?

It's been said, and maybe it's true, that "the young fedayeen show their sense of humour by removing the bolts one by one from the Western machine."

It's probably only with puppets, worked by strings or the fingers of the puppeteer beneath their silken costumes, that you can produce a really ghostly and funereal, a truly macabre show. The very name—shadow show—warns you what to expect. Death is conjured up by characters made out of cardboard or wood, or represented by ten fingers of flesh dressed as fairies or princesses. And not merely death, but the dead themselves, the whole empire of the dead. It's natural, really: silence survives everything. It's what every dead person turns into as soon as you mention his name. And these characters made of cardboard or dressed-up fingers, with movements stiff as the bones on the walls of the cemetery in Pisa; these figures tiny as dolls found in the cenotaphs of the Pharaohs—they are an unbridgeable distance away from the voice telling the story, or trying to give them a voice, pretending story and voice are theirs.

Their indifference to story and voice alike teach us that story and voice are not theirs, and that when we are dead anything anyone says about us is not only literally false but also sounds it. Puppets give us perhaps our clearest glimpse of the nullity of death. Whatever attempt may be made at realism, there can never be any accord between the voice, whether high or low, of the showman, and the angular antics of the dolls. Even naked, without any frills, my ten fingers have a life, a dance, that's already independent of me. So what will it be like when I'm at my last gasp?

All this to show that I know what a distance there is—but how can one measure a distance that's really a feeling?—between what Abu Omar was and what I say about him now that he's dead, drowned.

"You need to draw some distinctions among the feudal Arabs," he told me in September 1972. "The emirs, the owners of the oilfields, are all friends of America and often of Israel too. We're in a difficult position. If you seem to be calling religion and property in question and inventing a new morality you're bound to incur popular wrath. The Muslim religion and property—first in the form of land and then in the form of minerals—have both been pretexts for liberation: from the English, the French, the Italians, the Spanish, the Dutch, and even the Americans. We—and 'we' are the Arabs, despite your scowl when you hear anyone talk about Arabism and Arabness . . ."

"The two words don't mean the same thing. I don't reject

'Arabism,' which means belonging to a certain religious and linguistic community. But what about 'Arabness'? Can we talk about Latinness and Frenchness too? And what's the corresponding word for Israel?"

"We can discuss all that another day. But my 'we,' 'us,' includes you and me. It excludes the Arabs we've allowed to take the place of the people we drove out—the princes who without consulting either the people or the Koran have entered the service of imperialism. The oceans of oil have long since been turned into thousand-dollar bills or bars of gold—liquidities!—and are sleeping safely in vaults in the United States. Our policy isn't to attack the princes because they are Muslims, but because they are not. They never have been. God isn't even a word to them. Certainly not a name. Our princes know Gold, and that's all."

"So how will you go about it?"

"Carefully. They've got weapons, and guards well enough paid to be devoted. And they've signed their sovereign names to treaties with our former colonizers."

No, I can't get used to it. The mental image of Abu Omar is always there, not visible but present, every time I recall or think I recall his words. Is it a ghost speaking? I'm not sure I haven't made him into a marionette, the sort of doll whose slack lips showmen, and liars too, manipulate. It's difficult not to play the ventriloquist when you're making a drowned man, or a man who was shot, talk.

This morning I heard the most recent version of his death. There were nine of them in a launch going from Beirut to Tripoli when they were spotted and taken prisoner by a Syrian patrol boat. The Syrian army handed Abu Omar and the eight other leaders, whose names I don't know, over to the Kataebs. And they killed them. The Kataebs are the Phalangists led by the Christian Pierre Gemayel. It may seem rather theatrical to depict Abu Omar as a puppet, but the dead do become puppets when you try to talk about them, and you yourself become a shadow-showman.

Abu Omar's last thoughts about the emirs were more or less as follows:

"People scarcely mention their wealth, because it's as if you were encroaching on their secret life. Yet if you can't mention it you diminish them, because they only exist through their fortunes. All an emir can say to a fedayee is, 'We're both Muslim, and how can one Muslim deliberately harm another?' Poor Muslims feel pity, and fear the stern God who protects the emirs. But, Jean, have you seen how many workers the emirs eat up? Many more than your Dassault. Never a meal without a few Shiites done to a turn."

The last time I saw him he took me to lunch in a stone-built villa in Jebel Amman.

"Our host's a man called Zaahrouh. A Palestinian who used to be mayor of Ramallah. He's proud when anyone calls him a refugee."

Abu Omar was invited partly as a familiar of Arafat's, but mainly as a former professor who'd been a pupil of Kissinger. There was a Swiss chef, so we ate a lot of tasty dishes.

"Who are all the people in your reception room?" I asked.

"Envoys from King Hussein. He wants me to be in his new government. But not on your life. I'd rather take a gun and go and shoot some Jordanians."

Three months later he was Hussein's minister of transport, and he stayed in the post for three years. Was he there with the PLO's approval? Was he there as an intermediary between them and the King and, through him, America?

They remain dead, the people I try to resuscitate by straining to hear what they say. But the illusion is not pointless, or not quite, even if the reader knows all this better than I do. One thing a book tries to do is show, beneath the disguise of words and causes and clothes and even grief, the skeleton and the skeleton dust to come. The author too, like those he speaks of, is dead.

The fulfilment of a prophecy, or rather the sudden prophetic declaration and its sudden fulfilment later, are the equivalent, in an extra dimension, of a puppet show. Inevitably, in life as distinct from the vision of death, the representation of a gesture is all the more silent the more closely the voice of the presenter tries to imitate the voice of the deceased. That's why for a long time I didn't speak of Hamza or try to make him speak. According to several officials he'd died in the desert, silent with the obstinacy of the dead. Not only might I, I had to speak of him in the past tense.

The subjunctive makes a particularly becoming veil. The Muslim colour for mourning is white. But how could I lend him my voice?

What kind of torture had left his legs black? Too many unknown factors made me restrain my imagination, as far as I could. I'd been told Hussein's and the Bedouin's secret police were expert torturers, which didn't surprise me as I knew the Jordanian people themselves—though the Palestinians won't like my saying this—were very gentle. So their police were inhabited by a very subtle spirit of ferocity. No paradox there.

You might say a second people, the police, had distilled itself from, and arrogated power over, the population itself. Unless it's simpler and truer to think cruelty and gentleness can coexist comfortably in one person. Or again, unless cruelty, tired of itself in that form, dwindles into gentleness or even good nature, only to show its teeth again after a while.

Apart from the fact that his legs had been blackened I didn't know anything about the tortures inflicted on Hamza. I couldn't resign myself to changing him into a silent doll, but nor could I forget him, alive or dead. Should I bury him deep inside me? If so, in what form?

I'd changed Ali into a marionette by talking of him and making him use French words he may not have known, or perhaps because I myself couldn't recapture his tone. So what difference was I trying to make between Ali and Hamza, and why?

By transforming a fact into words and characters you create other facts that can never recreate the original one. I state this basic truth to put myself on my guard. If it's only a question of ordinary morality, I don't care whether someone's lying or telling the truth. But I must stress that it's my eyes that saw what I thought I was describing, and my ears that heard it. The form I adopted from the beginning for this account was never designed to tell the reader what the Palestinian revolution was really like.

The construction, organization and layout of the book, without deliberately intending to *betray* the facts, manage the narrative in such a way that I probably seem to be a privileged witness or even a manipulator. What I recount may well be what I experienced, but it was different in that the disparateness of my own existence had merged into the continuity of Palestinian life, though still leaving me with traces, glimpses of, sometimes severances from, my former life. Sometimes events from this former life became so vivid I had to wake myself up. I was in a dream, which I am able to control now by reconstructing and assembling its various images. Sometimes I wonder whether I didn't live that life especially so that I might arrange its episodes in the same seeming disorder as the images in a dream.

All these words to say, This is *my* Palestinian revolution, told in my own chosen order. As well as mine there is the other, probably many others.

Trying to think the revolution is like waking up and trying to see the logic in a dream. There's no point, in the middle of a drought, in imaging how to cross the river when the bridge has been swept away. When, half awake, I think about the revolution, I see it as the tail of a caged tiger, starting to lash out in a vast sweep, then falling back wearily on the prisoner's flank.

"Do the Palestinians ultimately want to get back the territory now called Israel, or do they go on fighting in order to save what makes them unique, different from all the other Arab peoples?"

"The second, I think. This generation won't see the creation of Palestine. Israel won't get peace, but Palestine will still be just a sort of family heirloom that's brought out to impress people at weddings and funerals. It will be nicer to say 'We're Palestinians' than to say 'We're Jordanians.' "

"Why?"

"As a Palestinian I have mythical origins, I'm descended from the Philistines. As a Jordanian I'm just a stereotyped product of British administration."

"You say *this* generation. What about the generations to come?"

"Some historians say that although the French Revolution happened without Napoleon it was Napoleon who created Europe. The Arab nations need a man . . ."

"Of destiny?"

"Who'll unite the Arab people whether they like it or not."

"And do you believe that'll happen?"

"Yes."

"You expect this Messiah?"

"Don't talk to me about Messiahs. I'm an atheist, as you know very well. Kaddafi has never been able to live up to his ambition, secret or avowed."

"Do you know him?"

"Yes. He's a good man. But he had a conventional education, from childhood right up to the overthrow of the Senussi. And he hasn't changed. Nasser could keep him within bounds, and after Nasser's death he thought his mantle had fallen on him. He didn't realize Sadat was bound from the start to be a godsend to the Egyptian bourgeoisie."

"Did you know Nasser too?"

"He was much tougher. Nobody's heir. Didn't suffer from Kaddafi's almost feminine nerviness. It was June 1967 that finished him. And—now you're going to shrug your shoulders—de Gaulle. We'll talk about the 'casus belli' some other time."

"What did you mean by a conventional education?"

"Believing in good and evil, and giving them capital letters. Kaddafi's naïve. That's the cause of his failures. He had to be *very* naïve to try to get together with Sadat!"

I had the above conversation with a member of the upper middle classes, one of the top brass of the resistance, in Beirut in 1982. He had met Assad the week before. I think he saw him as the federator of the Arab peoples. So he was really a PLO dissident.

"We've got some Fairy Godmothers in the camps."

"What's a Fairy Godmother?"

"Someone who does good. Someone who comes to the Holy Land to do good."

"I don't understand."

"That's because you're French."

When I arrived at Amman airport in 1984 I was met by the representative of the World Bank and his wife, who was an American. Or rather a Jordanian. She corrected people on this point several times. She was correcting herself.

"We've just come from the Algerian ambassadress's farewell cocktail party. Have you read her book?"

"No."

"Everyone's talking about it."

"How do you know?"

"She showed us her Press Book."

"What's that got to do with Fairy Godmothers?"

"She's one of them. She's given some of her royalties to the kingdom's poor. Would you like to meet the king?"

"No."

"We've got another Fairy Godmother. A saint. Everyone in America's talking about her and calling her 'The Saint.'"

"How did she get to be a saint? I'd be very interested to know."

"She helps the people in the camp at Baqa. Every morning she supervises the masons and the carpenters building houses."

"Are they building houses in Baqa?"

"Yes. The World Bank, which my husband represents here, lends money to the state, and the state lends it to young couples."

"What *is* the World Bank?"

"A welfare organization. Haven't you heard of it before?"

"Does it lend money? At what rate of interest?"

"Nine and a half per cent. It lends people here the equivalent of a hundred and fifty thousand French francs. Seldom more. Repayable over eighteen years. With that amount they have to buy the land and build at least a ground floor and one storey."

"How can they pay all that money back?"

"The Bank finds them jobs."

"And takes part of the monthly salary?"

"Naturally. But at least the head of the family is sure of a job and a roof over his head."

"What if he wants to leave before the eighteen years are up?"

"He can, but he loses his house. Unless he buys it outright."

"What if he belongs to a union or a political party?"

"Oh, King Hussein and Queen Nour, whom I know very well, can't bear people who are against them, especially if they've lent them money."

"I see, madam. And the Saint—what does she do?"

"She does good. A fortnight ago we had an American here who's writing a book about her."

"And she doesn't object?"

"Of course not."

"In that case I understand. That's what makes her a saint."

"I really don't understand you."

That—yielding to the temptation to be bought, or even hired, for eighteen years—must have been one of the reasons for the sadness I saw on the faces of some ex-fedayeen. And that was one of the holds America had over Jordan.

"The World Bank lends to us at so much per cent and we lend to you at so much per cent. With the money you have to buy between a hundred and a hundred and fifty square metres of land in Amman. The house mustn't have more than two floors. A group of architects has drawn up some plans—you can choose the one you like. One more thing: you pay back the money over eighteen years, but we employ you for the same period."

"Shall I own the house myself?"

"Of course. After eighteen years. When you've paid for it."

"And may I join . . . ?"

"The PLO? No. Israel wouldn't allow it. Neither would the World Bank."*

From 1970 on, and especially after September of that year, there was an incredible flood of Arabic publications on the subject of Palestine. First of all there were small magazines. Some were printed on expensive paper, white or glossy, in which Palestine, its people and the fedayeen disappeared under lyrical rhapsodies expressed in words and pictures. A pale obscurity covered everything like a pall of snow: everything, from the fence round a field to the sweating or bleeding fedayee, from a woman in labour through a wood of pine trees to the camps and the tins of food, was covered in a layer of words.

The words were always the same, and they ended up concealing anything to do with Palestine as it really was. Palestine was always an affianced bride, a mettlesome filly, a widow, an expectant mother, a pure virgin, the queen of the Arab world, the letter

---

* This was the case in 1984.

Alif, the letter Ba, with which the Fatah surat began, and so on and so forth.

These hyperboles helped to make the struggle known, but I wonder whether they didn't make it seem unreal, merely the excuse for a poem. Curiously enough, all these poems written and published in Morocco, Algeria, Tunisia and Mauretania, though they should by rights have winged their way to the Palestinians, actually fell back upon the countries where they were written. Apart from a few volunteers who hitch-hiked to the Middle East alone or in small groups, I wonder whether the Arab world wasn't delighted to be able to transform the struggle into verses. It saved an awful lot of trouble: you didn't have to travel to the battlefield, you didn't get wounded or killed, you proved to yourself and others how good you were with words, and by making the Palestinian struggle unreal you justified your remaining at the University of Tunis. No one goes out of his way for a war that doesn't really exist.

Many of these publications were printed on such luxurious paper I wonder whether it wasn't the PLO itself that supplied it. Or to put it more plainly, did all the poets receive remuneration for their talents? Daoud Thalami told me in 1972:

"Lots of Arabs want to be published in 'Palestinian Affairs.' The amounts they ask are colossal."*

It should also be noted that the number of poems increased after the Resistance was defeated by the Bedouin. But they spent more time anathematizing Hussein than urging renaissance. Tears come to the eyes of the Arab poets I'm talking about more easily than calls to battle to their lips. Then poetic production slowed down. I think there must have been a shortage of imperial Japanese paper.

To say people travel the world, and describe their travels, is not the same as travelling yourself. To say the Palestinians learned geography by going from one airport to another is not an act of terrorism. As the revolution isn't over yet, is it right, is it even possible, for me to try to describe a part of it? Even if it was temporarily flagging, it might revive at any moment. A nomad

*In 1982, too.

shepherd in Egypt or on the steppes of Mongolia might be a descendant of the XVIIIth Dynasty of the Pharaohs. He keeps his sheep, and the secret of his own royalty. And one day he will claim his throne and his sister's hand.

"Tell me, Jean, has there ever been a time since the death of the Prophet when the famous Arab unity actually existed? Under the Ommeyads? You've heard about the struggle between Ali and Moawiya, and the rivalries that started up as soon as Muhammad died. Under the Abbasids? The Ommeyad caliphate was still powerful in Spain. The Berber and Arab kingdoms were always fighting, even though all of them were Muslims. The Ottomans? The twenty-one Arab states we have now? Arab unity is just an aspiration. It reminds one of the three states of the Indo-European world, which never came into being but survived as an aspiration until everything went up in smoke in 1789.

"Take France. You've talked about the linguistic unity of the Arab world, but take France. France has had linguistic unity for years—I've talked to you before about how it happened—but beneath that unity, that rather monotonous veneer, there are all sorts of attempts at regional revival. In Brittany, Corsica, Alsace, Flanders . . . I'm like Monsieur Homais, aren't I?"

That was Lieutenant Mubarak in Beirut in 1972, in a lounge in the Strand Hotel. I can see the black bitch now in her leopard-spotted uniform tailored by Pierre Cardin. The lieutenant was on his own. He was on his way out. He said hallo to me and asked me how I was. Ajloun must have been forgotten. I saw Kamal Nasser and greeted him warmly, not thinking he'd be murdered three weeks later by some long-haired Israeli.

"Put this is your book. Incredible as it may seem, there are some tribes in our country who know—don't put believe; put know— that Israel gets rid of its dead by eating them. That's the explanation of the huge fruit they grow, so heavy it breaks the branches."

"What's the connection?"

"The richness of the fertilizer. Proteins galore."

His brother was a colonel opposed to Numeiri, so he must be influential in Khartoum now.*

---

*1985.

Since, as he'd told me, he felt, as a Black, that he only existed through his disturbing effect upon me, Mubarak was like one of those impressive places that will have the same effect on someone else in a hundred years' time.

A little while ago I wrote that though I shall die, nothing else will. And I must make my meaning clear. Wonder at the sight of a corn-flower, at a rock, at the touch of a rough hand—all the millions of emotions of which I'm made—they won't disappear even though I shall. Other men will experience them, and they'll still be there because of them. More and more I believe I exist in order to be the terrain and proof which show other men that life consists in the uninterrupted emotions flowing through all creation. The happiness my hand knows in a boy's hair will be known by another hand, is already known. And although I shall die, that happiness will live on. "I" may die, but what made that "I" possible, what made possible the joy of being, will make the joy of being live on without me.

Some time around 1972 Muhammad-el-Hamchari took me to see the Italian writer Alberto Moravia. We were to meet Wael Zuayter. Zuayter was murdered in 1973.

Strangely enough, Italy, which before had seemed so airy, struck me as ponderous compared with the vagabond life of the fedayeen.

I returned to them in May 1972, via European and Asian Turkey, Syria and Jordan. The following few pages tell something about Turkey.

A "strange separation," or rather a cold reprobation, kept me from approaching other people. After at least five years away from them, like a Muslim woman in a veil of stone, with a naked gaze more lively than profound, I sought in other people's eyes the thin silk thread that ought to link us all, the sign of a continuity of being that two gazes intertwining without desire should be able to detect.

For five years I'd lived in a sort of invisible sentry-box from which I could see and speak to everyone while I myself was a fragment broken off from the rest of the world. I couldn't lose myself in anything any more. The Egyptian Pyramids had the same value, force, dimensions and depth as the desert, and the desert had the same depth as a handful of sand. A shoe or a shoe-lace was no different, either, except that a habit acquired in childhood prevented me from putting the Pyramids or the desert on my feet, or seeing a rosy dawn around my shoes.

The best-looking boys had the same value and power as the others, but no one had any power over me. Or rather I didn't notice it. I was completely swamped in the animal kingdom and the human race, and my own individual existence possessed less and less surface and volume. Yet for some time I'd realized I had one. I was me, not just anyone or anything. Around me the world began to swarm with individuals, single or separate, and, if separate, capable of entering into relationships.

It was dark and I was in bed. I was thinking about those five years. Roughly five years, for how can you measure exactly a time which, though it had a beginning and an end, had no events to distinguish it, just as the space I travelled had no rises or falls? What's more, the beginning of those years never had a date attached to it: they didn't arise out of an identifiable event, but out of something which, though decisive, was unverifiable. Thinking of those five years I looked back with such sadness I decided I must rediscover that undifferentiated past.

But no sooner had I made my decision than there was a bright but diffuse light around me in the room, so noticeable that I pulled the blanket up over my head to check if it wasn't coming in through the skylight over the door. But even when my head was under the bedclothes the light was still there. Then it went out, but slowly, as I remember, and gently. It was a glow rather than a light. For a few seconds something in me was phosphorescent. I even thought my skin might have become luminous, as a parchment shade does when a lamp is lit.

"The almond aura of a Byzantine limbo," I recited to myself. Had *I* invented the word "aura"?

Who wouldn't have felt some fear, some pride, some shame, before starting to laugh? It was snowing in Istanbul.

By some aberration on the part of the authorities, some hippies were walking round outside the mosques, outside the Blue Mosque. They'd taken their shoes off and were walking barefoot. Their heads were bare too, unless you counted the snowflakes settling on their beautiful long fair hair. In the snow or anywhere else, single or in pairs, they were all alone, and so deliberately turned in on themselves I was sure they were getting in training to walk on the water some day. But for the moment they were in up to the neck. Even if they ever succeeded, scepticism and laughter would soon reassert themselves, for despite all the magical effects Islam, like Judaism, was a very opaque religion.

Both in Europe and in North America a wind was about to blow through the prisons and upset the nocturnal activity that had been going on there for so long—rotting, railing, groaning, wailing, dreaming solitary but proud. Prisoners young and old would suddenly refuse food and barricade themselves in their workshops, where the most adult occupation was making barbed wire and plastic Christmas trees. They would set fire to anything that would burn or smoulder and smoke: flames would leap out through heat-shattered windows.

The men inside thought they were taking part in a general orgy, but I couldn't help them transmute it into politics, as they'd have liked. I couldn't give up wandering. My time with the Palestinians was only a stage, a rest, a garden where you rest before starting out again, where I learned from my travels that the world was probably round.

I didn't believe in God. The idea of chance, a random combination of facts—a trick, even, of events, stars and beings owing their existence to themselves—such an idea seemed to me more pleasing and amusing than the idea of One God. The weight of religion crushes; chance brings lightness and laughter. It makes you cheerful and curious; it makes you smile. Claudel, the most religious of French poets, though he wouldn't acknowledge he knew it, expressed it the best when he wrote of "the jubilations of chance." Such blasphemy from such a square! And would Japan be what it is and where it is if it weren't for chance and the incalculable farts of the volcanoes?

Istanbul swarmed and shone with wonders described a thousand times by illustrious travellers and dreamers: the Golden Horn, Petra, Galata, St. Sophia, St. Ireneus, the Blue Mosque, the Red Sultan.

What are called the lower depths of cities in fact fly over them like a shot-silk scarf. The gambling alleys, the black markets, the false cripples, the false archaeologists, the brothels, the still-damp walls of ageless ramparts all belong to the bourgeois dream, the dream of a bourgeoisie still all buttoned up even when it's in its underpants and sweating on the beach. The huge pale whores in Istanbul were as unreal as the card-players in Ajloun. Brothels are chaste places in Turkey. The customers haggle with the pimps round a stove in the middle of the room, bargaining so closely they get it wrong and lose their stake.

Istanbul was still soiled by spurts of saliva. Stripped by Ataturk of their Ottoman robes, the Turks relieved themselves standing up, a bit of Western progress imposed by iron rule. The dreariness of the place was enlivened by graceful arcs of urine and saliva suddenly and accurately spouting from between teeth, moustaches and zip fasteners.

I don't know if it was by some atavistic compulsion, but my wanderings always took me straight to the popular and populous districts. Was it the same compass that guided me to the fedayeen?

Going up to Galata, near the Tower, one day, I saw a young man selling oranges under an awning in the middle of the pavement, almost in the middle of the street. The fruit was arranged in a pyramid, wide at the base but with one single orange on top. You see fruit and vegetables set out like that all over the East. The customers often choose to buy from the bottom or one of the lower rows, but the merchants know how to whip a vegetable or a fruit out and replace it with another before the heap can collapse.

The youth was smiling, and I suppose, vaunting his wares in Turkish, in which the word for orange must have several meanings. He had the gift of the gab, and I noticed how his hand moved swiftly from his eyes to his teeth to his crotch, then very rapidly back to his black hair, teeth and shining eyes, the object being to disturb rather than charm the passers-by. I was about to walk on, when something stopped me. I drew my head back to check that I wasn't mistaken. Over the orange at the top of the pyramid there was another one, suspended in the air a foot or so above it. It hung there motionless in air that was motionless despite the bustle of the street.

Levitation is quite a common notion in Turkey, but even if it were acceptable to a Western mind, even one in a body that had suddenly been lit up at night by inner fires, still, an Ottoman orange disobeying Newton and refusing to fall . . . ?

Perhaps it was falling, but was puzzled and had stopped in mid air?

My astonishment must have shown on my face. The young man showed me a few more teeth and flicked with his finger at the orange, free falling or ascending into heaven. It swung from right to left. Two smiles were exchanged. Around us a small group of Turks burst out laughing. The orange was hanging from an invisible nylon thread attached to the awning.

"Very pretty."

The young man gave me a stinging smile.

"Americano?"

"No"—in English.

"Deutsch?"

"No."

"Fr . . ."

"Yes, French."

He told me in gibberish how he'd fixed himself a little miracle. The Sufi I like best is al-Halladj, the marvellous fool, Al Husseini al-Halladj, burning to the end with friendship for the Loved One. The Sufi I revere the most is Bistani. The Tower of Galata cast a shadow in the moonlight. Did those young Turks think you can impregnate old men through the mouth?

Dreams of power explode into stories, legends and fairy tales. Words like king, prince, princess, hero, martyr, conqueror, tyrant and dictator must be there to make up for the wants of the storyteller or dreamer, while each reader or listener seizes on and identifies with them so quickly it proves he was waiting for them. He was waiting as a man in a thicket waits for the loveliest and most naked of young girls to come along the road, but more seriously, for should he go with the beautiful naked girl along the road to power, he'd abandon her if it rained or snowed, on the excuse that it's no use travelling with a dead body. I'd do better to go back and marry my mother and become king of Thebes. The sour love-affair of the Duke of Windsor and Mrs. Simpson doesn't make me change my mind.

You need to choose the right inspiration and a bard with plenty of breath. If you put two matches together and light them, they twine so close you can't separate their single ember. Two immortalities in one. And so with the bard and the power that he sings, as long as no one goes and touches what's left of the confused but splendid conflagration.

An old man travelling from country to country, as much ejected by the one he was in as attracted by the others he was going to, rejecting the repose that comes from even modest property, was amazed by the collapse that took place in him. By property is meant the almost universal law by which someone has a number of things or buildings or lands or people, external to himself, which he may dispose of, use, enjoy or abuse. A house is a building in which you can stay, in which you can move and walk about.

The desire to get rid of all external objects was this traveller's principle, so it must have been the work of the devil, God's devil, that after a very long time, when he thought he'd really divested himself of all possessions, he was suddenly invaded, one can only wonder via what orifice, by a desire for a house, a solid fixed place, an enclosed orchard. Almost in one night he found himself carrying inside him a place of his own.

At first it was just a house that he carried in his bosom, as the Fathers of the Church delicately put it when speaking of the Virgin Mary; though really it was in a part of the body that doesn't exist—in a place out of space, you might say. At once inside him and around him. As the house where he was born was never built, it wasn't that, but another, which he, an old man, lived in. In which he moved about, and where he looked through an open window at the sea, with the island of Cyprus in the distance. A kind of madness made him seem to say, though he never actually did: "And from here, out of danger, I'll watch a naval battle in broad daylight."

The battle did take place, but later, when all had evaporated—the house, the window, the garden, the sea, the shores of Cyprus. It was the war between Turkey and Greece.

God, who made Earth and Sky out of nothing, performed another wonder. To Saint Elizabeth, Queen of Hungary, obliged because of her position to move about in the pomp of a royal court, he gave a present. It was a nun's cell built specially to fit her and invisible to her husband and the courtiers, the ministers and the ladies-in-waiting. This personal and secret cell moved about as the queen-saint moved about, and only four eyes could see its inner walls—the queen's two eyes and God's, the four making but one in all, a Cyclopean orb with a single lid.

The Cyclops must have blinked. The single demon ravaging my mind had built me a house in an Eden-like setting, with the sea, though distant, visible and blue, an island awaiting its naval battle, an orchard of fruit and flowers, and silence.

It was a situation both filmsy and funny. I went on rejecting real property, but I had to deconstruct the property inside me, with its corridors, its bedrooms, its mirrors and its furniture. And that wasn't all: around the house was the orchard, with plums on the plum trees which I couldn't put in my mouth because everything had been for so long inside me. I was in danger of dying of indigestion through just eating the stones, or even of getting fat in this false hunger strike. I was waiting for the naval battle to take place opposite, so violent that in its first few seconds I'd be amazed and annihilated. Where was the Sufic poet's "waterless desert within a waterless desert"?

The situation made me laugh, and my laughter made me laugh again. I was getting better. To carry his house and furniture inside him was humiliating for a man who had shone one night with his own inner aurora.

That very minor miracle, of the man who shone like a glow-worm but as briefly as a firefly, made me think—for I did possess the power of reflection—of the miracle of the levitating orange, reduced to unmysterious logic by a nylon thread. And I guessed there would soon be a rational explanation, as of the inexplicable incandescence, of this pregnancy of house and orchard, sky and sea.

For my humiliation made me aware that it was *my* house, *my* furniture, *my* light and *my* interior. Did that last expression mean the inside of my house, or the vague, uncertain place put there to conceal a total void—my inner life, sometimes called, with equal lack of precision, my secret garden?

The house inside me made me something less than a snail, which at least has a real shell outside it. Less than a snail, which has both the sexes necessary for reproduction. How many have I?

Because it was happening in Turkey; because I could move my inner domain about there; because I wasn't far from Ephesus, where the Virgin Mary, mother and octogenarian, lived in a little stone house in which when she died she was carried up to heaven by angels—what had I to fear?

"You've never experienced anything like it," I said one day to Ferraj, to whom I'd related my miracle, as astonishing to me as the *mi'raj* to Muhammad.

"On 26 June 1970, on the first step of the escalator at Kuwait airport, I rose up in the air without moving so much as my foot."

"But you didn't go up to heaven."

"You don't start from Kuwait to do that."

It was in Turkey still that I was haunted. For a long time I'd battled against myself and the desire for possessions to such effect that all I had were the clothes I stood up in. No replacements, and pencils and papers had been broken or torn up and thrown away. But the world of objects discovered this void and rushed in to fill it. There was a great clatter of saucepans, for the house and garden didn't come ready to walk into, but pan by pan, tap by tap—the latter blocked in accordance with Kalmuk, Hittite and Turkish tradition. Once I'd sacrificed to the devil, that is built a house for a young Arab, objects, no doubt appeased and pacified, stopped persecuting me. From Antioch I went to Aleppo, from Aleppo to Damascus, then to Deraa and Amman. And finally to Ajloun.

The episode of the house inside me, on my inner plot of land, may have derived from Mahjoub's suggestion, when I drew his attention to the house at Salt in the sun.

"See how beautiful it looks on the rock!"

"The PLO will let it to you for six months if you like."

It immediately became dirty and grey.

The vague apparition in the sun of the house in Turkey started me off on a swift process of acquisition. It belonged to me almost the moment I saw it. I could arrange the rooms as I wished, furnish them as I liked, build arbours in the garden and plant it with vines and blue and white convolvulus. Last and most important, I could see myself going from room to room or sitting in an armchair looking at the sea and hoping for the pending naval battle. I'd own that too, as it would be part of the décor, part of the guaranteed view.

Fedayeen born in the desert had never seen anything so tranquil. They now enjoyed a peace known only to the rich. They had to enjoy it there and then, knowing it was the prerogative and product of the enemy, and so had to be fought. But it had to be enjoyed too, so they might know the enemy's weaknesses and be better able to attack them. So like the rich they lolled on divans and Second Empire chairs. Like the rich they knew this peace and luxury would last for ever unless, despite the soldiers and the police, the revolutionaries came. Came and seized the houses with the delightful views that allowed you to watch naval battles and the corpses floating on the calm waters afterwards, or the slaves working in the fields and displaying such aesthetically pleasing weariness it made the guests leaning over the balcony feel more peaceful still. For a few seconds the fedayeen, sitting in the armchairs or walking on the carpets, were the masters of it all, even enjoying the thought of their being driven out by revolutionaries who were themselves.

How could I be so near Tarsus and not go to see it before leaving Turkey? But I didn't really expect to find a family there called Saulovitch or Levy Bensaul. There may be an old Jewish quarter, but all I saw were great modern eggboxes like those at

Saint-Denis-sur-Seine. I told my young Turkish travelling companion how disappointed I was.

"But Cleopatra came here," he said in German.

"When?"

"Two years ago, when they filmed *Antony and Cleopatra* with Liz Taylor."

In Antioch all the hotels were full. In the last one I tried, the most expensive, I sat in the lounge and waited for a Turkish coffee. An Arab in a gallabiya sitting nearby tried to talk to me in several languages—English, Spanish, Greek, Turkish . . . I told him in very bad English I didn't speak any of them. The manager explained to him in Arabic that I was French and didn't speak any other language.

"If the conversation's not too complicated I can understand and make myself understood in Arabic."

We were in the part of Turkey very close to present-day Syria, in the old Willayet of Antioch, where Turkish and Arabic are equally common. My Saudi Arabian friend traded in cereals and dried fruit. He said he was using only one of the two beds in his room, and I could sleep in the other if I liked. As I had very little luggage I offered to pay for a couple of days in advance. He looked upset. He was glad to have the chance of talking to someone French who could manage a few words of Arabic. He invited me to Riyadh.

"But what are you doing in Antioch?"

He laughed at my question, then said:

"You go to Algeria to see a former French colony, don't you? When I was a child I learned a bit of Turkish, because what's now called Saudi Arabia was occupied by the Ottoman Empire. But also I have Arab cousins and distant cousins here. I enjoy seeing them."

"Are they emigrants?"

He laughed louder than before.

"No, no! But we belong to a tribe that was divided into five parts. A nomadic tribe—we were all nomads once. A lot of our people stayed in Arabia; some stayed in Transjordan—Jordan didn't exist then; a third section had to stay in Iraq; a fourth group remained in Syria; and some others settled in the *sandjak* of

Alexandretta. Alexandretta was given back to Turkey in 1937. My relatives owned a lot of cherry orchards, so in order to be able to keep them they learned Turkish."

Apart from the grotto at St. Peter's, I don't remember anything special about Antioch. I spent most of my time with the Saudi merchant. One morning, with assumed regret, he told me about what he described as Nixon's cool reception by Chou En-lai. He'd heard about it on the phone from one of his relatives in Riyadh. I was in his room, only half dressed, when he took the call, which left him as indifferent as an order for nuts.

"Even if Russia takes over from China, the Palestinians know the great powers will just make use of them. Like an unsolicited gift of no commercial value. A row of artificial pearls you throw in with a big purchase when the bargain's been haggled over for years."

His ornate manner, wrinkled brow and difficulty in rising from his prayer mat made me take him for a man of sixty or so, with enough experience to know all about political concessions.

"How old are you?"

"Thirty-seven," he said.

I still haven't thrown away his visiting card, with the name embossed on it in gold, once in English and once in Arabic.

Later on, in Beirut, Abu Omar gave me his version of the reception given to Nixon and Kissinger. Instead of dwelling on the ceremony, or lack of it, Abu Omar interpreted the event in terms of Palestinian politics.

"We've just seen through *The Thoughts of Mao Tse-tung*. I've always thought they were a firework display designed to conceal something, and now I know?"

"And what's the something?"

"The negation of the USSR. At least, to start with. After that, who knows?"

It didn't bother me to learn about the policy changes of Moscow and Peking. On the contrary, I discovered there'd long been a sort of débâcle inside me, and it's from that moment I date my certainty of a shipwreck to come, and in murky waters. Everything would seem to happen under the waves. The Palestinian revolution, desperate as a man who falls in the sea and can't swim, would make the same useless gesture as Abu Omar may have made when he was drowning. Moscow knows as well as Peking and Washington which side its bread is buttered. Red Spain was abandoned. So was Greece when it rebelled. What follows will describe not so much a revolt as a drowning, though the hope of some bright issue is indestructible.

Around 1970, 1971 and the beginning of 1972, some fedayeen still under Nasser's spell, which his death hadn't completely effaced, were sure they'd be able to act in and on the Arab world, and even on the Koran itself when properly interpreted. (There were a few members of the Muslim Brotherhood in the resistance; others probably kept it under observation from outside.)

The Palestinians had no idea the world would be frightened by such fervour. But many of those once favourable to the fedayeen's struggle to recover their land now turned against them, even when Begin declared Judea and Samaria what he, the journalists and the diplomats called an "integral part" of Eretz Israel.

The plane hijacks brought both fame and rejection. I was in Beirut when George Habash's men forced three planes to land in the desert at Zarka. I can still see the weary faces of the three PFLP (Habash) leaders lighting up when I told them how the capture of the three aircraft, tamely lined up in the desert in the sun, had won the admiration of all the young people in Europe. Or at least, I thought, those whose staple diet was comic strips.

The fedayeen on the bases (not to be confused with the camps around Amman), who kept watch on the Ghor, the cliffs and ravine of the river Jordan, Israel, the Ajloun area and all the rest of Jordan, dreamed of great upheavals in the Arab countries. No one knew the Palestinians would have to be driven from Jordan to Syria, from Syria to Lebanon, to Tunis, to Yemen, to the Sudan and Algeria, passing through Cyprus and Greece. Nor did anyone know that though they might be swallowed up in a great depression, they might climb out of it and find themselves once more.

Abu Omar again:

"The Arab world—you see it only from Paris—hasn't stayed

bowed down and motionless ever since Mehemet Ali in Egypt. He rebelled against the Ottoman Empire and the English. Then there was the Druse revolt in Syria in 1925, crushed by your General Gouraud; the Algerian war; the Moroccan uprisings; the Tunisian revolt that slung out both the French and the Italians and their quarrels over the famous rain map; in 1958 there was General Kassem against the English and the Iraq Petroleum Company; and neither Nasser nor Kadhafi left the Senussi kingdom unscathed. All of us tried to shake off our fleas. But there wasn't one war or uprising on the scale of the Palestinian revolution."

"Too much wealth kills, especially if it isn't earned. A mixture of eyes of convolvulus blue, brown, grey-blue, light green, bottle green and black. A jumble of accents, greetings and dialects derived from Arabic. All these have imposed on the Western world the energy buried in the sand. The population suggested enough couplings to block the straits. Underdevelopment was rolling in money. Arabism mounted until it became Arabness, then Panarabism—not armed, but proclaimed so loud the Palestinians would have been forgotten if they hadn't taken the form of a glorious golden cloud—gold again—floating over the Arab world, the oil, and the emirs they consecrate and justify. If the Palestinians' glory, that is their death, had been made of copper instead of gold, do you think the emirs would give them a single kopeck?"

It was in April 1984 that I heard the above from Rachid, sitting on a wooden chair by the door of the Salah-ed-Din Hotel in Amman.

Too much wealth kills, especially someone who hasn't earned it. This was aimed at the emirs, the passive beneficiaries of their oil. It also applied to the poor Arabs, who shrivel up their brains thinking about money.

Having seen the poor in Mauretania, I wanted to ask the Palestinians if there was any prostitution, hidden perhaps but flourishing, in the refugee camps here. Their answers, all given independently, were unanimous. They still surprise me.

"No. Not in the camps in Jordan. In Lebanon, possibly, before the massacres. But I don't think there was a single organization in Beirut. Too easily detected. There were isolated cases, but outside the camps."

"That's amazing."

"No. Palestinian women aren't famous for their beauty. Unlike the men."

Was this remark made just for my benefit?

Although you had your white, royalist terror in 1795, the word terror wasn't too terrible in French until lately. Jack the Ripper spread terror nicely enough in London, and so did Bonnot in Paris, but the word terrorist has metal teeth and the red jaws of a monster. The Shiites have inhuman jaws like that, it says in the papers this morning, and Israel must lash them to death with the poisonous tail of their army—the army that ran away from Lebanon. If you're against Israel you're not an enemy or an opponent—you're a terrorist. Terrorism is supposed to deal death indiscriminately, and must be destroyed wherever it appears.

Very smart of Israel to carry the war right into the heart of vocabulary, and annex the words holocaust and genocide. The invasion of Lebanon didn't make Israel an intruder or predator. The destruction and massacres in Beirut weren't the work of terrorists armed by America and dropping tons of bombs day and night for three months on a capital with two million inhabitants: they were the act of an angry householder with the power to inflict heavy punishment on a troublesome neighbour. Words are terrible, and Israel is a terrifying manipulator of signs. Sentence doesn't necessarily precede execution; if an execution has already been carried out, a sentence will gradually justify it. When it kills a Shiite and a Palestinian, Israel claims to have cleansed the world of two terrorisms at once.

The Shiites of southern Lebanon, infuriated by the way what they called the Palestinians' impudence called down Israeli retaliation, welcomed the Israeli tanks with showers of scented white rice, sweets, rose petals and jasmin. Today, 24 February 1985, the Shiites are taking over from the tired Palestinians and hunting the Israeli soldiers to the border.

You may remember Abu Gamal the Syrian, a pious Muslim who came and greeted me in my tent at Ajloun but wouldn't say, "I respect you because you don't believe in God." Now I know he was right. Right to refer everything to Islam, not so as to have an ally in the ancient faith, but so as to have one in fidelity to the Law of the earth, in which for so many centuries the Law was born and evolved. To go back so far in time is the same as descending deep, deep into yourself, unto death, so as to find the strength to fight.

After that . . . But why should one think of after. Now is the time for fighting.

Several images throw themselves at me, and I don't know why I choose the one I'm about to describe for the last time. The vapour from a boiler steams up a window, then gradually disappears, leaving the window clear, the landscape suddenly visible and the room extended perhaps to infinity. Another image: a hand and a sponge move to and fro over a blackboard rubbing out the chalk writing. That's all.

The farewells the fedayeen who are leaving take of those who will leave later on seem to have the same effect. First they all embrace. Those who are going to stay behind stand motionless on the path, and those who've been chosen to go down to the Jordan retreat backwards into the distance with a smile, both groups waving their hands in front of their faces as a sign of farewell, of effacement. Like the writing on the board and the steam on the window, all their faces disappear, and the landscape, all its tears wiped away, is restored to itself. The fedayeen to be sacrificed have been the strongest. Tired and waving the childish "Bye-bye," they have resolutely turned their backs on their comrades.

I don't think there was any strategic calculation in Abu Gamal's hesitation about answering me yes or no, but rather a premonition. And in the end he solved the problem not by renouncing his faith in any way, but by seeking it in his own profoundest depths and in the depths of the centuries that had fashioned it. An admirable detour via God himself, in other words via himself.

Eclipse is a word full of meaning. In addition to the sun, which is even more evident when eclipsed by the moon, every event, man or image eclipsed by something or someone else emerges regenerated; however brief their disappearance, they emerge cleaner and brighter than before. Vietnam eclipsed Japan, which had eclipsed Europe, America and all. "All" had done its share of eclipsing too.

The word also summons up the old image—Chinese, Indian, Arab, Iranian, Japanese—of a dragon swallowing the sun, which is eclipsed by the moon. In French the reflexive verb *s'eclipser*, literally to eclipse oneself, hovers between the usual meaning, to slip away, escape, and the figurative connotation, to disappear because of the brightness of another. Even obsession will never fix this word—it's always giving people the slip.

Starting off from the East, we see the uprisings and other swellings of youth being eclipsed all the time, and disappearing from History for a moment only to reappear strange and new. There were the Zengakuren in Japan in 1966; the Red Guard in China; the student unrest at Berkeley; the Black Panthers; May 1968 in Paris; the Palestinians.

These lively rings circling the earth were the opposite of other world tours and followed other parallels. The image of the sun-guzzling dragon may take account of gravitation, the law that governs the stars. But in the time it takes to think that prison is hollow, or full of holes and cavities, a man can imagine in each of them a time and rhythm different from those of the stars. In the middle of each hollow a song, not a cry, consisting of a single note. The wonderful word eclipse allows everything to be a star occluding something else.

A liar hides or thinks he hides, thinks he is eclipsed behind another lie; he plunges into infinite recession. Why did the Imam remain hidden? What was he trying to hide?

"You hide the fact that you're a believer and belong to the Alawite sect for fear someone might see you're something else again—not an Alawite but perhaps the real Imam, perhaps even the Jewish one?"

On 14 September 1982, at about eleven o'clock in the morning, French, American and Italian ships started to leave Beirut. I watched them flee into the blue of sea and sky, their nationals on board.

They were the deterrent force which ten days earlier had enabled Arafat and the fedayeen to leave Beirut despite the Israeli presence.

The French covered Beirut harbour as the Palestinians embarked. It was a strange ceremony, a sort of funeral, as if this man and his men, their emblem shattered, deserved a funeral mass sung to blaring music. But French soldiers also kept the Israeli and Phalangist patrols under observation, and cleared the mines from the Museum Corridor, the only route by which the Merkava tanks could sweep from East to West Beirut.

A few days later, between eleven in the morning and one, the French, Italian and American ships sailed away again with their soldiers.

"Why are they leaving so soon?"

On the balcony of Mademoiselle Shahid's apartment we all wondered that, passing binoculars round from one to the other and not believing our eyes. The ships were taking the deterrent force away from Lebanon, and the very same day, 14 September 1982, at half-past four, their departure was eclipsed by Béchir Gemayel's assassination.

At eleven that evening Israeli armoured cars and infantry entered West Beirut and eclipsed Bechir's death. The next morning, Wednesday, and for the next three nights, the Palestinian camps of Sabra, Chatila and Bourj Barajneh were bombed, and the civilian population tortured and massacred in an eclipse so brutal it blurred Israel's image.

We wait for the first of these events to emerge more plainly: France's betrayal of the civilian population when its soldiers slipped away and eclipsed themselves as soon as they'd cleared the Museum Corridor of mines in East Beirut.

They must have been between two and three thousand, the Palestinian and Lebanese dead, together with a few Syrians and some Jewish women married to Lebanese, all killed in the camps at Sabra, Chatila and Bourj Barajneh.

Dying with their eyes wide open, they knew the terror of seeing every created thing—man, chairs, stars, suns, Phalangists—

tremble, convulse and blur, knowing they were going to vanish because those who would be their victims were driving them to nothingness. The dying saw and felt and knew their death was the death of the world. *Après moi le déluge* is a ridiculous saying, because what comes "after me" is the death of all creation.

Understood in this sense, death is a phenomenon that destroys the world. To eyelids reluctant to close the world gradually loses its brightness, blurs, dissolves and finally disappears, dies in a pupil obstinately fixed on a vanishing world. So? The wide eye can still see the shine of the knife or bayonet. The brightness that slowly approaches, pales, blurs, disappears. Then the knife, the hand, the sleeve, the uniform, the eyes, the laughter of the Phalangist have ceased to be.

When the undertaker's assistants lowered the coffin, first vertical, then horizontal, the chorus burst out over me, the friends' adieu: "With my breath, with my blood..." In 1973 the voices rang out like trumpets. I'd been to similar funerals before. But now, when I hear the word Palestinian, I shudder and have to recall the image of a grave waiting like a shadow at the feet of every fighter. I note the mental image here to convey to the reader how it alone can express the deathly tremor produced by the word Palesti.

The fedayee went off towards the Jordan munching a last bit of gruyère.

A period desk, four shaded imitation candles, a few sheets of paper on the desk, a marble fireplace, a little clock with little columns, a mirror up to the ceiling—that's all the French require for Murat's drawing-room. Their leader too says lord knows what.

As the aristocracy know, it's a commonplace courtesy to pass over vulgar expressions. Words both noble and bourgeois yield easily to coarseness. But in the middle of the night, in the middle of the bed, between the sheets, an almost wordless language, or one that makes words mean their opposite, is forged between two lovers. Two, or often three—but here a touch of charlatanism creeps in. Wherever it occurs, this nocturnal language between two lovers creates a night. They take refuge in it even among a thousand or a hundred thousand others, who may have held their noses at the moisture of their reunion.

It's not that they invent new words, though they have nerve enough to do that before the very eyes of the victims. But to things and images and their sexual attributes—and what is not a sexual attribute to a couple of lovers?—they give a meaning unintelligible to the rest of us because it's seen in their own special light.

One or two hundred fedayeen together are courteous. Victorious or vanquished, they form a troop. But out of the crowd a glance swifter than a wink reveals two fedayeen as two lovers. Their rapid though invisible encounter, their way of talking to each other, makes us see them as one.

Don't think I'm still talking about desire, when now I'm really talking about something else. Lovers here means the opposite of what it did a paragraph or so ago. When you see B1 and B2 together (two fedayeen going from border to border, one a Shiite and the other a Sunni, but both Palestinians) you're seeing and hearing two lovers who are serious and chaste. Every word they say refers to explosives, silos, remote control, people known by names to do with money—Sterling A, Florin E, Ecu X, Mark P—all known to them alone, really to these two alone. Chaste, but so close that if one of them is sad the laughter of the other immediately fills the void in him.

I was talking to them about Amal.

"You're right," said B2. "Amal and a lot of the Shiites take a more and more fundamentalist attitude to religion. When a Shiite recites the Koran, especially the surats about the law, it's impossibly strict, especially when your mind's occupied by Liz Taylor's bosom. But when we use guns and bombs and gelignite and fuses, and when we shoot, either standing or kneeling or lying down, we do it all exactly the same as the Christians."

B1 whispered in my ear, but quite loudly:

"All the Shiites work for Mossad."

B2 burst out laughing.

"True enough. But it doesn't do Mossad much good—the information I give them as a Shiite comes from you, who are a Sunni."

"We're always squabbling, so people don't know. He and I will be united only in death."

When I was a kid, film actors playing members of the Foreign Legion used to talk like that.

Beirut airport was open, so I wasn't going to Aden.

In theory my last trip should have been Paris, Cairo, Damascus, Beirut, Amman, Aden, Paris. In fact it was Paris, Rabat, Amman, Beirut, Athens, the Ruhr, Paris.

The first thing that surprised me when I phoned Hamza was how gentle his voice was, and yet how full of real despair.

"Will you ever go back to your own country?"

"Which country's that?"

"Jordan."

"That's not my country. Jean, I'm done for. I've got some grey hairs. And often I'm in pain from my wounds."

"From so long ago?"

"Every time it's as much of a shock and it hurts as badly as at first, in prison in Amman."

"What about your son?"

"Yes, Jean?"

"Will he go back to his own country?"

"Yes, Jean."

And the despair in his voice was greater still.

"Which country's that?"

For the first time there was a touch of gaiety.

"Palestine."

That reassured me. We'd been talking to each other as best we could in Arabic, and his elision of the "a" in that last word, "Flestine," made it sound familiar, almost like slang.

Is love anything else but what wakes you up and sends you to sleep? Does it make you anxious too? What has become of him? Of her? Of them both? The question always presents itself as if it had chosen its moment. When one's very tired, too tired to think, and starts to day-dream. Or in a moment of pleasure. But what may they be suffering?

What had preoccupied me so deeply and so long was going to seek out its goal: marks on a thin, suspicious face, a few grey hairs, and some smears of henna on a withered skin.

Israel in a caftan with ringlets down to its collar. Was it a wall the Palestinian waves would come and beat against?

What if this book were only a mirror-memoir for me alone, in which I conjured up my own shape among a few others in a time not of their choosing but of mine? Perhaps I needed this story in the past in order to understand the time and place they'd taken on in my memory; so that via the writing I could see a little more clearly the struggle as a whole, its advances and retreats, resolutions and whims, altruism and greed.

For I saw only rarely, and then only part of the mechanism and not the whole thing.

But I don't understand any better now. I see something else, something that certainly oughtn't to have been transcribed in words arising directly out of events. But the events happened, and it doesn't much matter if I've adopted a tone that's rather casual, not to say lacking in piety. I leave on the water tracks already blurred, which the fighters would have liked engraved in marble. The book I decided to write in the middle of 1983 weighs less than the furtive gleam of a fedayeen stealing away from Ajloun. What can you understand of a hurricane when you're in the eye of it? How much do you understand when you see swimming on the water the down that's to fill a pillow?

No one beside the grave knew my shoes let in water, and that I'd leave the cemetery with bronchitis.

The metaphysical struggle goes on, impossible to ignore it, between Jewish morality and the values—using the word in its monetary sense as well, since a few Palestinians have got rich—the values of Fatah and other elements in the PLO. Between the values of Judaism and those of living revolutions.

It's now, as I'm about to leave this book, that I'd like to record one of the clearest visions I still have of Lieutenant Mubarak.

Still at Salt, but in the evening this time, I was surprised to see the world bisected. The image took the form of a person there at the moment when it happened. It's a moment that seems short when the knife is sharp, but which seemed long as Lieutenant Mubarak walked in front of me in the setting sun. He was the knife, or rather the handle of the knife that was slicing the world in two. On his left was light, because he was going from south to north, and on his right the opposite. The sun had sunk behind the mountains of Jordan and the last streaks of sunset, gleams of red and pink, lit up the left side of his head and body, while the right was already in shadow. The dark line he made as he moved along seemed to cast all the land to the east—the desert—into the shade.

The lieutenant, walking before me and separating light from darkness, was a modern projection of the Pope who saw himself as a knife dividing the world into two halves, one in Portugal and the other in Spain. At night, with his dark face and no doubt equally dark skin stretching over his muscles and sinews, Mubarak was more like an archangel than a human being. His limp had almost disappeared.

Is the justice of a cause to be measured by its bravery? Given the joy of a mind conscious that the body is in peril; the complexity of the causes involved; the rivalry of a group of males in the prime of youth; a patriotism as sensitive as jealousy; an ancestral tradition of raiding; a scarcely concealed love of looting and massacre so great and terrible the looter is in danger of dying before his looting; and that the torturer welcomes both the bliss and the hell of his torturing—given all these it would be unfair to deny Israel the thrills of bravery, pillage and torture.

As I am writing this book in the form of "Souvenirs," I must cheerfully accept the rules of memoir writing and dredge up a few facts.

I went to Damascus for the first time when I was eighteen, just after the Druse revolt. The city was devastated, and it had been devastated by the French army. This didn't surprise me, as the French army, of which for a few weeks I'd then been part, had the place in its grip: while it spared and perhaps even added to the exoticism of the place, for the first time in my life I saw a city in the power of young soldiers.

For me Damascus meant three things: exoticism, freedom and the army. Freedom because I'd recently left a very strict reformatory school; I'd been there for four years and the discipline had been harsh. I'd been a *colon* or inmate there; here the same word meant a colonist, a conqueror. And though I wasn't really one of them, I was, perhaps unwittingly, their janissary.

Since I knew nothing about building, I was ordered to help with the construction of a small concrete fort. When I arrived, the foundations had already been dug, on a hill overlooking and therefore threatening Damascus. The Tunisian soldiers knew no more than I did about building. However, in the eyes of a distant and unseen captain, it was my patriotic duty as a Frenchman to be responsible for their work and the successful construction of the fort. They were all older than me, and if they did as I told them they weren't obeying me so much as "a certain idea of France."

Arriving from Beirut by train, you passed by the spot where the Prophet is supposed to have halted, saying, "I shall not enter Damascus. A man cannot go to Paradise twice."

The river Barada was canalized by the Romans, and watered Paradise on four, sometime five different levels.

To the right of the train were apricot trees, and through the window on the left I could see a hill at the edge of a desert. On top of the hill were the beginnings of a building which the French officers referred to as Fort Andréa. Just before you got to Damascus, two branches of the Barada lying at higher levels than the three branches on the other side of the train made a sort of two-storey ring round the hill. There were green houses built on piles, like the ones you see in lakeside villages, and on the various banks of the river young Circassians were drinking glasses of raki.

Coming back from the centre of Damascus, from the Ommeyad mosque or the Hamidieh souk, I used to go through the Kurdish quarter. In the little mosques, during and after our games of cards, General Gouraud, who was responsible for all the ruins in the city and for what was called the restoration of peace, was described to me in much the same terms as those applied nowadays to General Sharon.

At Fort Andréa the Turkish soldiers and I did the same work, though I was in the Engineers. Our skins were eaten into by the cement. The fort was supposed to have a hexagonal tower in the middle designed to house a naval gun, I forget what calibre. I learned my trade as a mason as the fort took shape. It seems to me now it looked forward to its wedding with the naval gun from the time the first forms were in place.

But, indifferent to the forthcoming marriage, I spent my nights playing cards and learning a bit of Middle Eastern Arabic. It's only now I understand my rôle in the games. As later at Ajloun, with Mahjoub, card-playing was forbidden in the French army, so the Syrians had to hide. I was allowed to join in, though on my conscript's pay I couldn't have played for high stakes piled up in cash round the table. At about two or three in the morning every player cleaned up the pistachio shells from round where he was sitting.

I used to get to the fort late in the night, or rather early in the morning. A roisterer returning at dawn dead tired from the casino—that was me during my eleven months in Damascus in 1929. If a patrol became too inquisitive about the light from the candles and descended on the Syrians, who are as famous for gambling as the Greeks, the presence of a French soldier might have warded off the danger.

The captain of the Engineers came to see the tower with the formwork taken down, and like God he found the work good. He offered me a quarter of a litre of rum from a flask attached to his belt. The rum was warm from the sun and from his sweating thigh. He had a drink after me, spilled some rum and saliva on his sky-blue officer's uniform, pushed back his thrice gold-braided kepi, corked the flask, and blurted out something encouraging which I must have interpreted as "Good work! You deserve the Croix de Guerre with bars!"

It's the bars—"palm leaves" in French—that still give the Croix de Guerre its mystery. He was good enough and sober enough to add that the naval gunners would be bringing the gun in a week's time. And everyone was to turn out for the wedding, with guns, boots and feet shining with cleanliness. The day came. We were told some mules were coming up the hill with the gun carriage and—both I and the Tunisians were intrigued by this—the soul of the gun.

The captain told us about it first:

"The soul of the gun is on its way."

A naval gun, even hauled along on the backs and sides of

mules, was something noble, and we were mere sappers, there to dig trenches when things went wrong for the artillery. Just labourers, really.

"Present . . . arms!"

We presented our Lebel rifles in honour of a cannon dating from nearly eight hundred years ago. The gun, its barrel and soul (that is its core) dismantled, entered the fort on the back of two mules and between two rows of troops, peaceful but armed. I can still feel the thrill of pleasure and welcome running through the tower's cement. The gun was placed in position. As no one knows what goes on inside the head of a naval officer ashore, nor how, we still don't know why the lieutenant congratulated me on the good work. If I hadn't been using my right hand to hold my rifle butt as we presented arms he'd have shaken it with his white glove. He was holding his left glove in his left hand.

I heard someone say:

"In honour of Colonel Andréa, a French officer killed on the field of battle; in honour of your own good work, captain, and that of the young French sapper and these excellent natives, we shall now fire just one shot."

Are there any books, is there one book or even a single page on how spiders' webs are formed, at night, in the dark? I'm not sure whether observers have ever hidden in the gloom to see how the spiders set about it. But wait a minute—there's a book in Italian about southern Italy and Sicily which talks about Ariane or Ariadne hanging on to the end of a cobweb.

But at noon, right in the Syrian sunlight, someone was lucky enough to see a thread of saliva turn into a network of wrinkles, a spider's web become a whole continent. But above all, above all, how did that unbroken thread come to be?

The naval officer's idea was premeditated. The naval gunners' mules had been ordered to bring a case of shells.

The very word shell was enough to terrify us. What? Right here beside us? Was war so close, and glory within reach?

"Just one shot, men."

We came down to earth when he added casually, though still rather formally:

"A blank, of course."

The last word was almost drowned in a great peal of laughter. These sailors were such kids.

"A blank."

The report was somewhat muffled, but there was a definite smell of gunpowder. I opened my eyes again. Very slowly, almost too gently, as if to spare me from believing my own eyes, a spider's web appeared. Slowly the tower cracked; trembled, I think; and certainly collapsed into rubble. The noble naval gun pitched and tossed, reverting naturally to its motion back on its torpedo boat in a raging sea. It was rather like the movement of Tyrolean ticket collectors as their trains go round bends in the rails. And that reminds me that Austria once had a port, Trieste, and ruled all the seas.

The gun was swallowed up in the concrete.

The military hospital was a quiet place. The Syrians had made some changes to it when I saw it again recently. The doctors there cured me of the jaundice I'd deserved by my shameful incompetence. I was sent back to France for a month's convalescence, but my military career was over. I'll never have a statue put up to me when I'm dead, a bronze likeness of me on a bronze horse standing out in the shadows cast by the moonlight. And yet that tiny, grotesque but monumental disaster prepared me to become a friend of the Palestinians. I'll explain what I mean in a little while.

It was the Palestinian phenomenon that made me write this book, but why did I stick so closely to the obviously crazy logic of that war? I can only explain it by remembering what I value: one or another of my prisons, a patch of moss, a few bits of hay, perhaps some wild flowers pushing up a slab of concrete or granite paving-stone. Or, the only luxury I'll allow myself, two or three dog roses growing on a gaunt and thorny bush.

The prison was strong, its blocks of granite stuck together with the strongest possible cement and also with iron clamps; there were strange cracks caused by the rain. But one seed, one ray of sunlight or blade of grass was enough to shift the granite. The thing was done, the prison destroyed.

The distance between "Palestine shall conquer" and "Israel shall live" is that between a sword blow and a bud. And that chance metaphor, though it's only a figure of speech, makes me fear a military defeat.

Between the ages of six and eight I felt like a stranger in France, though the authorities did what's usually done in hospitals all over the world for cancer patients. France was all around me, and thought she was hemming me in all the time I was there, though really I was far away. All around me she circled, just as her empire, pink painted on the map, circled the globe; an overseas empire in which I could have gone all round the world without a passport, though only steerage.

That foolishly proud empire, never troubled before except by the empire of India, was invaded, almost without opposition, by a few battalions of handsome fair-haired soldiers. Whether it was because they had too much beauty, too much fairness, or too much youth, France cringed before them. I was there. Finally she fled, terrified. With my own eyes I saw a whole nation from behind, saw their backs running away, caught between the suns of June, of the south, and of the Germans. And where did that herd of backs and suns make for? For the sun.

In that ruined temple, mosses and lichens appeared, and sometimes kindness and even stranger things: a kind of almost happy confusion, elemental and classless. I kept my distance. In the pride I'd inherited from the former master of the world, I watched the metamorphosis with jubilation, but with the carefully hidden distress of being excluded from it.

Scenes like this took place. A lady with jewels on her fingers, wrists, neck and ears, was looking after two poor and naughty children. In the same second-class carriage a gentleman wearing an Anthony Eden hat and a number of decorations was carefully tending a poor old man who was injured, exhausted and dirty. A young lady with long green-painted fingernails helped an unfortunate woman lugging four cardboard suitcases, and patiently and incompetently untied the string round one of them to find a pair of old much-darned grey socks.

But how careful this sensitive nation is of its language, in which Berber means barbarian, hashischin an assassin, Andalou a vandal, Apache an apache, and so on with boches, wogs and the rest. The French, so proud of their colonies, became their own immigrant workers. They had the same greyness, and sometimes, briefly, the same grace.

Moss, lichen, grass, a few dog roses capable of pushing up through red granite were an image of the Palestinian people breaking out everywhere through the cracks.

If I have to say why I went with the fedayeen, I find the ultimate explanation is that I went for fun. Chance helped a lot. I think I was already dead to the world. And very slowly, as if of consumption, I finally died altogether, just to do the decent thing.

The different lengths of time it can take a viral infection to incubate may be so varied it's impossible to put an exact date not merely to its birth but even to its conception. To the moment when there's a slight histological or other jolt. And just as the origins of a revolution or of a family fortune or dynasty may be lost in minute changes of direction, so I can't really give a date to the beginnings of this book. Was it after Chatila? It took 1 November 1954 for France to realize she had to capitulate in a little spa in 1962. The Palestinians' newspapers don't say much about the period between 1920 and 1964 (when Fatah was founded). Europe and America don't want to know the Palestinian struggle had already begun even then.

The word exoticism might put me on the wrong track. Exoticism, the wonder you feel at what you see when at last you've crossed the ever-receding horizon. Beyond—but there's never any beyond except another changing horizon, necessarily a strange one, a foreign one. My long journeys became so familiar they concealed that crossing of the line, but in the end I thought that as I wrote this book I could make out, if only through a mist, not only France but also the West in general. Both France and the West seemed far away. They had become utterly exotic to me, so that I went to France as a Frenchman might go to Burma. I started to write the book around October 1983. And I became a stranger, a foreigner, to France.

Beirut was bombed by Israeli planes from 12 June to 8 September 1982, and whatever was still left standing after the raids was knocked down by the Phalangists. After that the ruins crumbled to dust. You don't often see a city reduced to dust: I'd seen Cologne, Hamburg, Berlin and Beirut. What would be left of Sabra and Chatila and Bourj Barajneh? I've gone down the main street in Chatila having almost to leapfrog over the corpses blocking the streets. The number of obstacles I've had to jump over in my life. The smell of decomposition was so strong it was almost visible, and insurmountable as a rampart.

In September 1984 I didn't recognize anything. The main street was much narrower than before. Cars moved along slowly and with difficulty. The noise of horns and engines and shouting made me think of the silence in a morgue or a cemetery, and I committed the blasphemy of longing for it. Temporary fruit and vegetable stalls were surrounded by jumpy customers, Palestinians, as variegated as the wares on offer.

"It's getting impossible to breathe the air in Israel," Rabbi Kahane had written, accusing the Israeli Arabs of poisoning or polluting the atmosphere. What I felt in the main street of Chatila two years after the massacres was an urgent desire to live, to grow, to consume as fast as possible so as first to swallow the world and then become impervious to it.

Newcomers to Amman find Jordan very attractive as they drive in from the airport, especially in the evening. I'll leave it to the reader's imagination to choose the colours he prefers among those so beloved of travel agents.

Springs, either natural or drilled and often surrounded by trees, appeared in the midst of stony gorges; and creepers at once sprang up everywhere, even over the rusty carcases of old artesian wells. Fourteen years after my first visits I couldn't recognize anything, but I realized straight away that the charm of the hills and of the darker and more distant mountains, of the valleys, gardens and villas, was just a painted veil hiding the ferocity of the Palestinian camps.

It would be interesting to ask some connoisseurs of courage and tactical invention about the fedayeen—Bayard, Crillon, Turenne, Napoleon among the French, and, according to theatre people, Lyautey.

For my part I've seen the fedayeen at ease in bravery and courage. But to my wonder and disillusion, they had no fear either of killing or of being killed; of doing evil thoroughly or of having it done to them. They paid attention to necessasry military stratagems, but it soon struck me they saw death as an eternity lasting only until their own victory. If they'd won they might without vainglory or trickery have offered the Israelis some territory, but they refused to be driven out of it for ever. Yet they were driven out, ignominiously, in the name of a morality prescribed by the invaders.

What I found most disturbing, and sometimes baffling, was their self-delusion. They were committed fighters, inspired by hatred of the enemy and the infamous characteristics attributed to him; the manly pleasure of combat male against male; the satisfaction of bearing aloft the banner of your group; by all the interlacing motives that lead to hand-to-hand fighting in which a dagger is still the ultimate weapon. And yet when the fight was over, how was it that none of the dead, whether friend or foe, got up and went and washed the blood off?

I saw and still see the fedayeen as capable of being angry with the Israeli dead for not wanting to wake up; for not being able to understand that death should last only a night at the most. Otherwise fighters would become murderers.

"Just because you kill someone there's no reason for him to stay dead for ever. And the cruelty of the Bedouin troops, the soldiers who danced so beautifully one day—the fedayee never really understood that. Nor even what leapt to a stranger's eye: their elegance in the midst of penury. By his mere presence, without even moving, a Bedouin soldier laid waste the meagre furniture, saved from the dustbins of Amman, that the Palestinians arranged so neatly."

If what Abu Omar said was right, it had taken only twenty years to give the Bedouin and Circassians a nationalist sense of belonging to the kingdom of Jordan. The kingdom only came into being in 1959, and then by such obvious artifice that I was amazed it could inspire the Bedouin with sentiments so new to them.

The country was made up of what used to be called Transjordan, which England bestowed on Hussein's grandfather, the emir Abdullah, son of the emir of Hejaz. Jordan struck me as a mess. The majority of the population were Palestinians, or wherever they really came from claimed to be immigrants from Palestine. In addition there were the Jordanians of the cities—Amman, Zarka, Irbid and Salt; the elusive Bedouin; and finally the Circassians, who could only be seen as colonists serving the interests first of the English and then of the Americans.

It's a poor country with a poor subsoil, except near the banks of the Jordan river. It seems only to have been created as a barrier between Syria and Israel in the north and the kingdom of Saudi Arabia in the south. But the Jordanians felt at home in Jordan, and saw the Palestinians' bid for power as sacrilege not only because of their demands but also because of the attempted *coup d'état*. Only the direct descendant of the Prophet could be the legitimate king.

Inside the quadrilateral temporarily granted to the fedayeen by treaties drawn up in the Tunisian embassy in Amman, the Palestinians in the camps and the soldiers on the bases behaved like an occupying power. In the Ajloun sector, where I lived, I saw harassed peasants unable to conceal the hatred in their eyes.

The Palestinians also made another mistake: they were hostile towards some customs and postal officials, and towards others in the postal and hospital services. True, these were only minor officials, but they were young and disposed to be friendly. So in July 1971 the Palestinians, cut off both from them and from the peasant population, were alone and surrounded by enemies.

"I think he was taken prisoner by the Bedouin and tortured. I'll make further inquiries."

And he added quietly in Arabic, no doubt thinking I couldn't understand:

"Hamza, from Irbid—I think he's dead."

It was Hani el-Hassan who told me this.

The camps had changed too. Canvas and dried earth had been replaced by torrents of concrete, overflowing from Brasilia, La Paz, Osaka and New Delhi, and out of them crept almost formless creatures. Like moss or lichen these beginnings of life would appear in the cracks of a ruined wall, in the almost invisible groove on a paving stone. And grass had sprouted in the cracks in men and women and children too. They were all born out of cracks in the concrete. But they still had what I'd thought had been destroyed for ever by Hussein's Bedouin, Dayan's pilots and the precautions of the World Bank: the light of their teeth and eyes.

Should I get used to that? Has reality got more imagination than my nightmares and my memories?

How does a journey really start? What reasons does one give oneself? Just as I didn't go to Amman in order to tell France about Hussein's brutality, so I didn't start out in June 1984 so as to give an account of the fedayeen strung out between Algiers and Aden. The fixed mark, the pole star that guided me was still Hamza, his mother, his disappearance, torture and almost certain death. But if he was dead, how would I know his grave? Was his mother still alive? Wouldn't she be terribly old? My fixed mark might be called love, but what sort of love was it that had germinated, grown and spread in me for fourteen years for a boy and an old woman I'd only ever seen for twenty-four hours? It was still emitting radiations—had its power been building up over thousands of years? In fourteen years my travels had taken me to more than sixteen countries. Under each new sky I could measure the amount of the earth's surface that power had irradiated.

I knew Ajloun had disappeared. Even if there'd been no new building, no tree cut down, no axe broken, there'd be nothing there that meant anything to me now. The fields, once yellow, would now be green meadow; instead of goats there would be cows. Just one gleam lit up my reverie, though it could scarcely be called a hope: perhaps I could go to the outskirts of Deraa, and before crossing the Syrian border turn left on to the road that goes through Jerash to Irbid. There, where no one would know me, I'd have a quiet lunch, certain I wouldn't be able to find anything of all I kept or thought I kept in my memory.

"If you want to visit the camps you have to have permission from the Minister of Information. But you've got permission already—I've spoken to him on the phone."

This sounded as fatal as a spadeful of earth. In 1972 Daoud had advised me to go to Jordan saying I wanted to visit Petra, but really to go and see how the Jordanian and Palestinian populations were still at loggerheads.

"We're trying to bring them together wherever we can."

Discreetly as I'd travelled, the people at the Ministry of Information, where I'd applied for permission to go to Petra, held on to my passport too long. But at the Jordanian embassy in Beirut I was given a visa within a few minutes. I showed it proudly to a hotel porter, a Palestinian.

"They gave it to you too quickly. If I were you I wouldn't go."

I did go. Four days later I was requested, to put it mildly, to leave Jordan, and taken back to the Syrian frontier.

And fourteen years later, here I was again. The representative of the World Bank and his wife were waiting for me at the airport. They'd been contacted from Rabat—the people there were afraid I'd be arrested on my arrival in Amman.

"Jean and I will go to Irbid on our own. If we can't get into the camp, or if we're arrested, let the minister know."

So we set out for Irbid—Nidal, a Palestinian woman friend of hers, and I. Nidal was a blonde and very beautiful Lebanese woman, an actress, who spoke French and Arabic. Nidal can be a woman's name as well as a man's.

I'd spoken a lot about Hamza, his imprisonment, his alleged torture, the Zarka desert, and what the PLO official had called his probable death. I mentioned that he might be in Germany, though despite Daoud's letter I couldn't see how he could have gone there, and especially not why. Or for whom.

The Palestinian resistance has never been one movement, but many. You had to join one and pretend to belong equally to all. But primarily you had to join the resistence of your choice and stay with it. Mine was Fatah.

Fatah has remained a popular organization. But at its centre, which became a centre of command, the bureaucracy of the resistance, perhaps unwillingly, has got mixed up with another resistance—that of the wheeling and dealing riff-raff.

The road from Namur to Liège, from Liège to Brussels and from Brussels to the Channel coast is perfect, and the motorway linking the Gulf of Akaba to the Syrian frontier is like it. It takes two hours to drive from Amman to Irbid, and on either side of the road lie well-cultivated fields. At the head of one valley I saw the Baqa camp, where I'd stayed for some time, and I was surprised to notice that it was in a hollow, whereas I'd remembered it as covering several sides of quite a steep hill. It looked like a jewel in that landscape, but that was because it was a long way away. What's more, I was catching a brief glimpse of it from an air-conditioned car: in those circumstances any misery can look enchanting, so long as you don't have to live in it yourself.

From that distance and from the car I didn't suspect that the clumps of greenery were rows of cactuses full of rubbish: old hairbrushes, toothbrushes and burned string beans.

The Roman remains at Jerash were as inhuman as ever, and as proud, knowing Latin scholars from the Sorbonne came to decipher their two-thousand-year-old inscriptions.

Our car wasn't stopped, and we found ourselves almost unawares in the Palestinian camp in Irbid. It was all but indistinguishable from the centre of Irbid, except that the houses were not so tall, only a ground floor and one storey. The streets, sloping gradually and almost aesthetically downwards, were as clean as those in the town itself, but poorer. The suburbs of Irbid seemed to consist of well-to-do houses surrounded by gardens. In the camp, all the front doors opened on to the street.

We stopped the car in front of the first house, and Nidal went inside to ask the way. Before giving us the information we'd asked for, a woman invited us in for tea. She smiled, and the second thing she said was, "We're from Nazareth." The suspicion which everyone had tried to warn me about in Amman and in other Arab countries didn't exist here. The Palestinians were quite ready to tell you where they came from.

An old man spoke to me, also smiling, and confirmed that we were already in the camp and that all the houses round about were Palestinian. No one complained about exile, war, money troubles or the difficulty of finding work. The house we were in sheltered a rather complex family group: a still young father, a very young son-in-law who was a soldier in the Jordanian army, three women and a large number of children. I give the details to show how visitors were immediately put in the picture by their hosts. It was also an invitation to us to be equally forthcoming: Who were we?

We told them, without hiding or embellishing anything. No one was bothered by the presence of a Frenchman, sitting on the carpet, propped on cushions. It seemed to them quite natural that Nidal should translate everything they said into French and everything I said into Arabic. I recognized the spontaneous confidence so typical of the Palestinians.

As my statement of my position has shown, I've never thought of myself as a Palestinian. But there I was at home.

I wasn't at home in Amman. I'd been told all over the Middle East and elsewhere that the camps were full of policemen and spies, and I'd been expecting sly faces asking long questions in short, inquisitorial sentences and refusing to talk about themselves.

"They're very secretive. If you ask questions they won't answer. If ever they do answer it's only to catch you out when you tell lies."

But they liked talking about themselves, liked explaining their position. If I'd ever felt any uneasiness it would have disappeared. But I'd never been bothered by the doubtful expressions of even PLO representatives in the West—they seem to live so far from the people—when they heard about my journey. Despite a few images that disappeared as soon as seen, there was a sort of peace inside me, like a bed of trust, when it came to the Palestinians. Other Europeans, but other Arabs too, had lied to me about them. But I was comfortable here. It wouldn't have taken much for the two men of the family to tell me about when they were fedayeen. I laughed when they laughed. When, after the tea, they waited for the women to bring cool drinks, I waited too.

The house, and especially the room where we were all sitting on the carpet, looked very clean. But in their smiles and frank words I thought, in 1984, I could detect signs of capitulation. Capitulation was there precisely in the attempt to conceal it, in other words in a change for the worse trying to pass itself off as a change for the better. For the change was really just another misfortune. The little street, and those we saw later, were covered with concrete, and sometimes a little stream of water ran down the middle, sometimes clean, sometimes not. The houses weren't new, but they were strengthened with a filler that was stronger than concrete or pure cement. The whole district seemed frozen in a kind of eternity in which nothing would ever get worse because it was stuck in this misery. Deterioration perfectly preserved in concrete.

Instead of a broom there was a vacuum cleaner in the room. The blades of the fan turned, but it didn't amuse the kids. The Coca-Cola came cold from a refrigerator that was both visible and audible. But life here wasn't lived in comfort. It was lived in resigned acceptance of comfort. Everything I looked at was clean but poor, with the sort of ascetic elegance that comes from the sure and felicitous arrangement of a few cheap bits of furniture bought perhaps at the hardware store. In the right place, a white plastic bucket can be a work of art. Allow me a platitude: the room smiled but sadly, like a Palestinian face.

I had the impression the struggle was only suspended. This family of ten or so had halted to get its breath back. Which told me, better than the sorrows of 1970, that to make life bearable we must take refuge in the temporary that seems to last for ever.

Nobody seemed surprised that we stayed only a few minutes, either. We were among taciturn people, where important things are said standing up. *Mezze* are small, tasty, swift but easy hors d'oeuvres eaten in the East before a long meal. A few minutes with that Palestinian family in Irbid was a *mezze*.

No one seemed to know any Hamza resembling my description. The young son-in-law, the soldier, who'd been silent, stood up and shook hands when we left, and smiled at us for the first time. I had the impression he'd been watching us mistrustfully; but when, as I sat on the carpet, I made a movement betraying an old man's fatigue, he was the only one to notice, and immediately slipped a cushion under my weary arm.

Out in the street, in the sunshine, we couldn't help talking of Hamza. It was nearly noon. Nidal went into a greengrocer's shop. She was wearing dark glasses to protect herself from her celebrity. She asked if there was anyone in the district whose name was Hamza and whose mother was a widow.

"He lives with wife now. His mother used to be a widow, but she remarried."

I made no comment. Obviously this Hamza couldn't be the one I was looking for.

"This one's a fake," I thought. "There must be real Hamzas and false ones. Anyway, one must be real even if all the others are false."

The idea of a widow who'd got married again didn't square with the notion that Hamza's mother's first and last greeting had conveyed to me, nor with the few hours I'd spent with her and her son. When you had a son like that you didn't marry again. That was my first reaction. Then came the thought, crude but sadly dubious:

"A woman over fifty and on her own might have remarried as a refuge from her country's misfortune and the sorrow of Hamza's torture and death. And yet she was the real head of the family, and does the head of a Palestinian family need the comfort of a second husband?"

"Can you take us to the house?"

"Of course. It's quite close, and I know Hamza's at home."

The imaginary fortress in which the West and even the Arabs themselves had imprisoned the Palestinians, reputed to be frightened, proud, timid and silent, collapsed before my very eyes. As easily as a grocer in the Puy-de-Dôme telling someone how to get to the local dentist's, the cauliflower seller led us into a nearby street.

He stopped by an iron door which I didn't recognize: I remembered Hamza's door as being of white-painted wood. Here, between the iron door and the house a few branches showed above a wall, proving that the house had a little garden and not a courtyard. But I believed in my memories, and even more in the durability of the things that had caused them. I might have said, "Because my memory is faithful to me, the world must be faithful too."

The greengrocer thumped on the door a few times with his fist.

"Who is it?"

"Me."

This exchange sounded to me like either a code or a practical joke. How could he be here, answering in such a ringing voice, so peacefully and naturally? Had he been changed? If so, why? And how?

What I relate seems ordered, but it's only set out like that to make things easier for the reader: in fact it was quite different. A series of fleeting impressions overlapped inside me, making time and even place quiver. Place was a sort of concrete step and iron door, with Nidal, the greengrocer and me. How wretchedly inadequate writing is! I may put down, "I thought that . . . ," but on the contrary I didn't think anything. Or rather I thought a whole ocean of thoughts succeeding one another like waves, each transparent enough for the links between them to be divined. Images rather than thoughts followed one another and yet seemed simultaneous: "What if it was a trap? What if the greengrocer was an informer? Was the iron door locked from inside? What about my plane to Sanaa? Had Nidal led me into an ambush?"

My questions were answered by a shock that affected my whole being. Through this shock, which felt almost like a bodily organ inside me, thought returned slowly, as if from the soles of my feet.

A handsome young man, apparently only half awake, stood in the doorway. He had tousled black hair, two or three days' growth of beard, but no moustache. He looked surprised, but held out his hand. Nidal asked him his name.

"Hamza."

I looked at him. He was handsome enough to be Hamza, or his picture or copy or replacement. But I was sure this young man was not my friend of a day who had lived with his mother. Yet he was attractive despite his sudden awakening and dishevelled clothes. If the other Hamza was in his grave, perhaps this one might take his place in my affection after a couple of days' grief and remorse. He was standing in the doorway. What did we want of him?

The only image that presented itself to me now was that of one or more fedayeen setting out on a mission in Israeli territory. But the way I felt it might be translated like this: "A sudden hole that seemed to be of human dimensions moved when they did, but behind them, like a shadow ready to receive them." Even today I still feel a similar sadness at the mere mention of a Palestinian. I've only got to hear the word and the hole is there. More precisely, I feel as I always do by a newly dug grave. Perhaps that's what the leaders dimly felt when they ceremonially leapt to their feet whenever a martyr came into the room.

"Like a shadow," I wrote. But it was a deep shadow, an oblong shadow made by picks and shovels digging up earth and rock. Thanks to this image I think I can understand, and keep before me, one of the Palestinians' special characteristics. All men are mortal—the apparent stupidity of the saying doesn't shock me. But if all men *are* mortal, not many of them have the courage to know it, and those who flaunt their knowledge are even rarer. The fedayeen didn't have the common European habit of keeping a cigarette jammed against their skull behind one ear, but they did have the knack of giving a crooked smile with a cigarette between their lips. And it seemed to me that in the oblong shape that followed them like a shadow there was a sign like a knowing wink. The white world moves forward without a shadow. I saw at once the oblong pit behind the young Palestinian. But I knew the leaders no longer rose as gesture of mourning.

"Do you recognize him?" Nidal asked me in French.

I was afraid to say no in case it transformed this Hamza into a sort of teddybear that didn't suit me and had to be put back on a dusty shelf.

"So I'm only a second-class Hamza," he might have thought.

"Ask him how old he is."

"Thirty."

"That's too young. Hamza must be thirty-five by now."

We were acting like cotton planters looking for a runaway slave. I at least must have looked like a horse dealer who's had a horse stolen but doesn't recognize this one's coat or teeth. He's not even sure about its name.

What anxiety was making this Hamza wrinkle his nose?

Nidal explained whom we were looking for in the Palestinian camp.

"This *is* the Palestinian camp."

Then he suddenly came awake, recognized Nidal and found her beautiful.

"There used to be three Hamzas in this district," he said. "Me, a martyr,"—one of the dead, that is—"and another one older than I am."

Then came the second shock.

"He's working in Germany now. But his mother lives in the next street."

"What do you think?" Nidal asked me. Then, to him I'll call Hamza II: "Take us there, please."

To explain my presence Nidal told him the woman and her son had put me up for a night fourteen years ago. I was passing through Irbid and would like to see her again if she was still alive. It was clear from my age and fatigue that I wasn't a Jordanian official, someone to be wary of.

"If you mean that Hamza and his mother, she's still alive. Very much alive, as you'll see!"

It was as if he meant, wonderingly, "All too alive!"

He accompanied us down the sloping street with every sign of confidence. But our comings and goings, Nidal's Lebanese accent, my speaking French and our general appearance were beginning to arouse some curiosity, perhaps nervousness. I was afraid some camp official might come and demand explanations. Heads, even bodies, turned to look at us as we went by. I was rather uneasy. Why had the young man made up his mind so quickly? He might be taking us to a political official.

The uneasiness I convey here by a sentence lasted only a moment there in Irbid. It was almost adventitious, for I was *sure* he was a friend. I weighed my feet down with imaginary soles of lead, so as not to skip along too joyfully.

No crowd gathered. Yet we must have seemed a very odd group—a Frenchman and two unknown young women being led about by a tousled young man obviously snatched out of bed at noon. (I realized I haven't said much about the second young woman: she was rather dull, but later on her presence helped show the mutual trust that had been generated.)

As I went down the gently sloping street I felt—I didn't know exactly what at the time, but as if I'd entered a world familiar to me. A friend was holding me by the hand. Of course I didn't recognize anyone. How many people had I met back in 1970? But none of the faces seemed strange. Nor did I recognize any of the houses outright, yet when I found myself outside one that looked fairly new, with three steps and no little courtyard like the one at

Hamza's place, I was certain I was looking at the house that had been in my waking dreams for fourteen years.

It was because of the slope that all became clear to me—gradually, patiently and unmistakably, through the angle of the soles of my shoes. Perhaps, when blind men go back to a place they've been to only once before, they know where they are by their balance as they walk. Perhaps signals transmitted through the soles of their shoes help their whole body to recognize a space it has been in before.

Hamza II pointed to the house.

"That's Hamza's house. His mother's there, and I should think you can see her."

I might have been wrong when I said I was in a world that was familiar. But I wasn't wrong. My feeling, or rather presentiment, was as explicit as what Hamza II had just said, and it was linked with the meeting I've described between me and Hamza and his mother. I was quite certain. It was in this house that I'd met them, and despite all the changes that same house was now in front of me.

At worst it might have been one or other of the two houses on either side of it; it couldn't have been the house opposite, because it had to be on the left as I came down the street. Another and very different clue was Germany. From Daoud's letter, backed up by what Hamza II had said, I knew Hamza was working, or had worked, in Germany. And I still don't know how, but that Palestinian house in the camp at Irbid had something German about it.

I didn't reason about this. I experienced it directly, as you know an apple is unripe before you pick it, just from its colour; or even without looking at it. The house wasn't built with materials from the Black Forest, but I sensed a parallel between it, or rather between the sight of it and the sound of the word Germany. Perhaps I even had a presentiment of the present-day link between Germany and the Grand Mufti of Jerusalem.

The front door was open. Nidal entered first. Then I went up the three steps. Nidal was already talking to a frail elderly woman whose white hair was just visible, parted in the middle and drawn back under a scarf to form a bun—no doubt a very meagre one.

This is what I felt: If this is Hamza's mother, she's already among the shades. If I ask too pointed and painful a question she'll fade away before my very eyes, and it'll be Hamza's late mother I'll have in front of me.

I cautiously held out my hand, and she touched it like a cat who's got its paw wet. She also said:

"Sit down."

She indicated a little sitting-room where instead of a carpet some blankets and cushions formed a comfortable little nook. With the agility that elderly women retain in all the Arab countries, she sat down on the wooden floor, her legs tucked under her, her body perfectly upright.

"Do you recognize this Frenchman?" Nidal asked.

"My eyes are very bad now."

"He stayed here with you and Hamza in 1970."

"Did he have a camera?"

"I've never owned a camera in my life," I said.

Her face showed no reaction. She'd probably forgotten all about me. All the Palestinians had lived through the savagery of the Bedouin soldiers, and she'd had to endure the time when Hamza was in the Zarka punishment camp. I wasn't certain myself that this was she. But little by little the rooms here came to reflect the layout of the house then. The sitting-room in which we were talking now had once been the mother's bedroom, where she'd brought me tea in the morning and declined to have any herself. Opposite where we were sitting was the door to the toilet, where I'd learned to use the bottle of water.

Hamza II, awake now, squatted down with the rest of us, observing with childlike wonder this strange confrontation. We were trying to be clever, to catch this poor woman out, telling ourselves, "It's for her own good."

While Nidal translated my questions into Arabic and the mother's replies into French, I had time to cast my mind back, to think up new angles of attack, to remember fresh details about the old house and interpret them in terms of the present. The woman's face was on a level with mine. It was very white, almost as white as her hair, in which I could see, amid patches of flaky skin on the scalp, some streaks of the henna that's applied to the hair and palms of a bride on her wedding day. She spoke in a very low voice.

"I remember my son coming here with a stranger one day, during Ramadan. It might have been a Frenchman—I don't remember."

"What's your son's name?"

"Hamza."

"What year was it?"

"A long time ago. Too long. I don't know what year."

"You can remember the month—Ramadan—but not the year?"

"Yes, Ramadan."

"You must remember this, then: your son Hamza introduced you to a Frenchman, and you had a gun slung over your shoulder."

"No, no—I've never had a gun."

I spoke to her, we spoke to her, cautiously rather than kindly, like policemen or examining magistrates overcoming their irritation and proceeding slowly, one detail at a time, soothingly, stealthily. I think at one moment we nearly got there. Nidal, her friend and I had become perfect cops. I was enjoying the dissimulation; I think grand inquisitors in the past and modern investigators must have or have had the same skills as bird-catchers. Her reactions made it plain she'd been accused by the police of having a gun.

"Right, no gun. Your son introduced you to the Frenchman, and told you he was a Christian but didn't believe in God."

Hamza II burst out laughing.

"Hamza didn't believe in Him much either."

"And you said to your son, 'If he doesn't believe in God I must give him something to eat.'"

"Oh, he didn't eat much. Just a sardine . . ."

"Two. Two sardines, two tomatoes and a little omelette. Not much . . ."

Everyone laughed except her. Nidal said, in Arabic:

"But this lady's describing Jean exactly. He's been staying with us for a week in Amman, and he hasn't eaten anything."

"Your son took me into his room and showed me a hole by the head of the bed. You and your daughter and I were supposed to hide there if the Bedouin got too close."

Nidal stopped translating when she got to the word "hole." Was it her profession as an actress, her skill at exploiting a moment of drama? At any rate, the first part of the sentence hung there in suspense, like a fine thread that would never snap. Then Nidal went on to translate the rest of what I'd said.

As soon as she'd finished the mother stood up and held out her hand to me.

"The hole's still there. Come with me and I'll show you."

There was no need to translate. She took me by the hand without asking the others to come too—this was something she wouldn't normally have done, but she was obviously excited—and led me into the next room. Here I saw a square trapdoor, which she opened. While I was still in Hamza's room, peering down the opening I'd known about for fourteen years, two young men came into the house, attracted by the bustle in the street outside.

The shelter symbolized the trust the Palestinians had reposed in me—Khaled Abu Khaled, Hamza, his sister and his mother.

I straightened up, looked round, and said in Arabic:

"This used to be Hamza's room."

"Yes," said his mother, also in Arabic.

For the first time she gave me a little smile.

The two young men closed the trapdoor so that it was indistinguishable from the wooden floor again. They were the mother's grandsons and Hamza's cousins. They'd been afraid we might be bringing bad news from Germany.

I recalled what Hamza II had said: "Hamza didn't believe in God much, either." It suddenly struck me he must have argued with his mother about his beliefs. Had she, as a Muslim, been shocked? His disbelief must have been well known to their Palestinian neighbours, and might have been due to his friendship with Khaled Abu Khaled. At any rate she'd come to accept it in the end. Whether she became resigned to it, I don't know. But the fact that she'd said I must be given something to eat showed she knew that unbelievers were in the habit of carrying on as usual during Ramadan.

That answer of hers had seemed extremely broadminded on the face of it, whereas in fact it was the logical consequence of her twenty-year-old son's independent ways. He'd discovered atheism at the same time as revolution, and Islamic customs had gone by the board. Anyway, her first words to me long ago turned out to be less striking than I'd thought at the time, when I put it down to typical Palestinian sensitivity and tolerance, a quality always discovered sooner or later in the struggle that leads to practical wisdom. But I didn't think any the less of her now I knew what had really led to her brilliantly simple answer. She was still a Palestinian, but she might have been a loving Christian mother whose adolescent son had lost his faith, and perhaps his reason, and insisted on eating meat on Good Friday.

"He's working in Germany."

She spoke aloud, turning towards either Nidal or the young Palestinian woman, but from now on addressing everything she said to me.

"In Germany," she said again, as if by invoking his distance from us she was still shielding him, saying he was too far away for anyone to do him any harm. She was protecting him by magic.

"You're talking too much."

This was the younger of her two grandsons—the more forward one, it seemed to me.

"But you haven't forgotten that Hamza went to fight that night, and that when the shooting got close you slipped into his room, where I was sleeping, with a cup of coffee and a glass of water on a tray?"

"I took the Frenchman a glass of tea."

"No, it was a cup of Turkish coffee. And was there a glass of water too?"

"Yes."

"Turkish coffee is always served with a glass of water. But not tea."

"You're talking too much," the young man said again.

The midnight memories of these two elderly folk, in which he probably saw some secret connivance, was getting on his nerves, partly because of his youth and partly because of his respect for Hamza.

The mother's eyes shone more brightly, and in a face and body bound for dissolution I found myself confronted with an ever-increasing force trying to hold me at bay. We weren't exchanging sweet nothings: I was trying to establish that I knew something; she wanted the past forgotten.

"You don't give coffee to someone who has to sleep."

"You wanted me to stay awake."

"The Bedouin were getting closer."

"You're talking too much."

Arab fiancées and brides use a lot of henna. It fades from the skin more quickly than from the hair. As I said before, Hamza's mother's hair was white and sparse. I'd got attached to it. It was still there even if I turned and looked at Nidal. That head was inside me. The little flakes of pink skin visible among the hairs were covered with henna and would never be otherwise. A young bride and a dead old woman, I'd noticed all this before, but now I'd become fond of it, in the same way as one is more attached to a defeat than to a victory. The Palestinians' victory over the Israelis at Karameh hasn't been forgotten, but it exerts much less fascination than the defeat at Deir Yassin. Every detail about Deir Yassin is gone over and over in people's memories, each new one examined under a microscope. And whoever studies them is moved less by the fact of defeat than by the inexorable first sign or signs of decline.

Defeat is something survived and gone over again and again, word by word. Victory is a given fact: no point in harping on it.

Absurd ideas presented themselves because of that head, though they were quickly dismissed:

"What about consulting Dr. Bogomoletz?"

"How about trying a new egg-and-honey shampoo, or royal jelly?"

"Or sea-water therapy?"

The more I looked at the wrinkles round her mouth and on her forehead the less I recognized the strong, cheerful woman I'd known before. So much so that the more proofs she gave me that I really had been here, that we really had met, before, the more I doubted whether all that had actually happened fourteen years ago. Doubt is not the word. It was more like the feeling you get when doubt gives way to astonishment and you say, "It's not possible!"

After it's been used in the bath for a long time and dwindled to half its original size, a piece of soap, amazed at the change in itself, might exclaim, "It's not possible!"

Before, my memory had been firmly imprinted with the image of a woman strong enough to carry a gun, and to load, aim and fire it. Her lips weren't thin in those days, nor faded to the same pallor as the trace of henna on her dandruff. I hadn't been present at the débâcle; I could measure its effects all the better. Hamza's mother had become as thin and flat as all the other two-dimensional shapes you saw in Jordan.

Beyond her faded dress I saw the flat cardboard dummies on display in fashionable shop-windows in Amman, trying to give life to a caftan visibly expiring. Hamza's mother was as flat as Hussein's tin crowns stuck up over all the streets and squares; as the first fedayee crushed to death by a tank; as the empty uniform on the coffin of a dead soldier; as a poster; as a barley loaf; as a plate.

But if she remembered these details so well from so long ago, she must have talked and laughed about them with her son. Why? And how?

"He's working in Germany. He's married to a German."

"You're talking too much."

Her grandson thought she was gaga. Perhaps everyone in the camp did, so as not to have to bother about her and her ramblings. To warn her like that was to put her back in the cage of old age. She straightened up wearily. She must have had enough of old memories and of her belligerent grandson. But perhaps he wasn't as suspicious as he seemed; perhaps he wanted to show how grown-up and manly he was compared with an old lady who looked like an octogenarian.*

Meanwhile Hamza II kept looking at Nidal. Did he find her beautiful because she *was* beautiful, or because she was famous? And also she spoke such good Arabic, with a Lebanese accent, and then all of a sudden French, a strange and probably barbarous language. Like many women, whenever she was speaking she thought she was thinking.

---

*I write "looked like"; but she really was an octogenarian: time spent in sorrow ages people. Though she'd been fifty fourteen years ago, she didn't merely appear to be, she *was* eighty.

For the first time, Nidal's friend said something in Arabic. Hamza II looked astonished. It turned out she and he had both belonged to the same organization, had even been in the same network and on the same operations against the same opponents. Both had got older; their looks, their names, their way of life had all changed; and they had met again here. As we looked on in astonishment they addressed each other by their fedayeen names and talked openly about their various operations. They were not new friends now, but old comrades. As they talked in a different language, time seemed to contract almost tangibly. The mother came back into the room just as the grandson who kept saying "You're talking too much" got up to go and look for her. But she was there. Her right hand was clenched; with her left she offered me an open envelope.

"Hamza!" I said, pointing to the photograph. He looked about twenty in it. Nidal looked. Her friend and Hamza II looked too.

"He was always laughing," said Hamza II.

What was Hamza II feeling? His name was the same as that of the distant hero whom we'd just glimpsed from so far away. But he wasn't the hero, and that "II" placed him farther away from the hero than complete anonymity would have done. He no longer doubted that I'd spent the night here so long ago.

Then the grandson's voice was heard, even sterner than before:

"But what language could you talk to one another in?"

He too probably saw he'd soon have to admit I'd been there before, though the moment was not yet come. His finicky admonitions had got nowhere, and he wouldn't be able to prove himself a great sleuth unless this last trick question uncovered something.

Everyone forgot Hamza's photograph and looked at me. I adopted a light tone.

"Hamza told me"—Nidal translated—"he'd spent ten months in Algiers when he was doing his army training. He learned a few words of French and a bit of North African Arabic. Those were the languages we used."

"He was there for six months," said his mother.

"Ten."

"I can't remember—it was so long ago."

She waited for Nidal to translate her answer, then added:

"I can't give you his address. I haven't got it."

Her right arm stretched itself out to me almost independently, and her fist opened and offered me a scrap of newspaper. It had some figures written on it—what are called Arabic numerals, though they're used all over the world. She explained to Nidal, without a smile, without any expression either of victory or defeat:

"Hamza's telephone number. You can phone him this evening. Direct dialling."

I'd got a plane ticket to Aden, but I didn't go. Aden, Sanaa, the two Yemens were too far: the journey would have been like waiting in an endless queue. As soon as I got back to Amman that evening I dialled the code of a town in Germany and then Hamza's number. Someone in Germany picked up the receiver.

"Hamza?"

"*Nam* ("yes" in Arabic)."

Even if I hadn't forgotten his voice the gentleness of this one would have surprised me. Once again I thought: "It's not the justice of their cause that moves me—it's the rightness."

He wasn't surprised at my having gone to Irbid. Hamza wasn't dead, as someone had dared try to make me think. We exchanged a few words in Arabic and German, which it seemed to me he spoke very well. He dictated his full address.

The worst had been death, alone, under torture. So the worst wasn't always inevitable. Or had the worst really happened anyway, *in that Hamza wasn't dead?*

But to return to the house in Irbid.

Something must have changed the mother's attitude, for she'd handed over the piece of paper with Hamza's phone number written on it, for me to take away. It showed signs of frequent handling, and if I did take it away we'd be severing the thread that linked her to her son. I said as much, but she was worn out again, too worn out to show any further sign of disarray. Mustering the courage to give me the paper seemed to have struck her all of a heap. I copied Hamza's number into Nidal's notebook and gave the dirty bit of paper back to his mother.

I must go back to when I was walking down the sloping street and felt as if I were entering a world already familiar to me. I'd thought for so long about that street and the white door into the courtyard—and in my memory the street didn't slope down; it was level. That was how I'd described it to the Palestinian manager in the Abu Bakr hotel near the customs post in Irbid in 1972. He'd warned me against going back there.

"I'd like to have news of Hamza and his mother."

"You've had a lot of trouble crossing the frontier. The police didn't want you here. At the moment they think you're in Amman, or at least on the way there. If they find you in the Palestinian camp in Irbid they'll take you back to Syria.

"That's all that will happen to *you*. But if you go into a house it's bound to be under observation by the Jordanian army. And you'll endanger anyone there who's already suspected of belonging to the fedayeen; you'll endanger any of the fedayeen who've taken the risk of letting you through; and you'll endanger me—I've promised the police to keep an eye on you until you leave for Amman."

So I didn't go back to the house. But I described it to the fedayee in the hotel, who said he'd try to find out what had happened. He didn't find out anything. Or he forgot. So many Palestinians had copped it.

"He was in the Zarka camp for a long time. He was injured, tortured. In the legs and the knees."

So part of Daoud's letter was true.

The mother pointed at me, suddenly laughing, though quite toothless.

"The Frenchman made us laugh. Hamza offered him his comb and he said he combed his hair every morning with a wet towel."

"It must have been me, to say anything so daft."

I can't remember exactly when I thought: "But if she can remember what I said so clearly, she must know I didn't have a camera. The photograph I've just seen shows Hamza when he was twenty, not twenty-two. She knows I couldn't have taken a photograph of him before I came to her place."

"Who took that photograph?"

"Khaled Abu Khaled."

I was sure then that the mention of the camera had been a trap. If I'd fallen for it I'd have proved myself a liar and wouldn't have been told anything. Lying sometimes has charms I may enjoy toying with even when writing this book. But at Irbid it would have been disastrous. A single hesitation would have made the mother suspicious.

It was then I saw that little face more clearly. It was pale and blanched, as if it had been washed in disinfectant, and marked with the dark spots of age and some remaining streaks of henna. Narrow and broad at the same time, her face was full of suspicion, malice, fear and defiance all at once.

I remembered very clearly how trustingly she'd welcomed me on my first visit, and realized how much time had gone by since then. The years between 1970 and 1984 had been a time of suffering and trial, and had changed that sturdy intelligence into its opposite—timid mistrust. She'd been worn down, but not completely extinguished, by affliction. Would she have enough time left to change back to what she'd been before?

But had it been so great a transformation, after all? She must be suffering from sciatica—she often rubbed her thigh.

But why had I felt that the place was familiar as I came down the street? I'll hazard an explanation. In 1970 I'd lived through that half-day and whole night in a state of great inner excitement, invisible to anyone merely looking at me, and the place must have imprinted itself on me. Just as with one of the modern lottery tickets where you scratch a blank space to find the amount you've won, the street, the place as a whole, had appeared to me not visually but in the mental configuration I'd unconsciously registered when I was there before. It was when I went down the street fourteen years later that I knew I'd gone up it fourteen years before.

And now all I've written before seems false. This account may be better:

In 1970, I think it was December, after drinking some tea in the mother's room while she was preparing the evening meal, I went for a walk up the street. I felt happy after my sleep, Hamza had come back tired but not wounded, there hadn't been another alert yet. By a tap in a wall I said good day to an old Palestinian woman who was drawing water in a bucket. I can't remember what she answered, but after she'd gone back inside her house a youngish man still in his pyjamas came out of it, walked over to me, returned my greeting and asked to see my papers. Rather annoyed, I rummaged in my pocket and showed him the pass Arafat had written out for me.

That trivial incident, quite insignificant compared with the warmth I'd experienced in Hamza's house, had made me mistrustful of these people looking for trouble. When I came back in 1984 the main thing I recognized was the tap in the wall. I'm not sure this is the right explanation, but if so, everything would be clearer. The image of the tap in the wall had always been there. Every time in all those fourteen years that I'd thought of Hamza, the fountain was superimposed on my thoughts. Affronts, or whatever has offended or hurt us, come back much more readily than kind actions. We don't usually remember unpleasantnesses deliberately; on the countrary, we try to fend them off. But when we remember happy moments the traces of some suffering, even if it was only fleeting or imaginary, surface too, insistent and often immutable reminders. Not every tap in a wall spoke to me of that past unpleasantness, but every recollection of happiness brought back the tap as well.

But it was still there in Irbid, and I saw it. It was still where two streets met, the one that led from the main road and the one that went to Hamza's place.

Writing this today I don't know why I didn't cry out in recognition then, as I did later when I saw Hamza's photograph: "The tap in the wall!"

The mother and I spoke almost together:

I: "The next morning I went to Damascus."

She: "When Hamza came back from seeing the Frenchman off he said he'd gone to Damascus."

She'd decided to address me directly in Arabic. Nidal whispered a translation.

"You see what we are now. But we've been in Spain, Holland, France, London (Leila Khaled), Sweden, Norway, Thailand, Germany, Austria."

As she said the words—Spagnia, Landia, Francia, Guilterra, Teland, Magnia—I saw quite clearly the popular emblem of each country. Hearing the names on the radio, had she found out the geography of the places where the fedayeen operated, where she might have thought her son was planting bombs?

Bullfights, the canals of Amsterdam, the Eiffel Tower, the Thames, snow (telj in Arabic—she said the word with wonder), Polar icefields, a golden Buddha, Franco, Hitler, waltzes . . . From her house she had conquered the world and moved Hamza about in it, and now described all that had been won and lost to her own Las Cases, like Napoleon on his island.

"We've been in Italy, Morocco and Portugal," she went on. "And where are we now? In Düsseldorf. Some Japanese came from Tokyo to kill Israelis for us at Tel Aviv." She pronounced it Tel Abeeb, as Arabs often do.

"Did Hamza buy you the colour television?"

"It's very small, and my eyes aren't good. I listen, but I don't often watch. I did yesterday though, in spite of the blur—I wanted to see Hussein the Butcher kneeling down and praying for the old man."

"Which old man?"

"Abdullah, his grandfather, was killed coming out of a mosque in Jerusalem. Are you listening, Frenchman? Long after his death they still pray to God to have mercy on him and save him."

When I left the house I realized I'd encountered the poetry of the fedayeen in the 70s: a total confidence, yet with prudence still awake.

I was afraid as I felt the warm outdoor air on my face. It seemed to me that everything in the house had been just a dream. I was afraid for the mother, for her two grandsons, for Hamza II and for Hamza himself. Our entry into the camp and our subsequent comings and goings couldn't have gone unnoticed.

"What can you expect? An elderly man from the North comes to this out-of-the-way spot and tells some tale to an old woman. She's glad to have avoided a trap about the stranger having slept here fourteen years ago. He's got a good-looking blonde with him, too, obviously European and speaking elegant Arabic with a Lebanese accent," said Nidal.

Was I really afraid? I did feel as if I were covered with a thin glaze of dread. But there was nothing left of the mistrust I'd been told about in Beirut, Rabat and Amman. Instead, there was an image. But where in me did it originate? A tuft of moss had sprouted in a crack in a concrete floor.

A few spores or the roots of a fig tree would prise up, softly or strongly, the paving-stones. And shatter them. This image was before me, not clear, but dim like the mental picture I'd had in the past of the tap in the wall.

We went back through the camp, accompanied by the grandsons and by Hamza II, smiling now, admitting, even boasting a little, that he'd been a fedayee. The streets were almost deserted: everyone was having the midday meal. A few young Palestinians greeted Hamza II. He answered with a nonchalant smile like the real Hamza fourteen years ago—or, if I may so express it, like Hamza I smiling like Hamza II.

When we got to Nidal's car Hamza II ostentatiously ignored my proffered hand, took me by the shoulders and embraced me twice. The grandsons smiled and did the same, perhaps more warmly. They all shook hands with Nidal and her friend.

Where could all the mother's coldness, dryness and mistrust have come from? From what dried-up stream? But the metaphor didn't help. No image applied so well as the words "dry" and "dryness" themselves, connoting the absence of all that flows, that is liquid, that spreads out and irrigates. In those two words all is fixed and motionless, as in the mother. Her eyes never shone— that would have meant something had stirred within her.

Twist and turn as I might for the words, my efforts showed the unease I wouldn't admit to myself: what had happened in those fourteen years to turn such a free and handsome woman into the one who treated us with nothing but guile and mistrust? For it seemed to me she gave me the piece of paper with Hamza's phone number on it merely out of weariness under so many pressures. The plural is significant.

She'd been gay before, defending her cause with her gun and proud of her son. Now she was dried up.

Though the eglantine, the wild rose, is the flower of the romantics and perhaps their symbol, it's only natural that I should prefer the fruit to the petals. The pink eglantine produces a warm bright-red fruit, a rose-hip. It's known in French as an arse-scratcher because its rubbery flesh contains some downy seeds which if I eat two or three of them make me itch round a certain hole.

When they fall, the petals of the eglantine reveal the fruit, tiny at first but very noticeable, because it's the same red as the penis of a dog in love. Five petals fall one by one from each rose on the bush, almost one a day until all that's left is a bramble.

In the same way I saw the Church stripped naked before me, teaching me that the stagnant water in the fonts came not from the Jordan but from the tap; that the birth of Jesus didn't date from the year 1; that unclean teeth could crunch the host without producing some internal miracle, and so on.

And so with the mother. Her son wasn't dead. He wasn't unique. He even had a son. What I'd taken to be a lapse of the memory had been a trick, or the vestiges of one. Hamza had two older brothers. Not knowing that, I didn't know what the mother felt about them—whether she mightn't be as fond of them as of Hamza. And where had Hamza got his unbelief?

"Hamza didn't believe in God much, either," Hamza II had said.

Perhaps he'd got his unbelief from his brothers? After all her meditations there wasn't much left of the mother: a few flakes of dandruff streaked with henna, a bundle of bones, a wan face betokening a woman's sex, a grey shift, a wild rose-bush without any petals, and the Church with the gilt rubbed off.

A gold rush was something that happened all the time. I found that out in the church of a little village in France. The candlesticks were made of gold, of old gold—you could see brown rust marks on them. They were religious and therefore sacred objects made of a metal lending itself to metaphor. But a stonemason in the village laughed at me: the candlesticks were gilt. And I learned the difference between artificial gilt, gold plating, gold leafing, vermeil and solid gold. But then the village priest laughed at the stonemason: he said the candlesticks were made of tin covered with a thin layer of copper.

That descent into the golden inferno and godly poverty made me careful at first and later blasé.

Renaissance, Louis Treize, Louis Quatorze, Regency, Louis

Quinze, Louis Seize, Empire, Louis Philippe, Second Empire—all the furniture, whatever its period, was made in Karachi out of wood, silver and mother-of-pearl. But each item was covered in gilt. This was the apartment of the UN representative in Beirut. He'd had the furniture brought here from home, some palace in Pakistan, no doubt gilded all over inside and out like the Sikhs' Golden Temple.

He lived on the eleventh floor of the building in Beirut where I lived on the eighth. He asked me up for a coffee, and I was astonished both by the gold on the ugly furniture and by the invitation. I'd come back from a Karachi full of buses, where everything was tied together with wire but seemed to be looking at gold—buses and tricycles with the tops up, looking at gold plate or gold leaf, silver paper, aluminium, with green predominating, or red, or yellow, each colour climbing over the other, and gold over all the rest. And in Beirut, on the eleventh floor, all this gilded furniture, so happy to show itself to me, was looking at the sea!

Although like all the inhabitants of Beirut he was afraid of bombs he was being very matey. A UN ambassador ought never to have invited me into his home.

He was living with a young and quite pretty Palestinian girl. She'd seen me in an Arabic bookshop in Paris and was afraid I might recognize her. The Pakistani knew no Arabic and spoke only English and French. She was the first and perhaps the only Palestinian prostitute I ever saw.

"No," he said, "I didn't meet General Sharon. He might have been quite friendly with my family but I didn't go near him. Shaking hands with him isn't part of my duties."

I went back to Chatila in September 1984. The house I was taken to had been destroyed but rebuilt and repainted. The women offered me tea. I knew four of them: the mistress of the house, her mother and her two young daughters. Everyone had been injured in 1982 except the ten-year-old son.

"The bullets and bomb fragments are still inside us."

I learned from them that the women were ashamed not so much at having been injured as at having bits of Israeli ammunition inside them. They were afraid they might give birth to monsters, and felt not only wounded but also raped beyond repair.

"The shrapnel lives a life of its own in our flesh, and worst of all, with it."

There were only a few sticks of furniture: two armchairs from who knows where, two divans of the same provenance, a low table. The walls were decorated with photographs and roughly drawn and painted portraits of the dead.

For all its bareness the house was not only clean: everything in it was arranged with elegance. This refinement was really enviable, arising as it did out of massacres and rubble, furnished at it was with debris, yet imparting a heart-felt sense of security and peace. Hamza and the Palestinians in general seem to carry such peace about with them; I saw it as a survival of the elegance of voice, manner and bearing handed down by an old, forgotten popular aristocracy. I saw many houses, many families like that among the ruins of Sabra and Chatila and in the refugee camps in Jordan. Sobriety and elegance in Palestine; lakes in Norway.

In 1972, two days before I was expelled from Amman and from Jordan itself, I witnessed something that would have been good for a page or so of sarcasm if I'd been able to write it down.

I'd been to Petra and back, and was sitting in the Jordan Hotel awaiting the return of the Palestinian contact I'd made. I had the hotel lounge to myself, because everyone else had been invited to a couple of cocktail parties being held in the lounges on the lower ground floor, which I never visited.

The strangeness of the event and of the place began with two notices at the top of the double staircase leading down to two vast cellars, probably all lit up and covered in gold. One notice was in English and Vietnamese and signalled the national holiday of South Vietnam; the other was in English and Arabic and celebrated the national holiday of Abu Dhabi. One notice was in honour of a country which in a couple of months would no longer exist; the other was in honour of a country which for me, who'd never been there, was just a sand desert dotted with a few wells.

From the corner of the black divan where, with my eye on the monumental hotel entrance, I awaited the Palestinian's return, I could see the almost simultaneous beginnings of both parties.

Two ambassadors, each seemingly unaware of the other—I was sorry they weren't wearing their national costumes, sky-blue and gold for the Vietnamese, embroidered white for the Arab—waited to shake their guests' hands before they went down the double stairs on the double red carpets. It was obvious that the guests, though covered with sashes and gongs, would be like the liquid in communicating vessels and move from one party to the other.

But first, between the entrance to the lounge and the top of the double staircase down to the double cave, an unforeseen ceremony took place. The embassy secretaries in their many-coloured uniforms, with their wives in silks and satins; the consuls, with their wives in lace; the bachelors in morning coats or evening dress, with their oafish looks—all the diplomats arriving for the parties were searched by six policemen who let through only one couple at a time.

The Italian ambassador was the first, and presented himself with his arms stuck out in front of him as if asking to be tickled. A Jordanian policeman felt him from neck to socks. Then came the Spanish ambassador, whom the policeman didn't touch, just flicking his hands over him as a tribute to the Franco government's refusal to recognize the state of Israel. Next, the Japanese ambassador: frisked. The Ivory Coast ambassador and his lady, despite her boubou: frisked. The Dutch ambassador: frisked. The Brazilian ambassador: frisked. Masses of other ambassadors, scintillating with decorations: frisked.

The policeman hadn't said a word to me. I sat on my divan, never taking my eyes off the door except to look at the silent homage being paid to the diplomatic corps after its ordeal by the South Vietnamese ambassador and the Arab of the Sands.

But the show was starting to flag. The diplomats and their ladies were still sprightly enough, making their entrances as naturally as if it were a matter of course for an ambassador to have his crotch and armpits and almost the soles of his feet gone over for the entertainment of one invisible Frenchman. But the athletic, moustachioed policemen were showing signs of fatigue after so much bending down and straightening up to feel soles and legs, pockets and shoulders. As if by a single unseen accord they fell into three groups of two, one of each pair standing in front of an ambassador, the other positioned behind. The policemen had invented Stakhanovism all by themselves.

If you want the white of a fried egg to look good you have to break the egg into some already hot butter. Then the white quickly loses its transparency and viscosity and turns into a kind of white enamel with a thin dark edge. That's when the egg should be served. If the egg is fresh the colour of the white is usually somewhere between off-white and ivory. This is due partly to the proximity of another enamel that's closer to green or sometimes red, but usually green. This second enamel also looks rather swollen.

The Charles II cross worn by the Spanish ambassador similarly consisted of a round of green enamel surrounded by a band of white. Later, in Amman in August 1972, I saw a harder white on the chest of the French ambassador—on the cross worn by a Chevalier of the Legion of Honour. The military attaché was wearing the medal of the Resistance. I noticed that the fineness of an enamel, whatever its colour, resided in two details: a slight swelling, subsiding near the edges, and a fine, almost invisible network of tiny cracks, probably due to the firing. If you examine a gong through a magnifying glass you discover much the same complex mystery as you can detect with the naked eye in a Chardin or a Vermeer.

I kept count in my head as well as I could. The countries of the Eastern bloc refused to recognize South Vietnam, while huge hands pawed the Moroccan, West German and Swedish ambassadors. Then the French ambassador made his appearance, representing eternal France, I suppose. His Excellency, the sash of the Legion of Honour round his neck, accepted the first policeman's genuflexion and the travels of two powerful hands up his legs and thighs, then the attentions the second policeman devoted to his sacred back. The ambassadress meanwhile stood by in a long gown, clutching her handbag as her husband was checked from top to bottom and pronounced not dangerous for the two cocktail parties.

The French military attaché, in dress uniform and more bemedalled than a Neapolitan church, appeared at the door and hesitated for the second immortalized by Turenne: "You tremble, carcase—but if you knew where I was taking you..." And like the Marshal he launched his trembling body into the fray and let himself be touched up before my very eyes.

The Pakistan ambassador; the Tunisian ambassador. It didn't surprise me that all the ambassadors' wives came in lace and emeralds and rubies, but where did their husbands get all the discs adorning their chests, each chest swelling like Victor Hugo's forehead, as if the chief object of every ambassador was to develop the largest possible showcase for gongs.

I even wondered whether their chests didn't start to swell as soon as the first medals were pinned on them—growing thereafter at the expense of the legs and head, so that the former became thinner and thinner and the latter stayed heavy but hollow.

Or perhaps their chests were pumped up?

This ceremony, like the reverse of a huge medal without any obverse, awarded for we'll never know what services rendered, came to a halt, perhaps to get its breath back. When the searching was over and all the diplomats had gone down into the private lounges, entering the bowels of the earth in order to emerge at the antipodes, a sort of peace descended even on me. Two of the policemen were massaging one another's backs with the same voluptuous relief as I've read that women of the 1900s used to feel when they loosened their corsets.

In the entrance hall a haze, a steam as of a Turkish bath, seemed about to float over the policemen: they were all stretching and opening their mouths to yawn. Then from the depths there emerged not the first but the last of the diplomats and ambassadresses, the military and cultural attachés.

The policemen braced themselves for another bout of searching. Their backs were aching, their hands and wrists were tired—but ready to start frantically frisking shoes and feeling up trouser legs again. I saw the same despondency and weakness in the eyes of the French ambassador as I'd often seen in warders searching me in prison: the ambassador was naked.

His wife had more pride. She nodded towards her husband and his attachés and said curtly, in English:

"That's enough games for tonight. I've been searched once already."

The cops were relieved, and straightened up.

As I looked at them all I realized how beautifully these Oriental cops used the most suggestive gestures to order the great men of Europe and the world to bend down, hold out their arms and proffer their backsides. They'd learned a thing or two from the impassive mask and almost invisible smile of Talleyrand.

The ambassadorial couples came up from the two lighted golden cellars. Their exhausted but upright backs passed proudly by the policemen on the way to their cars, which they got into, still almost upright. They recognized joyfully the curves of familiar backs in chauffeurs' jackets (English) or tunics (Belgian, German, French). Men and women alike got into their cars with the solemnity of people leaving a nasty smell behind them, to which their stern expression is the only clue.

A party. A fête. A ceremony. A celebration . . .

It may irritate me when a veteran tells me for the umpteenth time about the battle of the Argonne, or when Victor Hugo, in *Quatre-Vingt-Treize*, goes on about the forests in Brittany, but it won't stop me writing again and again that the days and nights spent in the forests of Ajloun, between Salt and Irbid, on the banks of the Jordan, were a celebration, a fête. A celebration that can be defined as the fire that warmed our cheeks at being together despite the laws that hoped we'd have deserted one another. Or as the escape from society into a place where people were ready to fight with us against that society. That exaltation may be felt when a thousand, a hundred, fifty, twenty or only two flames last as long as it takes the match that lighted them to burn out. And the only sound or song is that of the charred stick writhing until it's consumed.

This last image reminds me that a wake is a kind of fête. In fact, every fête is at once jubilation and despair. Think of the death of a Jew in France under the Occupation: he's buried in a country graveyard, and seven of the worst Jewish musicians come from seven different directions carrying seven black boxes. Badly but superbly the clandestine septet plays an air by Offenbach beside the grave, then each goes off on his own without a word being said. For the God of Isaiah, who is only a breath of wind on a blade of grass, that night was a fête.

The slight or subtle unease of the Mukhabarats as I looked at the mother's white hair and face was necessary for the celebration of the mystery, and made it possible for that strange encounter to become a fête.

Of course it's understood that the words nights, forests, septet, jubilation, desertion and despair are the same words that I have to use to describe the goings-on at dawn in the Bois de Boulogne in Paris when the drag queens depart after celebrating their mystery, doing their accounts and smoothing banknotes out in the dew.

But every more or less well-meaning organization is bound to be gloomy—not funereal but gloomy. So they put loudspeakers in factories for the music to cheer up the assembly-line workers and increase their output. The owners of battery farms say music makes hens lay more eggs. Any celebration of a mystery is dangerous, forbidden. But when it takes place it's a fête.

My Palestinian friend didn't turn up. As it was night-time by now I decided to go to his place, finding my way back to the street almost by instinct. His father's shop was still open.

"I'll take you to him," his father said in Arabic.

He smiled at me and didn't seem to resent my coming.

His son was in bed being looked after by his two wives. He was black and blue all over from the attentions of some policemen who'd wanted to know what I was doing in Amman.

"Leave at once! Get out of Jordan!"

"I'll go tomorrow."

"Go tonight."

The party in the two cellars was over. I forgot to say that a few minutes after the sleepwalking diplomats left, the cleaners, supervised by a policeman, found several decorations on the floor, with brilliants imitating precious stones. None of them was worth much, but the police superintendents would be able to amuse their kids with them. Or so I was told by the lift boy detailed to keep an eye on me and search my suitcase.

There were no explosions that night in the gardens of the Jordan Hotel, though the drivers all brought their national number-plates up close to the doors for safety. Instead of sleeping in my room, by a subterfuge about as effective as a suit of armour made of plywood I spent the night lying on a blanket in the bathroom.

Otherwise unscathed, I left Jordan the next morning by taxi, pleased in spite of everything with my glimpse of the diplomatic corps. The frontier between Jordan and Syria was closed, but they opened it to let me through.

"Is finish for you."

Nevertheless I went back fourteen years later.

"Intelligent? Them? Of course. The difference between the Palestinians and the other Arab peoples is due to their defeat. Once they were driven from their homes, their gardens, their sheep, their leeks and roses and kohlrabis by the Israelis they turned into fighting demons—demons dealing and accepting death to destroy not only the people who ousted them but also all other races. The fedayeen have declared war on the whole world. They have adopted the noble name of revolutionaries."

"Don't you like the word?"

"You know very well I don't. But in Algeria we fought the Algerian revolution . . ."

"Your bases were in Morocco and Tunisia."

"They were all over the Arab world, and in China and the USSR. The Palestinians could have had the same."

"You know very well they couldn't. The Arab world has never feared your liberation or your ideas. But the Palestinians frighten them all, great and small monarchs alike."

"So they tell people like you. They tell the Muslims something different. The Israelis have made them effeminate. But Islam is only half asleep. When it wakes up it will get tough. Take the rise of the Muslim Brotherhood."

He knew about the Muslim Brotherhood's arrogance, but that was all! The Algerian officer who came to see me all too often in 1972 didn't foresee the advent of Khomeini. The Sunni Muslims seemed the strongest then, and the Shiites still spoke and behaved timidly in comparison.

"If they win they'll fight a holy war, and you won't survive. The Muslim Brotherhood won't tolerate you. You'll have to be converted or die."

"I'll be converted. But don't you worry about me. What will they do to you?"

"When I go back to Algeria I can't even tell my sixteen-year-old son I don't believe in God."

"Would he kill you?"

"He wouldn't understand me. He wouldn't call the police—he'd call the lunatic asylum."

That officer's famous among the Palestinians and the Algerians, but he's dead. Why did he come and see me, just to exchange a few words? I never saw him again, except one last time in Beirut.

"You shouldn't stay. Everything's going to be destroyed. Bombs and shells will crush everything up together—men, women and children, sheep and horses and old iron—*they'll* turn them all into a mishmash that's more Islamic than Palestinian."

I wrote that down in September 1972. He died before me: his car was blown up by a bomb. An Israeli bomb?

Around September 1972 a sort of oppressiveness could be felt in southern Lebanon. It weighed down the movements of the fedayeen, and perhaps their thoughts as well: their joy in fighting and destruction disappeared. The heaviness was there as always when the leaders and their subordinates "thought seriously"—that's when they pitted their certainties against the weird certainty of their enemies that a God had promised *their* country to the descendants of a vagabond. Though it was necessary, it was burdensome to have to study every single troop movement. When the leaders went to Peking and Moscow and Geneva, did they think they were free to come and go? To talk to the people there as equals? Great empires tend to throw their weight about, and the PLO were in disarray.

The last thing but one the Algerian officer said to me was:

"The Middle East will be peaceful again when the Palestinians stop being so clever, stop trying to be knights in shining armour, and just have the same aims as everyone else who knows what's what: to cut their coat according to their cloth instead of going off killing and dying."

When I went back to Salt in 1984 I saw the houses with romanesque porches again, with their semicircular vaults supported on four small marble columns. They brought back my longing for somewhere to live, and a garden with a view of the sea and Cyprus in the distance. I don't know whether this nostalgia derived from a snail-like desire for a shell, or just the pleasure of letting my imagination free to float where it liked, like a body on the sea. The latter explanation is more noble. But less true.

One morning fourteen years before, Dr. Mahjoub, hearing me exclaim "How beautiful!" when I saw that particular little house at Salt, had said, "The PLO would let it to you for six months." This immediately made it uninhabitable for me. But all the other houses I saw at Salt reproduced so faithfully—or at least I thought so—the architecture and town planning of a little Byzantine city that I felt I wanted to live there for the rest of my life. That is, stay there for two or three hours; not more.

This time, in 1984, the sun lit up the house from behind instead of in front, because it was five o'clock in the evening. The romanesque porch was in the shade, which seemed to add to the ancient atmosphere and made it possible for me to sleep there, since darkness and old age put me in need of shelter. A couple of sailors suggested a lodging which would have shut me up in space and time. I looked back with regret to the house in Turkey, with its garden and its view of the sea and the coast of Cyprus, and the naval battle I'd have liked to see from my window, with drowned men floating on the now still waters.

When I wandered round Ajloun again in September 1971, I was bemused at first by the collapse of the Palestinian resistance, and when I tried to find the reasons for it, all I found was:

Reviewing all I thought I knew about the fedayeen, it seemed to me that the resistance, despite the catechism handed out to the fighters, exhorted them to be defensive rather than aggressive. The act of killing had become distant, shrouded in complex ritual: you needed a permit just to hunt partridges. Buying a gun or a carbine and choosing the cartridges or shot—all these were ceremonies that seemed to me to rob the act of murder of its substance. The meetings of the men, the vocabulary of hunting, the bustle of the women round the stoves before the hunters' return, the hunting songs, killing by remote control by pressing a trigger—all this no longer meant taking life but merely fulfilling a social obligation.

The Palestinians seemed to me to have lost direct contact—atrocious perhaps, but necessary when life is at stake—with the death of the victim. This aversion to murder in the midst of a brutal war was like an extension of the forgetfulness or aversion reflected in the chaste traditional dances: their eroticism had become stylized over two or three thousand years in the desert. At Baqa I'd felt as if I were watching the soldiers of Nebuchadnezzar, though really they were Bedouin who still knew the power both of the dance and of the chase.

Our daily diet came from Argentina in the form of tins of corned beef. Our worst crime was using a tin-opener to get at the bullock that had been murdered at La Plata. The Bedouin, as their dances proved, still had direct contact with death-dealing. But to the Palestinians a hunted animal had become the enemy. Even those who didn't catch it ate it, no matter if it was only a quail. To the Bedouin a Palestinian was an enemy. Killing an enemy is easy. The Palestinians never considered the Bedouin as enemies.

I can't not include in this book the truck that for eight months brought tins of food and loaves of flat Arab bread to Ajloun. It went from base to base, starting from Baqa Camp and stopping first at Ajloun to leave us our rations and then driving on to the next base. How shall I describe it? From what angle? The best observation point is certainly the eyes of the kids in the Jordanian village. They looked down on it from above and could see it was brimming over with loaves. The kids were hungry and so were their families, and there was our supply truck going all round the countryside feeding the fedayeen, with never anything for those children with eyes as big as their bellies.

So the expressions and gestures of the Bedouin must have been affected by the Palestinians' complexity and unease. They were as alike as brothers, but to the Bedouin the Palestinians represented the advance guard of a world they'd long been able to keep at a distance by means of a desert that had once been lethal but was now shockingly opened up.

This attempt at an explanation may have some validity. And yet sometimes, temporarily at least, many of the fedayeen would be possessed by the red madness of murder. I'll come back to the subject some time.

The defeat at Irbid of the Palestinians from Salt, whether through murder, flight, imprisonment or torture camps, showed me that the lightness of the fedayeen's way of life was due to the fact that death was always hovering over them. A horrible cliché, but every fighter did have this lightness of being because he knew he had no future. Mahjoub once told me: "In order to be a real fighter I never think of what I may be doing the day after tomorrow." No doubt that came from some catechism for the perfect martyr. The aims of the revolution were so distant that only its present moments were worth living.

That was what I thought, or rather something like it, yet I knew I'd never be cured. The fedayeen who'd become my friends, but with a friendship that was never laboured, were dead, imprisoned or on the run, or had regrouped to fight other battles in other countries. The trees—beeches, hornbeams, a few poplars—hadn't been harassed. They said nothing. But not a single tropism had yielded.

I crept away almost on tiptoe, like someone leaving a room in which even the bed is asleep.

When the "ferocity of the fedayeen" was mentioned, as sometimes happened, it referred mainly to rough treatment of things and never to actual cruelty.

I was always delighted when furniture symbolizing wealth and comfort was put to derisory uses. One night by the light of the moon, on a dry and stony bit of land somewhere between Ajloun and Irbid, I found myself in the middle of a conclave of high-backed Voltaire armchairs. It was in March 1971, and all the fedayeen on the base were living in the handful of villas the king had had built for his ministers. In a few hours the villas were emptied of these thirty-odd red velvet armchairs, which now stood in a circle on a ploughed field. Facing them were a couple more chairs of the same kind, one for me and one for the fedayee acting as interpreter. I think the river Jordan must have been rather less than a kilometre away. The Palestinians were expecting a lecture, but we spontaneously opted for the free flow of ideas, smiles, laughter and anecdotes.

Here's a list of the tiny objects that were handed round: cigarette lighters no bigger than an apple pip: transistor radios; boxes of matches; safety razors; packets of Gillette blades; leather-bound imitation Korans the size of a big toe-nail but hollow, with the name of God carved inside in Arabic; fountain pens; pencils; identity polyphotos; pocket mirrors; folding scissors—the wherewithal to furnish a Lilliputian house or a miniature mail-order catalogue. What actually happened was that everyone contributed a match to make up a box for me to take away with me.

It's time for me to take stock. From 1950 to 1955, I found Greece pleasant. In 1967 Japan was delightful. At the beginning of 1970 I was fond of the Black Panthers. From late 1970 to late 1972, more than anything or anyone else I loved the fedayeen. What happened? Greeks, Japanese, Panthers, Palestinians—had they been under a lucky star? Was it that I was easily impressed? Are they still as I remember them? It was so beautiful I wonder whether all those periods of my life weren't just dreams.

When a drawing has too many mistakes in it an artist rubs it out. Two or three rubs with the eraser and the paper's blank again. With France and Europe rubbed out I was faced with a blank space of liberty that was to be filled with Palestine as I experienced it, but with touchings-up that worry me. Like Algeria and other countries that forgot the revolution in the Arab world, my Palestine thought only of the territory out of which a twenty-second state might be born, bringing with it the law and order expected of a newcomer. But did this revolt, that had been an outlaw for so long, really want a law that would have Europe for its Heaven? I've tried to say what happened to it, but for me Europe had become *terra incognita*, and I'd had to leave it out.

Perhaps the massacres at Chatila in September 1982 were not a turning-point. They happened. I was affected by them. I talked about them. But while the act of writing came later, after a period of incubation, nevertheless in a moment like that or those when a single cell departs from its usual metabolism and the original link is created of a future, unsuspected cancer, or of a piece of lace, so I decided to write this book.

The matter became more pressing when some political prisoners urged me not to travel so much and not to spend so much time in France. Anything not to do with the book came to seem so far away as to be invisible. There was the Palestinian people, my search for Hamza and his mother, my trips to the East, especially to Jordan, and my book. But France, Europe, all the West, no longer existed. A trip I made to various parts of Africa and my stay in Ajloun detached me still further from the Europe and the Europeans who already meant so little. By the middle of 1983 I was free enough to start to write my *souvenirs*, which were meant to be read as reporting.

After giving his name and age, a witness is supposed to say something like, "I swear to tell the whole truth . . ." Before I started to write it I'd sworn to myself to tell the truth in this book, not in any ceremony but every time a Palestinian asked me to read the beginning or other passages from it or wanted me to publish parts of it in some magazine. Legally speaking, a witness neither opposes nor serves the judges. Under French law he has sworn to tell the truth, not to tell it to the judges. He takes an oath to the public—to the court and the spectators. The witness is on his own. He speaks. The judges listen and say nothing. The witness doesn't merely answer the implicit question "how?"—in order to show the "why" he throws light on the "how," a light sometimes called artistic. The judges have never been to the places where the acts they have to judge were performed, so the witness is indispensable. But he knows a realistic description won't mean anything to anyone, including the judges, unless he adds some light and shade which only he perceived. The judges may well describe a witness as valuable. He is.

What's the point of that medieval-, almost Carolingian-sounding oath in the courtroom? Perhaps it's to surround the witness with a solitude that confers on him a lightness from which he can speak the truth. For there may be three or four people present who are capable of hearing a witness.

Any reality is bound to be outside me, existing in and for itself. The Palestinian revolution lives and will live only of itself. A Palestinian family, made up essentially of mother and son, were among the first people I met in Irbid. But it was somewhere else that I really found them.

Perhaps inside myself. The pair made up by mother and son is to be found in France and everywhere else. Was it a light of my own that I threw on them, so that instead of being strangers whom I was observing they became a couple of my own creation? An image of my own that my penchant for day-dreaming had projected on to two Palestinians, mother and son, adrift in the midst of a battle in Jordan?

All I've said and written happened. But why is it that this couple is the only really profound memory I have of the Palestinian revolution?

I did the best I could to understand how different this revolution was from others, and in a way I did understand it. But what will remain with me is the little house in Irbid where I slept for one night, and fourteen years during which I tried to find out if that night ever happened.

This last page of my book is transparent.

TITLES IN SERIES

For a complete list of titles, visit www.nyrb.com or write to:
Catalog Requests, NYRB, 435 Hudson Street, New York, NY 10014

* *Also available as an electronic book.*